I0769084

As Long As Rivers Run

By Larry Ray Rather

As Long As Rivers Run
Written by Larry Ray Rather

Published by Forest Light Productions, LLC
Basalt, Colorado

www.forestlight.art

Cover Illustration by Tania Dibbs

Printed in the United States of America.

Hardcover ISBN: 979-8-9907625-0-3

Paperback ISBN: 979-8-9907625-1-0

Light of the Moon, Inc.
Empowering Independent Authors Since 2009
Book Design/Production/Consulting
Glenwood Springs, Colorado
www.lightofthemooninc.com

DEDICATION

This book is dedicated to my parents, Maxine and Ray Rather, who moved our family to Aspen in the summer of 1960. Their move allowed me to discover and explore the forests, mountains and meadows of Colorado's high country at a young age, and those early, curiosity-driven treks generated a deep love for the beauty of the western slope of Colorado.

After our move, my parents' ease in connecting with the diverse people who became our neighbors inspired me to seek out the stories of the Ute people, who first walked the paths I roamed as a child. Their history and legends, shared by generous Ute leaders and historians, have inspired this novel.

Although the story and characters I've created are fictional, many details of the novel are rooted in facts. For example, a treaty in 1868 conveyed nearly half of the Colorado Territory (16,000,000 acres) to Ute bands and families. A thirst for exploration and the dream of striking it rich drove a flood of men (young and old) to seek peace and prosperity in the Rockies, especially after the Civil War. As more and more white prospectors and settlers arrived, greed fueled conflict with the indigenous Ute peoples, but despite violent clashes and deadly misunderstandings, appreciation and curiosity sometimes fostered unlikely friendships.

I have spent countless hours researching the culture and history of Colorado in the late 1860s, and although I have written an imagined story, I have done my best to create a mystical tale that is plausible, if not probable.

ACKNOWLEDGEMENTS

My greatest appreciation goes to my family: daughter Hanna, sons Jesse and Evan, and former wife, Sharon. Their support through the long process of research and composition of this book was invaluable. My daughter and sons often served as sounding boards for my ideas, and Sharon wisely encouraged me to "Just tell a great story and don't worry if anyone likes it." Her words drove me on and allowed me the freedom to focus on dreaming up a rich and romantic tale.

Early in the process of writing this book, I befriended CJ Brafford, the director of the Ute Indian Museum in Montrose Colorado. Not only did she share historical knowledge, enriching stories, and details about her own Native American experiences, she also guided me to the 1969 publication Uncompahgre Ute Words and Phrases by Hazel Wardell, which served as my primary linguistic reference for the Ute words and phrases used in this novel.

Dr. Paul Salmen, my retired family physician, researched the means and methods of medical procedures in the late nineteenth century and imparted to my story his personal knowledge as a doctor and surgeon, both of which greatly enhanced the accuracy of several scenes. Thank you also to my Ute friend, Kenny Frost, who took the time to tell me his stories — and share his memories of friends and family.

I also owe a debt of gratitude to those who helped bring this book to fruition. My friend, Charlotte Edwards, offered unflagging technical support to help me wrangle my manuscript into a working format. Alyssa Ohnmacht and her team at Light of the Moon, Inc. who provided expert guidance and encouragement throughout the publishing process — and introduced me to my exceptional editor, Kristin Carlson, whose expertise, wisdom, and support kept me enthused about this project from start to finish.

To all these people, and to countless others (you know who you are), I offer my most sincere gratitude for the time, talents, and knowledge you have shared with me.

CHAPTER ONE

Boy Gets a Name

▲ ▲ ▲

The Ute Indian boy sat motionless at the river's edge and felt the world around him. He stared at the far bank where pine boughs bobbed, and white spray rose from an icy pool beneath a waterfall. The Beaver Moon wind swept his long black hair across his face as water drops froze on his leather leggings.

For three days he'd waited at the sweat lodge, built for his dreaming quest. The first day he bathed in steam from morning until dark then moved outside, wrapped in an elk-hide robe that his mother had given him. For the next two days and nights he waited for his forest helpers to appear. His uncle had told him the forest helpers would arrive in a vision to expose his medicine powers. Their wisdom would serve him throughout his life. There was no promise that a vision would appear, but by tradition, a Ute boy with two hands full of summers would perform the rituals to summon a vision. The creator, Sinawav, encouraged fasting, sweat bathing, and extended prayer.

He hadn't had anything to drink for two days when an unconscious urge moved him to the river, where he swallowed a handful of freezing water that cut down his throat like a blade of ice. His head spun when the frigid fluid hit his stomach. He slumped in pain and stared down at the rocks where a little bird bounced into his view. It was pinecone-sized and slate black. The boy knew it as *wah-we-chitch*, a water bird. He'd wondered before how such little creatures could swim in the most rapid rivers in search of food. They'd disappear in raging currents then reappear to skip across the ice and dive back in again. He and his friends had tried to catch them before, without success, and now one sat just inches from his knee.

The bird bounced closer, watching him with steely eyes. It bobbed and dipped as if daring the boy. Its feathers sparkled with water drops that mirrored the forest and sky.

The boy's world began to swirl in a collage of cloudy colors. A tapping sound within his head grew louder with every breath as his blood rushed to match the beating heart of the bird. Louder and stronger the pounding grew, like fireside drums calling his clan. His rumbling heart rocked his posture and dizziness pulled at his will.

At the boy's flinch the bird flared but was swiped from mid-air by fingers that wrapped around soft down. Though his feathers were soft, and his weight was light, the water bird was no fragile creature. He was the spirit of the mountain streams, and his strength had been honed by the river's course. The boy's arm jerked at the socket as the little bird, as stout as a stud, yanked him into the river. His fingers held tight to the bird, which surged with unthinkable power. The slashing cold cut at his senses as water pulled at his skin. His mind took flight as the weight of the water swept him downstream. He couldn't breathe in and he couldn't breathe out. The river swallowed him whole, and slowly his mind surrendered to the blackness. Trapped between worlds, he drifted and relinquished his past and all grasping for a future. His life froze at a point between breaths. Suspended between worlds, the boy's spirit and that of the water bird, became one.

Towed farther downward he felt a warmth in his chest. The pressure lightened and the struggle to breathe lessened. As his mind cleared, a new thought replaced his fear. As they sank deeper, a spark of light pierced the darkness and the river's depths brightened like sunrise. At the edge of the shadows air bubbles swayed upward, each sphere glimmering with a sparkle of light. The boy and the bird floated above the calico gravel and surveyed a boulder-strewn arch around them. Motion in a shadow revealed a fish as big as a sunken log, Grandfather Trout. His eyes rocked to the rhythm of his crimson gills. Across from Grandfather Trout was Old Man Otter, long whiskers swaying side to side. At the boy's glance the otter spun playfully, nose to tail, then settled back into his sandy nest.

The water bird moved between the fish and the mammal, and when the trio fixed their eyes on the boy, he heard their unspoken words. "Welcome to our world; this shall be your refuge."

The totems drifted apart, and beyond them shone the source of the light. Lying on the river bottom, rocking with the current, was a bundle of buckskin leather folded like a cocoon. It was the size of a baby wrapped in a papoose and it glowed with a golden light. Guided by knowledge that lived in his bones, the boy swam to the bundle and lifted it from the river's bed. He looked at the totems, which moved closer. Old Man Otter dipped his head, the bird darted upward, and the boy knew he was to follow.

With a kick of his legs, he shot up with the bundle in his arms. As he rose, he saw Grandfather Trout slip between the boulders as Old Man Otter laced his way downstream.

With the bird just beyond reach, the boy swam toward the margin of blackness that separated him from the upper world. Again, he entered the blurry space between apparition and reality. While one arm clutched the bundle, his other pawed at the icy darkness until his movement ceased, and the awareness of his spirit vanished.

• • •

The boy lay with his eyes closed, feeling pain in his shoulder and an ache in his hip. How long he'd been there he didn't know. He listened to the world around him. He could hear the river and feel warmth on his neck. The angle of the sun told him it was morning. He wasn't sure where he was, and he felt uneasy. A cool breeze brushed his body, and he remembered the gift robe from his mother. His mind wandered through the last few days, and he realized he was waking from a sleep he couldn't remember falling into.

When his eyes slit open, his body jerked, and his heart jumped in response to movement at the tip of his nose. He released a broken scream and scooted back across the rocks. Stopping when his back hit a boulder, he looked side to side searching for movement. Fear gripped at his throat and his mind darted in different directions. Slowly, he reined in his breath and saw that only the river moved. Drawn to motion at his feet, he saw little black feathers flipping across the stones. He grabbed one just before it touched the water and studied the delicate pattern. His heart slowed, and he sensed that he held his *medicine*. The tiny feather felt heavy with power. He drew in a breath and felt the labor in his lungs. A stir in the water drew his eyes to the black eyes of an otter staring back at him. The whiskered face disappeared in the current, leaving a circular ripple that bent with the river's flow.

On the opposite bank a water bird, wah-we-chitch barked at the stream. When the bird disappeared in the river, the boy's vision of the underwater world reappeared. He could feel the weight of the water and the lonely blackness, but he felt no fear. He breathed in deep, filling his lungs, then let out a long sigh. A flow of joy rode out on his breath, and a calm feeling settled in his gut as he remembered his dream. He didn't fully understand the intentions of the totems or the purpose of the golden yellow bundle, but he knew he'd received a vision and that his uncle would help him understand it.

His stomach growled, and he thought of his mother, Stone Calf, cooking. He could smell steaks sizzling on a firestone and knew that she and his sister, Star Flower, would be worried about him. For a moment longer he stared into the water, then he knew it was time to leave. The walk back to the village would take all day. He headed toward the sweat lodge with the little black feathers gripped between his fingers. He quickly gathered his gear and wrapped the elk hide robe around his shoulders before heading downhill. He'd moved downstream only a short distance when he saw two riders and three horses coming uphill. He recognized the horses and knew the men, his father Bow River and his uncle Good Bear.

On a big black boulder in the naked aspen forest, the boy took a seat and waited for the riders.

CHAPTER TWO

A Cape of Red Curls

▲ ▲ ▲

Tom Dunagan's buckskin horse cut a straight-lined trail through the dew-covered alpine grasses. Tom rode chin-up, scanning the surroundings in the method of a scientist. With the diligence of a hungry hawk he studied the land for clues to its history and the mysteries it held. He consciously recorded details like the seams in the rocks, the height of the trees and the tint of the water's color.

His thirteen-year-old daughter, Brooke Rose, rode behind him on a paint mare they called Tess. Three loyal pack mules followed her.

Brooke was wrapped in her father's union coat and wore a limp felt hat pulled low. Her curly, auburn hair sprang out in all directions below the brim. With the earnest intent of her father, her curious blue eyes surveyed the world around them.

In the cool morning air, a bank of fog rose slowly above the melt-swollen stream in the canyon below. Willows along the bank stood, lightly brushed with the green buds of spring. On the boulder-covered slopes, golden avalanche lilies glowed in the sunshine. The early morning light shot through heavy clouds and washed bright the western slope of the Rocky Mountains. Above timberline on an eastern fork of the Rio Colorado snowdrifts lingered in the cirques and the avalanche chutes. The perennial snow added a chill to the air. Early June, at twelve-thousand feet, is a time between seasons where winter's ash mixes with summer's promise in the plump willow buds and the song of the wren.

At the snowfield's fringe, water drops begin their passage on a journey to the sea. The flow of water to the ocean and returning with the clouds serves as a tireless heart pumping life into the land.

In the canyon far below them, the muffled grunts of a grizzly bear mixed with the sound of the stream rolling stones. The bear's head was buried in a marmot's den where he dug with finger-long claws. Every so often he'd analyze the air for opportunities and danger. If nothing changed, he'd dig in again, moving earth with determination. In the endless expanse of mountains and valleys, this giant of all carnivores was barely noticed except for his relentless digging.

Downwind of the bear and within rifle range, hid Bow River and his fifteen-year-old son, Water Bird. Bow River held a rifle and Water Bird gripped a bow with an arrow pressed to the string.

They were hunting the *Bunkara* or Thunder Fork of the Rio Colorado, so that Water Bird could learn the boundaries of their territory. They were tracking elk and curled-horn sheep, but they knew the canyon was home to the grizzly bear too.

They'd spotted the bear coming downstream, before he was lured upslope by the smell of spring-fresh marmot. Had he not detected the rodent's burrow he'd have cut their trail and the tables would be turned.

Bow River recognized the bear as a giant he had seen before. A discernibly torn ear stood half erect, while the other flopped forward. He was as big as a buffalo cow with a boulder hump on his back and paws like pots. He was old and thin from a winter underground, and he was hungry too. Because of his old age he scrounged for rodents and bugs. As his summer strength returned, he'd fill his belly with larger prey.

Bears of every color were sacred to the Utes and were killed only as needed. These monarchs of the mountains were celebrated in the narrative of the Ute tribes. The Grizzly Bear was especially regarded for its strength and ferocity. With a shoulder hump like a buffalo and the face of a wolf, he was the specific guardian of the high mountains. The sovereign ruler of the cloud-capped peaks and gemstone lakes. His preferred range was above the oaks and aspen forests. The same high country that was essential to the Utes for its abundance of meat, fish, and berries. The bears and the Utes shared the same range and had learned to coexist. There was little reasoning with the bears. As long as the Utes let them have their way, there was rarely any trouble. This hand-in-hand relationship was celebrated in the name of Bow River's family group, "The Yellow Bears."

From behind a large boulder, Bow River and Water Bird watched and waited for the bear to move on. Water Bird clutched the possible bag that hung on a leather cord around his neck. It held the power and protection of his totems — the water bird, the otter, and the trout.

Once they saw where the bear was going, they'd know which way to go. With hand signs and silent expressions, they plotted their path.

• • •

On top of the divide, Tom and Brooke stopped and studied a map that vaguely reflected the land before them. For nearly two months they'd followed its clues, and now they stood on the divide that split the continent and separated their past from their future. The sun warmed their backs as they looked across the sea of peaks and valleys. An unexplored land held by the Utes who made it their home. Tom looked west with anticipation, but a part of him wondered why he was here. He saw a wilderness ripe with possibilities but also fraught with peril. He harnessed his breath and wrestled with the notion of a father and daughter driving headlong into the wildest country on earth. He worried for Brooke, but he'd been more troubled by the thought of leaving her behind. She would be faced with some hardship, no doubt, but until they could settle again, he wouldn't be without her.

As the earth warmed, a dense fog rose up the ridges, and a damp cloud engulfed them. They started their horses downhill. Tom slowed his mount, keeping Brooke and the pack animals in sight. The fog was passing uphill when a sudden ruckus of branches breaking spooked the stock. Tom drew his rifle, as his horse side-stepped and pinned its ears downhill. Brooke's mare snorted and backed up the trail. The mules lunged uphill, stopped on a rocky point, and looked below. Hearts pounded, while eyes watched and ears listened, but the rumbling river was the only sound.

Through the thinning fog Tom saw a narrow trail leading downhill. He turned to Brooke. "Must have been a deer," he whispered.

Brooke focused into the fog and lightly nipped her lip. Her eyes were keen and concentrated. She unconsciously reached for the little glass star that dangled from a leather string around her neck — a gift from her mother, which she'd worn every day since her passing.

Tom leaned side-to-side looking into the fog then tapped his horse's ribs. On a series of game trails, they moved downslope. As they ventured deeper into the canyon, the fog got thinner and the sound of the stream grew louder.

When they came out of the mist, Tom caught a movement to his left. He thought a boulder had moved, but the truth quickly raised its burly head.

The Grizzly Bear pulled its muddy muzzle out of the dirt and stared at the riders above him. His black eyes glared through matted hair. Snarling, he bared white fangs.

Tom shouldered his rifle and fought to hold his horse in place. The startled bear spun downhill with a sharp grunt from deep in his gut. The defiant bark was as sharp as a shot, and Tom's horse reared as if hit by a slug. Like a runaway ore cart, the bear swung downhill, plowing a path through the wet earth. Rocks and mud flew as he wove through boulders and disappeared into the trees.

• • •

Bow River knew the alarmed bark of a startled bear, and he knew what he'd just heard. When he and Water Bird peeked over the boulder, they knew their morning hunt had taken a terrible turn.

On a dead run the bear spotted them looking over the rock and turned their way. He was on them before they could move and, as Bow River cocked his rifle, the bear leaped into the air. Water Bird stumbled backwards as his father's rifle exploded. The bullet hit the bear's chest with a *whap*, as he lunged over the boulder. Bow River reached for his knife just as the bear's nose slammed into his face like an ax. He flew backwards, dragging limp legs, and hit the ground as slack as soft leather.

From behind a stunted pine, Water Bird watched the bear standing over his father biting his shoulder and tossing him like a scrap. Then the bear rushed to where he landed and shook him as if killing a snake. Bow River's body flopped and twisted in the bear's powerful jaws.

Water Bird feared the bear's attention but knew he was his father's only hope. His arrows had little chance against the monster, but he had no idea where the rifle had landed. Desperation yanked him from what he pleaded was a dream, and a battle cry erupted from his gut. He charged the raging bear. Without looking up, the giant continued to rip at the man who'd blown a hole in his chest.

At nearly striking distance Water Bird shot an arrow into the bear's thick hide. The bear didn't flinch, just continued the one-sided fight as blood gushed from the bullet wound. Water Bird shot again, and the arrow struck close to the heart. With trembling hands, he steadied another arrow onto the string and was starting to draw when an explosion went off next to his face. *Kaboom!* He jumped sideways from the blast.

The bear was knocked to the ground by a rifle slug. Staggering to his feet, the creature turned toward the sound of the shot. He teetered side to side then plowed toward Tom Dunagan, who steadied his rifle and aimed again. As Tom targeted the monster's face, his mind flashed to his daughter, and he knew he must survive. He pulled the trigger as the bear plowed into him like a locomotive. Its nose hit his forehead, the back of his skull hit the ground, and darkness flooded his world.

An arrow flew from Water Bird's bow and struck the bear. He fumbled for another arrow before he realized the commotion had stopped. The bear was still. A man's arms and legs stuck out below the pile of fur. The bear arched up once then settled down with a rattling hiss.

Water Bird gawked in confusion at the man beneath the bear. A panic of loss gripped his gut as he raced from boyhood to manhood with the speed of a falling star. He ran and fell at his father's side, reaching out, unsure of what to touch or where to lift. He pulled off his coat to make a pillow and scooted it beneath his father's head. Bow River was motionless except for the blood that pumped from his arms, legs, and skull.

"Mo-if! Father!" Water Bird cried as if calling across a canyon, *"Mo-if!"*

Bow River's arms hung limp and flopped out to the sides.

Water Bird's chin quivered as he drew in a deep breath and glanced around the forest. He knew his father was alive, but he wouldn't be for long. Their horses were downstream, and their village was days away. He knew he needed help but could summon only himself. Hopeless surrender tugged at his will. He looked down at his father and began rocking gently back and forth. All he knew to do was something he had never done before. He shuddered, holding back a sob, pressed his lips together and started humming the Ute dying song. The chant started softly then grew as he remembered the rhythm. It brought a measure of strength as he performed a duty he hardly knew. With the wobbly tone of a sparrow the haunting song drifted through the forest. The woods grew dark as clouds settled into the pines. Water Bird knew he couldn't leave his father for even a moment. The man who had guided him as a teacher and companion was slipping away like the evening light.

At the crack of a branch, Water Bird's head jerked toward the sound. There in the shadows was a slender form that blended with the tree. The thin shape faded away as fog twisted through the forest. He watched the spot as the figure appeared then disappeared in the mist. He felt a different fear grip his throat. He stared at the spot and felt the flow of his breath over his pounding heart. Water drops tapped on pine needles as light rain began to fall. A breeze cleared the fog away and, where the ghostly form had stood, he saw only a curtain of spruce. He twisted sideways and slowly straightened, then movement in his lap drew him back to his father. "*Mo-if*," he whispered. Bow River groaned, and his body tensed.

"*Mo-if*," Water Bird said, louder, but Bow River went limp.

Water Bird let out a long breath and gently rocked his father. He looked down, listened to the stream, and remembered his forest helpers — the bird, the fish, and the otter. They had taught him: "This river shall be your refuge." He had to get his father into the cold stream to stop the bleeding. He wrapped his father in his arms and started to stand but froze at the sight of strange boots beside him. His heart held still knowing someone stood over him. He slowly looked up to see a cape of red curls framing fierce, ice-blue eyes that locked their gaze on him.

CHAPTER THREE

Gift Horses

▲ ▲ ▲

Jagged lightning slapped the earth, and thunder shook the ground. Murky clouds shot icy bullets while the churning winds pressed down with crushing force. The men on the knoll locked their arms and flattened themselves to the ground. They labored to breathe with their faces pressed into the dirt. The wicked wind ripped their clothes and worked to wedge them from the earth. Their horses squealed as flying gravel cut their hides.

The young man, Strong Horse, feared the spirits had betrayed them and death would be their only escape. His thoughts spun as he struggled to breathe against the sucking wind. His strangled mind drifted to a woman in a meadow flushed with color. Her black hair draped shoulders covered in beaded doe skin. Her fringed dress swayed side to side as she walked toward him with a teardrop sparkle on her cheek. It was Star Flower, and she was the reason he was here in enemy lands. He had come to steal horses and, if successful, he'd be wealthy with gifts to offer to Star Flower's father, Bow River, in exchange for his daughter's hand in marriage.

Closer and closer she walked toward him. His heart swelled with anticipation. He reached out for her, but the angry wind yanked him into the air. Higher and higher he spun until all he could see was the teardrop sparkle upon her cheek.

Whap! A slap on his back sent pain to the tips of his fingers. He coughed and spit out dirt. Through blurry eyes he saw his cousin Henry Eagle hanging over him with terror in his stare. Their friend, Arturo, coughed and shook beside them.

"Its' gone," Red Elk shouted, who was propped on his elbows watching the churning clouds.

"Look!" He shouted and pointed at the tail of the tornado that wavered below black clouds.

These Utes lived deep in the mountains and knew little about tornados. Their elders had spoken of the twisting, flatland storms but few had ever seen one. Now, they watched as one carved the prairie behind a horse herd that raced ahead of it. The same horse herd they'd been stalking for days and intended to steal that night before the storm appeared. Now they feared for their lives and yearned to run for the mountains. As the tornado chased the panicking herd, Strong Horse knew it was time to flee. He sensed their failure and the mistake of intruding into the land of their ancient enemy.

Beyond the twister stood the Arapaho village of the Spotted Bird Clan. People ran among the tipis as the funnel cloud plowed toward them. Mothers dragged children, running first one way and then the other. People scattered like ants into the forest behind the village.

The tornado coiled back up into the clouds just before it pushed the horse herd toward the river. For a moment, Strong Horse thought it was gone, but it slithered back down and exploded in the water. It cut a course onto the land and into the village as lightning danced and thunder rolled through the trees. The swirling wind swallowed the village and spit it out in splinters. People and dogs spun in the air like dust. The gruesome sight froze the Utes, who clapped their hands over their mouths as they watched the wind uproot the village. They winced at their dying enemies and felt naked before the powerful wind.

Eyes locked on the looming disaster, they didn't realize that the runaway horse herd had changed its course. The panicked animals had spun at the river and were now running back toward them. Strong Horse noticed first and yelled for the others to grab their mounts and cut off the herd at the foothills. Their own horses shied and reared in the commotion.

Quickly they circled the big herd and pushed the horses on with screams and taunts. At a frantic pace they drove the herd while watching their backs. The Arapaho's village was destroyed, but the Utes knew that angry survivors would be coming. For the next two hours, choked in dust, they raced to escape.

The evening sun glared in their faces then sunk below the clouds and disappeared. In darkness the air grew still, but the sky behind them still flashed with storms. They fought to stay awake through the night to keep the big herd moving.

As daylight neared, the steel gray heavens were pierced by lingering stars. The western sky faded from lavender to light pink on a base of baby blue. The setting moon floated above the prairie before slowly dipping from sight. The early summer air was crisp at dawn but promised to be angry hot before long. Grunts and huffs of winded horses mixed with the rumble of hooves. The smell of dust and lather floated in the air.

The stolen herd was a collection of every age. The oldest horses were stretched to the rear while stronger ones challenged for the lead. There were mares and foals, stallions, and old travois draggers. The horses were every color, and many were spotted across their backs and rumps. There were several red roans with silver and white feathered edges. Their color was the same as the red willows in winter, laced with silver tips. Many of the younger horses showed the same combination of colors.

Strong Horse rode at the point and although he was the youngest man, he was the leader. He wore a black headband with a single eagle feather. A fringed bag hung over his bare shoulder, and a beaded belt held a knife at his hip. In one hand he carried a quirt and slapped his horse in a regular rhythm. In the other hand, he balanced the reins and a rifle. He rode a leggy, black stallion with three white socks. On the horse's hip was a white handprint, and marks of valor streamed down its neck. A yellow ribbon hung from his bridle — a gift from Star Flower, which she'd given him at the Bear Dance the year before.

The men were all in their early twenties. Arturo, who flanked the herd, was twenty-four. To the north rode Red Elk who, like Henry Eagle, had seen twenty-two summers. Strong Horse had seen twenty-one.

The men had slipped away without their families' blessings. The elders knew that to go far onto the plains was dangerous. Their enemies, the Arapahos, Kiowas, and Comanches were strong, and the young men would be butchered if they were caught. But these were young men, not boys. They'd proven their skills with weapons and horses. If they chose to make a raid, there was no one who could stop them. War Raven, the chief of their Black Eagle families, warned them about their enemies. They would have to use all their wit to steal horses and get back alive.

The plan was to steal a few good horses that would be easy to drive back to the mountains. Now, their task was almost too much. They had a sprawling herd that they couldn't afford to cut down. Any old horses or cripples they left behind would serve as clues for the pursuing Arapaho. Nearly every horse of the Spotted Bird Clan had been stolen but if any horses were left, the Arapahos would be gathering forces and riding west. They'd have little strength after the tornado, but allied tribes would join in the chase of the arrogant thieves.

The Utes were weary, tired, and worn to the bone. It had been many days since they'd left the west side of the Snowy Mountains. For the time being they were rich with horses but tired and hungry. They'd hoped to be home by now but had traveled much farther east than they had planned.

As morning shadows faded, Strong Horse and his men searched for water and cover. If they found either, they could rest for a bit.

Thus far they had avoided their enemy's arrows, but it was the twisting wind that they feared the most. They rode with an eye to the sky and worried at the sight of clouds.

CHAPTER FOUR

The Weight of War

▲ ▲ ▲

Tom returned to a world of blurry light and searing pain in the back of his skull. He struggled to breathe from the weight on his chest and the coarse hair in his mouth. When he tried to move, he felt something pull at his arm. Through muffled ears and a cloudy mind, he heard the faint call, "Papa." Unsure if he was dreaming or dying, he strained to listen over the ringing in his ears.

"Papa." He heard it again and felt a tug on his arm. He recognized his daughter's voice, then panic set in as he fought to get out from under the bear.

His wide eyes met his daughter's and those of a boy crouched over a body in the creek. He struggled to sort out where he was and what had happened. He stumbled at the sight of the dead bear beside him. He felt the back of his head then studied the blood on his fingers. He looked at the boy and then to Brooke, and he knew he wasn't dreaming or dying.

Brooke stared at her father and watched him struggle to find his wits. When he opened his arms, she lunged to his side and hugged him hard. She shuddered for air, and Tom squeezed her back while watching the boy massage the man in the creek. When the man's arm moved, Tom knew he wasn't dead but would be soon if fate took its course. The last thing he remembered was firing a shot and the bear's nose at his face. He touched the knot on his forehead and studied the pool of blood at the bear's chest.

"Brooke, we need to find the horses and my surgical box."

"Up there," she said, pointing to the mules that watched from above. "I'll get em."

Tom turned toward the boy who stiffened and glared back at him. Tom stepped back and crouched down. His head throbbed, as he diagnosed the man from a distance. The stream drew away stripes of blood from his shoulder and head. The man groaned and tried to move, and the boy glanced at Tom then looked back down. Tom wanted to help, but first he had to get the man out of the water. If his temperature got too low, he would never recover. Tom scooted forward and the boy cowered over the man.

"I can help," Tom said.

The boy glanced his way then back to the man.

"I can help you," Tom said again and scooted closer. The boy huffed and rattled unfamiliar words in a tongue that Tom assumed was Ute.

Brooke came leading the mules, and the horses followed. She tied the mules and moved up next to her father.

"Papa, what should we do?" She looked back and forth between the men.

"We need to get that man out of the creek. I can stitch him up but this boy, might be his son, won't let me near him."

Brooke stood up and moved to the other side of the boy. She got down in a squat and inched forward. He squinted as she came closer.

"Young man, you need to let us help you, or this man will die. My father can help." Brooke glanced at Tom.

Water Bird looked back at her and huffed again.

"Please," she pleaded, her voice cracking with sympathy as her firm face softened. The boy stared back silently for a moment before he looked down at his father and spoke in a low voice.

"It's no use Brooke, he doesn't know what we're saying." Tom looked at the horses that stared at the bear. "We have to get into our gear, that surgical box, I need it."

His head ached at every twist and a part of him wanted to just lie down, but he couldn't. In the war he'd seen men with concussions fall asleep and never wake up. He knew that could be him — and probably the man in the stream too. He stared into the rushing water and struggled with his next move.

The little black bird swooped in and landed on a rock in front of the boy. The boy looked up slowly at the creature as it took center stage. It bobbed and dipped and stamped its feet while blaring chirps that pierced their ears. The boy glanced at Brooke, who tipped her head to the side and watched. The bird jumped into the shallows and spun and splashed in a ruckus. It jumped back up on the rock and stamped about, barking a rant.

The boy whispered something to the bird, and then the bird jumped into the water and disappeared.

"Papa, what did he say?"

"I don't know. He's talking to the bird."

The bird popped out of the water on a rock downstream and chirped then flew away.

The Ute man's moan drew every eye. The boy glanced first downstream at the bird that flew away and then to Brooke. He stood up and grabbed the back of the man's shirt and partially pulled him from the stream. The boy's face settled slightly. Tom stepped forward, but the boy didn't look up. Tom bent down and wrapped his arms around the man's body and tried to lift but couldn't. He glanced first at the boy and then at Brooke, then together they all lifted the man from the water.

"Over there," Tom barked and tossed his head toward a tree where they laid the man down. "Wood, wood," Tom snapped. He picked up a stick and shook it at the boy who hesitated then spun around grabbing sticks and branches with Brooke.

Soon a large fire boiled water, and the surgical tools were laid out on a log. Tom pulled a shirt from his gear. "Brooke, rip it into long strips." He got down on his knees and started folding and flooding the man's torn flesh. For nearly two hours he cleaned the wounds. Pieces of grass, gravel, sticks and pine needles had been ground into the cuts and scrapes.

He started the surgery on the man's shoulder first, it was the most severe wound and would take internal and surface stitching.

It had been years since Tom had sutured a large laceration but as he worked, he remembered the moves and some of the men he'd sewn up before. God damn the war. Those days were supposed to be over, but here he was again, trying to sew the life back into a man he didn't know.

An engineer by education, Tom had been forced into medical training at the height of the Civil War. When it was over, he and his wife and daughter moved west to leave the horror of war behind. But here he was again, fighting to save a life against daunting odds.

The boy watched every move Tom made. Tom could tell the boy was reluctant, but he seemed to concede that he had no better way to save his father. Tom checked his pocket watch and, after three hours, the shoulder was closed.

He moved to the man's skull, where the skin had been scraped to the bone. The slab of torn scalp started at his hairline and went halfway up his head. Tom felt the skull for soft spots but couldn't find any. After another hour, and fifty plus stitches, the man's scalp was sewn in place. Of the three spools of suture Tom had started with, he had only one left.

As bad as the man's head and shoulder were, it was his leg that worried Tom the most. There weren't any large cuts, only deep puncture wounds from where the bear had bitten his leg, trying to break the bones. The holes from its teeth had squeezed shut, and Tom pressed them open to clean them. He wrapped strips of cloth onto tweezers and drove them into the holes to twist out the dirt and hair that had lodged there.

It was early evening when Tom decided he was done. The boy and Brooke had stayed at his side the entire time. As Tom had told Brooke what to do, he thought the boy may have learned some new words in the process. When it was obvious that Tom was done, the boy took strips of dry green moss from the trees that he twisted and pressed into the wounds and patted them down with warm water. Tom didn't know the benefit of the poultice, but he sensed that the boy did.

Through the entire procedure the big Ute man never woke up. Tom knew he was trapped in a coma. Few people could survive that blow to the skull, not to mention the amount of blood he'd lost. Tom realized that the boy was right to drag the man to the stream. By getting him into the cold water, he may have saved his life.

Brooke started cooking bacon and biscuits right after her father knotted the last stitch. The boy gathered wood and piled it next to the fire.

After the horses were tied and unsaddled Tom and Brooke sat to eat. They talked very little as the dismay of the long summer day settled in. Brooke scooted next to her father, and he put an arm over her shoulder.

The boy sat on the other side of the fire near the man, who was wrapped in a blanket under a tarp. The boy nibbled at a piece of dry meat, and his eyebrows raised when Brooke offered him a plate of food. He didn't say anything, but the softening of his frown did.

As evening's dull light settled over the camp, the marsh sparrows lonely call drifted through the air. Tom lay down and folded a blanket over his shoulder. He felt the pine needles pack beneath his hip as he let out a hesitant sigh. He could feel Brooke's warmth near his back and soon knew that she was asleep.

On the other side of the tree the man breathed in ragged gasps. The boy sat near him and poked at the fire.

Tom breathed in deep and tried to forget the day, and the hundreds of stitches he'd sewn in the flesh of the man by the fire. He had cleaned the wounds the best he could, but he knew that infection was inevitable. He tried not to think: What if the man never woke up?

Tom could smell the bear that lay just outside of the firelight. He dozed off and drifted to the hills of eastern Kentucky where the rumble of distant cannon fire weighed on his weary mind. Nodding off into a bad dream, he imagined opening a tent flap. Woof! The pig-nosed snout of a bear shot toward his face. Tom sucked for air and sprang up in shock, looking first at the lingering fire then at the Ute boy who stared back at him, wide-eyed. Tom's heart pounded heavily, and his breath blew hard against his cheeks. For a long minute he stared at the fire coals, until he was sure there was no cannon fire — and no bear. He breathed a sigh of relief. At least he wasn't still at war.

He laid down and stared into the darkness. Three days ago, on the east side of the divide, he and Brooke had met a man who called himself Mustache Bob. Now, he remembered Bob's long moustache twitching as he'd warned them: "Watch out for bears and make friends with the Utes."

CHAPTER FIVE

Sleeping Snakes

▲ ▲ ▲

The morning sky bled red over the scattered Arapaho village. The crying of the women worried the wolves. The twisting storm had spared no family, and the dead were gathered and laid near the remnants of their homes. There was no time for formal mourning. That would come later. Everyone who could help was tending the injured and consoling the orphaned. Dead horses and dogs were scattered among the destruction and, as the morning air rose, so did the stench of death and the whine of flies.

In the center of the destruction stood Black Bull, the chief of the Spotted Bird Clan. He stood tall and gave direction to the weary. He was naked above the waist and his muscular shoulders rippled with tension. A pair of tattered feathers dangled from his hair and a brass studded war club with a green stone head hung at his hip. His head had been injured by a flying branch that had killed his youngest son. His wife and daughter had also died in the tornado. His remaining son, Badger Heart, stood close by.

A young man named Fisher brought word that he could find only about twenty horses. With so few mounts, and so many injured, the camp would need help to move.

Black Bull sent Fisher and an older man named Fox to get help, riding two of the strongest horses left. Fox knew the rough country of the prairie, and he would speed the search for other clans who could aid them in the hunt. They struck out within minutes with their orders to head west before turning south. Across the river they found tracks of the horse herd and quickly knew that thieves were driving the herd away. Fisher went back to tell Black Bull, while Fox trailed the treasure of stolen horseflesh.

For almost a century the Arapahos had bred their horses, and, in the last generation, they had added the spotted Appaloosas from the north. The introduction of different bloodlines had come at the cost of many of their ancestors.

When Black Bull heard the news of the thieves, his jaw clenched at the thought of the enemies who would gloat in their luck and rejoice in his loss. He couldn't chase them now, but as soon as help arrived, he would run them to their deaths. He hated his enemies even more for bringing the wrath of the churning wind. He would hold them responsible for the deaths of his people and the destruction of the village. He knew the thieves could not escape without losing some of the horses. The speed of their escape would depend on their greed. If they were heading west, they were probably Ute, if south, Comanche. Whoever they were, they were bold to come so deep into Arapaho land, and they must have come in force.

• • •

Strong Horse's band of thieves were three days from the Spotted Bird village when they knew they were lost. They couldn't find the trail that had brought them east, so all they could do was follow the sun. Fighting the thirsty herd, they found themselves trapped in rough country more than once. Every mistake slowed their escape and tired the horses.

Had the Arapahos chased them quickly, they'd have been caught. Although they hadn't seen any warriors yet, they knew they were coming.

The big herd was in trouble. Three old horses had died, and others were slowing the move. The youngest ones were stressed from near constant travel and little time to nurse.

As darkness fell the third evening, the weary herd stalled to a walk. They would have stopped, but Strong Horse led two mares with foals and if the pairs kept moving the others would follow.

The small bear stars were rising when Strong Horse's mount perked his ears and snorted. Other horses moved up alongside of him and marched with new purpose toward the smell of water. The herd broke into an easy lope except for the oldest horses that lagged behind at a slower pace. When they came to a shallow river that sparkled in starlight the horses waded in and sunk to their bellies. Stuck in the mud they drank from their knees. The men dismounted and stood in the river to keep the herd at the edge of the water. If they got in too deep, they'd never get out. The men also struggled to keep from getting stuck.

Late in the night the horses settled back on the bank and grazed while the men took turns watching the herd. During his watch, Strong Horse realized they'd have to leave some horses behind. They would rest the herd into the next day then set out with only the strongest ones.

Come daylight the river had started the culling. Two horses were stuck in the mud from the night before. One was dead and one was dying. A young sorrel filly stood near the bank with a broken leg. She, too, would soon feed the wolves.

Henry Eagle and Arturo waded out to a stuck horse and sliced an artery in its neck. The horse stood still, too weak to fight. With cupped hands against its hide, they caught the blood and drank it from their palms. When its nose sunk into the water they sliced along the spine and took the meat. On the bank they shared the horseflesh while Red Elk snored in the shade of his horse.

As the sun rose, the herd fought flies while the young ones lay on their sides.

Strong Horse rode to where he could study the herd and see the surrounding hills and canyons. When the other men joined him, the sun was high overhead. He instructed them which horses to leave behind — and how to use those cull horses to confuse the Arapahos who were surely coming.

They would leave the oldest horses, and any with crooked feet or legs. They would keep as many of the spotted roans as they dared. Strong Horse hated to leave any horses behind but knew they must to get home alive. They were all pained at the thought of sacrificing horses that were the very reason they'd risked their lives to come east. Among all tribes, the horse was the most valuable possession — next to its owner's life.

In late afternoon they drove the herd up-river to an area of tall grass just below a shallow crossing. On the east bank, they cut the cull horses from the main herd. Some foals were kept with mares to avoid separation problems.

Arturo and Red Elk drove the forty cull horses up the river beyond the crossing. The little herd grazed along slowly and were eased upstream into a narrow canyon. Late in the evening the two men slid from their mounts and caught the culls one at a time. They worked until after dark to catch and kill every horse. By the time they got back to the other men the moon was climbing into the sky.

The remaining horse herd had grazed up-river to the shallow crossing. Strong Horse caught two mares with babies, and Henry Eagle roped a spotted stallion. They entered the river and the rest of the herd followed in nearly single file. As the horses strung out in the moonlight, Strong Horse counted over one hundred and sixty head.

Arturo was last to cross the river and, before he did, he brushed the hoof prints from the muddy east bank. The tracks of the forty cull horses were left heading up stream past the crossing.

The half-moon was near the western horizon when the last of the horses made it to the west bank. The men and horses were rested and, as they left the river, Strong Horse coaxed them into a long stride.

• • •

Black Bull and Badger Heart sat on their horses and stared into the canyon at the stinking carcasses. Blood-soaked circles marked the sand where each horse had bled to death. Their throats cut by the Utes that had stolen them. Vultures circled, ravens squawked, and coyotes prowled the ridges.

Black Bull jerked the bridle and kicked the ribs of his sweat-soaked horse and headed back to the river. It was almost dark by the time they discovered where the big herd had crossed two days earlier. Black Bull knew that just a handful of thieves had stolen the herd. Without a word, a war party, armed for revenge, kicked their horses, and headed west for the Snowy Mountains.

• • •

All the horses ran with their ears pinned flat on outstretched heads. Nostrils bulged as bellowing lungs pushed and sucked for air. They'd been running full tilt since daylight, when Red Elk spotted a column of dust to the east. They'd moved the herd steadily through the night, knowing that the Arapahos would run their mounts to death to catch them. The mountains that loomed ahead marked the edge of Ute land, but the vantage of the rugged canyons was still half a day away.

Strong Horse knew the mountains wouldn't stop the Arapahos. They would become beggars without their horse herd. They'd chase the Utes to their tipis if they had to.

As they climbed the foothills, the big herd started to slow. Strong Horse knew they'd have to make a stand when they reached the slanted stone ridges.

At a narrow spot between outcrops Strong Horse brought the men together while the thirsty herd moved on. Red Elk was to push the herd up farther, then return to the fight. They didn't know how many enemies had chased them, but if they didn't fight now, they'd have to fight in the dark. The Utes had rifles but were low on bullets; they'd have to get in close.

A little above the canyon floor they hunkered down and waited. Thirst, hunger, and lack of sleep were overridden by vigilance. Standing hair pricked necks and backs. Sweaty hands gripped wood and steel.

The sun tipped west of center, and dusty air clouded the pines when the Arapaho warriors came up the crooked canyon. A big man was in the lead and another man with badger bars painted on his face followed. Behind him rode a dozen men. They entered the canyon in a tight group, pressing hard to catch the thieves by dark.

Kaboom! Black Bull's body flipped from his horse before the first bullet's echo was heard. Brains and blood splattered frightened faces behind him. Two men took slugs before they could spin. A horse dropped and its rider reached for a rescue, but both men were slammed dead to the ground. The others slid to the sides of their mounts and dodged for cover. Another volley put another man to the ground. Shots that missed men hit horses that stumbled beneath them. Another volley of four shots and two more men fell to the ground.

From a clump of trees just out of range the Arapahos fired back. The man with painted stripes on his face like those of a badger sprinted forward. He lay behind a dead horse until he dove to the body of the first man that had fallen. He lay beside the body for a moment then dashed away in a shower of lead with an extra rifle and a war club in his hand. The Arapahos moved farther back into the trees. Screaming rose in the afternoon air. A single shot rang out, followed by the sound of fleeing hoof beats.

Strong Horse and his warriors waited a moment then stood and taunted their cowardly enemies. They watched the Arapahos ride out of sight, leaving behind only lingering dust and the bodies that lay on the ground.

They climbed down and walked nervously in the direction of the dead. With rifles pointed at the motionless forms, they approached the nearest man, the one Strong Horse had shot between the eyes. They breathed hard with open mouths as their hearts pounded. Strong Horse looked back at the other men and then at the strong-armed man at his feet.

Strong Horse gripped his knife and screamed as he scraped the scalp from Black Bull's skull.

They all stamped and hollered in fright and delight as ripples of energy flooded their bodies. Scalps were lifted and bodies were hacked as the four Utes claimed their first battle plunder. The fear that had drug at their heels for days had fled with the Arapahoe. They felt a little safer with their wealth of horseflesh and merit. Yet, at their feet, their enemies lay like sleeping snakes. Relieved to be back in the mountains they grinned through guarded smiles. Proud of what they had done but fully aware of the weight of hatred.

They gathered the herd and bedded on a bald knob where they all guarded the herd through the night. Two more days and they would cross the divide into the Black Rock River Canyon and enter their village. Their families would hail their arrival in astonishment. Their adventure would seal their positions as valiant warriors within the Black Eagle family.

Only two moons had passed since they'd slipped away onto the plains, but the tale of the Churning Wind Raid would be told for many more.

CHAPTER SIX

Rose Creek

▲ ▲ ▲

The Ute man started to rustle. He'd been motionless most of the morning. For three days he'd drifted in and out of a dull consciousness as his fever fought infection. At times he'd thrash about and jab at mind-made enemies. Pain raked across his face every time he moved. Tom watched him with one eye and reached for a pan on the fire. He wondered if the man still battled the bear that had tried to kill him.

Tom's head still pounded from his own struggle with the brute. The wicked sights and sounds haunted him in a storied collage of his past. His tortured mind always returned to the horrors of war. Blood's echo pounding in his ears always milled into cannon fire.

For the first two days and nights the boy stayed by the man's side. Tom felt he could be the boy's father. The second evening the man woke and barely slit his swollen eyes, moved his lips, then sunk away again. The boy's face rose and fell with his father's movement. The next dawn the boy was gone but returned mid-morning with four gaunt horses. He picketed them across from camp where they grazed non-stop until afternoon.

Tom tried to talk to the boy on a couple of occasions. He could get across points like firewood, water, and time to eat, but when he tried to talk of names the boy only stared at his father, and Tom would let the matter go.

Brooke only ventured to the edge of camp to watch the boy or look at the horses. When she wasn't working on chores, she'd sit and draw or write in her journal. Tom watched one morning as she followed the boy toward the horses. When the boy heard Brooke behind him, he spun, and she froze in her tracks. One side of his lips edged up, hardly a smile, but he tipped his head for her to follow.

It was the third afternoon in camp and sunshine was cutting through the pines when the man's eyes snapped open. Tom came out of a crouch to check on him. With arms extended, palms down, he signaled to the wounded man to stop, relax, and lie back down. The man glanced around, sniffed the air, and started to rise. Then stiffening in pain, he let out a shallow sigh and sank back onto his butt.

"Brooke! Get the boy. His father's coming around." She jumped at his shout, glanced upstream and trotted away.

The boy was holding up a horse's hoof when she saw him. Caught for a moment, she didn't know what to say, "Hey! Hey, you," she yelled, waving her arms. "Boy, come. Come on. He's awake." He dropped the hoof and stared her way. "Come," she yelled again and pointed toward camp.

He took a couple of steps, then yelled as he broke into a run. She matched his stride as they ran through the trees. When they broke into the opening the man grunted through the pain, sat up and spread his arms. The boy landed in his arms and released a string of words. The man watched Tom and Brooke over the boy's shoulder as he listened. He pushed the boy to arm's-length and looked at the bear hide lying across a log, then pulled the boy back close. Tiny tears seeped from swollen eyes. The boy twisted from the man and flopped on his back, staring upward, whispering to the sky. The man lay back down and spoke softly upward too.

Tom reached out and pulled Brooke close. The boy sat up quickly, his watery brown eyes moved between Tom and Brooke. He sighed a heavy breath and his shoulders settled. His thin lips edged up slightly just before he lay back down.

The warm afternoon sun roused the forest while those in the

camp dozed. When Tom awoke, three large stars sparkled in the west and the robins whistled their evening farewell. He stirred the fire to life and scalded rags and surgical tools.

Brooke woke up, followed by the boy who glanced at the pots by the fire. Tom stooped next to the man whose eyes slowly opened. He lay still as Tom touched the row of stitches on his forehead. Each row was washed and dried before he used a rag to wallow out the puncture wounds. The man gritted his teeth while Brooke and the boy grimaced and hissed. For nearly two hours Tom checked every stitch, cleaned every cut and pressed every bone. When he was finished, he wiped and scalded everything again. Then the boy took more of the twisted green tree moss and pressed it into the wounds. Tom didn't know why but he surmised the intent of disinfectant. He stared into the pot of boiling water and wondered about his bedside manner. He'd mustered some during the war, but it was always a struggle to lift spirits of men who had little hope. But this Ute man had more than hope. He'd shown a resistance to death tempered from what Tom knew must be a hard-earned life. With motions and gestures, Tom encouraged the man's faith and resolve. With a wagging hand, the man motioned Tom and the others to come closer. He cleared his throat and glanced up and to the side. He started to speak then stopped and glanced up again. Lightly choking to form words he uttered, "Tank-oo." Then, stronger, he said it again, "Tank-oo."

"Thank you," Tom repeated.

The man nodded lightly, "Thank you."

"Papa, he said thank you." Brooke's eyes were wide.

"You're welcome," Tom replied with a soft nod.

The man smiled back and nodded, stronger this time. Brooke and the boy glanced at each other then back at the men. Tom knelt and offered his right hand. The man reached across his body with his good left arm, took Tom's hand and said, "Welcome. Welcome."

They stayed in camp for one more day before Tom was ready to move. With some difficulty, the Utes conveyed that their village was three days away, but the first day they moved only a mile.

Cliffs and bluffs clogged the canyon, and the Ute man struggled to explain directions between the rocky outcrops. Several times they had to backtrack with rambunctious horses. As the day went on, the man's pain increased along with his confusion.

That night the camp was cold as everyone settled into rest. The next day went better as they covered a couple of miles. The trail was still hard to follow, crossing glacier-polished granite along chasms of whitewater that deafened their ears. They stopped earlier the second evening and camped on a bluff above a waterfall. The boy knew the spot and pointed out a fire pit that they used. By the time they got unpacked the man was miserable. The stitches in his shoulder had torn apart, and he was reluctant to have them repaired. He conceded only after Tom's insistence. By firelight Tom pierced new holes and knotted new stitches. The man was stoic but when the stitching was done, he collapsed from exhaustion.

As Tom cleaned his tools, he wondered what to expect when they reached the Ute village. He knew it would be better for the man and his boy to be with their people, but how would they treat him and his daughter? He wasn't sure, but he knew he couldn't abandon this man and his son. He was deep into this situation now and couldn't leave if he wanted to. Not until he got the man back to his family. Then he would figure out his next move.

The next morning Tom knew they all needed to rest another day. He was determined to get as much food into the man as possible, and that meant staying put.

The man could barely get up to relieve himself for lack of strength. When he realized they weren't moving, he was bitter and snapped off words that Tom didn't understand. But he felt their meaning.

The boy was discouraged too. He knew he had to get his father home and he wondered why no one had come to find them yet. Surely, his mother and sister were worried. He was eager to be safe among his people, and he yearned to tell the story of how he and this white-faced doctor had killed the split-eared bear. The story was legend-worthy, providing his father survived. He thought of making a run for the village but chose to stay with his father instead.

• • •

The polished stone slabs along the river were warm when the boy decided to swim in the pools at the base of the waterfall. The churning water didn't scare him. In fact, no water did. The water was his refuge. He slid through the spruce and caught a crimson flash at the riverbank. The girl was sitting on the rocky shore with her knees tucked tight to her chest. Her lips moved as she looked across the river.

The boy wondered who she was talking to. Where was her mother? And why had these whites ventured so deep into their land? They weren't supposed to be here, but they weren't the only whites that crossed the divide into the reservation. This father and daughter were different though, not like the other intruders, with their little donkeys loaded with tools and pans. He liked the girl and her father, but he didn't dare trust them. They had saved his father's life, and maybe his own, but they were still whites.

He stepped into the sunlight just downriver of the girl. Her ivory face turned lightly pink as she straightened her back. He walked behind her and stopped at a column of rocks that skirted the river. He slid off his shirt and dropped his leggings. A piece of cloth covered his groin. With one tall step his toes bit into the rock and the next step launched him upward. He glanced back at the girl and caught her eyes just before he disappeared into a crevice.

When he walked onto the point above the waterfall, she covered her mouth with both hands. She looked much smaller to him now. He reached for the sky and filled his lungs just before he launched toward the swirling pool below. Like a spear hurled from a hardened arm, his slender shape pierced the water with slicing force. Down and down he went as air bubbles raced for the surface behind him. When his hands hit the sandy bottom, he crumpled into a seat and let the river nudge him side to side. Behind glazed eyes he watched a large fish that settled in the shadows. Its eyes rocked and its ruby gills wavered with the flow. He waited while the fish circled him twice then disappeared downstream. He held his seat a moment more, then, with powerful strokes, he surged upward. As he neared the surface, he could see the girl pacing back and forth. When his face broke the surface, she shrieked and stumbled backwards. As he stepped from the water, her face relaxed into a shaken smile. Her wide eyes bounced around his body where water beads rolled down his copper skin. She glanced up at the waterfall and lightly wagged her head. Soft words that he couldn't understand rolled off her tongue. He turned and pointed up to the rocks, making a motion with his hand, mimicking the path of his flight. With a whooshing sound he imitated his dive into the water. Her smile widened and she shook her head some more.

He turned toward the river and motioned her to sit beside him. He wanted to talk but didn't know how. He remembered the word his father had said.

"Tank-oo," he said as he looked at her.

"Thank-you," she said back.

"Thank-oo," he replied.

"Thank you," she said back, slowly.

"Thank you," he said confidently, and she nodded.

• • •

The little bird sailed in just above the water and landed upstream. Its slate black body blended with the stones.

"Wah-we-chitch," he said, pointing at the bird.

She tipped her head his way. "Wah-we-chitch?"

He dipped his chin one time, tapped his chest and said it again. He reached to the river, filled a hand with water, and put a finger in the pool in his palm. "Wah," he said. "Wah."

"Wah," she replied. "Water, wah?"

He nodded with a sideways glance then pointed to the little bird up shore. "We-chitch."

"Chitch?"

"We-chitch," he said back slowly. Placing an open hand on his chest, he looked her in the eye and said it again. "Wah-we-chitch."

She smiled wide, realizing that she had just learned his name. "Wah-we-chitch," she said, tapping a finger toward him. Water Bird sat up straighter.

"Wah-we-chitch," he agreed, matching her wide smile. She let out a gentle hum, looked out across the water and imitated the river with a waving hand. "Brooke," she said.

"Bok," he replied.

She said her name again. "Brooke."

He thought for a moment then said, "*Pahn-qwe*. Brook."

"*Pahn-qwe*?" She looked out across the roaring river. "Brooke." She made the sign for something little, showing him a little gap between her finger and thumb and pointed at a tiny creek that trickled into the river. "Creek. Brooke."

"Brooke," he said, pointing at the same small tributary. She nodded slowly.

Leaning back, she touched the petals of a wild rose that grew from a crack in the rock. "Brooke Rose," she said with a nod and high eyebrows. "Rose."

He held her gaze a second, his tight lips smiled. "Rose." He leaned back and touched the rose. "*Uckarth*. Rose." he said. Then, looking back to the little tributary stream, he added, "Uckarth Pahn-qwe."

"Uckarth Pahn-qwe. Rose Creek." She let out a slight chuckle, looked away, then looked back and put a finger to her chest and asked, "Uckarth Pahn-qwe?" He nodded *yes,* and she clapped her hands in front of her chest and sat up a little straighter.

The afternoon sun was hot, as Brooke and Water Bird climbed the bluff to camp. Tom waved her to where he sat, and the boy followed.

"Father, you won't believe. This boy dove into the big pool down there."

"I know he did. I watched."

"You did?"

"I couldn't believe it either. It looked like you two were talking?"

"Papa, we did, and I know his name."

"Really?" Brooke looked to the boy then back at her father, "Wah-we-chitch." She held up a palm and made a stirring motion as he said, "Wah—water, we-chitch—bird. The little black bird we've seen in the stream."

Tom looked at the boy, pointed a finger and repeated, "Wah-we-chitch?"

Water Bird nodded one time.

"Huh," Tom said with a slight chuckle as he bent back to his work.

"And I am Uckarth Pahn-qwe — Rose Creek."

Tom smiled. "Rose Creek. It suits you."

"Uckarth Pahn-qwe," she repeated. "And Papa, the injured man is his father, *Utch Noo-quet,* Bow River."

• • •

A deep, throaty holler bellowed across the valley. All heads jerked up and looked toward the mountain peaks. The cry sounded like a cross between a wolf and a coyote howl, but it was shaded with the guttural roar of a bear. Bow River sat up, his face strained, his brow pinched. Tom shivered as the eerie cry rang out again, then a similar scream from downstream echoed off the cliffs. Water Bird spoke, half hushed, looking uphill. Bow River replied, and Water Bird picked up his bow and disappeared into the trees.

"Papa, where's he going? What's out there?"

"I have no idea." He paused and looked toward Bow River. "I'm not even sure what it is."

A mule snorted, and everyone flinched. Most of the horses were tied at the edge of camp where they shuffled and glanced about with pointed ears. The booming shout rang out again, and Tom guessed it had to be human. Bow River struggled to his feet. He held his rifle and waved the barrel for Tom and Brooke to come closer.

"Brooke, we need to watch out for the horses. Could be thieves." Bow River looked at Tom and nodded.

Pops and cracks in the brush turned eyes and rifles toward the sound.

"It's Water Bird," Brooke hissed.

Water Bird tapped his fingers to his lips. He spoke silently with his hands, and his father signed back. No one spoke as Water Bird tied his horse close by.

For a second Tom wasn't sure what he'd just seen. Was it a gnarled piece bark on the side of a spruce tree or an old woman's face? He tipped to the side, looking, but couldn't see anything now.

"Brooke, get behind me."

"What is it, Papa?"

"I just saw a face out there." Tom looked to Bow River who nodded softly as if he understood.

Tom tossed his head in the direction of the face, and Bow River bent down to look. Water Bird stepped behind a sprawling pine with his father. Tom nudged Brooke, and they took cover behind the same tree.

The grating voice blared again, closer this time, a reply downstream was closer too. Bow River and Water Bird looked at Tom and Brooke, and their stern faces softened. Water Bird yelled into the woods, which brought a quick reply. Shoulders settled as father and son released sighs. Water Bird yelled out a string of words, and barely fifteen yards away a man stepped from behind a tree with his rifle marked on Tom. Bow River spoke, but the stranger still pointed his rifle at Tom's gut. Again, Bow River spoke, more forceful this time, and the man slowly lowered his gun and stepped forward. His eyes sprang open with concern when he saw Bow River.

The man looked similar in age and build to Bow River, but this stranger was slightly taller. He was dressed in gray leather. Two eagle feathers hung at the back of his head, a large brass ring dangled from his left ear, and a bar of red paint crossed his cheeks and the bridge of his nose.

When the stranger reached up and gently touched the row of stitches on Bow River's head, Tom recognized a brotherly concern.

He'd seen it many times before in the war. A brother's love was undeniable.

Water Bird stepped closer, and the man laid a hand on his shoulder.

Tom looked toward the horses, where three other men watched. They were naked above the waist, and each sported a different combination of feathers and jewelry. They all wore the same red stripe across their faces. Tom sensed they were dressed for war. He quickly reasoned they'd been under surveillance, and these men were here to rescue Bow River and his son. The three men stepped up and joined the conversation that seemed to be getting lighter by the moment.

As the afternoon eased into evening, everyone settled in. Each man made it a point to try to communicate with Tom and Brooke, and Water Bird joined in the effort. They gestured, pointed, and stared at Brooke's hair with bewilderment. When she looked at them directly, they'd tip their heads away, as if her pale eyes were blinding.

The fire was big that night. When food was shared, Tom offered biscuits, coffee with sugar, and stewed apples.

Water Bird told the story of the bear attack. His tale went on and on to the oohs and ah's and grimaces of the others. When he finished, they all looked at Tom and Brooke, stood up and stepped toward them. Tom and Brooke stood up to meet their approach. The men were serious as their eyes ranged over the father and daughter. The tall man with the brass earring stepped up first. He looked Tom directly in his eyes and offered his vertical hand, held chest high. Tom recognized the noble gesture of acceptance and clasped the man's hand with a *pop*. Each man stepped up and did the same, rocking slightly as they clasped hands. Then they approached Brooke and gave her the same direct look, followed by a tip of their heads.

Mid-afternoon a day and a half later, Good Bear, Bow River's brother, led six Utes on horseback through belly-deep grass along the river, which had slowed to a meander. Tom and Brooke brought up the rear with all the pack animals. Half a mile away,

Tom could see smoke hovering over tipis half hidden in an aspen forest. Fifty head of horses grazed unaware of their approach. But when they sensed the coming riders, they charged and galloped circles around the approaching horses and riders.

As they neared the village a cackle of whoops and hollers rang out. People began running their way. Some were mounted on horses, but most were on foot. Tom looked at Brooke who stared wide-eyed at the coming crowd. She flashed an uncertain glance at her father, which he returned. She looked back at the throng of people pouring from the trees and lightly nipped her lip.

Tom and Brooke were ushered to the edge of a camp that sat on a bench above the river. A large water spring covered in watercress gurgled from the hillside above the tipis.

From atop his horse Bow River talked over the crowd. His words and gestures caused eyes to swing to the newcomers and back to him. Tom didn't know the language, but he could read the intentions of the words. Heads nodded as concerned looks softened into subtle smiles. Bow River talked on, and his tone got more serious. The surrounding crowd became more sober too, except for the fidgety kids that kept their eyes on the whites, especially Brooke. Bow River finished with a lighter inflection that caused everyone to turn to Tom and Brooke. They sat on their nervous horses as the crowd moved around them. They were circled by kids, teenagers, and adults with curious brown eyes. They chattered like birds in a tree as they squeezed in to tap lightly on the strangers' arms and legs. Tom wasn't sure whether he and his daughter were being scrutinized or welcomed. Perhaps the gesture was meant to convey both.

Bow River and Water Bird slid from their horses and watched the crowd. They were joined by a woman and an older girl. Tom suspected he was seeing Bow River's wife and daughter. Bow River hugged them both with affection that was returned with touches of concern. The woman turned and walked toward Tom. Water Bird and two other boys, who led Tom's mules, rushed to meet her. Water Bird held a hand toward the woman then rocked his clutched hands at his heart. The woman swiftly wrapped both arms around him and mashed her face to his cheek. The interpretation was simple. This was his mother.

After some gesturing and nodding, he conveyed to the new arrivals that her name was Stone Calf.

Brooke looked softly into the woman's eyes, rolled her lips together and lightly dipped her head. Stone Calf returned the same slight bow. Tom and Brooke dismounted, and the woman turned and parted the crowd as she walked uphill into the village. The rest of the people waited then fell in behind Tom and Brooke.

The mules were tied off next to a tipi that was trimmed in ocher colors. Stone Calf stood at the open flap and gestured for them to enter.

Tom and Brooke looked at each other. "I guess this is for us," Tom said with high eyebrows.

Brooke met his look with the same wonder, dipped her head, and stooped inside.

The first evening at the Pony Springs Camp, Tom and Brooke were treated to a celebration they'd never dreamed to see. All afternoon, the women cooked as children piled wood high around a central fire pit. As the long days of summer eased into evening and the moon crested the mountains, fires were lit, drums pounded, and rattles shook. Tom and Brooke sat next to the fire as bowls of warm food were passed their way. They scooped out chunks of meat and roots from a savory, sweet soup. They weren't sure what the food was, but it tasted good. As the moon rose so did the drumming, and the dancers called out haunting songs. The white father and daughter sat next to each other and could only nod and smile as people offered them more food — and clothing made of soft leather.

As the moon arched west, Brooke leaned into her father. The high-pitched squeals of the children lessened, and the rumble of the celebration slowed. In the wee hours of morning Tom carried his daughter to their shelter. As the first birds whistled their morning songs, he dozed with ringing ears and aching cheeks.

CHAPTER SEVEN

The Pony Springs

▲ ▲ ▲

For three days the camp was quiet. Tom and Brooke laid low and patched gear. Tom appreciated the time to rest and mull over his situation, which he never could have imagined. His doctoring had saved Bow River's life, but he wasn't sure what to expect. Before long the sutures would have to come out, and he didn't know how that would go. The treatments he'd performed were being scrutinized by the people and, because Tom didn't know the language, he didn't understand what they thought of his methods. He sensed a mixture of admiration and suspicion. He was limited in his knowledge of the Utes, but the hospitality they'd shown thus far was reassuring.

Tom could rest during the day, but late at night he struggled to sleep. He kept second guessing his decision to leave his job in Denver and bring Brooke into the mountains. Prospecting had been his excuse. It had seemed a worthy endeavor at the time, but he cared little about amassing a fortune. Mostly, he yearned to explore. Throughout his life he'd been fascinated by nature and, as a boy, he'd discovered a cave full of minerals and crystals that had fueled an interest in geology. The seeds of exploration were furthered by his education at Western Reserve University, where a professor named Armstrong Perry, shared his adventures of exploring the west in the 1840's.

While at the university he met his wife Teresa at the neighboring Oberland College. They were married after graduation and moved to Toledo where Tom's family was. Brooke was born there in '55. Tom had worked in his father's shipping business and contributed to its growth. He and Teresa had owned their home — and shares in the company. Their life had been comfortable before the Civil War hit. After that, everything changed.

Tom had enlisted in the Union Army. Because of his education, he quickly rose in rank. As a captain, he was appointed to the position of surgeon's assistant and served in triage hospitals, tending to the sick, wounded, and dying. It was there that the knives of war cut him the deepest. He was not a trained doctor, let alone a surgeon, and he had to learn in the field with limited instruction. He made mistakes. They all did. The hospitals were always understaffed, and long shifts turned into bad dreams that haunted him still.

After the war he'd returned to Toledo, but his enthusiasm for the family business had waned. Within a year he and his small family headed west, lured by cheap farmland and a chance to start over. In September of '66 they bought a farm twenty miles north of Denver, but their stay was short. Teresa got sick on the way out west, and the doctors in Denver were baffled by her condition. Tom tried everything to save her, right up to the morning he reached for her in the darkness and felt her cold hand. He was devastated, and, if not for his responsibility to Brooke, he may never have survived the ordeal. He loved his daughter, but she couldn't replace the feelings his wife had kindled in him. Teresa had made his life easier, and she understood how the war had scarred him. Not long after she died and was buried, he sold the farm, and he and twelve-year old Brooke had moved to Denver.

After little more than a year they'd headed into the mountains and were now in Ute land, sleeping and waking in a tribal village. Tom looked up at the dusky tipi skin and studied the rawhide lacing that bound the pieces together. He admired the labor behind the awl-punched holes and needle-drawn sinews. He wondered if Stone Calf had been the maker. The wooden poles leaned in toward the apex of the room where an open triangle flap framed the blue sky. Light filtering through the thin hides cast a soft glow, and the painted diamond patterns on the outside of the tipi threw jagged shadows across the floor. Beaded decorations, like the ones he'd seen on headdresses and ceremonial jewelry, dangled from the pole by the entrance.

Brooke leaned against a rawhide box with her journal in her lap and hummed as she drew. Although he fought to admit it, Tom knew his wanderlust was driven by the loss of his wife. He was running from the fangs of war and, when Teresa died, those fangs nearly severed his will. His love for Brooke was the only thing that had kept him from becoming another casualty.

It was the morning of the fourth day when Bow River told Tom he wanted to meet him by the river. The midday air buzzed with life, as he and Brooke made their way to the sandy shore. Star Flower was next to her father when they approached, and she motioned for Brooke to join her downstream. The two girls sat on the bank, and Star Flower pulled out a pouch and showed Brooke what she was making.

Tom and Bow River sat on two logs looking across the river where horses grazed in the flats. Bow River looked strong. His shirt was beaded along his shoulders, and curly fringe dangled below his arms. A wide belt wrapped his waist and held a bone-handled knife, positioned just below his ribs. Two eagle feathers and a streamer of horsehair rippled against his neck. His braids were long and tight.

Tom studied the wounds on Bow River's arm and scalp, and he motioned for Bow River to show him his shoulder. Redness surrounded all the stitches, but none showed signs of infection. During the war he'd seen many men lose limbs from lesser wounds; infection was the usual killer. Tom wondered about the green leaf poultice that Stone Calf had kept applying to the cuts. He knew that nearly all Ute medicines were derived from plant sources, but he had learned next to nothing about any of them through his education or experiences. Because very few plants in the Rocky Mountains had been catalogued or scientifically analyzed in the scholarly books he'd read, any medicinal qualities they held were known only by native healers.

At first the two men struggled to talk, but gradually they pieced together enough words and hand signs to understand each other. Tom soon understood Bow River's most pressing question: Who did he work for, or was he on his own? Tom was caught off guard and didn't have an answer. He assured Bow River he wasn't working for the government and admitted that he'd wandered into the reservation by mistake. There was no boundary marker, so there was no way to know where the line was. Tom explained that he had come west seeking knowledge of the land. Bow River responded with an expression that conveyed dissatisfaction with his answer, but Tom couldn't offer a better explanation.

Bow River took a stick and drew a line in the sand between the two men. The scratch ran from north and southeast toward the divide. He looked up the canyon, *"Noo-vuv Ki-ve,"* he said.

Bow River translated the words *noo-vuv,* snow, and *ki-ve,* mountain. Then he placed a small piece of driftwood in the sand, splayed out his hand, and pressed the wood down with his palm. He looked east to the Snowy Mountains and pointed at the river, *"Bunkara-noo-quet,"* he said, and Tom knew that they were sitting on the bank of the *Bunkara* or Thunder River.

Bow River held up his hand with his fingers splayed wide, indicating that the Pony Springs Camp lay at the five forks of the *Bunkara* River. Farther west in the sand map, Bow River scratched another deeper line running north and southwest. He called it the *Rio Colorado,* and Tom knew it was the Grand River that started up north and ran to the Pacific Ocean. Where the Bunkara met the Rio Colorado on the map, Bow River tapped the sand and said, *Yampa Pagosa.* Tom wasn't sure what he meant, but he was curious to find out.

Bow River took his time to explain that Tom was welcome in their camp and advised him to stay with the Yellow Bears. He made his point with references to his enemies, the Cheyenne to the north, the Arapaho to the east, and the Comanche to the south. He invited Tom to stay in the safety of the Utes until he chose to go back to Denver. Tom recognized the generosity of the offer — and appreciated it. He could explore and record, basically prospect, without having to worry about trespassing or getting lost. He'd also have protection from Ute enemies, and from other Utes who might not be as welcoming as Bow River was. Tom admired this Ute man. He felt they were friends, and he sensed Bow River's eagerness to show him their territory.

Tom was grateful for the invitation, but he knew he needed to head back across the divide as soon as Bow River no longer needed his help. He was weary of the saga he and Brooke had survived thus far. He was lucky to be alive. He hated to think what Brooke's fate might have been if he'd been killed. The thought made him squirm. Deep inside, he knew he needed to go back to Denver to a comfortable life, good job, and safety for his daughter. He glanced down the river at Brooke just as she stood up and started walking toward the village with Star Flower. Both girls looked back at their fathers, who acknowledged their leaving. They walked with a buoyant step, watching each other's fingers and faces as they talked back and forth.

For most of the afternoon the two men sat, exchanging hand signs and choppy phrases, as they came to know each other better. Tom managed to convey that Brooke's mother had died. Bow River wrinkled his brow and tossed a pebble in the water.

• • •

Water Bird was busy every day moving about the village. He'd gained responsibility after the ordeal with the bear. He came by Tom and Brooke's tipi daily and seemed to be there to care for them. He'd show up with fresh food and gear. He'd hand them to Tom, but his eyes always glanced around for Brooke. Tom noticed his eyebrows bumping up whenever she appeared.

Tom and Brooke brought a level of excitement to the camp, and it was Brooke who drew the most attention. It took a couple of days before Tom was comfortable letting her out of his sight. All the people, especially the younger ones, noticed whenever she moved away from her shelter. The adults watched her too, with looks of concern. It was well known, even among the whites, that native children were often stolen to exact revenge.

Whenever she moved away from the tipi, boys and girls followed her at a distance. One afternoon, as she was dipping water from the spring, she turned around to the sight of three young girls holding little bouquets of flowers and feathers. It seemed that the bouquets were gifts, but the girls stood back until the oldest of the trio stepped forward and drew a white flower from her cluster. "*Sah-seet*," she said, holding the single flower to the side.

Brooke pointed at the flower. "Sah-seet? Flower." The girl's eyes widened with a slight nod.

"Sah-seet," the girl said again and laid her hand on her chest.

"Ah. Flower. Sah-Seet." Brooke pointed toward her.

"Sah-seet," the girl replied with a wider smile. She held out the flowers then pulled them back. Then she lifted a piece of her own hair and made a cutting motion as she pointed at Brooke's rolling red curls. With a playful smile, Sah-seet offered up the bouquet again. Brooke giggled. No one had ever wanted a piece of her hair before. The younger girls crowded behind Sah-seet and held out their own little arrangements. Brooke twisted a little smile then twirled up a lock of her hair and made the same cutting motion, and the girls nodded in unison. Brooke looked at her mane of red ringlets and tried to remember how long it had been since she'd combed it out. The second girl pulled a small blade from a pouch at her waist and held it out. Brooke took the knife, and the girls wiggled with anticipation. She pinched off a finger-long curl and sliced it free, then another, and another and she handed them to the children who gathered around her, the littlest girl, Sah-woof, bounced in place. They gave Brooke a bouquet of flowers and started to turn away, but Sah-seet turned back and pointed to the string around Brooke's neck. When Brooke drew out the small, glass, star pendant from under her shirt, all the little eyes went wide.

• • •

It had been about a week since they arrived at the Pony Springs when Good Bear and a man named Loma came to Tom's lodge to ask if he would hunt with them the next morning. Their plan was to go up the Stone Lodge Fork of the Bunkara for sheep and Tom's rifle would be a welcome addition. Tom felt honored and wanted to go, but he worried about leaving Brooke behind. The men noticed his hesitancy.

Just then Star Flower and a woman named Blue Jay walked up and spoke to the men. They talked back and forth, until Star Flower turned and directed a hand toward Brooke. The woman was clearly offering her company and protection. Brooke smiled and nodded. Tom felt his gut wrench. He wanted to hunt with the men and felt obligated to help support the tribe, but he'd never left Brooke before. The idea of leaving her with people he barely knew suddenly dug away at his ignorance. How dastardly some people would think he was for even considering such a choice. A buried prejudice reared its head, and countless ugly tales came to his mind. He understood that some were true and some false. Brutality was part of every culture; he'd seen it firsthand. But so was compassion and understanding. He'd always sought to live his life with a belief in the basic goodness of all human beings.

The Utes looked around with uneasy eyes. Good Bear glanced toward the horses, as if he were ready to leave. Tom felt that the men could read his thoughts and see his reluctance. Embarrassed by the bigotry of his distrust, he met his daughter's gaze.

"Papa, I'll be fine," she assured him.

Tom took a deep breath and looked up. Thoughts of Teresa darted through his mind. What would she want him to do? Just then, he caught sight of a little girl standing nearby with a lock of red hair on a string around her neck. He felt a softening inside. Brooke would be alright.

"Okay," he conceded. Brooke smiled at Star Flower, who replied with a little wink. Blue Jay kept her eyes on Tom.

Star Flower motioned with her hands.

Brooke watched, dipped her head once, and said, "Okay."

"Okay, okay, okay," Loma said, practicing a new word. Then, he pointed to the ridge where the sun would come up, and Tom knew he needed to be ready at sunrise.

The next morning at dawn Bow River and Star Flower were standing outside Tom's lodge. Within a minute, Water Bird rode up with Timber, Tom's buckskin gelding. By the time he was saddled, Good Bear and three other men showed up. Tom scabbarded his rifle, slung himself atop his horse, said goodbye to Brooke, and tipped his hat. She nipped at her lip behind a curled finger, swallowed, and gave her father a tight smile.

• • •

It was early July and the camp had swelled to almost seventy people. Every other day new families arrived to receive the welcoming hugs of those already there. Tom and Bow River met at the river every day. There, Tom checked on his patient's wounds, and the two men shared stories and knowledge. Tom's understanding of the Utes and their language was growing quickly, and he made notes every night.

The Yellow Bears were a secretive, close-knit family group, that ranged from their winter camps farther west to their summer territory in the *Pah-re Ki-ve* or Elk Mountains. They no longer traveled east for buffalo or made excursions toward Santa Fe or Denver. In fact, Bow River had never been to Denver. He, Good Bear, and Loma were the village elders, with Bow River having the final word in most of the decisions.

The Pony Springs Camp showed a history of use. The fire pit stones had sunk deep into the ground. Deep paths had been woven between the tipis, converging at the river, or winding toward the horse herd and the spring. The spring was sacred. The Utes had camped there for centuries.

Scattered throughout the village were antlers and skulls of buffalo, elk, and sheep. Some were wedged, vice tight, in the forks of trees. At the southwest side of the camp was a spot littered with flakes of chert and agate. Several big logs had been worn smooth from generations of Utes sitting on them while fashioning arrow-heads, spear points and knives from the harder stones. Above the camp, a tower of tilted strata poked the sky and cooled the village with an afternoon shadow.

Every evening men would arrive back at camp bringing in what they had killed that day, which usually included deer, elk, antelope, and mountain sheep. The meat was shared among all who needed it, but the hide belonged to the hunter. Whenever possible, the hunters brought whole animals to the camp, and everything from the intestines to the feet were salvaged. The meat that couldn't be eaten right away was placed on willow racks and roasted above smoldering fires. It was a constant chore to stoke the fires, and the smoky smell engulfed the camp and permeated everything. All the clothing, possessions, shelters, and people shared the earthy smell of wood smoke.

The Utes also captured young animals to keep as pets — from squirrels and chipmunks to foxes and magpies — and the children delighted in showing them off to Brooke. Everyone was involved in the village commerce. Any child old enough to draw a bow or catch a fish did so. Boys and girls raided birds' nests, trapped fish, and even ran down young animals when they got the chance. One afternoon, a teenage girl and two boys came into camp with four spotted elk calves, which they had shot with their bows after startling a herd that left them behind. The adults and older children congratulated the young hunters. The meat of the calves and their soft speckled hides were shared and admired. Trapping and hunting of birds like turkey, grouse and geese became a game, as much as a chore, for the children. And when colorful songbirds were caught, their feathers were traded as treasures.

One morning Tom saw men leaving camp, driving a small herd of horses and leading others loaded with meat and hides. They were moving trade goods farther north, closer to the trails that led to Denver and Salt Lake. The men wouldn't take their goods into town, but rather exchanged them with traders along the trails.

Through this shuttle system, the Yellow Bears acquired steel pots, knives, needles, and hatchets, as well as decorative items such as glass beads, brass rings, and ribbon and cloth.

Horses were the most valuable currency and created an economy within all tribes. They were central to the culture. They provided mobility, wealth, entertainment and even meat in the end. Every horse held a level of status and value. To the Utes, silver and gold rocks were of little use, but the value of horse flesh was supreme, which is why they had to be protected from predators and, more importantly, from thieves. The Utes were proud of their herds, and a good portion of every day was devoted to their care. They traded horses for the most expensive items like rifles, ammunition, steel traps, and tobacco. For a man to acquire a rifle from the trading post up on the Bear River, it could take as many as five horses — plus one more for a hundred rounds of bullets. The price for guns and ammunition was high, but if a man was careful with his shots, he could turn ten times the value of his trade in just a few months of hunting.

• • •

One late afternoon, a flurry of activity arose in the camp. The village was always busy, but the uptick of action so late in the day caught Tom's attention. Women and men gathered bundles and baskets and started taking down the racks that held their gear.

Water Bird and other boys met down by the river to drive horses into the meadow east of camp.

Brooke noticed the activity and asked Star Flower what was happening. With wide eyes she said, "It's time to move camp to the *Pe-en Pah-gah-root.*"

Tom understood the final words. "The Mother's Lake."

Star Flower looked to Brooke and made hand signs. Brooke did her best to translate them into English. "The Mother's Lake below the Brothers' Peaks?"

Star Flower nodded with a frisky grin. Brooke returned a knowing smile, because she and Star Flower shared a secret about a man who lived farther south — a man that Star Flower hoped to see this summer.

As Star Flower strode back toward her lodge, Brooke asked, "Papa, are we going with them?"

He heard a waver in her voice and wondered if she was feeling excitement or worry. His mind started to roil. The time was coming to decide the course of their summer. He looked out across the river, where boys riding bare-back caught spirited horses with braided ropes. The horses' squeals and the boys' shouts echoed across the grassy flat.

"Tom Gun!"

As the name rang out, Tom realized it was his new nickname. Bow River was striding his way. Grunting softly, Bow River looked upriver to the logs on the sand. Tom knew it was time to talk. He told Brooke to keep an eye on their horses and nodded toward the river. She headed that way, joined by Sah-seet and her sisters.

The two men moved upriver and took their seats. Bow River watched the horse wrangling taking place across the river then said, "We are moving camp." He looked west over his shoulder, *"Pah-re Ki-ve,* Elk Mountains, where we stay for the fish and the fruit moon. The berries will be ready soon. Are you coming?"

Tom was caught by the quickness of the question. He'd weighed his answer many times already. He knew he needed to take Brooke back to Denver. That was the smartest thing to do. He looked out across the river and silently rehearsed his answer again. He felt perturbed at the situation, at himself, and at Bow River. He knew what was best for Brooke. He knew the mistakes he'd made. He sighed heavily and twisted on the log to look for his daughter. He felt his jaw slide side to side when he saw her. She was wading nearly waist deep across the slow river. Hanging on her back were two little girls, who squirmed and giggled as water splashed their faces. Sah-seet coaxed them to the other side of the river. Tom uttered a little huff through a smile. He turned to Bow River to give his definitive answer, but Bow River cut him off.

"Tom Dun-a-gun you are brave man," he stated in clear, strong English. "I know you worry for your daughter. I too am brave, and

I worry for the safety of my daughter and all the children in our family." He leaned forward to see the girls walking through the tall grass. "We know the world is for our children. They are the most important. They are the ones we protect the most."

Bow River leaned back and looked at Tom, "You saved my life and probably my son's. You made it possible for me to carry on with my wife and our family. Your daughter Brooke, Uckarth Pahn-qwe, Rose Creek, is now like my daughter and I will protect her to my last breath. Tom Gun, I'm sorry you don't have a woman, and Rose Creek no mother, but you have a family here." Bow River stood up and looked across the river. "We leave in two mornings for the Mother's Lake. If you do not go, you should go back across the divide. I will send someone with you. You decide."

Tom reached for a stick as he watched Bow River walk toward the village. He scratched a mark in the sand, his definitive answer was still stuck in his throat. He understood well what he was being offered, a chance and permission to do what he'd come to the mountains to do. Protection too, but still there was risk. Life in the wilderness was a daily challenge, much harder than he'd figured it would be.

A high giggle caught his attention. The girls were crossing back across the river with help from the woman, Blue Jay. Brooke looked his way as they climbed the bank and walked toward the village. He knew she sensed his quandary. She'd been horribly frightened when he'd crawled out from under the bear, and nervous the days that followed, but she seemed to have let it pass. The welcoming people had made a difference. Now she seemed completely at ease. She was fond of Star Flower, who was almost like a big sister, something he couldn't be. Everyone was captivated by her, especially the children. She'd never had time to make friends in Denver, something he just now realized.

He knew the demons that haunted his life — and could only imagine what haunted hers. The remedy he sought fueled his yearning to explore. He wasn't sure what Brooke's longings were, but she seemed content to be where they were now. Life in the village was an adventure and a distraction. Tom didn't want to go back to Denver. He suspected Brooke didn't either. She had been so strong through all their trials so far. He needed to hear her thoughts.

The meandering arcs of the river shimmered golden as Tom made his way back to the lodge. Brooke had a fire going. When he dipped in under the tipi flap, she didn't say anything, but he could see she wanted to know if they were going on or not.

Tom kneeled at the fire and poured a cup of hot water. He ate warm elk in a broth of greens and thought through his question.

"Brooke." She looked up and rocked back.

Her hair was a darker red than her mother's.

"Brooke, I've been wanting to ask you: Should we go on, at least to the lake?"

She looked back into the fire, ran her tongue along the edge of her teeth, nipped at her lip a little, then looked up. "Absolutely."

An astonished little huff jumped out with Tom's breath, as the decision became heavier. Not only did he want to continue the journey, but Brooke did too. He finished the stew, set the bowl by the fire, and lay back on his mat. *Of course, she wants to go on. She was cut of the same lion-hearted courage as her mother.*

• • •

Tom heard the crackle of the fire before he woke up. It was still dark outside, and a robin whistled far away. He rolled on his side and saw Brooke writing in her journal. He rubbed his eyes and wondered if she'd been up all night.

"What are you writing about?"

She looked up with soft blue eyes a little red and swollen. "About Mom. I dreamed about her."

Tom's lips mashed into a tight smile. "What did you dream?"

"She was helping me." He could see a little blush about her face.

"I dreamed about her too." He always did.

"Really Papa, what'd you dream?"

Tom stared into the fire. "I dreamed she was standing in a

57

meadow of flowers, in front of a big rock mountain at the edge of a lake." As he said it, he realized the prescience of his dream. The mother of his child, standing on the shore of a mountain lake.

"The Mother's Lake," Brooke said, reading his mind.

"I guess we're supposed to go see it," he said.

Brooke's face broke into a wide smile.

. . .

By mid-morning the camp was abuzz in every direction. Some tipis came down, and others were left standing. Dried meat was packed in rawhide boxes, while some was tied in bags and cashed in the ground. Hides were wrapped and hoisted into trees or stacked with other bundles of goods to be loaded the next day.

Although Brooke had become handy at moving gear, she didn't have the experience of the Ute women. But, before long, she had plenty of helpers — as did Tom, who was learning to tie knots and fasten hitches he'd never seen before.

All day long, people prepared for the move. Late in the day a heavy rain came through, and everyone was forced into the tipis that were left standing. Tom and Brooke shared their tipi with two families they barely knew. They sat around the fire sharing food and words until late. Then everyone curled up to sleep. Round, brown, baby eyes kept watch on Brooke. She scooted her back tight against her father's and felt the warmth of the room as she drifted away.

. . .

It was still dark when the knock of horse hooves came through the camp. The fire was brought to life, and everyone grabbed food. Parents jostled children awake, their eyes in mild protest. By the time gray light lit the woods, people were packing horses and loading travois. Some of the older women left their chores behind and started walking and riding out on the trail, headed west from camp.

Tom and Brooke packed gear on their horse like everyone else.

Mothers snapped orders and pointed guidance while their families bent to the labor of packing and securing loads. This would be the first time the Dunagans would travel in the ranks of the Yellow Bears. The chore of moving a village of people and possessions was a huge undertaking. Shelters, bedding, clothes, food, pots, tools, and weapons had to be packed and loaded.

Half of a tipi hide was a full load for a horse, but a whole tipi could be strapped to a travois, which was then pulled by a horse. The triangle-shaped racks were strapped atop the horse's shoulders with two long poles dragging behind. When loaded, they could carry three times the weight a horse could carry on its back. Lots of goods could be carried on a travois, including kids.

As gear was tied securely, family groups mounted and made for the west trail. Tom got plenty of help, and, when he and Brooke fell in line behind Loma's family, everyone twisted and watched them with anxious eyes.

They didn't drive all the horses up the trail. Mares, foals, and older horses were left on the sage flats of the valley. They would eventually follow the big horse herd at their own pace. The handful of people who stayed at Pony Springs would look after them.

Tom knew the Utes felt safe for the time being. They were hidden well in their mountain fortress, and other tribes would be hard pressed to make a raid and escape with their lives. But still, everyone was watchful. The squawk of a bird, the bark of a dog, the direction a horse's ears pointed. The tribe noticed everything.

The country they traveled changed quickly from sage-covered flats to a narrow, red canyon squeezed by the creek. The left-hand ridge was a thousand feet high and covered in dark spruce and pine. The right side of the canyon, facing southeast, was just as high and marked by open ridges and swirling aspen stands. Both sides of the canyon were scarred with avalanche chutes. Mounds of snow littered with trees and rocks plugged the stream bottom. To the south, giant pointed peaks stood out like temples, their north faces mostly covered in snow.

The long line of people and horses moved at a steady pace, and no one spoke. The only sound was the scratching of travois poles, the squeak of rawhide ropes, and the clop of horse hooves up the canyon.

Tom wondered where they were headed. Why was it called Mother's Lake, and what about Brothers' Peaks? Bow River wouldn't tell him much, except that Wolf Song, Loma's father, might tell him the whole story someday. Bow River said only that the peaks were named for twin brothers, wolf and bear.

Tom knew a good deal about the surrounding geology. He recognized the red striations and cliffs as sedimentary layers, laid down over eons and infused with iron that gave the rocks their maroon color. He knew that, below the sedimentary layers, threads of silver and gold were formed by extreme pressure. Where those threads broke the surface, prospectors hit pay dirt.

They had traveled a couple of hours when the procession veered west up a tributary canyon. Young people, who had been working at the back of the line, left their jobs and hurried up the trail. Tom couldn't catch their words, but as they disappeared from view, he noticed everyone was talking more and pushing on at a quicker pace. Small kids riding with their parents jumped off and hurried up the trail as if running toward a party. They chattered and joked and giggled. At a bend in the trail, the old women who had left camp early that morning, sat in a group with their faces to the sun. They didn't move, and hardly anyone looked their way.

Star Flower had worked all day with her mother before leaving her post and riding up next to Brooke. With a girlish smile, she coaxed Brooke to follow her. Tom nodded his head, and they disappeared into the aspens. Tom tapped Timber's ribs, and he picked a pace to match the horses and riders around him.

The trail meandered through the aspen forest and, as they neared the southern edge of the grove, Tom could feel excitement all around him.

He stopped at the margin of a meadow full of pink, yellow and purple flowers, a kaleidoscope of color. Beyond, a mirror blue lake cradled a pair of pointed peaks that crowded the western sky.

Brooke rode up. "Papa, look." Her eyes were wide with wonderment.

Tom knew that everyone, except the littlest babies, had seen this sight before, yet every face around him shared the same amazement, as if this was the first time they'd ever been there.

Water Bird galloped up. His loose hair swirled around his bare shoulders as he slid to a stop between his sister and Brooke. Star Flower shared her brother's smile. Water Bird tipped his head toward the peaks and held two fingers side by side. Star Flower made the same hand sign and said, "Brothers' Peaks."

Tom and Brooke laid their reins across their saddles and made the same sign with their fingers. All the heads around them nodded, *yes*. A hum of prayers mumbled through the meadow like a swarm of honeybees. Tom took in a deep breath, certain that very few white people had ever seen the twin mountains before. A pair of nearly perfect pyramid-shaped peaks, as grand as any Tom had ever seen, stood like gigantic maroon bells against a sky of baby blue. Brooke stared at them, too.

As he looked at his daughter with the lake behind her, her mother came to mind. He hoped that through their eyes, Teresa could see the same meadow, flush with flowers, the shimmering lake, and the towering mountains.

People, horses, dogs, and kids made their way through the meadow and headed toward the lake. At the shore, buckskin-clad Utes with shiny black hair knelt on knees or sat cross-legged looking across the water. Tear tracks cut dusty cheeks; shoulders slumped with ease. Bow River and Good Bear walked around the groups and spoke to the families.

At Loma's call everyone walked to the sandy shore and stood as one, looking toward the peaks. The elder, Wolf Song, adorned in eagle feathers and fringe, walked to the front of the group and waded knee deep into the water with his back to the crowd.

Tom and Brooke stood at the edge of the group, and when everyone lifted their arms up toward the sky, they did too. Wolf Song spoke loudly, and his words echoed in the silence. His last words were repeated by the people, followed by a long pause where no one spoke or moved.

Tom held his breath. He felt a part of a centuries-old ritual, and the weight of the kindness shown by the Yellow Bears pulled his heart to the ground in humility.

Soon, a single voice broke the silence, like a bull elk's call across a meadow. When Tom saw Wolf Song's shoulder shudder, he knew the ancient song was coming from the little man standing in the water. His voice rang through the valley like bells from a cathedral and, when all the Yellow Bears let forth with the song of their fathers, the land shook. Young and old joined in the high, wild rhythm of an ancestral blessing, while naked toddlers splashed in the rippling shallows of their Mother's Lake.

CHAPTER EIGHT

The River Treaty

▲ ▲ ▲

The third morning at Mother's Lake, four men came over the south pass. Their arrival seemed welcome to some but worrisome to others.

Bow River and three men moved up the trail to meet them. Tom watched from camp and could see Bow River explaining the bear attack as he touched the scars on his arm.

The oldest visitor was near Bow River's age. He wore a red, striped vest. His hair hung down his back, gathered with a single feather. He and Bow River walked along the lake as the other men headed toward camp. Several times the men stopped and went back and forth, hands waving as they talked.

The people watched until the men turned around and headed back toward the tipis. When they got nearer Bow River called to Water Bird, who trotted through camp telling everyone to meet at the central fire pit. The people were waiting for news and were quick to gather. When everyone surrounded the smoldering coals, Bow River stepped up on the hearth. He rolled his lips together in no hurry to speak. The maroon peaks rose at his shoulder and the mirror-flat lake lay calm behind him.

Bow River looked at the man in the vest then explained that the families of the Black Eagle Band were moving north and expected to be at Sheep Lakes in seven days. It was there, on the south side of the divide, the two bands would meet for the summer gathering. Bow River explained that War Raven brought word of the treaty talks in Washington. Tom couldn't understand much of what Bow River said, but when he heard the words Washington City, he understood. All Colorado citizens knew that the Ute chiefs had traveled to Washington to negotiate terms of a new treaty. The Ute council included War Raven, Bow River's cousin, Archer, and other head men of the tribe.

Bow River and Archer had formed a solid alliance over many years. Their personal bond had been forged in childhood when they were stolen by Comanches and sold to the Mexicans. As teens, they had escaped and returned to the Yellow Bears with knowledge of the white people's ways, which included words from the Spanish and English languages.

Archer had become the leader of the Red Springs Utes, the largest of all the Ute bands. War Raven's Black Eagle band was part of the same group. Archer had sent War Raven to bring the news to the Yellow Bears, while he carried the news farther south.

When War Raven stepped up to speak, he was met with hollers and whoops from the crowd. Bow River went to Stone Calf's side, taking his place with his family who stood next to Tom and Brooke.

At stake in the treaty were the lands of the Western Colorado and the rights of the Utes. Although relations between the Colorado citizens and the Utes had been mostly peaceful over the past decade, there was competition for land.

Some Utes, and many whites, had overstepped the vague reservation boundaries established by the treaty of 1863. Neither side wanted conflict, but fear and greed drove both sides to defend and expand their territories. Leaders from both nations had negotiated a new treaty in the fall of 1867 and signed it in March of '68. It was now early July and the Deer Moon for the Utes. The mountain bands weren't all in agreement about the concessions their tribal leaders had made, but the agreement had been signed, swapping the Continental Divide or the Snowy Mountains for the security of the Utes' historic lands to the west.

Tom knew that he and Brooke were in violation of the new treaty by being on Ute land. Some Utes were not happy that they were there, but Bow River quickly quelled any misunderstanding. Tom and Brooke were family and not to be harmed in any way.

War Raven spoke for several minutes, his movements describing his travel by train to the shores of a lake as big as the prairie. He described the great houses and strange animals he'd seen. His stories brought laughter and quizzical faces. When he finished, Bow River took his place. War Raven sat next to Good Bear, where he received a welcome greeting from Fat Cow, Good Bear's wife.

Bow River started to speak, waving his arms toward the peaks behind him and then to the canyon to the north. With his movements everyone looked down the canyon and to the high ridges where the horse herd grazed. Heads nodded and smiles grew as they looked around the valley. As he continued, brows furrowed, and frowns formed. Not everything Bow River said was good news. An older man asked a question. Bow River had a definitive answer that made him nod his head. As Bow River continued to speak Tom noticed more smiles. Young children and teenagers looked to their parents and, as the grownups relaxed, so did the young ones. Family groups talked, and the voices grew higher and lighter as the conversations went on. Soon everyone was talking, and the attention had left Bow River. He raised his voice above the chatter, and everyone looked back to him. In a final sentence he spoke in a slow deliberate manner, and, with his last word, the crowd broke into a cheer that echoed across the lake.

Tom and Brooke looked at each other, not knowing precisely what had been said. Brooke looked to Star Flower, who grabbed her hands and started spinning her in a circle. Excitement wiggled through the crowd. Bow River walked toward Stone Calf. She met him with a hug. Wrapping both arms around his neck, she lifted herself off the ground. Bow River squeezed her tight in return.

Tom looked around and saw women with wide smiles and streaming tears. Men had watery eyes. Young children jumped and danced in place.

Brooke turned to her father, "What's going on Papa?"

"I'm not sure, but it looks good and seems important."

With one last word from Bow River the big group spread out. Some men headed out with rifles and bows while others went toward the horse herd. Women went back to their chores, and children played. Boys and young women gathered in groups and talked. Some couples slipped into their tipis and pinned the door flaps shut, while others walked together along the lake.

As the crowd moved away, Tom saw Blue Jay looking his way. When their eyes met, she looked down and turned away. Brooke glanced at her father, who put his hand on her shoulder, and they turned and headed toward the horse herd.

Tom and Brooke climbed up to a hanging valley just above camp where they found their horses. Tom caught the tall buckskin and the paint mare, and together they rode to the top of a ridge above the village. As they sat in the shade looking across the valley, Brooke asked, "Papa, how long do you think we will stay with these people?"

He looked at her then back at the village. "I don't know. I feel good to be with them. How about you?"

"These people have been so good to me, and I like Star Flower. I think she wants to learn more English and maybe how to read."

"Really?"

"Yes, and maybe Water Bird too."

Tom looked back out across the valley. "I'd planned on us returning to Denver in the fall. As long as we can stay with this group, we're safe, and I can prospect a little and learn the boundaries of the new reservation."

"Will the Utes get to keep this land?" Brooke asked.

"I think so, but I'm afraid no one knows where their territory will begin and end. Until the land's surveyed, I don't know how anyone will be able to define the boundaries —unless they follow the rivers. I think we're safe to stay with the Yellow Bear people until the fall. We'll know more by then."

Tom and Brooke stayed on the point above the camp and napped in the shadows. When they got up, they could see activity around the village. They rode their horses back to the herd and walked into camp. Brooke headed toward their lodge but was caught by Star Flower, and they walked down the canyon below the village.

Bow River had been waiting for their return, and he motioned for Tom to join him. They walked toward the lake where Good Bear, War Raven, Water Bird, and several other men were waiting. Tom and Bow River sat on a log at the edge of the water. The other men sat in the grass where they could look out across the lake. Around the shores groups of people had gathered while children splashed in the shallows. Across the lake young boys were fishing and, not far from them, Brooke and Star Flower sat face to face on a large rock. Their movements were happy as they tried to converse.

In broken English and hand signs Bow River began to tell Tom about the news from War Raven. With his fingers he described that there were seven bands of the Utes. Five that lived toward the setting sun side of the great divide and two to the east. Of the five bands on the west side two lived to the north and two to the south. The Yellow Bear Band was part of the Red River or Rio Colorado tribe of the Northern Utes, and War Raven's Black Eagle clan was part of the Red Springs Utes, who lived on the Black Rock River.

The treaty negotiations had gone best for the Utes who lived west of the divide — even though they would have to share their land with their cousins from the east.

The bands that lived in the valley of the Sand Mountains would have to leave there and live west of the divide. Tom knew that Bow River was speaking of the San Luis Valley, where farmers from the north and Mexicans from the south had moved in on the Utes.

Although no one knew the exact boundaries, Bow River explained that all the land from the great divide to the desert canyon in the west, and from the Bear River in the north to the Navajo River in the south, was still Ute land. If the Utes lived in this land and learned the ways of the white man, it would be theirs *as long as rivers run and grass is green*. This is what the American men who presented the treaty to the Ute representatives had said. The Utes were calling the agreement The River Treaty.

Bow River looked to Tom and tightened his lips. "Tom Dunagan, do the rivers where you are from always run?"

Tom nodded yes.

Bow River continued, "Do they flow big in the spring and get smaller in the fall but always run?"

Tom nodded again.

"Do the rivers always change, yet always run?" Bow River asked.

"Yes, they do."

"So, when the white man says as long as rivers run, he knows that here in our land the rivers always run?"

"Yes," Tom answered with a nod.

"Tom Dunagan," Bow River said. "If this is true, would you agree that this land shall be Ute land forever?"

Water Bird, and several other men waited intently for an answer.

Tom thought for a moment. "Yes, I agree."

The men looked at each other with solemn smiles.

Tom cleared his throat and said, "The American government is very large, with many chiefs, and like the rivers, the American government will change too."

"We know this," Bow River replied. "Two times before, the agreement has changed. We know the Americans are very strong. We cannot fight them and win. War Raven has seen the great armies. We know that we must be friends, but we will not give up more land."

"I understand," Tom said as he looked out across the lake and heard the laughter of children in the water.

The men sat without speaking and listened to the sounds around them. When Brooke and Star Flower's laughter caught their attention, they all looked across the water. The girls sat rocking back and forth, giggling.

Tom spoke up. "Thank you, Bow River, for letting my daughter and me travel with you. You have been very kind, and I will help you any way I can."

At that Bow River nodded. "Not everyone will be happy with

this new agreement or want to learn the American ways. But if the government does what it has said it will do, then there will be peace. So, this is good, and we are happy that this land is ours."

Bow River turned, looked at War Raven, and asked, "When you left the Black Canyon, was Strong Horse there?"

War Raven shook his head *no*.

"Before the Hot Moon, Strong Horse and three men went onto the prairie." War Raven looked concerned. "They went to take horses form the Arapaho, Kiowa or Comanche; they have not returned."

Bow River let out a low grumble and clenched his jaw. He stared up at the peaks then looked across the lake at Brooke and Star Flower.

"I have heard this. Who went with him?"

"His cousin Henry Eagle, Arturo and Red Elk."

Bow River let out a deep breath. "Those men are small in a big land, and none of them have been there before," Bow River said. "They are strong. If they move fast, they can get away, but the Kiowa and Arapaho will chase them for their lives."

The sound of his daughter's laughter interrupted his train of thought. Bow River paused, then added, "If Star Flower asks about this, tell her nothing."

The men nodded.

"We will look for Strong Horse and the others at Sheep Lakes in seven days, but now we will celebrate," Bow River said. "This is a good day for all Utes, the people of the sun."

CHAPTER NINE

The Motherless Child

▲ ▲ ▲

The celebration of the River Treaty lasted all night. People ate around the fires until dawn. Brooke woke before her father and after only a couple hours of sleep. They had planned to go hunting with Good Bear and Water Bird, but Brooke felt sick and asked if she could stay in camp. Tom didn't want to leave her but, when Star Flower came by and asked if she'd like to pick berries, Tom decided to let her stay.

At midday Brooke and a few women headed downstream below the lake. A half a dozen dogs straggled along. They skirted a hillside then climbed a steep draw where raspberries grew among the boulders.

The women carried grass-lined baskets slung over their shoulders so they could pick berries with both hands. Two of the women carried babies in cradleboards, which they propped close by as they worked.

The women rooted through the shrubbery, strong and efficient as bears. Occasionally someone would straighten and survey the area. The mood was light and the sun warm as the women talked and plucked the fruit. Before long everyone had bright pink lips and fingertips.

Among the women with straight black hair, Brooke stood out, her red curls hanging down her back. A piece of cloth tied across her forehead kept wayward locks out of her eyes. She and Star Flower worked side-by-side and talked, using the few words they could understand from their growing shared vocabulary. Star Flower encouraged Brooke, who struggled to pick berries among the thorns. The older women had gathered berries for years, and their experience yielded fewer pricks and high-pitched squeaks. Brooke's peeps brought chuckles from the other women.

As Brooke worked on her knees in the underbrush, she was lost in thought about her surroundings. She had a different sense of belonging now as she worked among women without her father around. She couldn't remember how long it had been since she'd been with only women.

Her mother and Mrs. Lankering in Denver were the only women she had ever known well. Although she thought of her mother every day, being around so many other women made her think about her even more.

Brooke had many questions that only a woman could answer. At thirteen years old, she yearned for someone to share them with. She could feel the tugs of womanhood when her mind wandered to the boys — especially Water Bird. She remembered watching beads of water run down his chest and across his stomach when he stepped out of the river, at the waterfall.

Startled from her daydream, she realized someone had just mentioned her father's name. She hunkered down and listened. Again, she heard the name *Tom* spoken by someone just out of sight. She slowly rose to see who was talking about her father. Blue Jay, Stone Calf and Grandma Chuka were nodding their heads. Grandma Chuka grunted lightly when she saw Brooke looking over the brush. Blue Jay went quiet, and all three women straightened up. Brooke had caught them talking about her father. But what were they saying? Blue Jay peeked over the brush again and bounced her eyes to Brooke. With a shared smile, they both bent back to work.

Star Flower moved next to Brooke, picked a plump berry from her basket, and moved it to Brooke's lips. Brooke opened her mouth and accepted the sweet treat from her friend, who winked and started picking again. As Brooke watched Star Flower, who lightly hummed as she moved her hands around bushes, a wincing pain bit Brooke's belly. She must have eaten one too many berries. She squatted down and squeezed her thighs and butt, as a warm flush moved up from her stomach and into her face. Momentary relief was quickly followed by another pain deep in her gut.

Driven by the intensity of her pain, she moved downhill, crouched under a spruce tree and pulled down her baggy pants. A few red spots stained the fabric gathered at her feet. Raspberries? No, the color was too dull for berry stains. It had to be blood. Her blood. She closed her eyes, frightened by the realization that her time had come. The bloody spots on the pine needles beneath her confirmed it. Womanhood had arrived.

Her sigh expressed both fear and relief. Alone among the brambles, she yearned for her father, and her eyes welled at the thought of her mother. She shuddered, wiped her nose and shook her head. With a tuft of grass, she wiped herself and scooted up her trousers. Uphill she could hear the women talking. The only way to go was up, back to the new friends that she now needed dearly.

Blue Jay saw her first and knew that something was wrong. Brooke went to where Star Flower was working and stood next to her without saying a word. When Star Flower looked up, she sprang to Brooke's side and grabbed her shoulders. "What's wrong?"

Brooke made a sick face and circled her belly with her hand. Star Flower traced a tear down her new friend's cheek with a finger, then pulled her close.

"What?" Star Flower whispered the word in English as she rocked Brooke in her arms.

Soon, all the women came closer and crowded around the girls. Their faces and voices were racked with concern. They loved the motherless child they called Rose Creek. Everyone touched her hands, shoulders and back. A little girl stretched her arm between the adults to touch her thigh.

When the flood of emotion lessened, Brooke caught her breath and pushed away from Star Flower's chest. A wrinkle of embarrassment rippled through her as she looked at all the worried faces.

Star Flower held her by the shoulders and looked into her eyes. "What?"

Brooke took a deep breath and held up two pink stained fingers then pointed between her legs. When she brought her fingers up, a silent moment passed as every eyebrow raised and everyone spoke at once. Their voices rang with lighthearted confidence, and their frowns turned into smiles. The gentle hands of concern became jostling gestures of congratulations. Brooke was crowded by women she barely knew, who hugged and kissed and shook her as if she'd just won a race. Between sniffles, she broke into a half laugh. What had been a lonely moment minutes before felt like a triumph now.

The women gathered their baskets and surrounded Brooke on the walk back to camp. The shaggy dogs trailed along, tails up with a trot in their step.

CHAPTER TEN

A Teardrop's Sparkle

▲ ▲ ▲

When the first tipi flaps moved at dawn, dark clouds draped the peaks. Tattered fog clung to the lake as misty rain thickened the air and made the flowers droop. It was the Trout Moon of mid-July, the warmest time of the year, but cool and damp the morning the camp planned to move to Sheep Lakes. A move that couldn't be delayed because of weather. The wetness was an inconvenience but nothing that should keep the bands apart. There was too much to share between friends and families.

Stone Calf and Star Flower had their tipi down and ready to pack before Water Bird and the other boys got the horses to camp. The prior night's storm had scattered the horse herd, and the boys were wet and frustrated when they arrived back at the village. Anxious women threw scolding slang in their direction, and it was returned with hot replies. Restless horses and yapping dogs rattled the camp.

Two hours after first light the sixty plus people and eighty horses were on the trail. Armed men led the way, followed by eager women including Stone Calf, Star Flower, and Brooke.

Tom and other men herded stock at the back of the convoy. The wet conditions and restless horses were proving a challenge. Gradually, the animals settled under their packs and picked their way up the rocky trail.

As the column climbed, the fog thickened. Before long both ends of the procession were hidden in mist. The lead group was topping the bench above the lake when a spear of lightning stabbed the north point of the Brothers' Peaks. The flash and crash sent a tremor through the canyon. In the valley between the peaks, boulders rolled and mashed into the timber. Within seconds another bolt slapped the earth, and the thunderclap startled the horses. Everyone covered their ears with their hands and winced as a deluge of hail broke from the sky. They scrambled for cover while hailstones splattered the ground and ripped the trees. They huddled with arms over their heads as the children cried. Horses broke free, threw packs and dragged them through mud. Others squirmed on lead ropes, as pellets of ice stung their hides. Stone Calf jerked Brooke off her horse at the second thunderclap, and they squeezed under a big tree.

Tom was near the rear of the herd and could do nothing to get around the horses that choked the trail. So, he hunkered down with everyone else and waited.

Runaway horses were caught if they could be, while others got tangled in their pack ropes and stood humped against the wind. Within minutes the hail turned to rain and the pounding lessened. The storm moved down the canyon with an ominous roar. The torrent was short but had covered the ground with hail. Dirt that wasn't white with ice was slippery mud. People crept out and started gathering pots and pans and parfleches. Their leather clothing dripped like the woods around them, and their moccasins slipped and slid on the wet rocks and soil. Children stayed put while their mothers searched through packs for dry clothes.

The caravan had made it barely a mile and now was scattered over half that distance. It would take hours to gather the stock and repack the loads. Some gear would never be found. Bow River and Good Bear directed everyone to gather their goods and repack. It was past midday when the group headed uphill again. The rain had stopped, and, as the skies cleared, the temperature fell. Most everyone jumped down from their horses and walked, shivering against the cold.

By early evening the group was only halfway to Sheep Lakes. Bow River insisted that they set camp early below timberline, so they would have firewood and shelter. Star Flower protested with clenched lips but understood the situation. As badly as she wanted to cross the divide, she knew everyone was cold and exhausted. Her father assured her they'd make good time the next day and be at Sheep Lakes by mid-afternoon. He said they'd still have time to stop and prepare to meet their new neighbors. This notice was met with reluctant sighs from Star Flower and the women who stood behind her. Star Flower was eager to get to Sheep Lakes because there she would find Strong Horse, the young man she hadn't seen since the Bear Dance in the spring.

The next morning the land was dusted with frost that shimmered silver in the slanted light. The camp was moving early after a cold and restless night. They stopped mid-morning in a shallow canyon just below the pass and unpacked several horses.

Near a tiny stream hidden by willows, they prepared for arrival at their neighbor's village. They bathed, painted their faces, and fixed their hair. The young girls washed together and helped each other get dressed and adorn themselves with decorations. The streams were freezing, and the shrieks and giggles were crisp.

The men and boys shared a separate area and helped each other get ready too. Mothers and grandmothers spent time going back and forth between the groups. Everyone's appearance was important and full-dress decorations were expected — and required to display the band's happy prosperity. Sharing their bounty with neighboring family members and friends was a gift that went both ways.

The young women hoped to see certain men for the first time in months. Star Flower's friend Green Willow Spring had danced at the Bear Dance with Tall Deer for almost as long as she and Strong Horse had. They were just two of twenty plus women and girls hoping to connect with the men and boys arriving for the celebration — who were just as eager to pair up with the women and girls. Water Bird had danced for two years with a girl named Blue

Water and was looking forward to seeing her. He was bringing her a beaded bag that had been made by his mother.

When everyone was ready, they assembled in their places and started the climb to the pass. Bow River rode in front on a copper-colored mare with wavy black lines painted down her hips and legs. Throughout her mane and tail, Stone Calf had tied colorful feathers.

He wore a headdress of eagle feathers tipped in red. It was held in place by a wide brow band with white ermine tails dangling at the sides. The side feathers sloped backward to rest on his shoulders. His tan war shirt had red stripes running down the sleeves, which were fringed with horsehair. Loma and Good Bear rode behind Bow River, followed by a group of young men that included Water Bird.

Tom was given the honor of leading this warrior group behind Good Bear. He wore a buffalo-hide vest with the hair turned in; yellow lion tracks were painted on the front. Blue Jay had handed it to him that morning without saying a word. When Bow River saw him wearing it, he made a wrinkled half smile and nodded slowly.

Behind the boys rode the women and girls, the youngest ones in the lead. The women would ride to the edge of the camp then dismounted to parade into the village on foot. Star Flower wanted Brooke to walk in with her.

Grandma Chuka had given Brooke an elk skin dress to wear. It was polished with wear, and its long fringes, curled with age, hung just below her knees. Along the hemline was a beaded floral pattern. Around her waist was a beaded belt with a small bag that rattled with chimes. The smiles of the women who surrounded her gave Brooke all the confidence she needed to wear the dress with pride. Next, they combed through the tangles in her unruly hair and divided it into two sections. Pulling her head from side to side as they went, they plaited two braids that framed her face.

Her light skin, copper with freckles, and her sorrel-red hair shone in the sunlight. Her braids were thick, and she wore a leather headband to hold them back. Her sapphire-blue eyes mirrored the sky and attracted the curious attention of the boys and girls around her.

Among the women, Star Flower glowed as bright as her name. At almost seventeen, she was the eldest of the unmarried girls. Her dress hung to her ankles but was neatly folded across her saddle. A colorful beaded band ran from her waist downward over her hips to just above her moccasins. Circling her body at her knees, waist, and breasts were rows of ivory elk teeth. The cuffs of her wide sleeves were laced with red ribbons. Slender triangles were painted at the edges of her eyes and ran nearly to her ears. Her hair was parted in the middle with the seam painted bright red. Her braids were wrapped in otter fur, and the tails of the pelts hung almost to her knees. Around her neck was a red and blue choker that matched a bag that hung at her waist. Tucked in her belt with her knife and her needles was a Blue Heron feather fan, a symbol that represented her status as unmarried. She had the look of a girl and a woman at the cusp of bloom. Brooke couldn't help but stare at Star Flower, who looked both elegant and wild. The trail was quickly crowded with young men and boys, who rushed forward to see her and the other girls.

At the back of the pack were the oldest men, who were given the honor of the rear guard. They too sported their grandest collection of coups and weapons.

It was late afternoon when the Yellow Bears topped the ridge above the Sheep Lakes. The camp below them lay at the edge of timberline. Thirty tipis scattered between the two lakes and just into the trees.

Just over the crest was a patrol of boys, stationed to announce their arrival. Dressed in only breechcloths, they galloped up and took hold of the pack strings.

When the camp saw their neighbors on the ridge, they pounded drums, fired guns and blew whistles. They would greet their guests in their common clothes. Next year it would be their turn to present a grand entry at the Mother's Lake. But this day the honor belonged to the Yellow Bear people, who had made the climb across the divide to bring gifts and good will.

As the band wove their way down the trail to the village, the anticipation welled on both sides. Hearts and drums rapped harder with every hoof beat.

Bow River rode into the cheering crowd, scanning the faces of family and friends who had watched this yearly presentation for generations.

As more riders squeezed in among the tipis the dogs barked, and the horses pranced with edgy excitement. When the men were all in camp, they dismounted and spread an aisle for their women to enter. There wasn't a somber face within miles as children ran up and hugged the hips of aunts, cousins, and grandmas. Wide smiles and teary eyes appeared on nearly every face.

The young boys and older men entered the village last, their heads high, their shoulders back. Their hosts strolled up with the same proud posture, offering handshakes, hugs, and back slaps.

Tom and Brooke stood together near the center of the crowd, their heads swiveling as strangers grabbed their hands and rattled off words they didn't know. They returned each gesture with kind responses that no one understood. But all smiled as if they did.

For half an hour the reception rattled with laughter, hoof beats and the rumble of heavy drums. Lines of children ran through the crowd followed by worried dogs. Babies squealed and giggled with jubilation.

Three rifle blasts quieted the crowd to a murmur. Everyone turned to the men holding the guns. Between them stood War Raven with his arms outstretched, palms down. He looked to the sky, turned his palms upward and started to speak. All the talking stopped, and children froze in their tracks. Everyone spread their arms to the sky and threw back their heads. Tom and Brooke did the same. They didn't know what War Raven was saying but when people nodded, they did too. Tom saw Bow River look at him before lifting his eyes to stare into the cloudless sky. Next to Bow River stood Water Bird, who looked at Brooke before tipping his head upward and closing his eyes.

War Raven's prayer was short. When he finished the Black Eagle people cheered for their visitors, who nodded and smiled.

The crowd crumbled into little groups that scattered in different directions. Everyone moved to tend to stock, unpack bags and settle in. Groups of women walked away arm in arm.

Bow River didn't need to give directions but watched as everyone headed to their tasks. As War Raven approached, he caught Bow River's eye and shook his head *no*. Strong Horse was not there.

Someone must have shared this news with his daughter already. He could see her in the distance, standing motionless as a river rock. Star Flower in all her grace was frozen in a stream of movement, the sparkle of a teardrop on her cheek. A little girl held her hand and stared up at her until Stone Calf and Blue Jay appeared at her side, wrapped their arms around her, and slipped her away.

Orange light lay on the skyline when the evening drums began to roll. Flames in the firepits matched the sunset. Tipis glowed from the dinner's coals and horses grazed on slopes drenched in amber hues. The Sheep Lakes lay framed in flowers, glimmering like naked rhinestones. Across their surface the scene was repeated on wavy ripples, caused by feeding fish. As the people wandered from their lodges the Trout Moon crested the divide with the promise of many moons to follow.

CHAPTER ELEVEN

Little Bouquets

▲ ▲ ▲

The families camped together for six more days. They worked horses, hunted, made food, and played games. Every night they drummed, danced, and sang the songs that told their stories.

By the third night, only the younger ones lingered by the fire to watch for the morning stars. Those who chose to sleep weren't bothered by the noise as babies snoozed and seniors snored to the drumming pulse that had driven their lives for ages.

Brooke stayed close to Star Flower and Green Willow during the nighttime gatherings. Girls of all ages sat close to the trio and mimicked their moods and movements. To be within twenty feet of Star Flower and her striking friends was to be within the group.

The boys hung close too, watching the girls until they were caught looking, then they'd act uninterested. But all the boys and young men were interested in Brooke. Although most of them had seen white women before, they had never seen one as captivating as she was. It wasn't only her unfamiliar beauty that intrigued the Utes, but her manner too. She was content and unafraid among the people, most of whom she had never met. She possessed a kind, courageous sprit that Tom attributed to her mother. Like Teresa, she had a genuine interest in everything around her, the seeds of a scientist looking to grow.

At thirteen years old Brooke was considerably taller than anyone her age — and taller than most of the women in the tribe.
Star Flower was four years older, and Brooke was taller than her
too. Most of her height was in her legs, which made her gangly
compared to the other girls. Her hips and shoulders were narrow
compared to those of most Ute girls.

Her slender frame translated to speed — a trait the Utes trea-
sured. When coaxed into a foot race, Brooke easily beat all the
girls and a bunch of young boys too. Water Bird and his friends
declined an invitation to race, assured that they'd have no contest.

As the fires burned into the night the young men found reasons to inch closer to the girls. They'd sit nearby to listen and talk
as if the girls weren't there. Then one of the girls would call them
on their antics and the playful banter would begin. When the boys
got flustered, they'd disappear into the dark or jump to their feet
and dance away to the drums.

Brooke and her new friends were talking when out of the darkness came three little boys. They bobbed together in a tight group.
Their smiles and jerky movements could not disguise their intentions. They marched up and stood in front of the girls, squirming
and giggling until Star Flower asked what they were up to.

From behind their backs came three little bouquets that they
held at arm's length toward the girls. The little boys dipped their
chins and twisted away but their feet stuck solid. The older kids
laughed and jeered at the little ones, who held their ground in a
display of innocent courage that the older boys lacked.

Brooke reached out to a boy called Ah-choo-pits, Cricket, and
took his offer. Water Bird and his friends hooted in admiration
of the little guy. Brooke reached for the shy hand he offered and
led him toward the fire. At the edge of the light she paused, then
dipped into the rhythm of the drums while Cricket pranced a circle around her. Everyone young and old stepped to the fireside,
caught the cadence of the beat, and bowed into the flow of the
drums.

• • •

The dawn burned red then spread to pink over cloud-capped peaks. Shafts of light cut through the fog and lit the earth where meadows and timber stands were tented aqua blue. Rosy-pink and purple flowers glowed like candles in the filtered light. People stood by their lodges and gazed at the heavenly sight. On a ridge to the south, men and women kneeled in prayer toward the rising sun. When the hollow sound of a wooden flute rang out across the hills all eyes looked to the heavens, offering their full attention to the spirits of the people. In just a few notes they recognized the tune of romance, the Ute calling song.

On a point of rocks east of camp stood Tall Deer, facing the village with his back to the rising sun. His hair and fringed leggings blew gently in the breeze. The flute pressed to his lips released a melody that captured every ear. Behind him stood a spotted horse with red circles painted around its eyes. Its head hung under the weight of a buck deer — the traditional dowry offered in a Ute marriage proposal. Behind the first horse, four younger ones waited patiently.

Tom and Brooke walked through the crowd with Bow River and Stone Calf. Star Flower trotted ahead. She knew the sound of the calling song, and she knew it was not for her.

At the edge of the village everyone stopped and looked to the man on the point. He lowered the flute and watched a young woman shuffle through the crowd. Her mother followed behind her, brushing her daughter's hair as they walked briskly to the front.

The girl, Green Willow Spring, was dressed in a tan leather skirt with a turquoise beaded shirt and held a heron wing fan. From the edge of the group, she stepped out into a sea of green. Tall Deer raised the flute again and played while the audience swayed. People hugged one another, as wide-eyed children openly stared at the pair.

When Tall Deer stopped playing, he turned away from the village and faced the sun. He stretched his arms to the sky and tipped his face upward. Then he turned to face the people. Arms outstretched, in his strongest voice, he proclaimed his wish for Green Willow Spring and called for her to be his bride. A flutter went through the people, who shuffled at the announcement.

Green Willow Spring looked back into the crowd where her father, Antoeka, stood. She watched him stare at the man on the hill, who returned his gaze. The man and his daughter exchanged a look, then a slight smile creased his lips before he nodded.

Green Willow Spring's shoulders settled, and her smile fell wide as she turned and walked through the tall grass toward Tall Deer. They embraced one another then slowly turned and watched the rising sun.

Brooke looked to Star Flower, who stood with her hands on her heart as she watched the couple on the point. Brooke twisted through the crowd and on her way to Star Flower, Water Bird's eyes caught her gaze and held it. Tom saw the long look between them and as Brooke walked on he saw Water Bird bend his body to watch her.

When Tom turned back to the village, he realized he wasn't the only one that had noticed the moment between Brooke and Water Bird. Bow River, Stone Calf and Blue Jay were watching too, but only Blue Jay smiled. Bumping her eyes wide at Tom, she said something he didn't understand. Then she turned, stepped through the crowd, and disappeared.

CHAPTER TWELVE

The Endless River

▲ ▲ ▲

The journey back to the Mother's Lake was made in a single day. The ride was mostly downhill, and the horses traveled fast. Light rain sprinkled off and on, and little was said along the way. Young boys and girls rode ahead of the main party and were soon out of sight. The Utes started from the last bench above the Mother's Lake camp just as the sun sank behind the Brothers' Peaks. Below them fires burned at the edge of the lake. The sweet smell of syrup and smoked meat wafted uphill.

The people who had stayed at the lake met the returning group with relaxed invitations. Horses were unpacked and shelters were set before everyone crowed the fires for food.

The Yellow Bear Band would stay at the lake for a few days before moving down valley to the Pony Springs. It was the beginning of the Fruit Moon of August when the wild cherries and plums would show the first blush of fall. The elk would signal the changing seasons too, with gathering herds and bugling calls.

On the last day at the Mother's Lake, riders came from the north with news that buffalo had entered the northern region above Bear River. This was good news because the Utes needed buffalo for everything from horn spoons to tipi hides. It had been years since buffalo had been seen in the Bunkara Valley, although the evenings often began with elders telling stories of the rugged mountain buffalo that once roamed the canyons.

Whenever riders came from the south, Star Flower, asked about Strong Horse but no one brought good news. It had now been four full moons since he and the others had headed east. Everyone knew that the longer they stayed on the plains, the lower the chance they would return safely. But Star Flower and the rest of the band would hold out hope until they heard differently.

On a cool clear morning the camp headed downstream toward The Five Forks of the Bunkara. It was a long day at an easy pace and the last horse and riders made it to the Pony Springs as the sun sunk in the west.

The next morning the camp was set near the spring as it had been weeks before. The Yellow Bears would stay at the Pony Springs until snow beckoned them to move to lower country. Until then they would hunt, pick berries, and dig roots until their packs couldn't carry anymore. Everyone worked to acquire food and prepare it for winter. The men brought in meat and fish and the women cured it. If the hunts went well and the berries were big the people would live fat for a while. Survival was always all about food for the coming season and what it would take to stave off hunger from moon to moon.

On a morning that most of the men, including Tom, had gone hunting, Water Bird found Brooke and coaxed her to climb the mountain to the south of camp. Stone Calf wanted her to stick to her chores, but she slipped away with Water Bird at the first chance.

Water Bird carried his bow and quiver across one shoulder and a square beaded bag across the other. They followed a well-worn trail from camp and came out on top of the tower rock that stood above the spring. From that point they could see the five branches of the river and farther west. Water Bird pointed out a wide-based mountain with three pointed peaks. *Mo-goo-weve*, he called it, thumping his fist on his chest like a beating heart.

"*Mo-goo-weve?*" Brooke asked, thumping at her heart. Water Bird nodded yes.

"*Mo-goo-weve Ki-ve*, Heart Mountain." Brooke said. Water

Bird nodded again with a smile. With a few words and sign language Water Bird tried to explain that there were three buffalo that lived on Heart Mountain, one in the rocks, one in the snow, and one in the trees. When he couldn't explain any more, he grinned and pointed at the western horizon and said, "*Toom-cah-ne-ah-gah*," winter camp.

They sat on top of the rocks, pointing and exchanging words in English and Ute. *Too-wutch-um*, the sun, *wah-teep*, cloud, *sah-seet*, flower, *ah-pitsah*, boy, *na-chitsch*, girl. They went on through birds, horses, stallions, and mares. They named everything they could see. When they ran out of what they could see and say, they sat and looked out across the valley then down at the cluster of tipis below them.

Water Bird stood up and smiled before he started up the trail. Brooke fell in behind him in silence.

They walked up the ridge in waist-high grass and flowers. As they climbed, more of the surrounding mountains came into view. To the southwest they could see the giant Eagles Lodge Peak shaped like a tipi. West of it stood the maroon-colored Brothers' Peaks with their matching pointed tops. To the southeast, shining silver in the late summer sun, more tall peaks loomed. In every direction, they saw peaks studded with inset jewels of lingering snow.

Brooke knew that she and her father had crossed the Continental Divide to the east of here. She could almost see where they had encountered the split-eared bear that had led to their acceptance into the Ute village. As she stared east, Water Bird pointed up the river and said something Brooke didn't understand, so he snarled with an ugly face and raised his arms above his head, fingers splayed like claws. Brooke leaned away, pretending to be afraid of his angry bear impression. Water Bird cracked a little laugh. Brooke curled her fist in front of her mouth to hide her giggle, but Water Bird's smile grew wide, and they both laughed at his silliness. They stared to the east a little longer then continued up the trail.

The ridge flattened out and opened into a long meadow bordered in spruce trees. They walked in the warm sunshine, talking quietly as animals moved around them. Elk cows and calves passed close by, and a mother fox moved her kits. An eagle circled them several times and hummingbirds came within inches of their faces. Water Bird did his best to explain that the *moo-tah-touch*, hummingbird, was a messenger that could spread the news of the people.

They sat under a tree, relaxing in the shadows. The afternoon light was tinted yellow when they got up and climbed farther up the ridge. They looked south at the line of pointed peaks that stabbed the sky and the countless canyons that tied them together. Brooke didn't want to leave the scene that punctuated the day they had shared. The Ute boy dressed in buckskin with bow and quiver and the fair-skinned girl stood in the hazy afternoon air, glancing at each other then back at the vista, enjoying the feeling that came with the scenery.

Water Bird looked to the south then jerked his head back and placed his hand on Brooke's shoulder as he gently pressed her down.

"What is it?" She tried to rise against his grip, but Water Bird placed a finger to his lips.

"Riders," he said.

Brooke eased upward to look above the grass.

"There," he said, pointing a finger held close to his face.

Brooke squinted and spotted the line of men and horses. They looked like a string of beads inching down the slope. Water Bird grabbed her hand and moved them behind a tree. "Closer," he said.

"Who?" Brooke asked.

Water Bird turned his palms up and lightly shook his head.

"But —" Brooke started but caught herself, knowing she didn't have the words to continue.

Water Bird came out of his crouch and tugged her hand, and she knew they needed to run. They dropped off the ridge into the cover of the trees, but instead of going toward the village, they ran uphill toward the riders.

Water Bird strung his bow as they ran.

For half an hour they ran without stopping. At a pass that cut across the ridge they stopped and hid behind a log. As they struggled to catch their breath, Water Bird searched the hillside across from them. He pointed to the party of riders, just reaching timberline from above. They weren't easy to see in the low light. Five men strung out through a big herd of horses. Their broken pattern and the spotted horses blended in with the rocky terrain. The man in the lead sat tall and rode a big roan horse with a white rump patch. Light reflected from a rifle across his saddle. The second man carried a spear decorated with feathers and tufts of long black hair.

Brooke could see the worry on Water Bird's face, and she wondered if the riders were Kiowa or Arapaho?

They watched the party disappear into the timber, headed their way.

Water Bird took strong and deliberate breaths as he stared at the spot where the riders had been. He twisted his fist up to his mouth and looked at the ground, then slowly bent his head to speak to Brooke.

Brooke felt her forehead wrinkle. The only word she recognized was *cha-vah,* which meant horse. She tried to read Water Bird's face and made a guess at the rest. "Strong Horse?"

Water Bird twisted his jaw and nodded slowly. "Strong Horse."

Their eyes widened together as their heads bobbed. "Oh my gosh," Brooke whispered. Water Bird put his fingertips on her lips. Brooke's mouth dropped open, and she did what she'd seen the Utes do. She clapped her hand across her open lips as Water Bird did the same.

With so much to say and not enough words, they looked at each other and shared a hushed sigh before trotting downhill. Water Bird stopped and placed a finger to his lips. When he shook his head *no,* Brooke nodded. She understood there would be no more talking, that Strong Horse, the lover of Star Flower, was on his way.

When they stumbled into the village at dark their knees were wobbly and their skin damp. The people stared as they walked a line toward their shelters.

Tom was sitting by his fire. He stood up as Brooke approached, but she walked past. "Hello Papa," she said as she dipped inside the lodge.

Tom stuck his head inside the flap. "Where have you been? I was beginning to worry."

"Water Bird got us a little lost."

"Stone Calf told me you went hunting. Did you get anything?" He waited for a reply.

"I'll be right out," she said.

Tom returned to the fire, where he picked up his journal and jotted a note.

Brooke came out and ate without saying much. It wasn't like her to be so quiet. Tom could sense a new distance between them. She was becoming a young woman, and he knew she would soon have secrets to guard, even from him.

Brooke stared into the fire and wondered if Water Bird was right. Would Strong Horse be coming to their camp soon? For Star Flower's sake, and for the safety of the village, she hoped so. If the approaching party wasn't led by Strong Horse, who was headed toward the village? An enemy tribe? White settlers? A knot of fear tightened in her stomach. Should she tell her father? She'd never kept a secret from him, not successfully. But if she told him what she'd heard, he would tell Bow River, which would cause a commotion, maybe even a panic. There was no choice but to trust Water Bird. She mashed her lips shut and reached for the string around her neck.

"Brooke, are you alright?"

"Yes, Papa, I'm just tired. Today was a big day."

She stood and glanced around the village. "Good night, Papa," she said as she disappeared under the tipi flap.

Tom leaned back and looked around the camp, where parents and children huddled around their fires. It wasn't like Brooke to go to bed so early. Maybe she was tired, but he felt a pinch of guilt for what he may not know. What she might be hiding from him.

He was grateful for her safety here, with him. Still, a small, internal voice told him it was time to start keeping a closer eye on his daughter — and on Water Bird.

Yellow light caressed the peak east of the camp as a choir of robins sang their morning songs. Pans clanked and fires snapped as women poked coals into flames. Dogs stretched then greeted the people that moved about the camp. Muted conversations filtered through the hide walls as families rose to start the day.

At the Dunagan's lodge, Tom was warming tea water. Brooke stepped outside, laced her fingers behind her head, and twisted her back from side to side. She'd had a restless night. Between the tipis, she could see Water Bird kneeling at a fire pit. Their eyes caught.

The flawless tone of the flute spread across the valley like the lonesome call of a young wolf. The melodious cry of the Calling Song spread like a shadow and quieted the birds while curious animals tipped their heads toward the tune. Everyone stopped what they were doing to take in the meaning of the sound.

Bow River was the first to step out and look toward the rocky tower above camp. Water Bird came to his side and together they stared up at the point where a man held a flute at his chin. Again, the melody floated over the village then stopped. Bow River told his son, "Go for your sister. Let her know that Strong Horse has arrived."

Water Bird turned and ran. When he stuck his head into his mother's lodge the flurry of movement inside stopped. Stone Calf and Star Flower riveted their eyes on him. He was prepared to explain, but instead he just nodded with a smile. The women scurried to grab clothes and jewelry.

People huddled and a murmur rumbled as they discussed the man on the point. His muscular outline stood against wispy clouds in a light blue sky. Behind him stood a roan horse with a white rump patch.

A sigh sifted through the crowd, and Bow River turned to see his daughter walking toward him. Her fringed dress was the color of golden sand. The yoke was beaded in red and yellow to match her jewelry and shining hair. Twisted strands of turquoise beads hung below her ears. Her braids were dotted with the little pink flowers for which she was named. She carried a Blue Heron wing fan with the handle wrapped in white fur.

She glanced up and down as she approached her father. He turned to meet her and spoke softly as she got closer. With one arm stretched toward the sky he wrapped the other around her shoulder. Together they turned to face the man on the rocky point.

The sound of the flute rolled over the crowd again and, as they listened, four riders appeared at the base of the cliff leading strings of horses. One horse had a large buck deer slung across its withers. The men stopped on the grassy slope and waited as the flute continued to call. When it went silent the man lowered it to his waist and called out, "I am Strong Horse of the Black Eagle Band. I have brought horses to offer, so that I may ask for the hand of Star Flower." He lifted the flute to his lips and blew into it again.

For several minutes the music played as everyone gathered behind Star Flower. Women and girls reached out to touch her shoulders. She looked uphill. Brooke stepped forward and touched her too. Star Flower turned and shrugged her shoulders with a nervous smile.

Stone Calf's smile mimicked her daughter's. She glanced at her husband and then to the man on the hill.

When the flute stopped playing, Star Flower looked to her parents, Bow River and Stone Calf. Bow River waved his upturned palm toward her and then toward the man on the rocky point. With that motion and a slight nod, he gave permission for her to go.

Star Flower took a deep breath. Her chin trembled and she caught a tear with the back of her hand. She looked to the ground and gathered her skirt. After a few steps uphill she raised the fan above her head then twirled it downward, resting it near her waist. She bowed her head and listened.

When Strong Horse finished speaking the men who held the horses yelled and whooped, as did the entire camp. Drums pounded when Strong Horse mounted the big roan horse and headed downhill. All five men rode to the edge of the village, leading a colorful array of horses that pranced and snorted.

Strong Horse dismounted and walked down the slope to meet Star Flower. When they came together, he hugged her, lifting her feet from the ground.

The people scattered in every direction as they set out to perform their tasks for the rituals of the day. Relief spread through the village now that the young men who had ventured onto the plains were home, with more than just their lives.

Throughout the day and on into the evening the feast went on as stories were told and gifts were given.

When the sun touched the western hills and the light spread out in colorful layers, Strong Horse and Star Flower disappeared up-river to a lodge on a sandy bend overlooking the water. Through the night they listened to the ripples and moved to the rhythm of the drums as the endless river carried their cares away.

CHAPTER THIRTEEN

Medicine Water

▲ ▲ ▲

The Yellow Bears stayed at the Pony Springs for almost two moons.

Strong Horse and Star Flower disappeared for days at a time, seeking privacy to celebrate their union. Sometimes, they returned to camp just before dark. Other nights they didn't come back at all.

After what Tom assumed was their honeymoon, Strong Horse began the work of sorting and training the new horses in the herd. He hadn't owned them for long, so he was still learning their ways.

Strong Horse's skills far surpassed the basics of hunting and fishing that a man needed to master to survive in the mountains. He knew how to make snowshoes, flint arrowheads, and horsehair ropes. He could ignite a fire with stone and steel, or just three pieces of wood and a string. He could catch an eagle, outsmart a coyote, and kill a buffalo with a spear. And now his bravery was legendary, celebrated in epic tales of horseflesh and coups.

For all that he owned and all that he could do, Strong Horse excelled at racing, training, and caring for horses above all else. Almost daily he spent time with one or more of his horses, building their trust and guiding them to develop the talents he'd need in a reliable mount — or to improve the value of a trade. Other men came to him for help and advice, which he modestly gave.

Of the forty horses he brought to the Yellow Bear's village, none were more exceptional than the one called Taowa.

The stud's dark edges were a chokecherry roan that faded to silver gray. His white rump blanket was dotted with black spots. Many of the new horses bore similar markings.

But Taowa carried a particularly honest eye in his sculpted head. When he stood tall on his shiny black hooves, muscles rippling across his shoulders and legs, his regal bearing reflected the courage of the man who had trained him.

Everyone in the village was interested in the new horses. There were purple and red roans with spots of every size. Some were aspen-leaf orange and black; others were steel blue and gray. The Utes had never seen so many spotted rumps. Appaloosa horses were still rare among their people. Over the years, they had traded for a few from the Shoshoni up north. The Arapahos now had fewer than they'd possessed before the raid.

Water Bird was surprised to receive three horses as a gift. For a young man of fifteen to own a horse was unheard of. To own three made Water Bird a young man of means. A stature that didn't go unnoticed, especially among the other young men and women. His gift horses included a young, copper-colored stallion with a white rump patch and black spots, a gray stud, and a flashy, black filly with snowflake-white dots scattered across her hips. They were young horses with years ahead of them to learn the tricks they'd need to travel and work in rugged terrain. Both stallions had been ridden, but the black and white filly had not. She was cantankerous right from the start. Her spirit was a challenge but would be a big asset with age. The first day that Water Bird tried to bridle her, she fought him as expected. But when she was still fighting days later, Water Bird didn't know what to do. He had helped his father with horses before, but he had never trained one start to finish. Bow River offered some advice, but he left it to Water Bird to make the decisions and do the work.

Strong Horse noticed and, after watching for a couple of days, he cautiously approached Water Bird with an offer to help. Water Bird was confident in his own ability but not too proud to accept

Strong Horse's advice. Together, in two days, they had gained the filly's trust enough to climb on her back while she stayed still, unless they asked her to move. At that point the training could continue. Water Bird knew that without Strong Horse's help the task would have taken much longer. Water Bird was proud of his effort and progress with the filly he called Snowflake, but he was prouder of his new brother-in-law.

Strong Horse had quickly become a respected man in the Yellow Bear Clan. Not just for his bravery and skill but for his sound judgment too. His wisdom and generosity reflected his good nature and his desire for all the people to prosper. Many suspected that his steady demeanor was partly the result of a happy marriage. Strong Horse was seven years older than Water Bird, and his bearing was that of a man even older. Many boys in camp copied his clothes, his walk, even his talk.

He had a powerful build that was still growing. His shoulders were broad, and his arms were long. He was lean but barrel chested, and his legs were thick as trees. He was fast and strong, and it was easy to coax him to display his athletic gifts. He accepted all challenges with a spirit of good sportsmanship and always made his competitors feel worthy.

All the women in camp, including Brooke, were enamored by his prowess, his kind nature, and his easy smile. But most of all, they all admired the special bond he had with Star Flower, who was impressed by his charming nature too.

He was always helping with chores. He made tools for others and wrestled with the kids. His presence brought an attitude of confidence and wealth to the entire clan.

Strong Horse's cousin, Henry Eagle, and a young man named Siska stayed at the Pony Springs when the other Black Eagle men went back across the south pass divide.

Siska was a few months older than Water Bird. On their first hunting trip together, Water Bird took them to the Yampa Pagosa at the junction of the Rio Colorado and back through the high lakes surrounding Heart Mountain. When they returned to the Pony Springs, they brought back sheep, deer, grouse, and a large mountain lion. Stone Calf made the lion's hide into an arrow quiver that Water Bird gave to Siska.

Siska and the other visiting men were all interested in Brooke. Water Bird understood why. Her beauty was undeniable. But he kept his jealousy to himself. After all, she was white, which made caution wise. When the time came for the other men to leave, Water Bird didn't mind seeing them go — although he would miss Siska. They'd become friends, and Water Bird had told Siska about his special regard for Brooke. Because they lived on opposite sides of the Elk Mountains, Water Bird had felt free to confide in him. Unlike the boys from his village, he trusted Siska to keep his secret.

The aspen leaves glowed with gold and the cottonwoods were close behind when Bow River knew it was time to head for winter camp. It was warm and clear at the Pony Springs, but still he sensed it was time to leave.

The fall hunt had been good, and the berries were plentiful, so moving all the food would be a consuming task. Most of the horse herd would carry supplies or drag travois. As they traveled west, they would harvest pinion nuts and roots, adding weight to the packs. The camp couldn't travel too fast, as gear would have to be moved and stored then moved again all along the way. It would take weeks to make the trip with an extended stay at the Yampa Pagosa.

October's Traveling Moon was at hand and the Cold Moons were to follow. It was better to get ahead of the ice that would soon choke the rivers. Four river crossings separated the Pony Springs and the Winter Camp, and each one presented a different challenge. They all harbored the risk of lost supplies and lives.

Tom and Brooke left camp in the first group of thirty or so people. Good Bear led the way, followed by Strong Horse and the other men and families. Bow River would lead the remaining people and horses in two days. Water Bird stayed with the second group.

The lead group traveled almost twenty miles the first day and made it to the Red Cliff River where it entered the Bunkara from the north. They would stay there until the other group caught up.

The first morning in camp Brooke went with the women into the rocky hills to collect pinion pinecones. Afterward, they baked them over coals to collect the pitch and loosen the nuts. Once the pinecones had dried, they spread them on hides and whipped them with willows. The delicious little nuts pooled in the middle. From there, everyone scooped them up in baskets, ate them by the handful and spit out the shells as they talked.

It was the second day of moving camp that the full width of Heart Mountain came into view. Until then, Tom had no idea how truly magnificent the mountain was. Like a majestic trident temple on a level plain, it rose from the valley in grandeur. Tom could see and feel the honor the people held for the mountain in their morning prayers.

Bow River explained that the mountain was the heart of their homeland and that the Great Circle of their existence rotated around it. When Tom wrinkled his brow in wonder, Bow River's smile said that was all he needed to know.

Tom recognized the mountain as a laccolith. Magma had been forced upward by internal pressure creating an uplift that never reached the surface. After eons of erosion the volcanic skeleton had been exposed. The mountain was a collection of three peaks that spread out east and west. The two western peaks were the tallest and looked nearly the same height. The eastern peak was about two-thirds as tall. But Tom's thoughts were limited to geology. For the Ute people, the mountain was far more than the result of a series of seismic shifts.

Water Bird eagerly pointed out to Brooke and Tom that the eastern peak was the home of the buffalo running west. It took them only a second to see the buffalo's likeness in the snowfield cliff and shadows of the peak.

Water Bird went on to show them an image of a buffalo in each of the other two peaks too. After a bit of study and imagination Tom and Brooke could see the outline of buffalos in each peak, one in the cliffs, one in the forest, and one in the stone.

The two parties came together about a week after leaving the Pony Springs and camped on a bench between the Bunkara and another river flowing from the southeast. The Utes knew the spot as the Fat Berry Camp and the other river as the Snow Stone.

Tom thought the water in the Snow Stone had a distinctive luster. As if a mirror lay beneath it, it had a metallic sparkle quite different than that of the Bunkara.

From the Fat Berry Camp, the men hunted the flanks of Heart Mountain, while the women picked berries and collected pinion nuts on the brushy hillsides.

After three days the caravan crossed the Bunkara in a shallow but swift crossing called the Eagle's Nest Crossing. Perched in the dead spire of a Ponderosa Pine was an eagle's nest that Tom thought must have weighed a ton.

When the entire village of forty travois laden horses, pack-mules and dogs left the Eagle's Nest Crossing the talk among the Utes was all about the next camp at the Yampa Pagosa. There was a discernible yearning among the people to get there. Tom and Brooke could hear and see the excitement among the people. Tom asked Bow River about the high mood he noticed in the crowd. Bow River just widened his eyes, cooed through a rounded mouth, then rattled off words that Tom couldn't discern.

When Brooke asked Stone Calf where they were going, Stone Calf stuck out both hands palms down and made a patting motion that usually meant, just wait. Star Flower just smiled and whispered something Brooke interpreted to mean *medicine water*, although the only part of the word she knew for sure was *wah*, meaning water.

Tom, Brooke and Water Bird were riding together in the middle of the pack when they topped a chalky bluff on the south side of the Rio Colorado. The leaders of the group were just stepping their horses into the river when the riders around Tom and Brooke goaded their horses to run for the water. A column of dust from the pounding hooves and the scratching of travois floated like fog around their heads.

Tom and Brooke held back to watch the people run toward a river that smoked like a forest fire. Columns of thick steam rose from forty plus pools of hot water that skirted the edge of the river. A layer of vapor hung low in the valley and swirled around the arriving commotion.

Brooke turned to her father and said, "Yampa Pagosa." They both nodded lightly. From atop their horses they looked over the juncture of the Bunkara and the Rio Colorado cradled in a canyon of red and yellow hills. The valley echoed with the whoops and hollers mixed with the rumble of a thousand hooves.

As they rode closer, the stinky smell of sulfur caused noses to wrinkle.

At the Stinking Water Crossing, the river ran slow but strong and was three to four feet deep.

Not everyone or everything was moved across the river that evening. A few tipis remained on the south side, but most of the clan crossed to the north.

Each of the families knew their tipi sites before they waded out of the river. Weary horses stood neglected as people went straight into the warm pools of water to wash their faces and arms.

Before the horses were unloaded people were already getting into the water. Others partially stripped, lifted their arms and eyes to the sky, and fell over backwards into the water.

When Tom and Brooke noticed that everyone, from little toddlers to grandparents, were either in the water or kneeling at the edge, they too stopped their horse chores and waded in to receive the blessing of the calming warm water.

The evening meals were quick that night or not at all. Some of the tipis were raised while others were laid out for the next day.

Tom and Brooke laid out their poles and hide covering as they watched people scurrying about, doing little tasks before they headed back to the water. They saw men, women, and children hurry to the different pools, strip naked and either tiptoe in or launch themselves into the water in a ball.

Bow River and Stone Calf walked by as Tom and Brooke were watching the commotion. Bow River gestured toward the water. "Big medicine," he said in an encouraging tone. At that, Stone Calf stepped over to Brooke, picked up a shawl, grabbed her arm and turned her toward the river.

"Hey," Brooke protested, trying to come up with anything to say, but Stone Calf couldn't understand, nor did she try. With Brooke in tow, Stone Calf moved down a path at a lighthearted but determined clip.

A nervous whirlwind started to spin within Brooke at the thought of getting naked in front of everyone. She had bathed before with some of the girls, but she'd never been naked in front of a boy or man.

A fretful feeling was building, something between fear and flight, when Stone Calf barked out in a deep voice. Suddenly, two boys on the trail ahead of them broke for cover. Stone Calf turned to Brooke and, with a wry smile, urged her to continue. They cut through a patch of willows and cottonwoods and came back to the riverbank. Brooke could hear the gaggle of women splashing and playing before she could see them. When she and Stone Calf came out of the shadows at the edge of the large steaming pool, the other women cheered and urged them on.

Stone Calf quickly pulled her dress over her head and helped Brooke to do the same. Brooke was still hesitant, but when the women and girls saw her modest protest, they cheered and clapped and hollered at her with loving encouragement. Brooke couldn't understand their words, but she knew the tone and couldn't wait to join their group.

As she stepped into the water the other women craned their necks to look between her legs at a little tuft of red hair that had recently appeared. They giggled, nodded their heads, and clapped their hands across their mouths.

Brooke and Stone Calf waded into the pool hand in hand and, when they were waist deep, Stone Calf gave the sign of hands patting down. They let their feet slide away, and they sank into the soothing warmth. When Brooke brought her head above the water, the dark eyes and wide smiles of her adopted family surrounded her.

As nighttime engulfed the river, the women grew withered and wrinkled in the warm water. As the grip of their many shared hardships loosened, coos of relaxation and acceptance rose into the sky.

CHAPTER FOURTEEN

East or West

▲ ▲ ▲

The Yellow Bears camped at the Yampa Pagosa for almost three weeks. The men hunted, while the women worked on hides, gathered herbs, and prepared food for the coming months. People lit fires in the evening along the river, where they washed and soaked in the warm water.

Tom knew that the Yampa Pagosa was a unique geologic formation. In his years of study, he'd never heard of such an extensive collection of hot springs, pools, and caves anywhere in the west. In the stretch of half a mile there were over sixty pools that oozed hot water. One pool was nearly thirty feet across and untouchably hot. It boiled like a kettle of soup on a blazing fire. Surrounding it were more pools of different temperatures where people could float in hot water and then swim into the frigid river to cool down. A series of limestone caves were heated by steaming streams. One popular cave was large enough to stand in and could hold thirty people. The smell of wood smoke and humanity saturated the damp walls.

Another cavern, called Grandmother's Cave, held a warm pool that drained into the river. A person could swim from the outside to the inside and lie on a sandy bank in the steamy warmth.

The men gathered in some of the caves, while the women

congregated in others. But many were shared by both men and women, with couples disappearing in and out of them all evening.

The first evening that Tom sat in a hot cave, the men drummed and sang songs. Firelight lit the pools where the people, large and small, soothed themselves in the water.

The Utes were rich, and they knew it. The Yampa Pagosa was rightfully theirs. Although different families from many directions used the hot springs, the Yellow Bears had called this territory home for many generations.

. . .

Wavy cirrus clouds streaked the sky the evening that Bow River announced the village would move west. The thick hair of the ponies and the effort of the squirrels signaled the approach of winter.

Tom planned to head toward Denver with Brooke when the camp broke up at Yampa Pagosa. He enjoyed traveling with the Utes, and he knew Brooke did too, but he had to head back. He hadn't prospected as much as he'd wanted, but he had a duty to return his daughter to civilization.

Brooke was losing ground in her schooling, and they hadn't seen his folks in almost four years. Knowing that he and Brooke had gone into the mountains, his parents would be worried by now. So would Mrs. Lankering, who owned the boarding house where they had lived the past winter. She had always fussed over Brooke and had agreed to hold their mail or send letters back east if she got any.

Tom had been keeping an eye out for anyone who could carry word back to Denver that they were safe, but he hadn't seen another white man since Mustache Bob back in May. The assay office where he'd worked before had offered him a job on his return, but he wasn't sure if the business would still be operating by then.

Knowing that it would be dangerous to spend a winter in the mountains, Tom had remembered the route back to the pass across the Snowy Mountains. It would be a long ride from Yampa

Pagosa, but they could make it if they left soon. If they could make it to the divide in three days, they could be in Denver in another seven to ten.

When Bow River made the announcement, Tom knew he needed to tell him of his decision. But before he told Bow River, he needed to tell Brooke.

She respected her father's decision, but that didn't stop her from questioning it.

"Do we have time to get back across the divide?" He couldn't answer with confidence, and Brooke could tell.

Tom rubbed his hand back and forth across his mouth and glanced toward the eastern horizon. He worried that he may have waited too long and wished he had told Bow River sooner.

As he revisited his plans, he realized that getting over the divide in three days could be difficult. He let out a long breath and felt a tight spot in his gut. All his plans would be in jeopardy if they couldn't make it across the mountains. How would Brooke fare over the winter if they couldn't make it back to Denver? That was his deepest concern. She watched him silently as he contemplated their plight.

"Papa, I'll be okay – whatever happens." Tom held her gaze and knew she meant it.

They could endure a lot if they were together. They'd already been through so much. He knew the elements could be taxing, but they were manageable. He was certain they could weather whatever was to come.

"Brooke, I'll tell Bow River in the morning that we are heading back over the divide." She nodded her head and pressed her lips together as she glanced at the gear scattered around them.

The next morning leaves raced along the ground as Tom looked for Bow River. Everyone hustled, packing gear into hide bags and blankets. Eyes glanced his way, but no one stopped working. He realized that his departure with Brooke could create additional problems for his Ute brothers and sisters. If Bow River decided to send someone with them, to help them cross the divide, the Utes would be down a man, and their escort would be in harm's way.

He knew Bow River would weigh the risks and send a man with them anyway.

A strong wind whipped through the camp, scattering gear and trash. People hollered and cursed the wind as they chased and grabbed their belongings.

Tom found Bow River leading three horses toward the village. Bow River stopped and waited with a serious stare. With hand language and a few words Tom told Bow River his plan to head back east to Denver.

Bow River's face wrinkled as if he'd taken a punch. Tom had seen that pained look before. The chief's jaw muscles bulged as he clenched his teeth. He looked to the South. Then he reached out, took Tom's shoulder, and turned him to face the same direction. A red cliff foreground framed Heart Mountain, shimmering bright with snow.

Bow River pointed south, spoke sternly, then pointed at his feet.

Tom didn't understand much, but he heard the words, *noo-vah,* snow, and *vutch* shoe. And he recognized Bow River's insistence that it was too dangerous. Tom gathered his thoughts, realizing that crossing the divide would require abandoning their horses and walking through on snowshoes. Bow River turned abruptly, and they stood face to face. Bow River's nostrils flared with each breath.

"*Cuch*! No!" Bow River snapped. He clearly knew the meaning of the white man's word he had used. His jaw angled to the side, and his eyes squinted.

Tom wasn't sure what to do and before he could do anything, Bow River took in a deep breath and rattled off so many words Tom didn't even try to understand.

Bow River held his hand at his waist. Again, Tom heard, "*noo-vah.*" Snow. Then Bow River went on, using more sharp words in a higher pitch of pleading. His arms swung up in the air, as he looked to the north then back to the south. He stopped and took in another deep breath then looked Tom in the eyes and, at slower cadence, he said a dozen words that ended with Brooke's name, Uckarth Pahn-qwe, Rose Creek.

"No," Bow River said again as he stepped past Tom with the horses in tow.

Tom knew Bow River was right. He had made his decision to return to Denver too late. Going east, he and Brooke would face near-certain death. They would have to go west with the Utes.

Tom was dazed, unsure if he'd just received brotherly advice or a scolding. He looked over the milling horse herd, hemmed in by the river where Loma and Good Bear sat on horseback watching him. At Tom's glance, they turned away and went back to work sorting horses. Tom looked at Bow River, marching up the trail, and knew he had no choice but to follow.

Tom stooped into their lodge, where Brooke's eyes were quick to find his. He stepped to the side and started packing gear.

"Well?" Brooke tipped her head and watched her father.

Tom turned around and sat down on the pile of blankets that served as his bed. "We're heading out tomorrow."

Brooke tucked her chin and held a silent stare.

He looked up and met her eyes. "West, we're headed west."

She looked at the tipi flap then back at him. "To winter camp?"

Tom looked at the floor and nodded. His jaw was hard with a rankled look of concern.

Brooke looked around at all the gear. A tight smile pushed up her cheeks, which she covered with soft hands. Her eyes widened as she lightly nipped her lip and reached for the string that held the glass star around her neck.

CHAPTER FIFTEEN

Gift Boots

▲ ▲ ▲

The Yellow Bears had been in winter camp on Roan Creek for seven days when, late in the night, the village awoke to the sounds of vicious dogs.

The people stumbled from their warm tipis with weapons in hand. Women scurried about stocking fires for light. People were yelling and kids were crying, as everyone hollered questions back and forth.

The dog pack sprang and snarled its way north into the dark. Tom stood next to Good Bear; both men held rifles at their hips. Brooke stood by her father with a heavy stick in hand.

Suddenly, Tom jumped sidewise as three men broke from camp at a dead gallop. They disappeared into the dark with chunks of ice flying from horse hooves. Rifle blasts rang out and everyone froze. The crowd quieted and then another blast blew from Bow River's rifle. He stood with the gun pointing up and to the north.

The barking dogs were farther away. Over their continued ruckus, Tom heard the screech of voices. Bow River moved into the darkness with a cluster of men behind him. He yelled out, and shrieks rang back above the yapping dogs. Again, he yelled out a question and when the reply came back, he looked around with a worried scowl at the men behind him. As the men returned to the firelight and waited with their rifles ready, Bow River yelled into the darkness one last time.

From out of the blackness came the first figures hobbling toward the village. Their bodies were bowed, heads hung down. Loud talk went back and forth between the groups.

Meadow Song yelled then ran into the dark. Other women followed her.

Bow River and Loma walked out briskly to the first man who came into sight. As soon as they got to him, they both started yelling back instructions to the village. Everyone scattered in different directions. As more people came into view, more ran out to meet them.

Brooke stood with her father and felt the gasp of the village as the people came into sight. The haggard troop was comprised of men, women, and children in ragged buckskin clothes, black with ash and charcoal stains. Their tattered moccasins were bloody, and every eye was wet with worry and exhaustion. A pungent, stinky odor drifted into camp with them.

Some of the people coming in from the darkness fell to their knees in tears, too weak to take another step. The Yellow Bear women stepped forward to meet them.

Brooke ran up next to Blue Jay, who was helping haul a travois loaded with crying children.

"Here." She handed Brooke a little boy then flailed her arms toward the village, barking orders. Brooke knew to take the boy to the waiting care of the people.

Blue Jay grabbed a small girl and handed her to Green Willow, and she and Brooke ran for the tipis.

The little boy squealed and squirmed, reaching back for his mother. Brooke could feel his rough skin on her arms as she trotted into the light. In the fire's glow, she saw the red skin and scabs that covered his body. As the baby wiggled in her hands, a rank sweet smell packed her nose, and she caught vomit at the top of her throat. The poor little one was badly burned.

At the first tipi, Grandma Chuka took the baby and shooed Brooke back toward the people coming in from hell. As Brooke ran back out, others were coming in helping those who still hobbled along. People who couldn't walk were drug on hide sleds. Cries and sobs drenched the darkness.

For hours the people of the village toiled in mud and snow, as over forty fire victims were brought in from a disaster no one took time to explain. They brought the living inside and hauled the dead into a pile. Bundles of herbs and pots of grease were dug from packs, so they could be warmed by the fires and soaked in boiling water.

Tom stood by a fire and looked around a room of crying kids and moms and dads. He felt a familiar weight in his gut and took a deep breath to push it away. He'd been here before, but this time the kids were younger, and their parents were with them. Brooke looked up from where she knelt by Stone Calf, who was peeling black skin from a little one's leg.

Tom couldn't seem to get away from human carnage. He knew what to do; he'd done it before. Burns were common in triage, but this time he'd have only Ute medicine to work with. He wasn't sure it wasn't better. It probably couldn't' be worse. Tom sunk his hands in steaming water and started cleaning and peeling burnt flesh. As he and others worked, several women wrapped plant leaves and shredded bark into poultices, which were placed on burns and cuts. Others made bandages of rags and leather, which they fastened together and tied to patients with rawhide string.

Every member of the Yellow Bear family was up all night, salving wounds, sharing food, rocking babies.

The sun was high, and the day was starting to warm before the village settled to a murmur. It was the next afternoon before anyone took a deep breath and closed their eyes. By early evening the tale of terror was traveling through the tipis.

This was the Gray Horse Band of Uinta Utes, a people who ranged between the upper White River and the Utah Territory. They had come over the divide at the head of Roan Creek and struggled southward into the Yellow Bear's camp with no food and few belongings.

In the night, they had awakened to the roar of a wildfire fueled by high winds. Everyone who could get away was forced into the river. From the icy water, they watched helplessly as their village was leveled and family members were burned to death. They hadn't buried their food supplies yet, so all they had to eat had burned up next to their tipis.

A woman named Little Owl, who had left the water to save her niece, was badly burned and died the next day, leaving her niece an orphan.

The next morning, it had begun to snow and Red John, their leader, knew they had to move fast or the whole camp could die.

Their horses had been scattered and only a few could be found before they gathered up and headed south. They knew the Yellow Bears were in winter camp under the Roan Cliffs, and they were the closest band who could help them.

Now, everyone worked to comfort and feed the unfortunate souls. The Gray Horse band had lost everything, including their lodges, blankets, clothing, and food. For the time being, every lodge in the village would be packed to the poles with people.

The next morning under a cloudless sky, Red John stood in front of Bow River, Good Bear and Loma to thank them — asking for nothing more than the generous help they had already given.

Bow River assured Red John that his families were welcome in their camp. He knew that forty more mouths would stress their winter supplies, but these people were friends and family. Their survival was crucial to the survival of the Yellow Bears.

It was late in the Beaver Moon of November and the low country hills were bare. The coldest part of winter was coming and, if the weather held, they could hunt the elk herds upstream.

Bow River called for everyone to the center of the village where he spoke.

"All my brothers, all my sisters, all my friends, we are forced together so that we all will live. It is early in winter, and the ground caches are full of meat and grain. Our friends have lost everything, and we will share. We must work to kill more animals, gather more wood, and collect more nuts. The winter will be long, and we will be thin in spring, but spring we will see. Make room for our friends for they too are Utes, people of The Sun."

With the additional people in camp, more meat and hides were needed to make it through the winter. Three days after the Gray Horse band arrived a hunting party of fourteen men and sixty horses were readied for a trip upriver.

Elk herds wintered in the hills north of Heart Mountain to the Yampa Pagosa. Bow River knew that if the hunters could get there before the valleys filled with snow, they would find elk.

The day before the hunting party was announced, Bow River and Good Bear met Tom on his way out to the horses. Tom knew that this was a pointed intercept not just a chance meeting.

The horses grazed in the tan grass along the river and for a moment, the men watched them. Tom could feel orders coming.

"Tom Gun," Bow River said, "You and Rose Creek came to our village and because of you, I am here today." The three men looked at each other, then Bow River looked back at the horses. "When we were at Yampa Pagosa, Good Bear had a dream. He saw a long string of horses loaded with meat and behind them was Heart Mountain."

"That's good," Tom replied as he looked at the men.

Bow River raised his chin a little. "Tom Gun, you were riding with the group in his dream." Tom looked out over the horse herd, as did the other two men. "Tom Gun, you must go to the Bunk-ara. We need your rifle to bring back meat. Good Bear saw you there. Without you, those ponies may come back without meat — or not at all."

Tom wasn't sure about giving any credence to the logic of a dream, but he was in no position to say so. A slight hum slipped from the back of his throat as he thought about Brooke, certain that Bow River and Good Bear had thought of her safety too. In that moment, Tom knew he could trust his daughter's life in their hands.

"Okay," Tom said. His chin scrunched into a half smile. Tom was honored with the appointment and grateful for the trust he shared with these men. He took a deep breath that swelled his chest. Bow River and Good Bear stood tall, then turned to walk downslope toward the horse herd.

The hunters for the trip included mostly Yellow Bear members, though a few Gray Horse men joined them too. Every man carried a rifle.

Good Bear would lead the party with Loma and the newest member of the clan, Strong Horse.

Water Bird would be the youngest hunter to go. His father gave him one of his two rifles to take on the trip.

Bow River and Red John agreed to stay at the village and see to the horse herd and the gathering of more food. The remaining men and boys in the village would stay close to protect the camp and hunt nearby. Everyone would tend to the injured people of the Gray Horse Band as they were able.

The next day it was snowing lightly when the hunting party gathered at the edge of the village. The men and horses milled in a group while women loaded food and blankets. At the edge of camp, young boys held the pack strings and watched quietly as the hunters prepared to leave.

The hunters were dressed in their warmest winter gear. They wore fur hats with blanket coats and buffalo robes. Elk skin leggings and shirts were lined with rabbit and beaver fur. Each man wore decorations of beads, feathers, and brass. Most of the Yellow Bear men wore the hard-soled, knee-high moccasins with antler buttons that were a badge of the band.

Tom had seen the winter boots before, stowed away in the people's gear. He was pretty sure that Mustache Bob, whom they had met on the east side of the divide back in May had worn the same boots. Tom could still hear his auspicious words: "Make friends with the Utes and watch out for the bears."

Tom still wore the jeans and leather boots he'd left Denver in. The jeans were patched with leather and canvas. He wore them under loose, elk-skin leggings that were blackened with grease and smoke. He'd long ago given up on socks and now lined his boots with scraps of fur and loose elk hair. For all his efforts, his feet still got cold.

Stone Calf, Fat Cow and several other women in the clan had given Tom and Brooke extra clothing.

Brooke had worn through, or grown out of, all her white-girl clothes, except her father's wool army coat. Like the Ute girls, she now wore leather skirts and leggings and shirts made of blankets or furs.

Brooke stood near her father and watched the activity swirl around them.

The men were loaded and ready to leave when Good Bear gave a blessing to the village and to his fellow hunters.

Star Flower pulled the pack ropes tight on her husband's extra horses then took the lead of his roan stallion and waited.

Strong Horse helped other men and women ready their packs for the trip. His wife waited with his horse. He moved to her and ran the back of his hand along her chin line. Tipping her face upward, he kissed her on the lips. Before they parted, Strong Horse ran his palm across her stomach and around the small of her back then pulled her close again. He climbed atop his horse and watched as the other hunters shared their goodbyes.

Brooke faced her father at the side of his white horse. "Brooke, I'll be back in a few days," he told her in almost a whisper.

"I know Papa, I'll be okay. I know this is what we need to do."

Tom returned her smile with a nod.

She reached her arms around his neck and kissed his cheek. Tom held her back at arms-length for a moment then wrapped her tight in a long hug.

"Tom Gun," a voice called. He and Brooke turned to see Blue Jay step alongside Tom's horse.

In her right hand she carried a large leather bag tied tight. In her left, she cradled a pair of moccasin boots lined with thick brown fur.

Appreciation welled, and Tom's throat tightened.

Blue Jay pushed the gifts toward him.

"Thank you, thank you," he said on a long exhalation.

Brooke smiled wide as she watched him reach out. Tom took the gifts with a slight fumble and a half bow. A rattle of words he couldn't understand passed among the men and women, who now seemed as much family as friends. Tom smiled. Blue Jay nodded and moved off through the crowd.

"Papa, these boots are wonderful. Let me show you how they tie." Brooke adeptly wove the strings of the lacings around the buckhorn buttons. "See, it's kind of a trick to get this top one wrapped twice and folded back on itself, so it won't slip."

"I see." Tom nodded lightly and reached to his daughter for another hug. Over his shoulder Brooke saw Water Bird. When her eyes caught his he smiled.

Snow was falling lightly as the hunting party rode away. Women's voices rang out like coyotes, and goodbye drums rattled. Young boys looped circles around the hunting party as the men started up valley.

Tom stood in his stirrups and looked back. Brooke was dancing with friends, her red hair bouncing as she stomped the earth in beat with the drums. Behind her stood Blue Jay and the other women, who watched and laughed at the exuberant young dancers. Tom caught Blue Jay's gaze and felt safe that many eyes would be watching his daughter while he was away.

As the men rode upriver the temperature fell and the snow came harder. Everyone was wet and chilled by the time they finally stopped late in the night. The men tied up the horses and hurried to slip out of their clothes and into the warm waters of The Yampa Pagosa.

CHAPTER SIXTEEN

Hunched Against the Cold

▲ ▲ ▲

Tom and Water Bird crouched behind Strong Horse, who knelt with his rifle ready. Seven elk came out of a shallow draw. Steam blew from their noses as they labored through deep snow. The little herd moved to the opposite hillside as Strong Horse raised his rifle and aimed.

Kaboom! The lead cow stumbled with the first shot, and the next cow dropped with the second. Tom fired, and a young bull rocked forward, staggered to its feet, then fell dead. A yearling standing next to a fallen cow shuddered when the hot slugs struck its side. The other three elk spun and ran for the ridge line. The hunters steadied their rifles on trees, and the shots sounded like one. A cow stumbled and a bull spun downhill. With the bull's every lunge blood sprayed, until he fell, motionless in the snow. The final fleeing cow disappeared over the ridge.

Strong Horse ran and grabbed a wounded cow by the ear, drew his knife and cut her throat. He backed away as the animals thrashed, trying to escape, before surrendering and sinking into the snow.

Strong Horse looked to Water Bird, who was struggling to move a cow he'd killed. He was working to roll her onto her back. Strong Horse joined him. When the cow sunk in the deep snow, ready to be gutted, Strong Horse gripped Water Bird's shoulder. Strong

Horse turned to the east, facing the spot of the sun that was covered in icy clouds. Then he raised his arms, tipped his head back, and took a deep breath. Water Bird raised his arms to the sun and felt the slightest blush of warmth on his face. He looked down at the elk, thanked the animal for its life, then drew his knife.

Up the hill, Tom was about to shoot a wounded elk when Strong Horse yelled for him to stop and save the bullet. Within a couple of minutes, the bull settled to the snow and his eyes glazed gray.

Strong Horse waved to Tom, and they started cutting meat together.

They needed to gut the animals before they butchered them to save the kidneys, livers, and hearts. Once they cleaned the animals out, they cut them into pieces, which they tied onto the horses. They had to work fast to keep the chunks from freezing solid as stones.

It was early morning, and the sun had not yet touched the men. A day of work lay before them. The air was icy cold, and soon their hands were wet with elk blood that froze quickly. The daylight would be short in early winter, and the western horizon told of another storm on the way. As sunshine crept toward them, it pushed colder air into the canyon.

When the final two elk were ready to be quartered the sun had reached the men, but the cold remained. Water Bird went for the horses and returned with the ax to split the carcasses, but first he cut logs for a fire. With the work ahead of them, and the terrible cold, the fire was needed.

Through the morning they worked together with little talk. By the time the sun centered the sky they had three elk ready to load. As the day wore on the labor and the cold took their toll. Blood froze to their clothing and their hands stiffened.

When the sun touched the mountains in the west, they had gutted all the elk and four loads of meat were ready to pack back to camp. They would have to return for the rest of the meat the next day.

The storm that had held off all day now closed around them as they climbed out of the canyon. By the time they reached the ridge line the wind was driving a light snow that fell heavier as darkness came. They were covered in sticky snow when the fires of the Eagle's Nest Camp came into sight.

At the edge of the fire's glow, they unloaded the meat in stacks and hurried toward the crackling flames. The other hunters welcomed them to the warmth. Slabs of fresh meat sizzled on flat stones and a pot of coffee wobbled on the coals.

The men were glad to be in camp, but everyone was nervous about the cold. Near the big fires the flames were searing hot, but a short distance away the air was painfully cold.

Good Bear and Loma had never experienced cold like this. They worried about their families at Roan Creek, and they worried about the men in the hunting party too.

Two of the men couldn't get warm no matter what they did. A young man, Charo, of the Gray Horse Band, had become sick and lay near the fire wrapped in a hide that quivered as he shook. The other man stared stone-faced into the fire and said nothing.

Loma and Good Bear knew they needed to head toward winter camp the next day. They would stop at the Yampa Pagosa and soak in the hot water and take the men who were sick into the hot caves before they headed on.

The group decided that Loma and half of the men would leave in the morning for Yampa Pagosa. The remaining men, under the direction of Good Bear, would gather the meat still in the hills. If they got the meat back to camp with plenty of daylight, they would continue to the Yampa Pagosa. Strong Horse, Tom and Water Bird were part of the group designated to retrieve the remaining meat.

The other men joked about the warm springs and the steamy caves that awaited them. The allure of the warmth helped the men settle in despite the freezing weather.

The next morning the men split in different directions. Loma and five others headed for the Yampa Pagosa with eleven loaded horses.

The sun was high overhead by the time Strong Horse and the other hunters returned to camp with the last of the meat. The men in camp had twelve horses packed, and three more carried the last of the meat from the day before. They wasted no time and were soon ready to head downriver.

They gathered at the Eagle's Nest Crossing. There, one by one, they would ford the river in the shallows above a pool covered with blue ice.

The men stood on the bank and shuffled in place, slapping their mittens to shake the cold. There was a little kidding as they prepared to get wet again in the sub-zero weather.

The river wasn't too deep, but the water would come up on the sides of the horses. If one stumbled, the rider would surely get soaked.

The intense cold made the river freeze from the bottom up. Every stone was wrapped in ice, making the crossing slow for the heavily loaded horses. Some of the horses crossed by themselves, but others needed to be led into the water.

The sun was shining, and the men were anxious to be heading back. Once they crossed the river, they could be at the Yampa Springs by dark. They'd spend a night there then move on the next day toward the warmth of their lodges and their women at Roan Creek. The village would celebrate their return. The twenty-two elk the party had killed would add greatly to the food store. Although more would be needed, this first resupply would stave off hunger through early winter.

Before entering the river, each man stood by his horse and stripped from the waist down. They tied their leggings and boots around their necks and across their shoulders. They needed to keep as dry as possible. If a man's clothing got soaked, his life was in peril.

Once across the river they would dismount and dress. The six men and twenty plus horses should make the crossing quickly if everything went well.

Loma entered the river first, holding his rifle shoulder high. When he was halfway across, Eagle Moon followed.

When Eagle Moon was almost across, Tom eased Timber into the water. Chunks of mushy ice bumped the horse's legs as he took careful steps on the slippery bottom. Tom raised his bare feet above the water and reined in his horse, while the two pack animals behind him entered the river.

Water Bird waited for Tom to get halfway across the river before he started to strip. He'd made crossings like this before but never in such cold. This time he had to keep his rifle and clothing dry while balancing against the weight of two horses on a lead rope. He was the youngest man on the hunt, and his father had allowed him to go only after a request from Strong Horse. He knew some of the Grey Horse men wondered why he was there. He had Strong Horse's support, and he carried his father's rifle. Those were his endorsements.

He slung his leggings across his back and tucked the ends under the strap that secured his medicine bag, which held the power of his totems. His boots were stowed close to his belly under the same strap. With the rifle and lead rope in one hand, he steadied his horse then jumped up and wiggled onto his horse's back. The horse stood perfectly still. Water Bird's naked crotch settled onto the horse's warm hide, and for a moment the thought of icy water lapping at his thighs didn't seem so frightful. In a short time, he'd be on the other bank, slipping back into his fur-lined clothes.

The big horse snorted hard when he entered the river. The blast caused Water Bird to grip harder with his knees and lean forward, hugging the horse's neck. The pack animals paused at the edge of the water but came with a tug.

Water Bird glanced back at Strong Horse who was seated on Taowa, watching him and nodding approval.

Water Bird's Appaloosa, Surrocco, was proving his worth again as he moved, coolheaded, across the riverbed.

They were just about to reach the north bank when Water Bird heard the water thrashing behind him and felt a tug on the lead rope. He gripped the rope tighter and leaned forward, then he felt a slip inside his shoulder and a rush of pain stabbed across his chest. The cutting sensation spread and dug into his guts like a burning spear. A rush of painful heat radiated from his shoulder, as the joint separated under the strain of the lead rope.

He groaned in agony. His right arm wobbled at the shoulder. He gritted his teeth and held on to the rope as the packhorse struggled back to his feet. Surrocco stood still, drenched but standing.

Water Bird's face scrunched in agony as he leaned over Surrocco's neck. As he gasped for breath, he felt the jolt of his arm bone pop back into the socket of his shoulder. He let out a piercing cry and dropped his head to Surrocco's neck. He glanced back, searching for Strong Horse. Pain flooded his senses, and his stomach roiled with vomit. Behind him, a riderless horse shook off a spray of water.

Water Bird straightened and twisted against the pain, looking back for Strong Horse. But all he saw was his riderless horse staring at the water. A man's hand bobbed up in the rapids and, in an instant of panic, Water Bird knew it had to be Strong Horse.

Screams came from the north bank where men scrambled to remount. Others plunged their horses into the river at a full gallop.

Water Bird gasped for breath between rushes of panic and pain. He jerked on the reins and spun Surrocco around, slamming his bare heel into the horse's ribs. The big horse lunged toward the south bank. When they hit solid ground, Water Bird ripped off his shirt and ran down the bank yelling at Strong Horse, whose body floated through the rapids before disappearing under the blue ice.

Water Bird's rigid body hit the river like a lance, and he disappeared into the water as the other men ran back and forth along the bank. With powerful strokes he surged downward into blackness. His eyes were glazed by the cold and with every push of his limbs, his body became stiff. The shrieking pain of his shoulder was numbed by the cold. He couldn't breathe in, and he couldn't breathe out, as the water pulled at his arms and leg.

A faint tapping grew louder as his head throbbed and his mind drowned in the cold. He sighed in surrender as a stream of bubbles sifted through his lips and all motion ceased. His mind and body were adrift between worlds of future and past. His limp form sank slowly toward the icy river bottom.

In the world above him the Ute men and Tom tromped the

bank. Some of them ran down below the pool. Others waded into the pool and stood with arms held out.

Water Bird felt warmth in his fingertips, then a speck of light lit his senses. He was beyond the cold and, as the underworld brightened, a small black dot raced ahead of him.

At the river's bottom, the water became crystal clear and full of warmth and air. He paused in the stillness, and there, at the edge of the shadow, were his totems: the bird, the fish, and the otter, spinning in a playful circle.

He felt a painful tug on his shoulder as he was pulled into the light. Grandfather Trout floated just beyond his fingertips, where bubbles floated upward like tiny clear stars.

On a sandbar behind Grandfather Trout lay a golden leather bundle, rocking gently in the current. Water Bird swam to the bundle, picked it up, and spun toward the surface.

Water Bird broke through the ice at the end of the pool and stood up with Strong Horse draped across his arms.

Men on the bank yelled in disbelief at the sight of the young boy holding the man. They ran out into the rapids, grabbed the body, and dragged it to the snow-covered bank. They jumped and scampered, fighting the cold and yelling to each other. They were screaming his name, as if somehow Strong Horse might hear them and return.

Loma dropped to his knees and cradled Strong Horse's head on his lap. He twisted and shook him and yelled his name in his face. Loma's leggings turned red with the blood from Strong Horse's head.

Strong Horse's arms dangled at his sides. Water drops dripping from his fingers created little frozen mounds.

Good Bear was first to release the high-pitched notes of the dying song. The other men joined him.

Tom knew that if Strong Horse could be saved, it would have to happen fast. He broke through the circle of men, took Strong Horse's body, and laid it flat in the snow. The other men stumbled backwards, yelling in confusion. With mouths agape, they stood back. When Grey Wolf reached out to pull Tom away from the body, Good Bear shoved him back.

With both hands placed squarely on Strong Horse's lower chest, Tom pushed. Again, and again, he pressed with the power of his full weight. Each time, water rolled from Strong Horse's mouth. Tom bent over his face and pressed his lips to his mouth, forcing air into Strong Horse's lungs. Again, he compressed Strong Horse's chest until more water squished out with a cough, a gasp, then a quiver.

A twitch and a slight sound from Strong Horse sent the Ute men stumbling backwards again. When Strong Horse's eyes cracked open, the people wailed in disbelief and clapped their hands to their mouths. Strong Horse's eyes grew wide with a look of distant focus. He sucked in again then choked up more water. Tom pressed on his ribcage, and Strong Horse took in a long breath. He looked at the men around him. His lips came together and crept up at the edges.

The men started stomping and whooping.

Strong Horse reached up and pulled Water Bird close. As if telling a story, he spoke softly with a look of conviction. Water Bird nodded and locked eyes with Strong Horse.

Tom caught his own breath and rubbed Strong Horse's belly preparing to pump again.

Strong Horse set his jaw with a look of determination. Then he took in a full breath through clenched teeth.

His face loosened, and his eyes relaxed shut, as if drifting into sleep. Then they snapped open as his body arched hard. He trembled and twitched, then went soft and motionless.

Tom clasped his lips to Strong Horse's mouth and forced in air again. He could taste the blood that oozed from the man's nose. Again, Tom pushed on his belly and went back to his mouth, blowing harder this time. Strong Horse's eyes remained still and flat. Tom pinched his nose and blew deep into his lungs and held his lips close waiting for a push back of breath that never came. Tom pulled away, looked at the man below him, and knew the look he saw. Like so many times before, the stare of death looked back. Tom's mind swirled through all the dead faces of war and stopped on Teresa's.

The thought of his dead wife suddenly draped the scene with a curtain of loneliness, and he yearned for his daughter. How foolish he'd been to leave her.

He felt weak against a sly enemy that could dispatch the strongest of men at any time. This deceptive land of earth, sky, and water, so bountiful at one bend and so brutal around the next.

Water Bird crowded against him, staring down. He tried to speak in English but couldn't. Tom knew the question and answered. "I'm sorry, he's dead."

Water Bird held his stare and from deep in his gut raised a woeful moan that cut the frozen air. The men who had danced a moment before knelt and joined in the dying song.

On a bend in the Bunkara, beneath an eagle's nest, they wished goodbye to a beloved son and spirit.

In the cottonwood forest, ash piles still smoldered. Good Bear barked out orders that sent the men gathering firewood. Every man was soaked to the skin, and their leather clothes froze and stiffened as their feet and fingers went numb. They'd have to work fast to save themselves.

Strong Horse was left by the river where a mist of vapor drifted from his body. Taowa stood nearby, hunched against the cold.

CHAPTER SEVENTEEN

Arms in the Air

▲ ▲ ▲

The sun had tilted west by the time the hunting party was ready to move again. They'd wrapped themselves in dry blankets and switched wet clothing for bloody hides laced up with leather strings. They'd made the river crossing and helped each other bundle up on the north shore. By the time they were ready to move on, the sun was two fingers width from the horizon. It would be after dark when they reached the hot water of Yampa Pagosa.

Strong Horse's body was trussed up in a hide and strapped to a mule. The men had to push hard against the frozen corpse to fit it into the pack frame. His possessions were already spread out among those who rode silently. They had lost a powerful leader, who because of his courage and kindness, had risen swiftly within the tribe. The raid on the Arapaho's horse herd and the battle with Black Bull had galvanized his valor. The generosity he'd shared through his horseflesh plunder had touched every family within the band.

Water Bird couldn't stop the tears that crept down his cheeks. He had lost his friend and brother. His heart ached for Star Flower. If she grieved as Ute women traditionally did, she would slice her arms and breasts, chop off her hair — and maybe fingers too. The thought of her tan skin scarred, her screaming, her ragged hair, made a frightful knot in his gut. When he shuddered, his aching shoulder drove daggers of pain across his chest. The cold and the sickness of death made his vast world feel tiny.

Tom was stunned. How could the strongest man on the best horse have been thrown and knocked unconscious? He knew that a blow to the back of the skull had killed Strong Horse, but it still seemed impossible.

Loma's group made it to Yampa Pagosa by the time the sun hung low in the afternoon sky. After the stock was unloaded, the men hurried into the hot water pools. They kidded each other as they stripped and tiptoed across the slippery rocks before sinking in.

It was just before dark when the first runaway horse loaded with meat came in from upriver. Alakar, who was staking out horses, grabbed a mount and headed out looking for Good Bear's group. After riding for a distance in fading light, he returned and told the others about the stray horse loaded with meat. They knew something was wrong when pack animals loaded with meat came in first. Loma and three men headed back upstream looking for the others. Across a snowy flat lit by starlight, the men hollered for the lost hunters. In a while, they got a reply.

When the fires of Loma's camp came into view, the returning hunters had little will to keep moving. Their bodies and minds were numb with cold. Slabs of meat were roasting when they arrived. While some tended to the food, others unloaded packs then crept toward the warm water. Everyone knew the body strapped to the mule was Strong Horse, but no one spoke about it. The men who unloaded the body chanted as they worked. The frozen corpse was set away from the fires and hot pools.

What should have been a relaxing occasion was instead serious and somber. Through the night men went back and forth from the fires to the warmth of the water and steamy caves. Hardly a word was spoken until late in the night when Good Bear explained a plan. In the morning he, Tom, Water Bird, Loma, and a few other men would ride upriver to entomb Strong Horse's body in a place where others had been buried. The men who stayed behind would pack the camp. When Good Bear's group returned, they would be ready to go. The entire party would travel through the night, arriving at Winter Camp just after daylight. There was a chance that scout riders would discover them before they got to Winter Camp and notice the absence of Strong Horse. By trying to time their arrival at daylight they might avoid some of the hysteria that would develop. Strong Horse's death would be a grave announcement, and it was crucial for Good Bear to tell Bow River first. No one was to leave Yampa Pagosa ahead of the rest of the party. If anyone came along, headed downstream, they were to wait for the entire group or risk their own death at the hands of Good Bear.

After a short sleep in the steaming pools, the men rose and started loading the horses. Those that stayed at the springs climbed back into the water as the others headed up the river.

Good Bear's group rode into the dark with the body and three extra horses.

When the blackness was split by gray light, the ashen gray cliffs of the canyon were revealed. Clouds hovered at the clifftops and tiny snowflakes circled in the breeze. The river's roar smothered the sound of hooves on the rocky trail.

They traveled until mid-morning then turned up a narrow side canyon. They spread out, so that each horse had room to negotiate the trail that wound through the willows. They climbed around and over icy swells where the stream had frozen upon itself. The men stayed mounted, as their horses tested each step. They slipped on the ice, but the riders remained upright, trusting their mounts to sort out the path. At the base of a cliff the trail moved onto a narrow bench just wide enough for a horse and rider. The giant stone face was stacked hundreds of feet above and below them. Tom watched the string of men move out across the ledge without a stop in stride. They cut a sharp contrast against the chalky cliff. Dressed in beaded buckskin with brass earrings the Utes rode ponies of sorrel, black and choke-cherry roan. Their feathered headdresses bobbed as they crossed the bench and disappeared around the bend, one by one. The trail crossed a creek and came out at the edge of a small turquoise lake. On a narrow land bridge, they crossed where the outlet waters ran beneath the horses and fell out of sight. The lake's surface rattled with the sound of silver streams falling from icicle spears. Mounds of moss clung to the ledges and rained down water drops like beads on a string. Rippling rings crossed each other and spread in every direction. The men studied the emerald water and curtains of ice above and below. They pointed at the trout that darted around the lake. A little black bird bustled about the water's edge then jumped on a log and barked at the riders. Tom marveled that within the ancient stone formations hung a lively lake, teeming with motion. Loma twisted in his saddle and spoke in signs. Tom made out the words, "Spirit Lake Hanging in The Sky."

The men circled above the pool and rode toward a grove of pines. The trees were adorned with the skulls of horses and other forest creatures. Heads of bison and big horn, coyote and wolves were strapped to the trunks or dangled from branches. Some held patches of wrinkled hide and waxy eyeballs. Tom felt each empty stare that followed their passing. He studied a human skull in a tree fork and felt the hair on his neck lifting his shirt. The sweet smell of forest duff and death drifted in the air. The Utes stared ahead and rode with shoulders slumped. Water Bird warily glanced side to side. On a central trail, they wound their way through the woods then came out on a cliff overlooking the river.

No one spoke as they unlashed the body of Strong Horse and tightened the lacings of the supple hide they'd wrapped around his frozen body. They tied ropes around the hide cover for handles, Tom tried to take one of the loops, but Loma took his place. The four Ute men carried the body ahead of Tom. They moved along the bluff until Good Bear stopped at a crack in the cliff face. It was a few feet wide at the top then receded to blackness. The men dragged the carefully wrapped corpse of their brother and scooted it to the edge of the crevasse. As they lowered the elk-hide shroud into the darkness, Strong Horse was returned to the land of the endless spring.

Good Bear looked across the canyon, raised his arms and spoke. In long rhythmic phrases he talked to the ragged cliffs gouged by the silver river. Tom didn't know the words, but he knew the tone of credit, honor, and thanks. The men stepped up beside him and held up their arms to the clouds that hid the yellow sun, and together they sang.

Good Bear spoke to Water Bird, who went to the woods and led up the three extra horses. Water Bird watched with curious eyes as the elders taught without words.

The horses barely moved when the knives slid down their necks. Glistening blood ran down and pooled at their feet. They stamped at the tickling flow and twitched their tails as if shooing flies. The black gelding was the first to stumble, staggering to gain his footing. The gray mare with a white stripe down her nose pressed her hips backwards and stretched as if rising from a nap. She straightened and swayed slightly as her eyelashes sagged. The gelding fell first and then the mare laid down and stopped breathing. The mighty Taowa was the last to succumb. His head slumped. He lowered to his knees and allowed his hips to fall to the ground. He rolled to his side and his legs swung in a slow trot. When his hooves stopped moving, his ribs did too. Tom's heart pounded at the loss of the magnificent animals that honored the death of Strong Horse. The chiefs stood motionless holding the leads until the horse's eyes lay open. Good Bear murmured a few words and let out a deep sigh. He looked at the men, wiped his cuff across his cheek, then walked to the trees where the other horses waited.

The men mounted, turned downhill, and rode back through the skull forest in single file. When crossing the land bridge at the lake, each man, including Tom, raised his arms in the air. As they started down the narrow trail, a north wind broke over the canyon rim and slammed the snow-laden cliffs and trees. A cutting snow squall twirled around the riders then swept its way downstream.

CHAPTER EIGHTEEN

The Hunters Return

▲ ▲ ▲

The hunting party rounded a point above winter camp just as sunlight streaked the high mesas. Blue smoke hung in the trees above the scattered tipis. The first dog bark brought out a pack that raced toward the riders.

The men kept a steady pace to the edge of the village. When they stopped, tipi flaps flew open as women and men hollered hellos. The early morning arrival had caught the camp unaware as everyone lingered under warm bedding.

Bow River and Stone Calf scooted about at the first dog bark and stumbled to slip on boots and blankets. Star Flower sat up in bed and quizzed her parents as they slipped outside. Brooke sprang up beside her. "What's happening?" Her voice shook. Star Flower spun toward her with wide eyes, smiling.

"They're back." The girls giggled and scurried from bed, grabbing clothes. Brooke was out of the tipi first, spotting her father as he stepped down from his horse.

"Papa!" She ran toward him.

Bow River walked briskly toward the hunters but stopped when he saw his brother with his family at his side. Good Bear wrapped his arms around his wife while his children hugged him at his hips. His shoulders sagged as he moved about greeting his family. Behind them stood the overloaded packhorses with their heads hanging low. Beads of frozen sweat dangled from their belly hair. Bow River knew they'd traveled all night at a pushing pace. He'd been confident in the hunters he'd sent, and from the look of the weary men and stock he knew they'd found elk.

Stone Calf stood next to Bow River and watched the haggard hunters with their hollow eyes and distracted smiles. Bow River caught Tom's eye as he hugged Brooke, whose toes dangled above the ground while she scanned the crowd behind her father.

Bow River and Stone Calf walked forward and, when Good Bear saw them coming, he loosened his hug with his wife. His smile hardened but then relaxed when he looked down at his children. Beyond Good Bear was Water Bird, who struggled to loosen a pack. Stone Calf approached Bow River with a question. "Where's Strong Horse?"

Bow River rose on his toes and leaned to the side. He looked over the horse herd then walked toward Good Bear until they stood face to face. Good Bear could see pain in his brother's eyes.

Bow River couldn't even get his question out before Good Bear dropped the bad news. "We lost him. We lost him in the river." Good Bear's words trailed off to a hollow whisper. "He's dead."

Bow River's chest rose as the words ricocheted through his head. He yanked Good Bear closer and snarled. "What?"

Good Bear stared downward, then he slowly nodded his head *yes*.

"No," Bow River pleaded with a ragged sigh.

Stone Calf screamed then fell to her knees, throwing her head from side to side. Grandma Chuka ran to her daughter and fell beside her.

The shock whirled through the village like a dust devil as the other hunters spilled the news. Wails of grief rose, and people darted in different directions. Frightened horses, still loaded with packs, trotted away from camp. Bow River watched the mayhem erupt. As his mind raced and his heart pounded, he turned back toward his lodge and waited for the door flap to move.

Star Flower stepped out, dressed in a fur-lined coat and a Lynx hat. Her wide eyes flashed as she scanned the frenetic scene. She knew her mother's scream, and her heart twisted when she saw her on her knees. Above her mother stood her father and brother. She frantically scanned the crowd for her husband. She looked back at her father whose tight frown quivered as he lowered his gaze and stepped her way.

"No," Star Flower moaned. She trotted toward him then broke into a run. Bow River caught her as she rushed by, and they spun around as he fought to slow the pitiful scene. She looked into his eyes and felt the spear of the tragedy pierce her heart.

"Please, please," she pleaded.

Bow River rocked his daughter. Star Flower pressed her face into his chest and begged, *"Cuch, cuch, cuch."* No, no, no. Then, she crumpled to her knees next to her mother.

Brooke watched from a distance then pulled away from her father and slid to the ground in front of Star Flower. She wedged in to hug her, but Star Flower tore away and ran for the tipi. Brooke fell on her backside. As she tried to scramble to her feet, Water Bird grabbed her arm. Her wild eyes cast into his. He returned a stunned stare. Brooke glanced from face to face of the family members who stood like trees, watching Star Flower disappear into their tipi.

People darted about and dogs howled, but Star Flower's family didn't move as her cries blanketed the village like the blue smoke in the trees.

Brooke stepped back to her father who wrapped an arm around her. They sat on a log, and Tom described what had happened. He couldn't explain why. All he really knew was that Strong Horse had wound up in the river, busted open his skull, and died. Brooke fought back tears of disbelief and anger. She couldn't believe this could happen to such a man and the husband of her dearest friend. Now, Star Flower was her only concern.

"What will she do?" Brooke asked her father.

"She'll be in mourning for who knows how long."

"What do you mean?"

Tom glanced toward the mesa then back to Brooke. "She'll cut off her hair and cover her face in ashes." Tom looked away before he continued. "And she'll cut herself."

"But why?" Brooke shook her head hard, as if shaking away a bad dream. "Why would she cut herself?"

"That's how she will grieve, Brooke. She might cut her face and arms." He hesitated. "Or cut off her fingers."

"No," Brooke snapped. "Papa, she can't. She's going to have a baby."

"What? Aw, damn it."

"I can't let her." Brooke started to walk away.

"Brooke, you can't stop her."

"Oh, yes I can." She spun around with a stomp.

"Brooke, it's their way. You've seen the other women in camp. Some of them are missing fingers."

"Star Flower is different. I can't let her. I won't."

• • •

When Star Flower's family stepped inside their lodge, she was kneeling at the fire. Around her lay chunks of black hair. She put the knife to her scalp and cut off another handful and threw it to the floor. When she heard them behind her, she whipped around and cast a wicked glare. Blood ran down her arms. She opened her shirt and put the blade to her breast just as Stone Calf grabbed her arm. Star Flower shook her mother away and scrambled for the door. She grabbed a hatchet and bolted out the flap. Stone Calf lunged for her, but Bow River stopped her and held her back. She folded into his arms, sobbing and choking on choppy breath. They trembled together in surrender to the disaster of tradition.

When Brooke got to the lodge, she flung open the flap and stuck her head inside. The family jumped.

"Where is she?" Brooke shouted, "Where's Star Flower?"

No one moved. Water Bird tipped his head slightly west, and the others swung their eyes to his.

Brooke stepped out and saw Blue Jay walking toward her. She ran to her and grabbed her by the shoulders. "Where's Star Flower?"

Blue Jay shook her head and opened her mouth, but no words came out.

"Blue Jay!" Brooke screamed. "Where is she?"

Blue Jay's head bounced back at the blast and her eyes swung to the river trail. "Rio," she said, tossing her chin to the west. The two women held eyes for a moment, then Brooke broke away at a run.

Spots of blood dotted the well-worn path that led through the willows. Brooke knew the trail to the hole in the ice where the women drew water. She burst into the clearing at the river's edge and never slowed down.

Star Flower was on her knees with her hand splayed across a log. Her trembling right arm held the hatchet above her head. Brooke froze in horror for a split second before charging Star Flower like a buffalo, slamming into her with a heavy grunt. The hatchet, which had been poised to strike, twirled in the air.

Star Flower screamed and twisted as she searched the ground for the hatchet.

"No. No. Stop. You don't have to do this," Brooke yelled as they fell to the ground and rolled on the rocks and ice.

At the edge of the river Brooke sensed the icy water slithering by. She struggled to hold on to her friend as her mind raced for a way to save both their lives. In a tangle of limbs, she worked to keep the hatchet from Star Flower's hands while her friend tried every lever to break her hold.

"Please, please, Star Flower. You don't have to do this. You don't have to do this," Brooke begged. Fists and elbows flew. Brooke ducked her head and squeezed to hold on, just hoping to slow the battle, but her grip was starting to wane as exhaustion pulled at her purpose. She was losing strength and needed help, but no one was coming to the rescue. She needed more than might; she needed the perfect words.

Brooke often wondered but never knew where the words that leapt from her mouth came from. But there they were. In perfect Ute, she yelled: "Stop, stop. Your baby, your baby. You're going to kill your baby. For the love of Strong Horse, save your baby."

The name Strong Horse and the word *baby* battered Star Flower's determination. Her husband's death and the birth of a baby fought against all reasoning. The pain in her heart was fueled with rage, but the lump in her womb kindled to counter her torment. In a flash of clear thinking, she knew that only the birth of their baby could temper the loss of her husband. The man she'd dreamed about and waited for wasn't coming home. Only their baby could soften the blow of losing Strong Horse, who would never lie down with her again. At that thought, her will broke, and the war against what she couldn't change melted away.

Brooke felt Star Flower's body go soft, and they slumped into a heap. Out of strength and out of fight, they cried like children. The minutes passed in the river's flow, then they gathered air and cried some more. Between sobs, they acknowledged a shared pain and a shared love for one another. No words were needed as their minds raced to the past and into the future. The frustration of loss and change cut them both.

Star Flower leaned back, tipped her head to the sky, and raised the dying song from deep inside her body. The haunting melody rose to the sky and settled across the valley plain. Great packs of wolves heard her cry and joined in the ghostly song, while nervous horses watched the willow thicket. In the village husbands hugged wives and children held hands as they stared toward the weary river that carried their tears away.

CHAPTER NINETEEN

Winter Moons

▲ ▲ ▲

It was late December in the Hunting Moon when the men returned with the news about Strong Horse. The Cold Moon of January and the Snow Moon of February were yet to come.

Star Flower remained in the family lodge for weeks and was never seen outside except at night. The ash on her face was ever present, and as the scars on her arms healed, her belly grew. Brooke tried to visit her every day, but Star Flower barely acknowledged she was there.

With the cold came more snow that kept everyone close to their warm lodges. The people tended to the horses and gathered firewood. Their food supplies were good but promised to be low by spring. Like the bears that slept through the winter, the people laid low and planned for the spring.

The death of Strong Horse, the loss of two burned Gray Horse children weighed on the spirt of the camp. Great energy was required to struggle against the environment — but great joy could be found in the earth's bounty. Memories of the good times and the bad mirrored the flow of the warm seasons and the cold.

Tom and Brooke felt the pain of their hosts as they struggled against old age, sickness, and death. These realities seemed neither good nor bad. They were just part of life in a domineering wilderness.

There were twenty-six tipis in winter camp where Roan Creek entered the Rio Colorado. Sixteen belonged to the Yellow Bear Band, seven to the Gray Horse, and two were Black Eagle lodges. Tom counted one hundred and twenty-seven people and guessed there were four times that many horses and mules.

Within the Yellow Bear Band there were six main family groups, who spent the winters together. After the spring Bear Dance, the band would split into two groups and spend the summer along different drainages toward the Continental Divide.

On a Cold Moon night, when the snow sparkled like the stars, the elders announced a gathering. Everyone squeezed around a central fire in a big lodge lit with torches.

The headmen sat closest to the fire, surrounded by the rest of the people. Two older boys tapped on flat drums as the crowd gathered inside. Babies suckled and rolled big eyes, children chatted, and grandparents whispered back and forth.

Star Flower sat by her mother. Her face was black with soot, and her ragged hair was matted tight to her head. It was the first time that many of the people had seen her, and no one was too bashful to stare.

The council began when Bow River stood and spoke in rhythms for several minutes. The crowd listened and occasionally called out words.

At one point, Bow River directed his words toward Tom and Brooke, who sat next to his family. They couldn't understand everything, but they heard their names, Tom Gun and Rose Creek, several times.

When Bow River sat down, Good Bear stood up and told the story of Strong Horse's death, without saying his name. He described the valiant rescue by Water Bird, who listened with his head down. Water Bird rose when his name was called. His posture was humble in front of the revered men he faced.

Loma stood up beside Good Bear and, from underneath a hide, he pulled out a rifle. He held it in both hands and offered it to Water Bird.

Water Bird stood still with his eyes fixed on the gun. His lips parted, and his hand crept upward as if to cover his mouth, but he stopped himself.

Loma frowned lightly and gestured the offering again.

A murmur floated through the crowd, as everyone realized that Water Bird was being given Strong Horse's rifle. It had been retrieved at the river crossing, and the elders had decided that it should be his. He swallowed hard and looked at his mother, who smiled and nodded. Star Flower was seated next to her and trembled lightly with her head bowed down.

At Water Bird's first step forward, the drums rumbled. The crowd saluted him as he stepped around the people to stand in front of the elders and his father. Each spoke before Loma handed him the rifle. Water Bird studied the gun then spoke to the three men standing and the seated elders. Then he walked through the crowd as kids ran up and touched his arms. He looked at his sister, who had been staring at the floor. She cracked a gentle smile, and her mother wrapped an arm around her.

Brooke sat next to Star Flower. As Water Bird walked by, she tapped him on the arm. Again, the flat drums rattled, and the crowd chatted as Water Bird took his seat.

Bow River, still standing, turned his attention to Tom. With an upturned palm, Bow River gestured for him to stand. When he did, Bow River puffed up his cheeks and blew toward the crowd, explaining how Tom had tried to save Strong Horse.

Every eye turned to Tom, some wide, some narrow, some piercing, some soft. Curious frowns and hard stares conveyed a mix of suspicion and wonder. No one had ever heard of someone being brought back from the dead, not even for a moment.

When Bow River finished speaking, the eldest men began to talk among themselves. Everyone else listened in silence. The men went back and forth until Loma's grandfather, Wolf Song, stood.

In a shallow voice he spoke to the elder men then pointed a crooked finger toward Tom.

Bow River cleared his throat. His words came out in a hesitant mixture of English, Ute, and Spanish.

"Tom Gun," he said, "You have been with our families for

seven moons. You and Rose Creek have worked hard. You have hunted and shared your horses and guns. You have showed us that the whites can be good people." Bow River paused, his gaze still fixed on Tom.

"Wolf Song is very old," he continued, glancing across his shoulder at the old man. "He speaks of an animal that lives on the plains where you came from. This animal has a tough back like a stone and, although he is slow, he is very strong. It is said that he never dies. Most of us have never seen him, but we know he is there. He is called *I yatch*, the life giver." Again, Bow River paused and looked at the clutch of old men seated beside him.

"Tom Gun, you are like *I yatch*, the life giver. Your medicine saved my life after the split-eared bear tried to rip it away. And you blew the wind into Strong Horse to give him a chance to live. All the men saw this. Strong Horse passed on to the land of the endless spring but, before he left, he smiled and spoke to Water Bird. Everyone saw this. His smile in the face of death will forever give hope to the Yellow Bear people. To know that the land of the endless spring is just across the river, we will not fear to go there. Tom Gun, you are big medicine. For this I give to you horses." Bow River held up his hand with five fingers widely spaced. "And now we will know you as *I-yatch Noo-i*, Turtle Wind."

At Bow River's final words, the flat drums rumbled, and brass chimes rattled like rain. Tom looked around the lodge at the smiling faces of the young and old. Brooke stood up and clapped her hands, and soon everyone imitated her.

Bow River spoke above the clamor, then everyone stood and made their way toward the flap.

Outside the lodge heavy drums thundered around big glowing fires. The people filed out of the lodge and moved to the warmth where they pranced against the cold to the rhythm of the drums. They danced into the night and ate from bowls of warm stew as their spirits rose and the temperature fell. Brooke and her friends danced while the boys piled wood on the fires and kept the drums rolling. The village was halfway through winter and still had food and, although many cold nights remained, they knew that the next full moon would bring green grass.

The black sky was pierced by a thousand stars and each one was reflected in the snow a millionfold. The Milky Way moved west, and a big star climbed in the east when Tom and Brooke crawled into their tipi. From under a fur blanket, Tom watched his daughter jotting notes in her journal. Her jawline looked so like her mother's.

Outside, big fires popped and crackled, and the murmur of voices drifted away.

The next morning the village was quiet, and the tipi flaps didn't move until steam drifted from the hides. The people rested safe in their isolated land and waited for the thunder to wake the bears.

Star Flower stepped out into the sun. The smooth round mound of her baby belly pushed her skirt tight. Her reddish-brown skin was brushed clean, and her raven black hair was neatly trimmed below her ears. She picked up a water jug and headed for the river.

CHAPTER TWENTY

Gift Wood

▲ ▲ ▲

As the days grew longer the work outside did too. In the warm afternoons the women stretched hides that had been frozen all winter. Young women, including Brooke, were expected to help with chores. One day when Brooke was unsure about the work, Grandma Chuka jokingly made the point that if she hesitated, she'd risk getting a willow across her butt. Brooke dove right in and quickly proved her worth at sewing and shaving hides. The women were surprised and pleased at the skills of the young white girl.

Along with her ability to work, Brooke also shared her words. She taught the women and children, and even some of the men, the names of objects in English. When Brooke scratched letters in the dirt to describe an object, the Utes sometimes struggled to understand, but often, they would scratch out their own depictions to express their comprehension. The children picked up the different translations more easily, and they were interested in the use of written words. They enjoyed seeing their names written, and they all worked to draw out the letters Brooke showed them. Younger children most often played the games of reading and writing, but several of the older kids did too. Sah-seet, who was close to Brooke's age, and her younger sister Sah-wof came every night. Some evenings Brooke read to a dozen young people, sitting by the fire.

In addition to a dozen blank journals, Tom had purchased one book of fiction in Leadville when they'd passed through. The book, *10,000 Leagues Under the Sea,* was a fantastical tale that had captivated Brooke and her father. Although her new audience understood few of the words, they listened to Brooke with wide eyes, as if she were a talking spirit. Water Bird sometimes came to listen too. He'd lounge at the edge as if he were there as a babysitter, but Brooke could see him deep in thought and sensed he was as intrigued by her words and stories as she was by his.

One night, when Brooke was almost done reading, the children lay at her feet with heavy eyes. Softly, Water Bird spoke into the quiet. The children twisted toward him, rose up, and sat on folded legs. He was clearly telling a story that they knew. Now and then, they joined in, jumping on his words, until shyness cut them short. Brooke caught only the name, *Yo-go-vits,* Coyote, the common prankster of the Ute world. As the story continued, Brooke could feel tension building in the room. Water Bird stopped to take a breath, and all the wide eyes in the room stared back at him, hanging on his next words. He hollered the last line of the story toward the top of the tipi. Hearing his final howl, the children rolled with laughter. Brooke didn't understand everything he'd said, but she couldn't stop herself from laughing with the children until tears streamed down her cheeks. As the giggles died down, the little ones gathered up their blankets and chatted their way out into the cold.

Every few weeks, Star Flower's baby belly showed more. As the baby grew, Brooke's interest in it grew too. Green Willow was even further along than Star Flower, with a belly that made it hard for her to bend over. During the long days, while the women cooked food, built and maintained shelters or made clothing, the three friends often worked side by side.

The men concentrated on their weapons, horses, and hunting. There were twelve rifles in the village. The men who didn't own guns used bows and arrows and spears to hunt. Everyone from the youngest to the oldest needed a bow and arrows, and they worked at crafting them. They used cedar, willow, and spruce, experimenting with different lengths and girths. The arrows were easily lost if they didn't hit their mark, so the people always needed to make more. Different people specialized in different aspects of the production. Some of the elder men were renowned for the arrowheads they made from white agate and hard black stones. Other men, and some women too, carved and cured arrows and fletched them with feathers. Everyone worked for the benefit of all. The Utes traded work and goods to maintain a continual flow of raw material and food.

Tom had eight horses and three mules. The gift horses from Bow River were some of the finest in the herd. Most of the men kept one or two horses picketed close to camp. They switched them in and out of the big herd every few days. Although the camp was secure, the men were vigilant to keep horses and weapons at hand. No one told Tom what they wanted him to do, so he followed the moves of the other men and tended to his horses as they did.

Tom kept busy during most the day, but he, like everyone else, took naps. Sometimes it was difficult to sleep through cold nights. Everyone made up for lost hours of nighttime rest by napping in warm tipis during the day, which resulted in a partially nocturnal life of chores and stories around the fires at night, following typically idle days.

He and Brooke would often write together in the evenings. They'd compare notes and drawings back and forth and discuss what they had seen and learned. When they'd ventured into the mountains, they'd brought twelve leather bound journals and twenty pencils. As time went by, they wrote more and more concisely and drew smaller pictures.

Tom never had to gather firewood. It just showed up at his lodge. He'd come back from tending the horses and a fresh pile of wood would have appeared by his tipi flap. No one ever stepped up as the provider. One cold morning he heard an armful of wood hit the ground outside, but by the time he poked his head outside, whoever had brought it was gone. He suspected the deliveries came from Water Bird, so he thanked him one day. But Water Bird denied gathering wood for him. He told Tom that the gift-bearer was most likely a woman.

On a warm afternoon a few days later, Tom heard wood landing on the dirt outside. He hurried out in his bare feet, grabbed a stick, and trotted through the tipis searching for the one who had delivered it.

The women working outside their lodges watched him as he scampered through the slush. Can't Cook Enough and her daughter were cleaning pots when they saw him coming with the stick. They smiled when he stopped in front of them and struggled not to laugh. He held up the stick, realizing he didn't have the words to explain. Can't Cook Enough covered her mouth but couldn't cover her laughter. She took a few steps down the path and pointed. Tom was surprised that she seemed to know who he was looking for.

He turned a corner, and there, walking ahead of him at a busy pace, was Blue Jay. He started to call out her name, but the words stuck in his throat. The sight of her silhouette stopped him in his tracks. The undulating flow of her hips in the fringed dress momentarily banished his words.

He choked out her name and, when she spun around, he felt caught in his stare. But her look softened as she looked him up and down. She turned and walked toward him without hesitation, coming so close that she had to look down to keep from stepping on his toes. With a crooked smile she waited.

Forced by her closeness to look her in the eye, Tom stammered.

"Turtle Wind," Blue Jay said without blinking. A question hung between them.

Tom struggled at the sound of his new name and tried to remember why he'd left his tipi. The rough branch in his hand reminded him that he had been tracking the source of his firewood.

Blue Jay glanced at the stick in his hand, then her eyes came back up to study his face.

"Uh, thank you," he said as he wiggled the stick. He took a slight step backward.

She followed his step then reached out and gently laid her a finger just below his nose through the cleft of his chin. Tom stiffened at her touch as the alluring scent of this woman, combined with the smell of wood smoke, wafted up his nose. For a moment she stared into his eyes with a half-smile, then she slid her finger down his chin and made a fist. Lightly thumping him on the chest, she took a step back, spun, and walked away. Then, she rounded a tipi and disappeared.

Tom stared down the path after her, but his cold feet were anchored in the mud.

He flinched when he felt someone else standing close by. A woman held a bucket. Her grin was wide, and her eyebrows arched high. Wagging her head, she turned and walked away.

Tom looked down at his bare feet in the mud, held out the piece of wood, wanting to explain his behavior. But the woman was gone, and he had nothing to say for himself, so he tiptoed back toward his tipi.

CHAPTER TWENTY-ONE

Whitefish Crossing

▲ ▲ ▲

The river ice was breaking up when visitors started showing up at camp. Some stayed several nights while others stopped briefly before riding on. They drove packhorses loaded with furs and meat, headed for the agency on White River or the trading post on Bear River farther north. Some men would go on to Denver, depending on the political climate in the area. If the Denver citizens were quarrelsome or the Arapahos were on the prowl, the Utes wouldn't cross the divide.

What supplies the local trading posts could offer determined how far the Utes had to travel for goods. If the nearest outposts gave a fair trade and were stocked with the essentials — guns, ammo, pots, and pans — the Utes could stay closer to home. If not, they were forced to go on to Denver at greater risk.

The River Treaty had established the White River Agency as the headquarters for the Red Springs and Yellow Bear Utes. The agency was supposed to provide supplies to the Utes to compensate for their loss of hunting territory. The government also provided the Utes with farming tools and instructions on how to use them. Their mission was to teach the Utes to grow their own food. If they could farm, the thinking went, maybe they would stop being nomadic and stay on their reservations. When Utes traveled beyond their territory, they risked violent confrontations with government officials and Colorado settlers.

The Utes had little interest in farming, but they were enticed by the gifts that the government offered. For the past ten years the Yellow Bears had received presents and supplies at the old fort in Middle Park, but it was hard to know when the supplies would be there, and the rations were often spoiled. So, the Yellow Bears stopped making the trip.

Water Bird learned what he could about the agency. Ever since Tom and Brooke had shown up, he'd taken a greater interest in the white man's ways. He was willing to explore anything that could improve his favor with Brooke.

While checking his horses one day, he asked Tom about raising enough food to feed the people. Their conversation wasn't easy, because Tom could translate only simple phrases from the Ute language, but he clearly recognized Water Bird's interest in his tone. He explained that the government wanted the Utes to raise not only plants but animals too. When he explained that there would always be a need to raise horses, Water Bird nodded his understanding.

The visitors to the camp had heard that Strong Horse had died, and they all wondered how. They'd been told about the white father and daughter who lived with the Yellow Bears, and they were eager to see the man who had saved Bow River's life — and had almost brought Strong Horse back from the dead. But they were even more interested in seeing the tall, red-haired girl, who was so quickly learning their language.

Not everyone was happy to see whites on Ute land, but their mistrust was quickly quelled when the visitors learned that Turtle Wind and Rose Creek lived under the protection of Bow River and his family — no one dared test his allegiance to the visitors.

Most of the men who came to the camp brought horses for trade. All the Ute bands knew about the spotted horses that Strong Horse had stolen from the Arapahos, and everyone wanted to trade for them. The Yellow Bear horse herd totaled over four hundred. About a quarter of the herd were mules and burrows, which were valued too. The herd had grown over the summer, and almost a hundred foals were expected in the spring. The horses were the wealth of the band and, because the Yellow Bears had so many, they had substantial leverage in trades. The visitors would challenge the speed of their horses against those of the Yellow Bears and, once the winners were determined, the trading would begin.

Bow River's black and white stallion was well known for his speedy colts. Water Bird's new stallion Surrocco was highly admired too. His orange color, a striking contrast to his white rump patch dotted with big black spots, drew a lot of attention. But it was his long thick muscles that rendered speed and attracted offers. A Red Springs Ute attempted a trade five good horses and then six, but Water Bird never considered the exchange. He knew Surrocco was exceptional, and he believed the horse's greatest value was in the medicine power of his lost brother, Strong Horse.

• • •

Spring's first thunder echoed late one night, and the people knew the bears were waking. The next morning Bow River announced it was time to move. The village had camped under the Roan cliffs for over three moons, and every day the women searched farther for wood and the horses grazed farther downstream. It was late in the Green Moon of March when the village started packing to move.

Bow River told Tom that, if the river crossing went well, it would take seven days to get to the Big Tree Camp. There, at the forks of the Red Springs and Black Rock River, the Utes would meet other Ute bands, and the families would come together for the Bear Dance.

The next morning, when a sliver of pink stripes lay in the eastern sky, the people began their move. Dogs and wild pets romped along with the group as they started down the trail.

The winter-thin horses stepped out quickly and those dragging travois pulled lighter loads than they had in the fall. The people moved easily with the weight of winter behind them and the light of summer growing every day.

Brooke rode next to her father and felt the warm air caress her cheeks as her horse pushed at his bit. Her mount fought to run when rumbling hooves came up from behind, but Brooke held him back as the pounding got closer. Water Bird, Sah-seet, her older brother Cimarron, and a few other kids reined back their horses to draw up beside her. Their smiles were as wide as their eyes, and their gestures said, "Come on, let's run!"

"Go!" Tom quickly conceded before Brooke's eyes met his, and the excited troop sprinted away on their mounts.

The river rolled tawny brown with snowmelt water. White-headed eagles sailed the river's course and watched from atop naked trees. The men pushed the horse herd downstream then held them off in a side canyon until the women and pack animals entered. The river was crowded on both sides by sandstone cliffs, which restricted passage to one horse at a time. It was late in the evening when the people emerged from the canyon into a wide basin hemmed with pink cliffs to the west and low treeless hills to the south. Square-topped palisades loomed to the north, and a line of gray cliffs strung out beyond them. Tom studied the blocky formations, which looked like shale with seams of coal pinched between the strata. Some of the black stripes were a foot wide, while others were as much as thirty feet in thickness.

Along a sweeping bend in the river, they dropped packs and made camp for the night. Some people threw up brush shelters, but everyone else just rolled out hides and built fires around them.

The next morning a warm wind blew down the canyon as everyone worked to pack camp, but the delighted energy of the day before was absent. Women barked orders as extra attention was directed at packing the supplies. Everyone except the smallest children fretted about arranging their goods. Water Bird and all the young people scurried about, trying to please the mothers and grandmothers who commanded the day. Couples were seen in pointed conversations that ended with the men nodding their understanding.

The sun was high and spreading warmth when the big troop of people and animals headed downriver. Tom and Brooke quietly took their place in line like everyone else. The women who had been so bossy earlier now rode stoically with their eyes dead ahead.

Brooke caught a look from Water Bird who rode up beside her. She looked around at the other stiff faces then back at Water Bird. He tucked his bridle reins under his leg and explained with hand signs what was happening. She conveyed the message to her father. "Papa, Water Bird just told me we're coming to a big river crossing."

"Something about this one is different," he replied. "I can feel it."

Few things were more frightening to the Utes than a big river crossing. They could shelter against bad weather and kill their enemies, but they were often at the river's mercy. Having to float their belongings, including their children, across the big rivers was the root of nightmares. Everyone got wet and cold. Gear got soaked, ruined, and often lost. People and animals died, and it was usually the youngest who were swept away. But it wasn't only children who drowned. Teenagers, young husbands, old women, even chiefs had been lost. Children got braver with each crossing they made, but they all remembered brothers, sisters and friends who had been pulled under. Everyone carried endless pain for those who had been lost in a river. The memories spurred determination cloaked in fear. No one was safe from the river's wrathful reach. The very force that gave life to the land had the power to suck it away. The recent loss of Strong Horse made the river's vengeance even more cutting. The Utes often skirted the rivers for miles to find a good crossing, and they understood that they never crossed the same river twice. Currents moved, banks collapsed, sandbars shifted. The rivers were always changing. The same spot where they'd crossed safely one year could become a death trap the next.

The party wove in several lines through the cottonwood forest along the river. Horse hooves clicked, branches snapped, and travois poles scratched the ground. Over fifty horses carried gear, and nearly another hundred carried people. The procession turned south and came out on a wide gravel bar where the river braided into several strands. The main channel divided into four branches. The three closest braids were each as big as the Bunkara, and the fourth one was as big as the other three. The three nearest ones funneled downstream into the fourth which spread into a wide pool. Below the pool was a run of swift rapids that crashed into a gray cliff. Bow River and most of the men and women rode out to the first channel and surveyed the layout. The rivers they'd crossed before were small compared to this section of the Rio Colorado. At other crossings the horses were hurried through the river before gear got soaked or stripped away, but at this crossing there were four swift channels, or one long deep pool to cross. Either route seemed more treacherous to Tom than any crossing they'd made before.

It had been a year since the Yellow Bears had seen the crossing, and then, like now, they'd passed through before the highest runoff had carved new channels. The women huddled in groups and pointed to the south bank. The men discussed options before directing everyone downstream, where the cottonwoods bordered the river.

At the river's edge, stacks of logs were tied together with weathered rope and rawhide. Tom knew they were rafts to ferry gear and people across the river. Without orders, everyone bowed into their work, preparing for the crossing that the Utes called the Whitefish Crossing.

As Tom watched the preparation, the enormity of the chore took on literal weight. Until then he hadn't thought much about the amount of baggage that the people carried. He knew everything was essential. There were eighteen tipi skins rolled into thirty-six bundles, which weighed one hundred and fifty pounds apiece. Each tipi required twelve, twenty-foot-long poles. Every family carried bundles and leather boxes full of bedding, clothes, tools, weapons, and food.

Brooke pulled out a journal and jotted down notes as Tom gave her figures.

"Papa, it comes to about twenty-six thousand, three hundred and sixty-one pounds. There are one hundred and four people, four hundred and forty-two horses, thirty-three dogs and I don't know how many pets, especially if you include birds, mice, and squirrels. More than six-hundred lives hang in the balance," she said.

Tom blew a light breath.

Brooke looked back at him from under high eyebrows. "At least half a dozen more lives will be carried in women's bellies, and one of those bellies is Star Flower's."

He looked across the river, wondering what the odds were that everyone would make it to the south bank. He turned to Brooke and stepped closer. "I don't know exactly how this is going to go, but I need you to be brave and trust that we are with people who have crossed this river for centuries as part of the migration circle of their lives. You understand?"

Brooke bit her lower lip as she looked across the river and nodded. "Yes, Papa." She turned to the trees where Star Flower was bent over a pack, tugging on a rope. "Papa, I have to help," she said, as she moved toward her friend.

The travois were unloaded and repacked with gear that could get wet. The pots and pans, metal tools, and extra tack were bundled in lighter loads to be hauled either on travois or packhorses. Heavy items and things that would take on water couldn't be dragged through the channels without risking a wreck. If the horse slowed down or staggered, the travois could flip, entangling the horse in ropes and poles. The gear would get soaked and sink, pulling the animal down with it.

The heaviest loads that needed to stay dry had to be floated across the river on the rafts. The tipi skins, food, bedding, and personal bundles were stacked in separate piles. The big coils of rope that had been braided over the winter were stacked out too. At least a hundred horses were tied in the forest, awaiting their tasks. The boys held the rest of the herd away from the river to keep herds from mixing and getting in the way.

When the crossing started, the oldest and youngest horses without loads were pushed to the river first. The older horses had made the crossing before and knew how to swim for their lives. The Utes used them to lure the younger horses forward and draw them into the water. The boys and men who had held the horses away from the river would be the first to cross. Once they were on the other side, they would establish a receiving core for everyone else. Like the old horses that led the young ones, the men guided the boys.

When all the preparations were complete, the families stood together and waited for Bow River, Loma, and Good Bear to check everyone's gear. The chiefs walked calmly and held quiet councils with different groups, then they walked toward the river. Good Bear signaled for Tom to join them, and the four men walked to the edge of the water. Good Bear waded in up to his knees while Bow River, Loma, and Tom waited on the bank. When Good Bear raised his arms to the sky, Tom glanced over his shoulder and saw everyone, including Brooke, do the same. Family groups, from toddlers to grandparents, stood with their arms held high and their eyes to the sky.

Tom didn't recognize all the words Good Bear spoke, but he could discern the elder's intention. He was calling down a blessing on the crossing. When he dropped his arms, Bow River turned and hollered to the boys who wrangled the free horses. They disappeared into the trees and yelled out as they circled the herd and pushed them south.

Eighty head of horses moved toward the river with the younger horses competing for the lead. When they neared the channel, the yearlings lost their spunk and pushed back against the bigger horses that bumped them forward. The older horses crowded the bank to prevent a retreat. The herd stalled at the edge of the water, where the bank dropped off several feet, but the men hollered them onward, offering no reprieve. An old gray gelding reared slightly then lunged off the bank into the shallows. Another horse followed, then two, then three. Then, as one, the herd poured off the bluff in a shower of spray.

They drove across the first rivulet and into the next. The boys came out of the first channel with triumphant faces that immediately sagged when they saw they still had to cross a rocky bar and push into the next swift river braid. When they came out of the third channel the horses wobbled across the rocks toward the fourth and the boys, and some girls of eleven or twelve, shared a look of shock as the older men rode up beside them. Their shivers hid their desire to cry, as the men rode beside them to offer them merit and bolster their grit. They too were cold and stunned, but there was no going back.

The horses shook every time they came out of the water. They twisted and stumbled on the cobble, but they never stopped moving south. As they walked toward the biggest channel, they coughed and nickered. The young horses looked punished as they stumbled along with their ears splayed out flat. The boys and girls followed close behind with their own whipped look.

What had been a laborious task crossing the first channels became near panic, as horse and riders entered the fourth river channel. The river's strength pulled everything quickly downstream. The channel was swift but narrow, and with their last bit of strength the horses stretched for safety.

The old gray gelding still led. With churning legs, he arched toward the bank and pawed for solid ground. One by one, every horse stumbled to its feet as the south bank came under foot. The colts and yearlings came out farther downstream, but every horse made it.

Water Bird watched from the north bank, remembering how good it felt to be cold and shivering on the south side.

While the first herd was being pushed across the river, the women loaded packhorses and travois for the second group to cross. Once the animals were packed, they were pushed to the crossing. With little resistance, the horses entered the river. They swam the first channel and crossed the rocky bars, then swam the next two. By the time they got to the big channel, their sides heaved heavy, but their instinct lured them on, and they waded into the swift channel and climbed out on the south bank. The men and kids hurried to unload the packs and spread the gear out in the sun. With enough gear across the river to start setting a camp, it was the mothers and children who would come next.

At the edge of the first channel, families gathered to sort out who was going to carry which child on which horse. The horses were twenty-five of the biggest bellied best swimmers.

Brooke's mare Tess was in that group because of her steady nature and size. Star Flower carried the little girl, Sah-wof, and Brooke insisted she ride Tess. Star Flower agreed once she knew that Brooke would ride her father's black horse with the last group to cross over.

There were roughly fifty parents, babies, and little kids to get across. Babies were tied in pack boards, toddlers were toted in big slings, and little kids were tied to adults with makeshift harnesses. Moms, dads, and grandparents took on the inherent task of carrying their children, but everyone, including the teenagers, helped.

Tom had never seen Bow River so assertive. Everyone was his responsibility. From the little pets to the horses and the unborn babies, his reign was paramount. Every day he patrolled each soul, but at the edge of the big river his authority took on greater command. Like great generals Tom had watched in the war, he instructed with calm surety that spread trust. Everyone stood by his side and took orders to carry out his plan. Those who weren't chosen to carry children were directed to take a position down from the crossings to rescue gear — and save lives. Brooke, Tom, six men, and four women were told where to go and how to prepare for what was to come. Loma led them into the water, and they strung out in single file.

Brooke took her position on the first gravel bar between the first and second channels about fifty yards below the crossing. The shock of the cold and the pep of her horse made her heart pound. She breathed deeply to shake off her terror as she looked at the stretch of river in front of her. She was only thirteen, and now other people's lives could be in her hands. The chill made everything more daunting. She untied the rope from her saddle and held it in one hand, gripping the bridle reins in the other. Her horse fought his bridle, wanting to follow the other horses, but Brooke popped his bit and he settled back.

Blue Jay was directly across from her, between the second and third channels, and Sah-seet was a little farther down.

Sah-seet was younger than Brooke and smaller too. Brooke wondered how worried she was and if she had done this before.

Reasoning told her she had, even though she could see her own nervousness reflected in her younger friend.

Charlie Snow, a father of three, started across first with his little girl on his back. Bluebird, his wife, came next with a toddler in front and a cradleboard on her back. The little boy cried but went quiet when the cold water climbed his legs. The families stayed close to each other as they entered the river then spread out, depending on how their horses moved in the water.

Brooke watched each horse enter the first flow and then the next, and although the children looked frightened, the parents remained stern. Every horse had to swim in every channel, so for several yards they drifted downstream. They'd come out of a channel and walk back upstream to regain the angle then wade in again. One after another the parents and kids crossed the currents and, each time they came out, the horses twisted and shook while the riders gripped and squeezed to stay on.

Brooke was amazed when the first families climbed up the south bank and helped their kids to the ground, where they crumpled in relief. Large fires were already burning. The children huddled around them, while their parents worked. Mothers rooted through packs for dry clothes while men and boys wrangled weary stock.

• • •

A high-pitched scream cut the noisy scene in half. Above the rushing water and clatter, a desperate cry pierced every ear and heart. Brooke jerked from side to side, searching for the source of the screams that had suddenly stopped. A different yell rang out, and she saw Blue Jay racing her horse up the gravel bar.

In the third channel was Little Owl. She and her daughter, Berni, were on a horse that looked to be sinking. The horse was motionless and nearly submerged under the water. Little Owl frantically wrapped one arm around Berni just before the horse rolled downstream and twisted the mother and daughter underneath. The horse's motionless legs rolled up from the water, and Brooke knew the horse was dead. She crammed her heels into her horse's ribs, and he bolted into the channel. She was in deep water when she saw Little Owl's head pop up. She bobbed and twisted and screamed. "Berni, Berni!"

Brooke was kicking her horse out of one channel when she saw Blue Jay urging her horse into the next channel just downstream from Little Owl. Blue Jay threw a rope in front of Little Owl, who grabbed it while frantically searching for her daughter.

Brooke broke out of the water and crashed through willows and log piles headed toward Little Owl, who was pulling herself up the rope while Blue Jay dragged her toward the bank.

Brooke's gut clenched in panic when Little Owl let go and was pulled back into the channel. She was drifting toward the dead horse, where Bernie's little head bobbed, and her skinny arm hung on.

Brooke and Blue Jay braced themselves as the tragedy floated farther away. They watched with dread as Little Owl struggled to close a gap that only widened. The reality of their helplessness unfolded before them.

The crashing went off like a bomb when horse and rider hit the water downstream. When horse and rider emerged, it was Sah-seet who whipped her struggling horse. With eyes glued on the drifting dead horse, the young girl screamed a battle cry. In a few seconds that felt like hours, Sah-seet's horse drew up alongside Little Owl, who grabbed the horse's mane.

Sah-seet whipped her horse harder, trying to make up ground at just the right angle to keep Berni from drifting out of reach. As they neared the floating carcass, Little Owl screamed, "Berni!" The girl glanced up just as her mother snagged her by the hair. Sah-seet's big horse swam for his own life, and to save three more. When the horse hit the bank, he staggered and fell. Sah-seet jumped off and dragged Little Owl, who was carrying Berni, up the bank.

When they heard the little girl's frenzied cry, Brooke and Blue Jay drew in a relieved breath. They watched from across the channel as Tall Deer and Tom leapt from their horses and ran to hug the women and the child, celebrating their safe arrival. Loma got to the scene just before Little Owl's husband, Quikants, appeared and fell to his knees.

Through blurry eyes Brooke watched her father examine the scene in the method of a scientist, a doctor, and a father, and she knew lives had been saved.

In a short while Loma waved Brooke and Blue Jay toward the bank where more parents waited for the rescue riders. Brooke crossed back through the second channel and took up her position again. From there she watched, with her gut twisted tight, as Little Owl and Berni, along with the rest of the parents, reached the south bank. Loma crossed over to help on the south side. Before he went, he sent the rescue riders back to the north bank to help with the rafts.

Tom could tell that no one wanted to ride the rafts. If a person could hold onto a horse, or hold onto someone holding onto a horse, it felt more secure than riding on a powerless raft. Babies could be slung to their parents' backs, small kids too, but it was the eldest and heavily pregnant women who had no choice but to ride the rafts. The risks were numerous but if they wanted to cross and get to the Bear Dance, they'd have to trust their lives to a raft.

Getting the first raft across the river was tricky. It would be empty except for one man, who would have to swim to safety if the raft was swept away. The men would push the raft into the river as far as they could. Then, pointing the raft across the river, they would wade waist deep, then belly deep, then up to their chests into the water. When they couldn't go any farther, they'd shove the manned raft toward the south side of the river. That solo rider was usually one of the best swimmers. He'd spool out a rope from the back of the raft, and when he got closer to the south bank, he'd throw another rope to the men on the south shore. They'd secure the front rope to the south bank to complete a towline. Once a towline was secure, they'd use it to shuttle rafts, supplies, people, and pets across the river.

Water Bird stood on the front of the first raft. Tall Deer, Charlie Snow and Quikants pushed him into the current. Neck deep in water, the three men shoved the raft off then swam back for the north bank. Water Bird was naked above and below his breach cloth. A knife hung on a belt around his waist. His hair was held back in a long braid. Around his neck on a cord was a small leather pouch full of little black feathers, his medicine power. He rode the raft, watching the muddy water that boiled around him as he reeled out the rope from the back of the raft. He felt the current growing stronger as he crossed the river and balanced his stance against the rocking logs.

On the south side Bel-a-kook stood waist deep downstream from the raft, struggling to keep his balance. He yelled at Water Bird to throw the rope, but Water Bird waited. If he threw the rope too soon, and it fell short, the raft would be lost; but, if he waited too long, he'd get below the men, and the current would work against them. He held on and flexed his knees, ready to throw the rope. The raft lurched when it touched the main current. Water Bird stumbled and caught his balance to heave the coil of rope. It landed in Bel-a-kook's arms. He tossed it to Widget, who wrapped it around a tree.

When Water Bird saw the rope tied around the tree, he knew it was time to swim for the north shore. He glanced in the murky water and saw what he thought was a piece of driftwood below the surface, but it soon twisted into the round face of an otter. He turned and took three long strides, then dove off the back of the raft. He swam three powerful pumps and was rising to the surface when he felt something cinch around his ankle. He hit the end of the snare with a jolt that yanked at his hip and jerked him backwards. He immediately knew that he was tied to the raft by something that no one had seen. The tug on his leg dragged him backwards into the main current. The weight of the raft and the force of the water held him underwater. He pawed for the surface but couldn't get his face to air. He crunched his body around and grabbed for the strap with one hand while he felt for his knife with the other. He touched the knife on his belt, and it slid around to his back. He couldn't reach the knife, or the strap that choked his ankle. Pain burned in his shoulder, and a haunting reminder of past tragedies gripped his mind. He twisted on the tether strap as he grabbed for his knife, which remained just out of reach.

Slimy hair slid across his face, and he gritted his teeth. The slickness coiled around his neck and slid around his chest as claws scratched at his ribs. He pushed at what twisted around his waist, and his hand bumped the butt of his knife. He drew the knife from its sheath and felt the steel blade cut into a finger as he gripped harder to his only hope.

With the strength of near death, he folded against the water and swiped at the strap of leather that held his life. The pop of the strap felt like freedom, but the drag of the river held on. With the knife in his teeth he broke the surface and sucked in air. He dove into the water with restored strength and swam hard. Over and over, he threw powerful arms and kicked at the pain in his legs. Each time his head came up he heard voices getting louder. When his toes touched the river bottom, he stood up in waist-deep water. He coughed hard and wiped his hair from his face. He rubbed his burning eyes, and, through the blur, he could see someone coming closer. He shook his head and rubbed his eyes again then clearly saw sparkling blue eyes, pink lips, and stardust freckles. Brooke was coming toward him with Stone Calf close behind. As they closed the distance, Old Man Otter sunk out of sight.

Later that night, around big fires on the south bank, people told the first stories about the girl, Sah-seet, White Flower, recounting the day she pulled a mother and daughter from the mighty Rio Colorado. Water Bird sat not far from Brooke and listened. As the fires dwindled and the people made their way to bed, Water Bird walked to a point on a bluff and lay down under the stars. As he drifted into sleep, his totems appeared behind his closed eyelids. The bird, the fish, and the otter had arrived to share the night sky.

CHAPTER TWENTY-TWO

Three Pipes

▲ ▲ ▲

Crossing the Rio Colorado was a two-day ordeal. The first day to cross the river and the second to dry out gear and prepare for the push to the Big Tree Camp. The testy women from the day before were more cheerful and full of energy as they prepared for the next leg of the journey.

Heading south in the shadow of a giant mesa, Tom and Brooke topped a rise and saw the San Juan Mountains for the first time. The snow-covered peaks shimmered silver across the southern horizon.

The clan traveled fifteen miles the first day and camped near a small stream that came from the base of the mesa. They spent two nights in camp, hunting antelope and deer in the foothills, before they continued. Four days from Whitefish Crossing, the Black Rock River and the Big Tree Camp came into sight. Shale gray hills loomed above the valley, where hundreds of tipis were strung along the river. Clusters of ten to thirty lodges wove through the trees for half a mile. Tom guessed they were riding toward a village of over a thousand people. He felt his own pulse in his ears as he studied the sights and listened to the distant sounds. When he and Brooke had left Denver, he'd planned on skirting the eastern boundary of the reservation. Now, studying the view of three hundred unfamiliar tipis, he guessed they were near its center.

On the sagebrush flats beyond the camp a huge horse herd flowed over the hills like floodwater. Pushing one way and then the other, as stallions fought for power under a twisting coil of dust. When the Yellow Bear's horses topped the ridge, they spread out along the crest with ears pinned to the distance. A spotted gray stud was the first to break for the big herd. Behind him raced the rest of the free herd, bucking and twisting. No one tried to stop them. Instead, they fought to hold onto the ones they rode — and to slow down the ones with loads.

When they neared the village, paint-faced riders on decorated horses raced uphill toward them. They screamed like warriors facing enemies, rather than relatives welcoming family members. The riders were young boys and girls, who charged and bluffed each other with playful taunts. As the riders wove through the caravan, Tom and Brooke held their reins tight. The rowdy greeting committee swarmed the visitors and merged with the group, as they loped toward the village.

The Yellow Bears entered the village with Bow River in the lead. When they stopped and dismounted, they handed off their horses to waiting boys. People poured from the lodges and hurried toward them. Families greeted one another with hugs and shoulder claps while Tom and Brooke drew glances and stares. Most people had heard something about the pair of outsiders, mostly fireside tales of their grit and courage. Their entrance into the great village would not go unnoticed and, in fact, was anticipated. Some of the Black Eagle people spoke to Tom and Brooke while others stood back and seemed reluctant to approach. They tipped their heads together and talked behind cupped hands, while others just stared.

Tom and Brooke were with friends, but not everyone was happy to see them. The Utes had good reason to distrust white people. Their presence almost always signaled a brewing storm.

Tom dismounted and stepped close to Brooke just as the little boy they'd met at Sheep Lakes, Cricket, stepped forward with a wide smile. Above the noise he spoke in Ute. "Hello Rose Creek, I've been waiting for you."

Brooke smiled and tipped her head to look down at the little man. She understood every word he said. She stooped and hugged him close then held him back and said in perfect Ute, "Hello my friend, Cricket, I've been looking for you too. You have grown so much I didn't know you."

His lips rounded open as he listened to her words, then he clapped his hand across his mouth and backed up a step.

The crowd grew as people came to meet the new arrivals and get a look at the whites who had lived with the Yellow Bear people through the winter. A line soon formed in front of Star Flower as people took turns speaking to her and caressing her with gentle touches. She struggled to hold back tears while sharing a gracious smile that consoled everyone she met. Together they honored the memory of Strong Horse without saying his name.

His brother, Eagle Dog, came forward with a man and woman behind him. Everyone stepped aside. The woman spread her arms and hurried toward Star Flower, pinning her arms to her sides in a strong hug. Star Flower couldn't hold back her tears as she and Cedar Bird, Strong Horse's mother, rocked side to side, crying. When they caught their breath Cedar Bird held Star Flower back, looked down at her rounded belly, then hugged her again.

Stone Calf and Blue Jay stepped up to the women, as did others who wrapped their arms around the heavy-hearted pair. Brooke came close, and a young woman she didn't know reached out and pulled her in closer. Together, they all cried over their loss again.

It was early April in the Flower Moon when the people arrived at the Big Tree Camp. The camp was named for an ancient cottonwood as wide as a horse is long. Tom had never seen a bigger one from Ohio to Colorado. He spent part of the first day measuring and sketching it. It was near the center of the village that sprawled around it. Some Utes scowled at the attention he gave the tree.

Just north of the tree a tall brush corral was built. It took two days to drag the branches that built the walls. On the eastern side, people hung two large gates that scraped against the ground. When the corral was finished most of the people in the village could fit inside. Bow River explained to Tom that the annual Bear Dance would take place here, in the shadow of the old tree.

It was during this time that the chiefs held counsel concerning the issues that faced the tribe. The Bear Dance Council of 1869 would address the treaty signed the year before. The agreement contained the boundaries of the new reservation, along with guidelines that encouraged the Utes to forgo their nomadic traditions and pursue a life based on farming.

Agriculture was the ambition of most Americans, but it held little allure for the Utes. For centuries they had roamed, only loosely corralled by their enemies and the landscape. They had little interest in changing their ways.

The treaty moved the Capote Utes from the east to the new reservation in the west. More people on less land added pressure on the game herds, especially as the Utes tried to improve their lot through the meat and hide trade. As they sought an economy based on selling animal parts, they carved into the very resources that fed them. Simple things like steel pots and knives improved conditions, but these things cost money, and the currency the Utes traded away was sometimes the food they needed to survive.

If the deer, elk, antelope, sheep, and buffalo did not have enough time and space to replenish, they would vanish. With a high demand for meat and hides and a diminishing supply, the Utes were destined to starve if they couldn't learn to farm. Not everyone realized the precarious nature of their plight, but some of the oldest and some of youngest people did. It would take generations to develop farming skills. A few Ute elders suggested that they consult Tom; other leaders argued that they had nothing to learn from a white man. In the end, they agreed to ask for his opinion but insisted that no matter what he said, they would come to their own conclusions.

. . .

Water Bird poked his head into Tom's tipi and told him to come to the council lodge before sunset. It was a warm evening and the breeze smelled of smoke and musty forest. The big village clamored with pots, pans, and crackling fires. The aisle between the tipis bustled with children and pets in the last free light of the evening. Tom and Brooke headed to the center of the village. Star Flower caught up with them, and together they walked to the big lodge.

When Tom stooped to enter the door, he was met by a hundred eyes — which all shifted to Brooke when she stepped in behind him. Some eyes narrowed while others widened, but none of them looked welcoming. Brooke arched back from the room of stony faces. Her father nodded to the door, ushering her out with his eyes. She readily complied.

As she stepped out, shoulders settled, and frowns softened. Within the room sat the leaders of the Ute Nation. He saw Bow River, Wolf Song and Loma. The other leaders he'd never met. In a group of young men toward the back stood Water Bird. Two older boys at the back of the lodge rapped lightly on rawhide drums.

The tall Ute called War Raven pointed out Tom's seat between Loma and another man he didn't know. The unknown man with a hard-set jaw glanced up at Tom and scooted to the side with a huff. Tom could feel hardened eyes boring through him. Not everyone appreciated his presence here. His intentions were good, but how could they know that?

Once Tom was seated, three long-stem pipes were unsheathed and handed to Wolf Song and Wooden Bull. Two of the pipes were lit, and the elder men blew smoke in the four directions. When they finished, they passed the pipes to a line of men and two women seated to their left. There, Good Bear sat wrapped in a grizzly hide, the bear's wrinkled face perched atop his head. Around his neck hung a wreath of bear claws. Tom had never seen him dressed like this before. He'd seen Good Bear as grandfatherly, but now he looked unfamiliar and menacing.

To his right was a woman dressed in black feathers with a crow skull tied in the part of her hair. She held a staff covered in feathers, decorated with a bear skull strapped to the side. Tom had heard mention of The Woman Crow, and he knew this must be her. The only other woman in the room wore her hair pulled back, and her face was painted yellow. She was wrapped in a lion skin with the fat tail coiled in her lap. Tom deduced that the animal headdresses marked their wearers as part of an unparalleled alliance of elders and shamen.

When the first pipe was passed to Tom, he held it up and admired the polished wood and stone. He looked at Loma, who nodded to let him know he should smoke.

Tom drew deep on the pipe and let the sweet smoke fill his chest, then he slowly exhaled a cloud into the room. Before it cleared his lungs, he knew he'd taken too much. His head felt full, and the room began to swirl. He braced a hand to the ground, dropped his head and took a deep breath. The spinning slowed as fresh air moved across his lips. A bump at his arm came from Loma, who was handing him the second pipe. Tom glanced up at the other men, who sat with their heads in their hands. A man across the room stared back at him with bloodshot eyes and a lost stare. Tom had smoked many times but never had he felt so stunned.

Loma grunted and Tom knew he had no choice, so he put the wet pipe stem in his mouth and drew in. The smoke felt cool as mint, and he held it in until his mind started to turn before letting it go. He looked around the room and felt vulnerable yet not afraid. In every eye he saw the same powerless stare he knew he wore.

Once the pipes had circled the lodge and the drumming stopped, the room got very quiet. Bow River looked at the man seated to his left and then at Tom and said, "This is Archer. He and I lived with the Mexicans near Santa Fe when we were small. There we learned to speak Spanish and your words too."

Tom nodded. He knew the story of how the Comanche had stolen Bow River and other children and sold them to the Catholic churches. Bow River and another boy had escaped in their teens and found their families hundreds of miles to the north. Archer must have been the other boy. Now, the man sat staring forward with his shoulders back. His build was short and powerful with a broad torso and thick legs partially tucked beneath him. His light-colored leathers were beaded in colorful diamond patterns that ran down his sleeves. The tips of his long braids dangled at his waist.

Bow River spoke again, and Tom realized the address was directed at him. Other men were introduced including Wooden Bull and Black Feather, and elders seated near Good Bear.

Bow River settled in his seat. Archer looked around the room at every set of eyes. He twisted to see the young men standing in the back. Then he looked directly at Tom and said, "Tom Gun, we have all heard of you and your powerful medicine. You are Turtle Wind. We know that you, Water Bird, and your daughter Rose Creek saved Bow River from the Split-Eared Bear. We have all seen where you sewed him back together."

Archer spoke in a slow cadence in nearly perfect English with a hint of a Spanish accent. His pronunciation was precise and practiced.

"In your hands, you held the life of our brother." He made the hand sign for Strong Horse's name. "You helped him smile at his own death." A murmur rippled through the crowd as heads bobbed slightly.

"You are a brave man, Turtle Wind," Archer continued, "And so is your daughter. We know what she has done. You have been strong to live with us and help feed our children. Now, Turtle Wind, we want to know what you know about the white man's government agencies on the Black Rock and White Rivers." He looked around the room as if searching. "Turtle Wind, tell us what you know of these forts and what they mean for our people."

Archer looked at Bow River, translating English to Ute for the men in the room. They watched his face and listened to every word. When he stopped, all the eager eyes settled back on Tom.

Tom shifted his crossed legs and cleared his throat. He felt trusted but wasn't sure how to answer.

"The government has created agencies to provide a safe place where you can get food, supplies, and information to make your lives better." Tom looked at his moccasins, realizing that the weight of his words teetered on a balance of truth and hopefulness. The truth was the Ute nation was doing okay without the help of the white government. The Utes were one of the richest tribes in America, and they knew it. Their horse herd had never been bigger and there was still plenty of game.

"To be honest, I don't know the full intention of the government," Tom continued. "I only know what I've been told and what I've read." Tom waited for Bow River to translate. "I hear that these agencies will soon have sawmills for cutting lumber and a grain mill for grinding wheat. They will stock herds of cattle, sheep and horses for work and for breeding your mares."

As Tom listened to Bow River translate, he knew that his explanation sounded hollow. His words about the government horses would mean little, because the Utes already had better horses than the whites. The Utes didn't need bulky work horses because no one needed to drive a team or plow a field.

When Bow River finished translating, Archer mashed his lips together, looked at Tom, and said, "Tom Gun, we believe you. You are our friend, a brother. We want to hear what you think, not what we have already been told. We want to know what you believe in your heart." Archer tapped his chest.

Tom let out a long breath. His fears were realized. These men wanted more than just the political answer. They wanted his truth. The faces around him understood the direct question pointed his way. They wanted to know his beliefs, his opinion, his gut intuition, and they'd know if he lied.

Tom felt a pang of guilt for his weasel-worded answer. He had to go deeper, which would expose his own fears of the government's reservation policy. Tom rested his fist on his lips and stared into the glowing coals, knowing his own greed to explore had landed him here. The time had come for him to be truthful with himself — and with the people who surrounded him.

"There are so many white people that they cover the land to the east of the Utes," he said. "A number far greater than the buffalo herds, the leaves on the trees, or the stars in the sky. And this mass of people is set to flow over Ute territory like flood waters.

With them will come the weight of the plow and the point of the pick."

Tom's eyes relaxed back into the warmth of the fire as he waited for Bow River to translate.

"There are many among the whites who want life to be good for the Ute people. They wish for you to be free in this land. They have worked to secure a vast piece of your homeland, so that you may raise your children and your ponies without fear." The room of dark eyes urged him to go on.

"The fathers in Washington are thankful that the Utes have been peaceful and have become friends with many white people. This good will does not go unnoticed." Tom waited for one of the men to translate but they said nothing, so he continued. "Other tribes who have fought the white armies have not fared as well. The Pawnee have been forced from their land and now live squeezed together like prairie dogs. They cry in hunger and sleep in the cold."

The lodge was motionless as fifty men seasoned in stealth sat silently. Bow River broke the stillness with a sigh then translated slowly and clearly. When he finished, he looked to Tom for more.

"Among the whites are good men who have plenty, and other good men who have very little. But there are some whites who don't have as much food or freedom as the Utes do. Their children also get sick and die. They have very little, and they want more — more of everything. Their bellies are never full. They are like hungry ghosts. These poor white men will kill and steal like the Comanche." Tom paused as conversation rattled about the room.

Tom knew the council waited for his final words, so he chose them in his mind first. "I believe that the intention of the government is good. It is in the interest of everyone to live in peace. No one wants to die, but the white nation is very big, and the leaders cannot control everyone. Not everyone agrees. No one can fight the United States government and win. All the tribes together will not defeat the white men who rule this land. The Utes might win many battles but, for every white man that dies, there are one hundred to replace him."

Tom waited and watched the crowd. When Bow River finished translating, Tom continued. "The Utes, the people of the sun, should protect their land and be friends with the whites. The whites have many good things that you can use. Over time it will become easier, and everyone will learn to trust and help each other."

Tom looked back into the fire. "My friends, you have horses, game, and land from the Bear River to the San Juan River, the great divide to the Green River out west. A land as big as some countries in the world. If the Ute people accept this land and work to be friends with the people of Colorado, I believe we can live here in peace." Tom paused then added, "May we all live in peace, for as long as rivers run."

Archer loosened his shoulders, straightened his spine, and removed his gaze from the fire. He spoke first to Bow River then to War Raven and Wooden Bull. Bow River paused and glanced to the smoke that lingered at the top of the lodge.

An anxious knot wiggled in Tom's gut as he wondered what he might have set into motion. The lodge rumbled with conversations. Some of the voices were edged with anger. Others sought to soothe.

Tom could tell that not everyone was happy with what he had said. Three men in the back bickered sharply. A younger one jabbed a finger Tom's way, until another man slapped it down. The two men came chest to chest but settled down when others stepped between them. The younger man, who had a bright red stripe where his hair was parted, shot Tom a hard stare.

When Wolf Song stood up, the room became silent as everyone turned to listen. He waved his arms, pointed at the chiefs, the shaman, Tom, and Water Bird too. Then he said something that made everyone, including the serious shaman, laugh out loud. All eyes turned to Tom. Strangers looked his way. Some shook their heads; others smiled slightly. Tom knew he was the point of jest, and that was good.

The group went quiet as Wolf Song's words became serious again. Pensive faces returned as the room listened to the old man's last words. Then Archer took charge. He filled a new medicine-pipe and handed it to the woman in the lion skin. She spoke toward the sky then started the pipe around the room.

Loma savored the taste as it drifted from his mouth. Tom marveled again at the stone pipe before he drew in the third blend. The smoke was light and drifted in and out easily with the taste of lemon grass. He handed the pipe to the man next to him.

As Tom gazed at the fire, his mind rested and his heart kept beat with the drum. He breathed in deep and let go of his worries as an ease settled into his body. A peace he'd never known. In the lodge full of warriors, he shared the calming essence with his brothers — and two sisters.

Flip of the Shawl

▲ ▲ ▲

Throughout the winter Tom had heard people talking about the Bear Dance. Whenever people spoke of it, they had a lilt in their voices and subtle smiles on their faces. Since they'd left winter camp, talk about the Bear Dance had only increased. Tom and Brooke asked questions and took notes. Everyone was excited to tell them about the upcoming celebration.

As they put the pieces together, they learned that the Bear Dance was the most sacred of all Ute ceremonies. A celebration of the circle of life, the dance represented the sanctity of their greatest totem, the bear.

The annual event was the most significant social gathering of the year, because all the Ute bands would attend, along with friendly neighbors from other tribes. The different groups would travel from all directions to participate in the courtship, commerce, and councils that marked the occasion.

During the dance itself, men, women, girls, and boys would let their interest in one another be known. One man would be charged with making sure that all celebrants adhered to tradition. This overseer would also be called upon to pair couples who struggled to make connections on their own — from young people who were too shy to older folks who might need a companion. The overseer, called the Cat Man, wore a mountain lion skin over his buckskin leathers and directed the sequence of daily activities with authority.

Each day for four days, the dancers would keep moving until someone dropped from exhaustion. After this first collapse, the dance would end for the day, but the celebration would continue through the night — until the dance started up again the next morning.

• • •

It was the third evening in camp, and the night before the dance, when Blue Jay told Brooke to be at her lodge before daylight. The next morning when Brooke arrived, the women were excited for the ceremony. Stone Calf, Star Flower, Blue Jay, Fat Cow, and her young daughters were all in different stages of getting ready.

Blue Jay handed Brooke a doe-skin dress with a beaded collar and long fringe and said, "Here, young girl, put these on. I have a shawl for you, too."

Brooke held out the clothes and looked back to Blue Jay, "I don't need these," she said, "I'm not dancing."

The women stopped in their tracks and looked at each other.

Brooke repeated her assertion. "I'm not dancing. I don't know if I'll even go into the corral."

Blue Jay stepped forward, "Why not?"

"The dance is for couples, and I'm not Ute. Besides, I'm only thirteen going on fourteen. I don't know the dance, and no one will want to dance with me."

Fat Cow's girls looked wide-eyed and nervous. Blue Jay chuckled and looked to Stone Calf, who lightly wrung her hands.

"Brooke," Stone Calf started then corrected herself. "Rose Creek, you could dance with any man." She turned her palms up and her head lulled side to side. "Little Cricket, old Black Feather, or any young man — any boy in any band would be joyful to take your hands." She wagged her head as a smile crept up. "You don't have to have their babies. Just shake with them a little, like this." Stone Calf tossed her hips side to side then front to back, and the

182

room burst into howls of laughter at this serious woman, who now exuded the frisky spirit of the bear.

When they caught their breath, they were all holding hands and Brooke willingly conceded. "Okay, okay, okay."

The women mimicked the ridiculous phrase, "Okay, okay, okay."

Once they had the answer they wanted, the women began to comb and braid her hair., fussing over the fiery tendrils around her face. She stripped out of her everyday clothes and accepted the garment the women held out to her — a soft, highly adorned, deerskin dress.

"Now, walk like this," one of the women said, swaying from side to side with each stride. Brooke did her best, but her attempt to walk with a wiggle made them all laugh.

These women ruled the roost. They also did the hardest work. They gutted the buffalo, stood the tipis, packed the ponies, and wrapped the dead. They cried like wolves and fought like lions. They bore the babies, nursed the babies, and buried the babies too. Outside the power of Sinawav, the women were ultimately in control. They tied the strings that bound the most important gift, the gift of life, born of the purest gift of all, sex.

Without their women the men had nothing, and they knew it. Everything they did was about surviving so that their families might live to experience the circle of life, which began with the pleasure of touch. Life could be hard and cold and dangerous, but the purest reward of life was life itself in moments of soft, warm peace.

These women loved Brooke so much that showing her their most sacred ceremony was their highest wish. The Bear Dance was an essential to their existence. Without the romance of the dance there would be no new lovers and little hope for a future. They had never dreamed that Brooke would not attend. She and her father were considered family, and many people thought they might live with them forever. No one discussed Brooke and Tom returning to their previous lives. They had found the Yellow Bears with guidance of Sinawav, the all-powerful director of their lives.

Good Bear believed that Turtle Wind and Rose Creek had come to the Yellow Bears to help bridge the river that flowed between their worlds. The band shared the belief, and Tom and Brooke were allowed to participate in all the workings of the Yellow Bears to help build that bridge.

The Bear Dance ceremony began the morning after the chief's council. Shortly after first meal the sound of heavy drums and growler rasps rumbled from the brush corral.

Family groups wandered from their lodges as children zigzagged through the crowd. Couples walked with purpose while groups of young people walked light-footed toward the plaza.

By the time Brooke and the women made their way to the brush corral, a column of dust lofted into the sky. When the gates opened every curious face twisted toward them. At the far end of the plaza stood Good Bear with a lion skin draped across his shoulder. As the Cat Man, he had received the highest reverence from the other noble elders of the tribe.

Men and women had arranged themselves on opposite sides of the plaza, forming lines running north and south. The women stood on one side, men on the other. They started out close to each other, face to face. Then, to the beat of the drums, they sauntered backwards. At the signal of the Cat Man, they came together again. Married couples paired across from each other, and the strength of their bond was on display in their dancing.

With their chins held high, the women led by Stone Calf greeted everyone with wide eyes and big smiles. Each of the women wore a tassel of Brooke's hair as an earring or a charm. When they reached the other women, they knelt before the dancers.

Brooke could feel her heart and the rap of the drums against her breast as she walked across the plaza. When they reached the other women, they knelt beside them and watched the dancers. Brooke watched with her mouth slightly open as she gently rocked to the rhythm. Her head twisted from side to side as she listened to the lilt of laughter and dance. Clothing was trimmed with ribbons, beads, feathers, and flowers. Everyone bounced and wiggled to the influence of the instruments. She was caught up in the sights and sounds and barely noticed the way the women watched her, wondering who her partner might be.

Brooke saw Blue Jay in the crowd. She could see her father watching her too, but he quickly looked back into the crowd when she noticed him.

Fat Cow walked to where her husband sat and brushed her shawl across his face with a playful twirl. Good Bear jumped to his feet, grabbed her hand and together they crowded into the lines.

Water Bird was kneeling on the west side of the plaza. When Brooke caught his eye, he held her gaze a moment before looking away.

Brooke looked at the dancers then back at Water Bird, just as a girl flipped her shawl across his face. The girl tipped her head and twisted slightly. Water Bird looked up with a pointed gaze while the boys around him watched and shuffled. He stood up, dipped his head, and headed toward the lines of dancers. The girl was Blue Water. Brooke had met her at Sheep Lakes. She looked beautiful, her face angular and her shape womanly. She was as tall as Brooke and showed more signs of being a budding young woman. Her breasts were bigger and her hips rounder. Brooke suddenly felt hungry and a little dizzy from the whirlwind around her.

Water Bird was focused on Blue Water. After a few moments of smiling and talking, they picked up the dance step and moved to the tempo. Brooke caught herself staring, and she was about to move toward the gate when she felt a hand on her shoulder. She looked up at Star Flower, who met her with a soft smile. Star Flower rocked gently to the rhythm, watching the dancers as she rubbed Brooke's shoulders.

When the sun crossed over the brush corral and tilted west, people headed toward the shade and food. Brooke was sitting with Star Flower when she saw Water Bird headed toward the gates. He stopped and spoke to Tom, then he and another boy left the plaza.

The drumming continued through the afternoon and when the sun fell behind the corral walls, the fires were lit. Some of the dancers danced into the night, but most of the people left early.

Brooke went to their tipi not long after dark. She folded her buckskin dress, crawled between the covers, reached for her journal, and with the stub of a pencil, started to write.

When she entered the plaza the second day of the Bear Dance, Water Bird wasn't there, and neither was Blue Water. She knew that the young men tended the horses and did most of the hunting. There were over three thousand horses and almost that many people to feed.

She hadn't seen a lot of Water Bird since they arrived at the Big Tree Camp. He was popular and often followed by young admirers. Everyone knew of his exploits, which had contributed to his wealth of horses and his possession of a rifle. Besides his social standing, Water Bird was popular because of his character. He was looked up to, much like Strong Horse had been, and the story of him swimming below the ice to save Strong Horse was told at nearly every gathering of the people. He was young, strong, helpful, and kind to everyone young and old. Little ones knew his name, as did the elders. Every young girl between the ages of eight and eighteen knew who he was — and paid attention to where he was going.

At mid-morning of the second day, Brooke was sitting in the shade when a little girl came up and stood in front of her. It was Wren, Cricket's sister. She shifted from leg to leg and spoke at a pace that Brooke couldn't catch. When she paused, she glanced back and forth between the women. Stone Calf rocked her jaw and winked at Wren, who smiled back. Stone Calf leaned into Brooke.

"Rose Creek, this is Wren, the sister of Cricket. She is hoping you will flip your shawl for her brother."

Brooke rose to her knees and looked through the crowd for the boyishly handsome Cricket. He and some other boys sat with their backs against the wall. Cricket fiddled with empty hands.

Brooke nodded at Wren, who jumped in place and wiggled with excitement.

Cricket's friends saw Brooke coming and, as she neared, their eyes widened. Heads around the plaza twisted to see Brooke approaching the little group.

Cricket looked up and scrambled to his feet. When Brooke got so close that she had to stop, she smiled widely at the little man and playfully tossed her shawl across his cheek. Then, she spun away and walked toward the dance lines.

She didn't have to look to know he was behind her, his chin held high. At center stage, they fell in line with the other dancers, briskly pacing back and forth to the rap of the drums and the growl of the wooden rasps.

In a cloud of dust, the people swayed into the afternoon. Smiling faces settled into looks of contentment. Brooke danced with Cricket until the mountains were brushed in evening light then promised to see him the next day. As she and Blue Jay made their way to the gates, Water Bird came running around a corner. He was out of breath and stammered to sort out his words. He swallowed hard, stomped his foot, and hollered, "Horses! Horses! *To-wutch!*"

"Babies," Blue Jay said. *"Cha-vah to-wutch?"*

"Cha-vah to-wutch!" Water Bird said, nodding his head.

"We have horse babies," Blue Jay said in perfect English.

"Yes," Water Bird said, clear and crisp. "By the river, come! Come with me." He held up one hand. "Five babies."

"Oh yes, please let's go," Brooke said, grabbing at Blue Jay's hand.

Blue Jay held back. "Go, go!"

Brooke spun and ran for the river, as Water Bird scrambled to catch up.

Amongst some cottonwoods they came upon two young men who were watching over six mares and their new foals. Brooke knew two of the mares belonged to Water Bird. One was maroon with black spots on a gray rump patch, a gift horse from Strong Horse. The other was a black mare with white front socks, a daughter of Bow River's black stallion. Her foal was marble gray with tiny black dots across his back and shoulders. Water Bird walked up to the mare, laid a rope across her neck, and coaxed Brooke closer. The little colt inched forward and stretched out his nose to touch their fingers. The other curious colts crept in and surrounded them.

Water Bird reached for Brooke's arm and, as he moved, the little horses spun on rickety legs and lumbered away with their mothers' noses at their tails.

Water Bird led Brooke through a patch of willows and into a stand of trees. Brooke caught a glimpse of a horse standing in the shadows. As she got closer, she knew it was Tess.

The mare bowed her neck and pranced in a circle as they approached. Water Bird stepped aside and beckoned Brooke to take the lead, signaling her to move slowly. As she approached, the mare nervously pranced with her nose to the ground.

Brooke guessed what lay just out of sight, but she still sprang back at the sight of a colt, curled in the leaves. Her hands flew up to her cheeks, and she squealed. "Oh my word, I had no idea."

Tess snorted and pawed at the ground with an attitude Brooke had never seen. Water Bird chuckled and pulled Brooke back.

"Tess baby," he said. "Taowa's baby."

"No." Brooke said with the whoosh of a sigh.

Water Bird nodded.

"How do you know?"

Water Bird tossed his head lightly as he stepped around her. He squatted down close to the foal and held his hand out. The mare took a step back.

He traced his finger down the white blaze on the foal's face. "Taowa," he said. Brooke instantly remembered the face of the big stallion. The horse that Strong Horse rode when he fell in the river, the horse that had died beside his grave. The blaze on the foal's face was the same as Taowa's. She bit at her lip and nodded slowly.

Water Bird ran his hand along the foal's back. Scrambling to its feet, the foal took off behind its mom. Brooke and Water Bird stumbled backward, and Brooke landed on her butt. Water Bird held out an arm to help her up.

• • •

That evening, back in their lodges, Brooke stared into the fire and thought back across the trails that had brought them to The Big Tree Camp. She'd written so much she was almost out of paper. She'd recorded the horses, the hunting, the camps and the weddings, the births, and the deaths. With each event she had also reported something about Water Bird. Watching the small flame, she thought about his excitement over the foals and remembered his hand, pulling her up from the grass. It felt good to be near him. But seeing him often made her think of the farmhouse on Chip Creek, where her mother had taught her by lamplight. How she wished her mother could meet this boy.

"How many foals did you see down there?" Tom asked.

Brooke had to think. "I guess it was eight by the time we left."

"Wow, there must be over a hundred in all the herds."

"Probably." She looked back into the fire and thought of the laughter she'd shared with Water Bird when the gangly foal had jumped up and run away. Then she remembered Water Bird's bright-eyed smile and how he had looked at Blue Water. She felt a subtle twist in her belly at the thought of Blue Water's beauty and the outline of her figure. Brooke glanced down at herself then back into the fire.

"Papa," she said.

Tom raised his head.

"I'm not sure what to say or what I'm trying to say." She stopped and clenched her lips. "Papa, I think I want to ask Water Bird to dance, but then I don't."

His brow tightened.

"I'd like to flip my shawl at him, but I don't know what it means if I do."

Tom twisted on his bunk and stared into the fire. "I suppose it didn't mean much to you to dance with Cricket, but it might be something that he will remember forever."

"Oh, no Papa, it meant a lot. I'll never forget it, but you don't suppose he thinks we'll get married. Do you?"

"He might," Tom said with a smile. "But that could change if you ask Water Bird to dance. What's most important is what the invitation means to you."

She turned back to the fire and rested her chin on her fists as her father continued.

"Our invitation to the Bear Dance is an honor. I think you should dance. You may never get this chance again."

Brooke rolled away from the fire and stretched out on her blankets.

"At the end of the summer, we'll be going back to Denver," Tom said. "Then we'll head back east in the spring."

Brooke reached for her journal and twisted her head toward the fire.

"The thing is, we'll be leaving here in a couple of days, heading back to the Bunkara. We'll spend the summer there then head over the mountains in the fall. I'll let Bow River know when the time comes."

The tipi fell silent until Brooke crawled under her covers. She knew this would be her only Bear Dance. If Water Bird and Blue Water were to be together, Brooke wouldn't be in the way after this summer. If she could just enjoy the adventure, everything would work out fine. If she resisted the temptation of Water Bird, she would be able to finish high school and hopefully even go to college.

Brooke was destined for her mother's alma mater, Oberlin College in Ohio. She'd heard about the dating parlor, where her mother and father had met. She was confident that she could be an outstanding student at Oberlin and make her mother proud. Maybe she would meet a good man there and get married. If she wanted to. She liked Water Bird. A lot. But she was in the middle of an extended adventure, not her real life. The reality was: He was Ute, and she was not.

"Brooke?"

"Yes, Papa?"

"Go have fun tomorrow and enjoy this time. It won't last for long."

• • •

Brooke was at Stone Calf's lodge early the next morning. The women chatted and laughed as they sorted clothes and jewelry for the final day of the dance. By the time the women entered the brush corral, couples were facing off in the dance lines. Brooke and the other women knelt on the west side facing east. Stone Calf got up and disappeared soon after they arrived. Minutes later Brooke saw her and Bow River smiling across from each other in the dance lines.

Brooke drew a lot of looks. It seemed all the young people were watching her. She knew they wondered what she might do the last day of the dance, and she suspected that one of those who wondered was Blue Water. Brooke had only seen her a couple of times in the last few days, surrounded by other girls and older boys. Brooke guessed she was fifteen, maybe sixteen, surely old enough to marry if she were asked.

Brooke could see Cricket in a group of children. His playful teasing of another girl about his age told her that he wouldn't be heartbroken if she didn't ask him to dance. The last day was the day that the couples danced until they couldn't dance anymore.

Later in the morning Tom came in with a group of men. They sat along the west wall looking east toward the woman. It was mostly married couples who danced on the final morning. Groups of boys and girls hung to the sides and watched the adults.

Brooke noticed that the girls were dressed more extravagantly than they'd been in the days before. Many wore multi-colored furs across their shoulders with ribbons woven into their braids. Their buckskin dresses were beaded in yellow and red and accented with elk teeth and colorful feathers. Bells and shells tied to their clothes tinkled and chimed when they moved. Blue Jay spent extra time that morning on herself, and on Brooke, adding jewelry and other decorations. The last day of the dance reminded Brooke of a Sunday social, but instead of the popular attire of hoop skirts and paisley vests, the dancers wore extra-long fringe and dewclaw chimes.

Just before lunch, when the big gates opened, a group of nearly twenty men and boys strolled into the plaza. Their arrival had been anticipated by the excitement that swept through the girls like a breeze across still water.

The boys were dressed as flamboyantly as the girls. Some had paint streaks in their hair and across their cheeks and arms. They had all donned feathers of some sort. Those who were renowned for valor wore eagle feathers clipped and shaped to explain their merit. As couples joined the dance lines, excitement rose like a column of dust from the plaza.

Neither Water Bird nor his friends entered the corral in the first group of men. Tom came up and kneeled behind Brooke. His touch on her shoulder caught her off guard. Together they sat and watched the dancers. They were watching a young girl decorated in orange flicker feathers when the end of a shawl brushed her father's face. They both rocked back to see the tall figure of Blue Jay looking down with an inquisitive smile. Tom chuckled lightly and held her alluring gaze.

"Papa, you better dance. You may never get this chance again."

Brooke could see a blush spreading across his face. He held his eyes on hers for a moment then reached up for Blue Jay's hand. Together they walked toward the lines.

Brooke had never seen her father blush, and the people noticed him taking his place alongside Blue Jay. Once Tom found his step, he gave Brooke a coltish grin from afar. She'd never seen her father dance before, certainly not like this, and she'd never seen that kind of smile on his face either.

Brooke was still catching her breath from the excitement when she noticed the big gates being dragged open. In walked Water Bird with a group of his friends. From out of nowhere a tightness seized her ribs as she watched the young men cross the plaza like heroes.

Brooke thought of her mother, and what she might have thought of the girls approaching the boys for a dance. She thought it over for a moment and reasoned that Teresa would have thought it was quite acceptable.

Brooke glanced to the side where Star Flower sat. Her eyes widened when Brooke looked across the plaza toward Water Bird. He sat taller than the other boys, and his features looked more like his father's than she'd noticed before. His arms were bare, except for a pair of white stripes just below his shoulders. Around his neck was a bear-claw choker. His hair was held back by a flat-bone and two eagle feathers. On a long necklace that hung below his heart was a small leather pouch the size of his thumb. She knew it was his medicine bag, which held the totems of his power — the treasure that made him Water Bird. She knew about the bag, but she'd never really thought about the meaning of its contents before.

Her father's words returned to her. "Brooke, you'd better dance. You may never have this chance again." She stood, glanced at Star Flower, then walked across the plaza with one end of her red shawl in her hand.

CHAPTER TWENTY-FOUR

Silver Star

▲ ▲ ▲

Soft rain fell the morning the big camp scattered like ants from a hill. Ghostly clouds danced on the mesas as the Yellow Bears traveled up-river toward summer range. They were twenty-three lodges and just over a hundred people. There were nine new foals in the horse herd. Six with spotted or speckled rumps. Men from the other bands wanted them, but no trades were made.

The band traveled fifteen miles that first day. A good distance considering the effort required to break camp and sort the horses. The next day they continued upstream then branched to the west onto a muddy water fork.

The evening fires were being lit when Standing Man and Quinn of the Black Eagle band rode into camp. They marched through the village to find Bow River. They bore bad news, and the people crowded around them.

Tom, Brooke, and Water Bird were walking toward camp when the first screams sliced the calm. Ponies in the meadow threw up their heads and turned toward the village. Water Bird took off at a sprint and Brooke ran behind him. By the time Tom got to the crowd, the women were wailing, and the men argued and stomped. Bow River exhaled a low growl and clenched his fist.

Henry Eagle of the Black Eagles was dead. Murdered and scalped, his body thrown over a cliff. He and Fist of Crows had been hunting together on the rim of the black canyon. They had separated and, when Fist of Crows found Henry Eagle, he was lying on a thin ledge down in the canyon. Fist of Crows climbed down and found him dead. A rosewood arrow with Arapaho marks was broken off in his chest.

The men groaned at the details while the women scurried to gather their children.

Standing Man had more to tell. As Fist of Crows climbed back up the canyon, he came face to gun barrel with the killer, who was splattered with blood. His face was painted with the lines of Oo-nah-pooch, the Badger. As Fist of Crows clung to the top of the cliff, the killer held the gun at his nose. He could have blown his head off, but instead he walloped him across the face. Fist of Crows fell back to the ledge, where he'd been trapped for two days with a broken arm.

Bow River's jaws ground together as he studied the news. He bickered with Loma and Good Bear. They were mad, as were the rest of the men and women.

Bow River looked at the horses along the creek. Within the herd were paints, grays, sorrels and roans, and a lot of spotted-rump Appaloosas from the herd of Black Bull. Bow River knew there was a price to be paid for the death of Black Bull and those stolen horses. He knew too that the Utes would be blamed for the tornado that slaughtered the Arapaho village. The Arapahos would never forget, and now they were coming for retribution with an installation of terror.

According to Standing Man, there had been only one killer, most likely Badger Heart, the last living son of Black Bull. Bow River's guts roiled at the thought that somewhere, on a shield, hung the bloody scalp of Henry Eagle. He remembered that word had come in the winter that Red Elk, another of the men of the Whirling Wind Raid, had disappeared. Everyone thought he had gone north courting a Shawnee girl but now Bow River feared the worst. He was probably dead. The men discussed the need to be on the lookout for a vengeful warrior who marauded through their mountains, Badger Heart.

The next day the band moved over the divide into the Snow Stone Fork of the Bunkara. They struggled over a pass in deep snow. Two hundred horses were driven ahead of the people and the pack animals to break a trail. A band of heavy mares and those with foals brought up the rear. They traveled only a short distance that day, due to the reluctance of the horses in the deep snow. Scouts were sent out ahead and behind, searching for signs of any lone riders.

They pitched camp on a sagebrush flat above the Snow Stone River. This was the first evening since the Bear Dance that the women set up the tipis and unfolded all the bedding. Late in the night Tom heard rain, which soon became a soft muffled huff of snow that sagged the tipi poles. He stepped out the next morning to a clear sky and a foot of fresh snow that covered everything. Looking north, Tom recognized the giant shoulders of Heart Mountain and knew they were in the summer home of the Yellow Bears.

After the outside fires were lit, and blankets and clothes were propped up to dry, Bow River and Loma found Tom and told him that he was needed to go on a ride. He thought they were going to tend the horses or hunt. The Utes who gathered for the ride were not the men he expected. Good Bear, Loma, and two elders — Wolf Song and Pah-chook — joined Bow River. Tom understood why the chief was there to lead the outing, but he had no idea why two of the band's oldest men were joining them. When they set out, everyone in the village watched them leave.

As they rode up the river, Tom saw new geologic formations. From his saddle he saw seams in the rocks that held lead and galena, quartz too, which he knew could carry gold.

After a couple of miles, Bow River turned uphill. It took a little while, but he found a narrow trail that climbed through the thick brush. The melting snow made it slippery for the men and horses. On a knoll that poked from the hillside, they dismounted and climbed around a shale cliff. Bow River was standing over a hole when Tom came up. It was a trench dug into the hillside for about twelve feet. The rock face at the end of the cut was white as the snow around it. Tom thought at first it was quartz, but it was less opaque and denser. The men stood and watched him as if waiting for an explanation. He climbed to the end of the cut where the white stone was exposed. "Marble, snow stone," he said. "Who dug the hole?"

Bow River tipped his head to Wolf Song and Pah-chook.

"Why?" Tom asked with hands held out and a shrug of his shoulders. He knew the stone wasn't good for spearheads. In the time he'd spent with the band he hadn't seen a single piece of marble. The Ute men didn't answer his question with either words or signs. When they could tell Tom was stumped, Bow River pulled a quiver bag from around his back. He untied the lacing and carefully drew out a long-stemmed pipe that Tom had never seen before. He knew it was special as soon as he saw it. The stone bowl was shaped like an inverted "T" and made of snow-white marble. A bear's face was carved in the side of the bowl. The men grinned when Bow River handed him the pipe. He studied the carving and knew at once that he was seeing something a white man had never seen before.

He glanced at the cut in the hill and knew that this was the only prospect that meant anything to the Utes.

Tom handed the pipe to Bow River, who passed it to Wolf Song, who then led them all to the bluff overlooking the valley. There the men sat down and smoked the white pipe.

• • •

The Yellow Bears camped for almost a week along the Snow Stone before they moved into the Bunkara Valley. The second night on the Snow Stone, a baby boy was born to Tall Deer and Green Willow Spring. The family surprised everyone when they stepped from their tipi one morning with a baby that no one knew had arrived. Good Bear performed a new baby greeting ceremony before the camp moved another ten miles. They stayed away from the Fat Belly Camp at the Eagle Nest Crossing, where Strong Horse had died. No one had spoken of the incident or mentioned his name since the night in winter camp when Tom had received his name, Turtle Wind.

The Yellow Bears reached the Pony Springs Camp in early May at the start of the Green Moon. Like geese returning to their nests, the Utes revolved back to the heart of their land with the circle of the seasons. It was spring and the aspen forests were bare, but on the forest floor yellow and purple flowers pushed up through matted leaves. The landscape was bare but filled with the buzz of new lives and the return of old ones. The days grew longer by minutes, and every morning new birds, animals, and insects buzzed through the woods with the ambition of life. Nests to build, eggs to lay, calving grounds to find, dens to dig and babies to have. With the bloom of sunshine came the bloom of life.

By the time the clan camped at the Pony Springs. Star Flower's expectant belly was so full that she struggled to stand, let alone walk. She had ridden a travois the last days coming up the river. She was in pain, but she never complained. Tom noticed her discomfort, as did her mother and Blue Jay. Life was disagreeable at many turns for the Ute women, yet they carried on with steadiness and an appreciation for every day.

Tom and Brooke heard a few of the women teasing Star Flower about the big baby she carried. Although the banter was fun-loving, Tom noticed wrinkled brows of concern. One morning Grandma Chuka and Stone Calf had a spat. Tom couldn't understand everything they said, but both women frowned and seemed concerned that the baby might be growing too large.

Losing babies and children was dreadfully common among the Utes, and almost every woman wore the scars. Bow River told Tom that Blue Jay had once been with child, but the baby, a boy, had died at birth. She'd nearly died too. She was married for another three summers without getting pregnant before her husband had disappeared in the Red Spring Mountains. Many thought that Blue Jay had never married again because she could not have children.

As the Hot Moon of June approached, most of the band moved to the Mother's Lake camp. Bow River's family stayed behind at

Pony Springs to wait for Star Flower's baby. Everyone knew that she was carrying Strong Horse's baby and, although no one mentioned his name, the people all knew that this baby would be the child of a hero. The women agreed that the strength of a baby boy within the band would be welcome, but a girl would be every bit as important in the women's minds. The women ruled the roost, for only they held the power to bring forth life.

Everyone knew that it was at the Pony Springs where the seed of Star Flower's baby had been planted. She seemed content to be back where she had been married. There she would have her baby, and another circle would be complete.

For the Utes, life was one circle after another. Returning to the Pony Springs completed the circle of their annual migration coinciding with the seasons. They understood that the circle of water drove the circle of the seasons, which drove the circle of life, from birth to death to birth again.

Light pink clouds layered above the eastern peaks the morning that Tom, Water Bird, and two other men saddled their horses. They were headed up an eastern fork of the Bunkara after whatever meat they could find. They were about to leave when Brooke ran up to her father. Her excitement was sweet.

"Papa, Star Flower's water broke last night, and she's starting to push the baby."

Tom shook his head in wonder for Star Flower and his daughter, who were learning the ways of motherhood from Ute mothers young and old.

Tom knew that if Brooke were in camp all day, she'd probably be right in the middle of the birthing. His first thought was that she was too young to see what might happen.

"Who's with her?"

"Her mother, of course. Blue Jay, Fat Cow and Green Willow are there, too."

Brooke frowned lightly and put her fists on her hips.

Tom had brought a child into the wilderness and now a year later, she was a young woman of fourteen with the fortitude of someone twice her age. He knew there was no way Brooke was going to miss the birth of her best friend's baby. She'd protected the baby's life once before on the icy banks of the big river. She felt invested in this child. Tom did too.

"I'll be fine Papa. Don't worry. I'll stay out of the way."

Tom rocked his jaw and looked at the men who waited. Water Bird tipped his head toward the trail.

"We'll be back this afternoon," Tom said, turning his horse up-trail as Brooke trotted toward the tipis.

The hunters found a few sheep in cliffs not far above the creek and shot four of them. The animals were hard to get down from the rocks, and it was late evening before the men came within sight of the village.

Brooke came running to meet her father before he dismounted.

"Father, we need you," she blurted.

"What's wrong?"

"It's Star Flower, Papa. Something's not right."

Tom dismounted and gripped her shoulder. "What's the problem?"

"The baby's not here, and she's been trying all day."

Tom looked up to the sky.

"They've been asking for you."

"Who has?"

"Everyone. Blue Jay has been with her all day. She keeps asking for you. Papa, she's nervous, I can tell. We all are, Papa, she's real hot."

Tom looked over at the tipi, knowing that Blue Jay would do all she could to protect Star Flower and her baby. But childbirth was risky, even under the best circumstances, and the odds for complications would be much higher out here. Tom felt emptiness in his gut, a feeling he'd known before when asked to do things he knew little about. He'd pulled bullets out of bodies, amputated limbs, even removed eyeballs. But he'd never delivered a baby. Calves, lambs, even colts, yes. A human being? Never.

Tom looked back at Brooke. Her eyes pleaded for help.

"Okay, let's go see."

Tom stooped into the tipi, and every head jerked his way.

Nearly a dozen women looked at him. Some of them welcomed him, and others didn't. None of them looked happy. Grandma Chuka called out orders in a harsh tone.

Blue Jay knelt by Star Flower, who rolled from side to side on a tall pile of furs and blankets. Her face was wet with tears, her hair soaked in sweat. Clusters of herbs, feathers, and burning sage filled the room. The smell of sweet smoke and sweat made Tom's head swim. He lifted a silent prayer. "Oh God, help us, please."

Blue Jay gestured fervently toward Tom, who felt an urgent weight settle on his shoulders.

"Brooke, I'm going to need your help," he said. The room went silent. Blue Jay knelt between Star Flower's legs.

Brooke squeezed in beside Blue Jay, who looked exhausted.

"Papa, they've tried all kinds of things. They had her standing and pushing on her side and her back. Nothing's helped. She's getting weaker."

"I know," he swallowed hard. "Have they seen the head yet?"

"Not yet."

Tom put his hand on Brooke's shoulder, and she turned his way. "I need you to go dig out my medical kit. Go into my gear. It's in the bottom of a pannier in a leather bag. Hurry! And bring the surgical basin too."

Brooke darted out the flap.

Star Flower groaned, and Tom moved next to Blue Jay with his hands held out to keep them from touching anything. He called for water and rags in a cobbled mix of English and Ute. Everyone scrambled to place what he needed within his reach. He looked at the blanket that covered Star Flower's lower body, and Blue Jay lifted it up so he could see where he had to go. Tom looked between Star Flower's legs just as Brooke broke through the flap with a bundle of gear.

"Got it, Papa."

"Put everything into a pan of water." Tom heard the tools hit a metal pan with a clank.

Brooke reached for a jug of water but froze when Grandma Chuka barked, "No, no, no."

She pointed to a pot of hot water that swirled with a mixture of herbs and leaves. Her voice was firm. When Tom met her scowl, she shot him a resolute nod. In triage, he had been taught that cold water staved off infection, but the women who stared back at him didn't agree. Blue Jay leaned to the side and rinsed her hands in the nearly scalding water before looking back at him. She gestured and urged him to follow her lead, so he dipped his hands in the steaming water and rubbed them together furiously. With his teeth he cleaned sheep's blood from under his fingernails.

"I need more light," Tom, said. "Light. Fire." He looked at Green Willow, who piled on more wood, and he felt the heat on his back as the room brightened. Star Flower threw her head back and arched against a push.

Tom stared across the room at a bundle of feathers tied to a sparkling rock, as his fingers felt inside Star Flower for anything that might be a baby's head. His eyes moved up across her belly, and between her breasts to her flared nostrils. Her face wrinkled, her lips curled, and Tom braced for her determined push. He watched the contraction rise through every muscle and felt it land at his hands. She gritted her teeth, biting her own lip to hold back the urge to scream — until she couldn't. Her searing screech split the sultry air. Her mother, Stone Calf, held Star Flower's shoulders down while Fat Cow patted the blood from her lip.

As Tom stared out across the room, he felt the slightest bump at his fingertips. It was there then gone. "Well, hello there," he said in a soft voice.

He closed his eyes and fought the urge to react, but he knew what he felt. A foot.

Star Flower arched and pushed and relaxed. A tiny foot pressed against his hand again; it should have been a little head leading the way out. The baby was upside down. He looked down at the dirt floor, trying to hide his heartache. Star Flower had pushed all day against a baby that wasn't coming out. He looked up across her belly and sought for words that could never convey everything he needed to say. As he slid his hand out, she heaved against the baby that he feared would never get a chance to run. He knelt on both knees and dipped his hands in the hot water again. This time, it turned pink with blood. Anxiety tightened his chest at the sight of blood and the chatter of the women, who noticed too. He knew that Star Flower couldn't push so hard much longer. The women had delivered breech babies before, but they couldn't get this one to turn. He couldn't either. They all looked to him for a miracle. How could he explain that the only option they might have to save the baby would almost certainly kill the mother? He rubbed his forehead with his forearm. He had nothing to offer, no hope, so he said nothing. The moment was still, but his relentless mind scoured his history for anything that might help.

"Papa," Brooke broke the silence. "What's wrong? What can we do?" Never had he considered having to hide his helplessness. He hadn't felt this kind of futility since the morning he'd felt Teresa's cold dead hand in his own. He rubbed his fingers across his lips. He couldn't speak. Worthless anger jabbed at his heart as he fought a hatred for the world.

Blue Jay laid her hand on his shoulder. She stared softly at the floor, looking too exhausted for emotion. Her eyes climbed to his and her clenched lips bent up slightly. Her look told him she'd been here before. She knew the situation inside Star Flower. Her hands had felt it too. How many times had she bowed to the weight of her world, surrendering to the circle of life and death? An accidental sigh escaped his chest as he looked up at Stone Calf.

Tom knew he had done all he could. At some point, he must concede. He wasn't a miracle worker. Despite the name the Utes had bestowed up upon him, and his reputation for saving lives, Turtle Wind had no special powers.

"Brooke, I can help her with the pain. In the bottom of that bag is a little bottle of laudanum. Let's try to get some under her tongue. Soak a little piece of leather and get it inside her cheek. It will take a little while to work."

Brooke moved quickly under watchful eyes then moved to put the pain medicine in Star Flower's mouth. Stone Calf stopped her with a hand across her daughter's lips.

Brooke tipped her head with pleading eyes, "Please, please," she said and touched a finger inside her own mouth.

Blue Jay spoke to Stone Calf. Tom didn't know what Blue Jay had said, but Stone Calf's shoulders settled, and she moved her hand from her daughter's mouth. When she nodded, Brooke placed the tincture between Star Flower's cheek and tongue.

The crack of the fire was all that broke the silence as all eyes wandered across the floor, searching for a miracle.

Pop! A black stone dagger pierced the tipi skin. People stumbled sidewise. Bow River cried out, and a scratchy voice answered back. A shudder went through the tipi as eyes shifted, then settled on the knife sticking through the hide. They all watched it wiggle as it slid slowly downward, splitting the taut hide.

The wrinkled hand that gripped the knife slid through the slit. Then an arm and a shoulder pushed their way in, followed by the head, then the body of a gray-haired old woman.

Brooke held on to her father.

Blue Jay said something in Ute.

Brooke repeated the words in a low tone then said, "Papa, it's The Woman Crow."

Tom looked at the old woman without speaking. He remembered her from the council lodge at Bear Dance. She had disappeared from there, and now he wondered where in the world she'd come from.

The Woman Crow's eyes darted around the room, before they settled into a stare directed at Star Flower. With the knife in one hand and a fist full of green, stringy tree moss in the other, she circled the room as if floating. Everyone bowed their heads and closed their eyes. Tom and Brooke watched and listened. A ragged chant filled the air as The Woman Crow moved around the space. Once, twice, three times she circled, then she stopped with a loud wail that made everyone jump. Tom peeked up just enough to see her standing over Fat Cow. The woman's cloudy black eyes shot across the room and caught him. He felt a different kind of fear creep down his throat. He looked at the floor and closed his eyes, listening to The Woman Crow's chant. Then the room fell silent.

Only the crackle of the tipi skin told of her departure. When Tom opened his eyes, her black stone knife lay at his knees and the Woman Crow was gone. He stared at the obsidian stone instrument that sparkled like broken glass. Wrapping his fingers around the handle, he felt the edge with his thumb. It split his skin with a mere touch, and he remembered how the obsidian knife had split the tipi skin as if it were cutting lard.

Across the room, Stone Calf, Fat Cow and Blue Jay huddled on their knees, talking intently face to face. Fat Cow stared at the split tipi skin through which The Woman Crow had disappeared.

Tom said his thought aloud: "The baby is still alive."

Fat Cow nodded her head, *yes*, and placed her hand on her belly. All eyes turned to Tom. He looked at Blue Jay, who placed her hand on her own lower belly and made a quick slicing motion up and down.

Wishing the scene were a dream, Tom was frozen in the dark moment. He felt Brooke twist and stare at the side of his face; it snapped him back. He looked at her and came back to the moment, slowing his racing mind. He hadn't seen Brooke's birth, but he remembered the first moment he'd seen her pink skin and the cranky look on her face.

A disbelieving huff jumped from his chest when he read the look on every face. Everyone knew the baby was alive and, if he didn't do something, both mother and baby would die. He knew that babies had been cut from their mothers and lived. A new emergency operation called a Caesarian section had made it possible to save some babies, but it was rare for a mother to survive the procedure. Tom looked at the women across from him. Their faces reflected a desperate desire for him to try something — anything. The glint of the stone knife caught his eye, and his mind shot to the sparkling blue eyes of a boy on an operating table during the war.

Here it was again. The war was still winding its way into his memory, wedging itself in the present. Just before he had cut off the boy's mangled leg, his blue eyes had been scalded with fear. Tom would never forget that look. Weeks later, hobbling on a crutch, the boy had stood up straight and saluted him. As their eyes locked, they'd shared a sparkle of relief and gratitude for what they both recognized as nothing short of a miracle.

He looked around the room again and locked eyes with every face. Some nodded. The trusting eyes of his adopted family looked back at him. What if this were Brooke lying before him? He couldn't imagine asking anyone else to do what he was considering. He looked at Star Flower's tranquil face, then up to the face of her mother, who watched over her with ardent hope.

He swallowed and felt his heart settle. He would try to save them both. He'd seen miracles before, and he had to reach for one now. He looked at Star Flower then back at Brooke, noticing the silver streaks around the edges of her irises.

"Brooke," he said in a calm tone. "I need everyone out of here except you, Blue Jay, Fat Cow, Stone Calf and Grandma Chuka. Help me get everyone else to leave," he said.

Brooke barked out names and words in Ute and waved her hands as if she were sweeping the room. All the bystanders turned and shuffled toward the door.

Brooke spoke to Stone Calf, who knelt with both hands resting on her daughter. Stone Calf looked up, wrapped a blanket around her shoulders and moved off to the side.

Brooke whispered to her father, "I told them that before Turtle Wind could work any magic, everyone but us had to leave." Brooke tipped her head to match his.

He exhaled and pulled his shirt off over his head. Kneeling over the pot of steaming water, he plunged his hands in up to the elbows, twisting at the heat. He held his hands in as long as he could before pulling them out. Then he plunged his hands back into the water and held them there as long as he could.

In another pan he placed knives, needles, and the obsidian knife. Then he pulled out the surgical basin and sunk it in the hot water. Grandma Chuka dropped more green tree moss into the steaming water. Tom looked up at her. She held his stare and nodded. He wondered again about the plants the women were using — and hoped he was right to trust their instructions to use hot water instead of cold. He would need every advantage he could get in these rugged conditions. Maybe if they'd used hot water in the field hospitals during the war, more men would have lived.

He fished out the basin and placed the needle, tweezers, and razor in the hot water. Here he was again with his tools of tragedy. How much pain these tools had caused and cured. Now he hoped, one more time, that these tools could save a life — or two. He stared at the seam where the pieces of the surgical pan were joined together, and in the crevice, something glittered gold. He didn't remember seeing it the last time he used the pan. But before he let himself ponder what it was and where it came from, Teresa came to mind.

How easy it had been when Brooke was a baby and his wife was in good health. Her death was still his hardest challenge. Every time he worked to save a life, it seemed he was trying to save Teresa all over again.

He carried his tools in the pan of water and knelt at Star Flower's side. Brooke knelt across from him, and Blue Jay and Fat Cow were to his right. Stone Calf moaned a chant beneath her breath. The room felt resolute and warm.

"Brooke, the laudanum is having its effect. Be ready to give her more when I say so."

"Yes sir."

Tom reached for the razor, but Fat Cow grabbed his arm and held out the obsidian knife instead. He laid down the razor, held out his hand, and Fat Cow placed the stone knife in his palm. All the women nodded their approval as he plunged the knife in the steaming water. He had no choice but to trust them again.

Everyone held their breath as Tom touched the obsidian knife to Star Flower's belly. Her tight brown skin split apart faster than expected, and streams of blood ran downward. Star Flower wailed, a bloody scream that sent shivers through the tipi. Fat Cow shook her bowed head at the curdling cry. Star Flower tried to sit up, but Grandma Chuka shuffled to her head and firmly held her shoulders down. Straining against the old woman's strong hands, she passed out cold.

Tom knew he'd have to work with speed and precision. He

knew a lot about human anatomy, but it was hard for him to tell where Star Flower ended and the baby began.

"Brooke, here, pinch this. Now this. Hold this back." Tom handed her wide tweezers, and she pulled Star Flower's belly skin back.

Through an eight-inch cut Tom squeezed his hands inside her. He gently but firmly pushed organs and tissue to the side, feeling for the baby. He couldn't see anything in the dark, bloody soup. There was too much blood. He gently pressed both hands downward and toward her spine. Then his hands felt something hard. The baby's head. He stared across the room at a bundle of eagle feathers and let his fingers crawl deeper. Those were shoulders, he was sure. Star Flower started to twist. He knew if she came to and struggled, they'd lose everything.

Tom's eyes shot to Grandma Chuka. "Hold her. I've got to stop the bleeding." With one hand, Tom grabbed tweezers from the basin and eased them down his wrist until he could use them to clamp a vessel, which he pulled upward.

"Brooke, you have to tie this off," he snapped. Brooke grabbed a string of tendon from the boiling water and tied a knot below the clamp. It slid right off.

Blue Jay stepped in, gripped the slippery string, and tied the vessel shut.

"Not too tight," Tom said. Blue Jay slowed down and pulled the knot snug.

Tom set aside the knife and examined the muscular sack. The uterus was just above the intestines at the level of the open cut on her belly.

"Hold this open for me," he barked to Brooke. "I need to make another cut."

His daughter froze.

"Brooke, now." Tom said, loud and firm.

In as calm a voice as he could manage, he said, "Brooke, I need you to muster your strength right now. Get down here and hold this incision open, so I can make the next one." He was breathing heavily. Brooke shook her head, overwhelmed by the gore.

Resolutely, Blue Jay stepped forward and kneeled next to Star Flower.

Blue Jay deftly slid her hands around the flesh sack that Tom had revealed in Star Flower's belly, holding the incision site open. An involuntary shudder ran through Brooke's body, as she watched Blue Jay establish a gentle but firm hold that made it possible for Tom to access the uterus.

Tom rinsed the stone knife in the scalding water, and Blue Jay nodded *yes*.

He took the knife, turned the blade up, and delicately poked the point into the uterus. He'd barely slid the knife an inch when a massive gush of watery red fluid sprayed upward. Everyone gasped and sputtered as blood splattered every face.

Tom shouted, "I can't see!"

Fat Cow wiped his face then mopped Blue-Jay's forehead.

A silent moment passed. Then Blue Jay took a deep breath, and Tom smoothly slid open a small slit. Slipping two fingers inside the uterus sack, he guided the knife forward. In one long, steady stroke he opened the uterus with surgical precision.

Something wiggled inside the sack. The baby must be alive.

Tom nodded to Fat Cow, who reached into the incision that Tom now held open.

Her left hand searched, then her right arm disappeared almost to the elbow. She worked her fingers behind the baby's head. Soon, an oval face poked up through the cut. A collective gasp was followed by wobbly exhales of disbelief. Fat Cow was about to lift the baby free when Blue Jay stopped her with a shout.

Fat Cow froze. The little face that had appeared was marred by a blueish tint. Blue Jay reached out and slid her fingers under the umbilical cord, which had wrapped itself around the baby's neck.

As soon as Blue Jay unwound the pulsating noose from the baby's throat, she tied a piece of sinew around it, grabbed the knife, and sliced the cord clean through with a single swipe. Tom watched as Fat Cow slipped her arms under the baby and lifted the tiny bundle into the world, then handed her to Blue Jay.

Tom let out a short gasp when Fat Calf reached back into the slick cavity of Star Flower's belly and carefully extracted a mass the size and shape of a liver. The placenta. Tom would never have thought to remove it. In a typical birth, the mother would push it free shortly after the baby was delivered. But this wasn't a typical birth.

The tiny girl lay in Blue Jay's arms. Too still for anyone's comfort.

Tom felt a hand on his back, and a finger dug into his skin. It was Stone Calf.

The only thing he knew to do was what he'd done before. Try to blow life into the helpless babe. He closed his eyes and as his lips neared the baby's mouth, a sharp squawk and a heel kick to his nose bounced his head back. Everyone gasped at the ball of baby that erupted with the squeal of a pup.

Every face was flushed with shock, and they glanced at each other, unsure of what came next. In unison they hollered with joy and grabbed for each other.

Blue Jay handed the baby to her grandmother, Stone Calf. The infant girl was alive, but her mother was in grave danger.

"What is it, Papa?" Brooke's voice rattled in her throat.

"She's losing too much blood. We need to stitch her up."

Star Flower's skin was waxy and turning blue.

"Here, quick, quick," Tom said, as Brooke helped him clamp down one blood vessel after another with the tweezers, so he could tie them off. With every knot, the bleeding slowed a little.

Green Willow poked through the flap with her week-old baby slung across her chest. Blue Jay motioned her in, and Stone Calf put Star Flower's baby to Green Willow's breast. The baby stopped crying and started to suck as the tipi went softly quiet.

Through the night, Blue Jay, Fat Cow and Stone Calf stitched Star Flower back together with elk sinew; there was no other choice. They sewed up her uterus like they were lacing a water sack, bringing her skin together with knots that were tiny and tight. A skill Tom knew he couldn't match.

Star Flower lay motionless for hours, and Tom worried that she might never wake up to recognize her baby or her family, but for now she still breathed. Brooke leaned into her father, and he rocked her in one arm, letting her sob like the baby in Stone Calf's arms.

Blue Jay hollered to the crowd outside, and the people rumbled with relief.

A dozen women crowded around Star Flower and clasped their hands together. Blue Jay and Fat Cow held Brooke's hands. They all rested their foreheads on Star Flower and spoke with their eyes closed. Together they said a prayer of thanks — and lifted a plea for protection of the new mother's life.

When Tom stepped out through the tipi flap, the crowd was gone. A single figure stood silhouetted against the gray dawn. Above him the morning star sparkled large. Tom walked up beside Bow River and gazed up. "*Tella-t-peke*," Bow River said and pointed at the star.

"Tella-t-peke?"

"Silver Star," a voice said from behind them.

The men turned to see Water Bird step forward. Beside him came Brooke. She turned and pointed toward the tipi where the new baby slept, "Tella-t-peke," she said.

Tom nodded. "Silver Star."

CHAPTER TWENTY-FIVE

The Silver Star Claim

▲ ▲ ▲

It was mid-June in the Flower Moon when Tom and Brooke climbed the hill above the Pony Spring. They hiked in the bottom of a wide gulch that angled to the southeast.

Two days before, across the valley, Tom dug at an outcropping that showed mixed deposits of lead and silver. He'd finished for the day and was packing gear when he noticed a pyramid of rocks. It had been stacked neatly at one time but now sloughed downhill. Saplings that grew up through the edge of the monument gave an indication of its age. He stood still and studied the stack of stones. He hesitated to concede that the pyramid was the corner monument of a prospect, but he suspected he wasn't the first person to dig at the outcropping. He fought through the brush and found two more corner markers. Forty feet from one corner, a blaze mark scarred a crooked spruce, which confirmed his notion of a predecessor. He scratched the hair at the edge of his hat. In the fourteen months he'd been in the mountains, he hadn't seen any evidence of prospecting.

A prospector, Corky Black, crossed his mind. While Tom had been working at an assay office in Denver, Corky had shown up at the door right at dark. Tom was trying to close for the day but agreed to work one more sample. That pouch of rocks proved to be the richest sample ever weighed by that office. When Tom was done, the covert prospector bought a couple of maps and headed out into the cold. The next morning Corky Black was found dead in his hotel room with nothing on him. Tom had to tell the undertaker the man's name. Corky Black was part of the mystery and allure that had drawn Tom to explore on his own. Based on Corky's maps, Tom guessed that his strike had been west of the Collegiate Peaks, and that was just where Tom and Brooke found themselves now.

On the south side of the valley and about a hundred feet higher in elevation, Tom pecked at a gray crease in a rock formation. Brooke leaned on a short shovel and half-heartedly watched her father dig. She'd helped him prospect a little before, but she'd never understood how he chose where to start digging. Now, she was beginning to recognize the gray stones with stripes of tarnished green that her father looked for. They had worked a couple of hours at four different spots and were starting the fifth when Tom stopped mid-swing with his pick held above his head. Brooke wasn't paying attention but, when she didn't hear the rhythmic knock of the pick, she looked up to see her father frozen as if staring at a snake.

"Papa, what is it?" Tom didn't answer. "Father, what's wrong?"

Tom slowly lowered the pick to his waist.

"Nothing's wrong," he said as he stared at the last scratch made by the pick. "Come here, Brooke."

She struggled up the slope in the shallow scree. Tom offered his arm. When she got close, Tom reached down with his hand and brushed away the loose dirt.

"Oh my," she said. "Is that silver?"

"Yes." A streak of silver sparkled against the dull gray rock that bound it.

"I'll be damned," Tom, said, "I've never seen silver like this. It looks nearly pure."

"Really, Papa, I've never seen raw silver." He looked up at his daughter as a wide smile puffed out his cheeks. Brooke ran her finger down the glistening streak.

"Usually, you don't see that shine until it's been poured into bars. This is called thread silver. I never saw raw ore like this at the assay office." Tom reached out and touched it again. "See how it disappears in two directions. This is the apex of the vein."

Tom looked up and down the slope for any sign of old diggings or monuments, any clue that someone else had discovered this ore. He didn't see anything out of the ordinary. Only the sound of a dog barking down in the Ute village broke the silence.

"So, what do we do Papa? Is this Ute silver?"

"Until the reservation is surveyed, there's no way to know." Tom looked up and down the slope again. "If this ore is on Ute land, Bow River and his family could be the richest people in the west." But in his gut, Tom knew that the government would never cede such valuable territory.

"We need to mark this spot, and I'll file on it when we get back to Denver." Tom took the shovel from Brooke and threw a scoop of dirt onto the silver streak. "If it's not on Ute land, anyone has a right to stake a claim."

"The land should be theirs," Brooke protested.

"We can't control the government's decision. What we can do is protect the interests of the Yellow Bear Band by staking the claim before someone else does."

Brooke looked as if she doubted her father's integrity for the first time in her young life.

Tom paused and looked down toward the village where tipi tops poked through aspens. "For now, we'll stake out three claims here, one on each side of this one." He studied the gravel slope dotted with shrubs and trees. "We'll need to name them all and get them measured."

It took most of the afternoon for them to build eight monuments that marked the corners of the claims. They were piling up the last rock marker when Brooke stopped and said, "I know what we should call the middle one."

"What?"

"Silver Star."

"Perfect," Tom said. "Perfect." He grabbed the pick and shovel, while Brooke packed the rock hammer in the bag and slung it across her shoulder.

The south side of the village was empty when they came off the slope. They could hear a commotion of voices and a dogfight coming from near the river. As they got closer, Tom could tell that something or someone was the center of attention. Voices were high and happy and, when Tom caught a glimpse of a wool hat, he knew someone new was in camp. Brooke squeezed between Blue Jay and Stone Calf. Tom followed.

At first sight there was no question that the ruckus was for the man in the middle. Tom recognized him quickly. The squirrel-tail ends of his mustache were longer than they'd been a year before, and his green beret was faded nearly gray. A big yellow dog and longhaired black one bounced around at his side. It was Mustache Bob, the prospector they'd met on the Twin Lakes Fork a year before. No one else could have a mustache so long that it swooped below his chin and got lost in his clothes. He was the man who had told them to watch out for the bears and make friends with the Utes.

When he spotted Brooke and Tom standing among the Ute his eyes widened and his bushy eyebrows jumped. "Well, looky here," he bellowed as a wide smile spread his mustache. He moved through the crowd and held out his hand for a shake. The Utes crowded around to see the meeting of the white men.

The yellow dog leaned his shoulder into Brooke's leg. She kneeled, and the overgrown pup lapped at her face. The kids jostled to pet the dog and laughed as Brooke got a tongue washing.

Bow River appeared with Water Bird at his side. Bow River walked up to Bob and grabbed his shoulders in both hands then said something that made Bob throw back his head in laughter. Bob shot back a rebuttal in Ute, and the entire crowd howled with laughter. After a kindly smack on the back from Mustache Bob, Bow River reached over and grabbed Tom's arm to pull him closer. He stood between the two men and introduced them with their Ute names. Tom as Turtle Wind, and Bob as Squirrel Face.

After the introductions, Bow River pulled up his sleeve to show the scars on his arm then pulled back his hair where the zig-zag stitches on his scalp were still pink. The noisy crowd grew quiet as everyone listened. When Bow River finished, Bob looked at Tom and nodded without speaking, then reached out and shook his hand again. When the gathering broke up and Bob headed down to the river to pitch his tent, he was followed by a couple of women and some kids.

It made sense to Tom that Bob would know the Yellow Bears and be friendly with them too. He had talked about the Utes and the rugged land where they lived when they'd met before. Tom remembered the winter boots with deer antler buttons he'd seen in Bob's tent on the Twin Lakes Fork. He quickly reasoned that it could have been Bob who'd staked the claims on the north side of the valley.

That evening the central fire was lit before the sun went down, and the dancing and singing carried on until the Big Dipper circled the North Star.

The next morning Bob was at Tom and Brooke's tipi when the sunlight reached the camp. He carried a pot of coffee and greeted them with an enthusiastic "Howdy!"

Bob was eager to hear how they'd managed to stick it out with the Utes for over a year.

It took all morning for Tom and Brooke to recount the adventure of the great circle they'd traveled. Starting with the bear attack, then summer camp, the death of Strong Horse, winter camp, to Bear Dance then back to Pony Springs and the birth of Silver Star. Bob could hardly believe what he heard, but Star Flower and her baby, Silver Star, were alive, which stood as a testament to their tale.

Bob explained that the year before he had waited on the Twin Lake Fork until mid-summer for his partner to return, but he never did. Bob had crossed the divide in late August and spent a few weeks in the headwaters of the Bunkara before he'd headed back to Denver for the winter.

"What about your partner?" Tom asked. "Did he ever show up?"

Bob shook his head and stared into the fire pit. "No," he said. "Never saw a whisker."

The three sat silently and watched the smoldering coals. Brooke looked to her father, who met her glance. Bob sat up straight, cleared his throat, and went on.

"My partner headed to Denver a year ago last fall, carrying some ore samples." Bob looked at Tom, who sat waiting for more. "They were good samples," Bob said, with a cocked eyebrow. "Damn good, we thought. I don't know what happened." He wagged his head at the fire pit. "Might have died or got killed, he'd have come back if he could. He wouldn't quit me." Bob's eyes flashed to Tom then back down. "I don't know, he just disappeared." Bob poked at the coals with a stick.

Tom understood Bob's partner had carried a sample, so they must have made a strike. Somewhere there was a claim.

"What about your strike, your claim, and the samples you sent to Denver?" Tom waited for an answer, but Bob just stared into the fire. Tom knew that prospectors could be tight lipped about their business.

"Did you ever find the samples or a record of the claim?" Tom asked directly.

Bob twisted his gaze toward Tom and took in a deep breath, "No, I never found the sample, and I checked every district office from here to Cripple Creek. The claims were never recorded. I never found our names nowhere, makes me think he never made it to Denver. I asked every old boy we knew. Not one of them had seen hide nor hair." Bob looked back to the fire and took a draw of coffee.

"He'd have snuck in and out of town as best he could, trying to keep our strike a secret. He was probably robbed and throwed in a river."

"Ah damn-it. Did someone else get the claim?" Tom had to ask.

"No-no," Bob's voice rose, "The hole is still there. I been thinking he might still show up. He found it you know, the good ore."

They all looked back into the dying coals of the fire.

"We came west together after the war," Bob said without looking up. "We fought together too, at Shiloh and Cedar Creek. He saved my ass — I mean neck — a couple of times." Bob glanced over at Brooke then back into the fire.

"Your partner, what was his name?"

Bob looked out across the camp toward his tent where his black mule stood fighting flies.

"Charles," he said. "He never liked that name. Charles. Charles Taylor Black."

Brooke's eyes darted to her father, who stared at the side of Bob's face.

Tom wasn't surprised by what he heard; he'd been figuring the facts the whole time. It all made sense, and the winter boots were the key that brought it all together. The same style boots that he and Brooke and every member of the tribe had worn all winter — and the same boots that had gone to the grave on Charles Taylor Black.

"Corky?" Tom asked flatly.

"You knew him?" Bob's head twisted, and a look of anxious surprise followed his narrowing eyes.

Tom nodded. Bob's jaw shifted side to side as he stared at Tom, waiting for more.

"I worked in the assay office of Madison and Howard, Denver, spring of '66 to the spring of '68. Corky Black came in November of '67." Tom paused. "Right at closing time."

"Well, I'll be goddamned," Bob blurted, twisting toward Tom. Brooke sat up straight.

"He came in right at dark. I was trying to close, but he convinced me to measure one more sample. He was courteous, and I could tell he was in pain, so I didn't want to send him away." Tom stared into the fire pit, grabbed a stick, and poked the ashes.

"Now, wait right there. You're telling me you met Corky Black. Shorter guy, thick black beard, black hat?" Bob's voice was sharp and sounded suspicious.

"Ute boots, horn buttons, rawhide soles," Tom added.

Bob scrunched his face and tipped his head.

"I could tell he was hurting," Tom said. "Couple of times he made a hissing sound. I thought it was maybe his back."

"His back was always hurting," Bob snarled. "But he kept digging and working, digging and working." Bob cut himself off. "Go on."

"I tested the sample, gave him the results, sold him some maps, and he left." Tom looked out across the camp then back at Bob. "I saw him again the next morning,"

"Yeah?"

"I saw him in the back of a wagon. Just his boots, but I knew it was him. I'd never seen boots like that before. He was in the undertaker's wagon."

"Oh, goddamn it!" Bob sighed and spit in the fire. "What the fu — what the hell happened?"

"I went to Harrison's Morgue that evening, and Mr. Harrison told me he died at Miller's Boarding House the night before."

"Why'd you go looking for him at the goddamn morgue?"

Tom stared back at Bob before he spoke. "Corky Black was the last man I spoke to that evening and nearly the first man I saw the next morning, and he was dead. I wanted to know what the hell happened. Corky Black brought in the richest gold sample I'd ever seen, and we both knew it. He trusted me with what I knew. He trusted I'd keep my mouth shut, which I have until right now."

Brooke reached over and put her hand on her father's shoulder.

"I went to that morgue," Bob said, "Spoke to a tall guy with a short-cropped beard. Said he'd never heard of a Charlie Black."

"Well, I told him his name was Corky, I didn't know it was Charles. Harrison should have recognized the name Black."

"Na," Bob said. "Didn't know nothin'."

"I told Harrison his name was Corky Black," Tom said, "I told him to put that on the cross."

"Cross?"

"The cross on his grave. I paid to bury him."

"Why'd you do that?"

"Harrison was just going to dump him in a hole if someone didn't claim him by the next day. I couldn't have that," Tom said. "If you'd have gone to the graveyard, you'd have found him."

"What about the ore?"

"Harrison said he found nothing on him, no name, no weight sheets, nothing, only a bag of clothes with empty pockets."

"So, he did get robbed." Bob's eyes bounced back and forth between Tom and Brooke.

"Harrison never said anything about a robbery," Tom replied, "Just said it might have been a heart attack."

"How'd you say that sample cooked?" Bob asked.

Tom waited a second before he answered. "It measured out very well. Eleven, eighteen, and forty. Gold, silver, and lead. Like I said, it was the richest sample I'd ever measured."

Tom felt badgered, and he knew why. He was the last known person to see Corky alive. He knew about the ore, and he knew what maps Corky had bought. Tom had used the knowledge of the maps to get pointed toward the west slope. And now here he was, sharing coffee with the dead man's partner two hundred miles from where the ordeal began. Tom knew that Bob was putting two and two together.

Tom thought that Corky would have hidden the sample and the weight sheet if he were staying at a boarding house. Unless he died before he could hide them. In that case, someone else probably got the ore and the papers.

For the first time, Tom wondered how Corky got to Denver. "What was Corky riding?"

"He had a sorrel mule," Bob replied. "Dark ears, white socks, called him Ted." Bob thought for a minute then said, "He had a burro too, light colored, gray and white."

"And you've never seen them again either, huh?"

"Nope," Bob said flatly as he stood up and stepped toward his tent. He turned back toward Tom and Brooke. "Well at least now I know for sure, he ain't never coming back. Thanks for burying him."

Tom could hear his anger and his pain as he walked away.

"Papa, it kind of seemed like … well—," Brooke started.

"I know," Tom spoke up. "I know what you're thinking. I felt it too. I was one of the last people to see Corky Black alive. I was the only one who knew about the gold, and I'm the only one who had a clue about where he might have found it."

"What do you mean, Papa?"

"I only know that Corky bought maps, showing where the Ute land would be once it was surveyed. Remember, I asked about Corky in Leadville and that store owner, Mr. Benson I think it was, said he remembered Corky coming through there in October, headed up from the south. It was just blind chance that we took the Lake Fork cutoff and met his partner."

"But Papa, does Bob think you had something to do with Mr. Black's death?

"Brooke, I don't know what he thinks, just that he knows I knew about the gold." Tom paused as he thought some more. "He's probably wondering how we found our way here."

"Yeah, but we still don't know where the gold came from. It may not be from anywhere around here."

"You're right, Brooke, but chances are, if Mustache Bob is in this neck of the woods, that gold is too."

They sat back down, and Tom thought of the last year. He hadn't panned any gold. Hadn't seen any shiny yellow lines that suggested the possibility. Then he remembered. In the seam of his surgical basin, he'd seen something gleaming. The night Silver Star was born, he must have spotted a little gold dust caught in the crevice of the pan. The birth had been so harrowing that he had forgotten that puzzling moment. Tom stood and marched off toward their tipi.

"What are you doing, Papa?"

"I've got to find something," he said, as he dipped under the tipi flap.

That was the last that Tom and Brooke saw of Bob and his dogs that day and the next day too, but his tent remained pitched down by the river, and two of his three mules were in the horse herd. It seemed he would be sticking around.

• • •

Each morning Tom checked in on Star Flower and the baby. Star Flower still lays in the same place where she'd given birth. The evening after Silver Star was born, Tom had been amazed to see her awake and smiling slightly. She was now nursing the baby and eating elk liver and blood soup with a little help from her mother and aunt.

Grandma Chuka spent time with her too. She burned small bundles of sage and bark that filled the tipi with a sweet smoke. Then she packed Star Flower's sutures with a poultice of leaves and rubbed speckled green grease across her belly. In two days, Tom could tell the stitches were healing surprisingly fast.

The third day after the birth, Star Flower developed a fever and drifted into delirium. She screamed and thrashed and had to be restrained to her bed by the strong arms of her family. The air inside her tipi was sweltering hot from the fire and the boiling water.

Tom knew Star Flower was in severe pain and nauseous too. He hadn't been able to get all the blood from her abdomen — and he could only pray that she would absorb the excess and fight the infection. Every day, the women reached out tender hands to coax any excess blood from her womb.

A steadfast stack of firewood sat outside the tipi flap. The women continually fed Star Flower concoctions of roots and leaves, but her face was rapidly growing thin. Her cheeks had begun to sink between her teeth, and her full lips were chapped and shrunken.

Tom had no idea of the science behind the remedies Grandma Chuka used, but they were the only options. Tom had assisted in successful operations before under difficult circumstances, but this procedure had been done almost on the ground with only buckskin and cedar bark to wipe and clean the wound. He wouldn't say it, but he doubted anyone could survive such a crude surgery.

Stone Calf kept watch on her daughter's milk, which continued to flow for the baby's hungry lips. The baby, Silver Star, would wake to eat then fall asleep in someone's arms. One day, when Blue Jay handed the baby to Brooke, she held it out like a pouch of water. Blue Jay stepped behind her and pulled the baby tight to her chest, where the baby nuzzled her face. Tom hated for Brooke to be a part of the misery that clung to Star Flower, but he couldn't keep her away. She'd flush and stamp her feet if he tried to stop her from being involved. He could see and feel the ordeal wearing on everyone close to Star Flower, including his daughter. She was only fourteen and living through adversity that most women would never know in a lifetime. He was glad when she was willing to go with him on excursions away from the camp. Her long periods of silence told him she carried a heavy weight for the people she had come to love like family, and it wrenched at Tom's gut, too.

By the coming of the Trout Moon in late June, most of the Yellow Bear band had moved to the Mother's Lake Camp. Only five lodges and Bob's tent remained at the Pony Springs.

It was ten days after the birth of Silver Star, and Star Flower hadn't moved for two days. She had grown stronger for the first few days after the birth but, since then Tom had seen nothing encouraging about her recovery. He marveled to himself that she was still alive. The fits of pain and rage had passed, and she'd gone deathly quiet. She responded to nothing, not even the touch of her baby at her nipples. Yet the baby, Silver Star, continued to grow stronger and more active every day, as if she were drawing her mother's life into her tiny frame. Her little squalls could be heard through the tipi hide, and her every whimper assured the camp of her beating heart. The first morning that Stone Calf, now a grandmother, carried the baby out into the light, her frail cries summoned all the creatures, wild and tame, to pass close by.

It was a still evening, just before dark. Golden clouds rested on lavender peaks, as Tom, his daughter, and Water Bird made their way to Star Flower's side.

Tom and Brooke followed Water Bird into the damp warmth of the lodge. Bow River and Stone Calf kneeled beside Star Flower's bed. Water Bird stood behind them. The baby slept silently at her mother's side. The round room was full of family and friends, including Mustache Bob.

Squatted next to Stone Calf was The Woman Crow, who'd appeared from nowhere. The ghostly shaman sat with her face down and awkwardly rocked.

Stone Calf looked at Tom and Brooke with cradled eyes on heavy cheeks and said nothing, but they knew to move closer and kneel.

The Woman Crow rose and crept around the lodge with a bundle of black feathers in one hand and a crooked staff in the other. She made a guttural chirping sound as she stalked the room. When she passed behind Tom she stopped and hovered over him, spreading her arms like wings, and swaying from side to side. Tom and Brooke stared forward and watched the fur blanket across Star Flower's chest rise and fall to the rhythm of the rattle. The Woman Crow circled the room, landed next to Stone Calf, and lowered her head.

Stone Calf shifted and reached out to cover the baby's arm with her hand. Brooke looked at Water Bird and could see that tears streaked his cheeks. When he saw Brooke looking at him, he made no move to hide his sadness.

Stone Calf's cry broke through the silence, as she leaned forward and buried her face in the fur blanket that covered her daughter. Star Flower's eminent passing weighed like black earth on every beat of every heart.

It was late in the night when Tom and Brooke left the lodge with some of the others. Brooke held Water Bird's gaze for a moment before they left.

Outside, Tom curled his arm around Brooke and pulled her tight as they walked back to their cold lodge below the starlit sky.

Hours later, Tom heard his name in his sleep. "Tom Gun!"

"Papa, it's Water Bird," Brooke said as she sat up in the dark.

He flipped the covers away and sat up.

"What's wrong, Papa?"

"I don't know."

They crawled through the flap and saw Water Bird silhouetted against the gray dawn. The morning star hovered over his shoulder.

"What is it?" Brooke asked her question in Ute.

Water Bird just said, "Come," then turned and headed away.

Tom and Brooke followed. As they neared Star Flower's lodge, it glowed gold from the fire inside. Voices volleyed back and forth.

Tom was bending down to go inside when Brooke slipped around him and slid under the flap. He heard her squeal before he was halfway in. When he saw his daughter's friend, his jaw dropped. Star Flower was sitting up with a haggard, but fully alive, look. She glanced down at the baby then back at Tom. Tom fell to his knees and crawled closer. The family laughed through swollen eyes and ragged breathing. Brooke scooted up to Star Flower, who started to cry again at the tears of her friend. Star Flower reached out a weak arm and hugged Brooke while everyone in the tipi rocked and wiggled with cheer.

Later that morning, after the bird choir sang, Blue Jay told Brooke and Tom the story of how Star Flower had suddenly sat up in the night as if she were awakening from a dream. How she had held her baby up, as if seeing her for the first time. How she'd cradled the baby's mouth to her breast.

Tom knew that Star Flower's fever had finally broken, but he didn't understand how or why.

Later that day, with Mustache Bob's help, Tom talked with Bow River and Good Bear. Neither of them knew when Woman Crow had left or where she had gone. They never did. They never knew when she would show up or where she would go. She wasn't Ute, and many said she was from the desert country far down the Rio Colorado.

As the four men stood at the river's edge, Bob translated for Bow River.

"Turtle Wind, again you have saved lives, and our family will carry on." Bow River extended his hand to Tom. "The Woman Crow drew in the power of the sun, and you, Turtle Wind, acted with courage to help deliver new life to the Yellow Bears."

Tom searched for the words to match his gratitude. But there were no tidings to express the respect he felt for these Ute men so, instead of using language, he pressed his palms together and gently bowed to each of them, in a gesture the Ute had not seen before but understood. The two chiefs brought their palms together and returned the bow.

CHAPTER TWENTY-SIX

Rose Creek Waterfall

▲ ▲ ▲

Water Bird and Brooke rode through the meadow east of the Pony Springs. The morning air was warm and buzzed with life. All that Brooke knew for sure was that she was going somewhere she had never been before.

Her father and the other men had left before daylight to hunt on the Hunter's Fork of the Bunkara. Brooke stayed in camp to work with Stone Calf and Blue Jay, but when Water Bird suggested that they take a ride, the women insisted she go.

Water Bird led the way along the river that bowed through the grassy flats. Near the upper end of the meadow, they tied the horses and climbed uphill beside a fast-flowing stream from the south.

The hike was steep, winding through tall spruce trees that clung to the rocky benches and moss-covered forest floor. Pink luminous flowers lined the stream with a showy ribbon of color.

Water Bird climbed ahead of Brooke and extended his hand to help her at every ledge. On each rise they were greeted with a greater display of crystal water, rich green forest, and pink bouquets. Water Bird watched with gratitude each wondering look that crossed Brooke's face.

At the edge of the stream Water Bird cupped a rosy flower in his hands and said something she couldn't quite understand, but she heard her name and sensed Water Bird's tender meaning. She tipped her head to the side, and her hair fell over her shoulder. With an adoring smile, she honored his pairing of the magnificent setting and her Ute name, Uckarth Pahniqwe Rose Creek. Brooke stared up the stream and felt a flutter inside her chest, knowing that Water Bird was reaching for her heart.

He stood up and bounded to the next level of rocks. His eyes were bright with happiness as he motioned for her to follow. With the grace of a buck, he leapt from rock to rock, and she followed his lead. Her excitement rang out in laughter, as perturbed squirrels barked at their intrusion. The sound of crashing water grew louder with every step they climbed.

Water Bird suddenly stopped and spun around. Brooke met the gaze of his round brown eyes. The tip of his nose was a finger width away. He turned slightly and she could see the spectacle he wished to show her. Her eyes widened as she took in the magnificent sight.

A silver waterfall as tall as the trees sliced a backdrop of stone, dotted with moss and flowers. The water fell straight as an arrow into a pool where it scattered in a spray of rainbow colors. The spray dampened her face. A small black bird skittered along the edge of the pool then disappeared.

Brooke licked the moisture on her lips and brought her eyes back to his waiting face. Without thinking, she took hold of his arm, which was damp to the touch. He looked down at her grip then back to her gaze.

As Water Bird's eyes slid closed, so did hers. As warm flesh touched her lips, a swirling sensation twisted inside her and spread in every direction. She felt the tip of his tongue, and a tickle bounced through her body like fireflies. Her head spun as her fingers dug harder into his arm.

She had never felt anything like this before, but she knew what it was. If she didn't control this feeling fast, she wouldn't. And if she waited any longer, she couldn't.

She hesitantly pressed his kiss away, let out a deep breath, then stared into his dark eyes.

Water Bird echoed her long breath, which made them giggle, but the waterfall swallowed every sound.

Brooke's eyes circled his chiseled cheeks, and for the first time she noticed the golden flecks deep in his eyes that held her tiny reflection. She loosened her grip but lingered a second, just for the touch. She licked her lips to discover a new taste that added to her thirst. As she released his arm her mind said, *run, run now*!

She lurched to the side with a short squeal and scrambled away, knowing he would follow. At the sound of his steps her heart raced, fueled by a tantalizing fear. Her laughter rattled as they darted through the woods like the lynx and the hare, with Brooke running from the man she so hoped would catch her.

She swerved around a giant tree, positioning its trunk between them. They sprang from side to side as he reached, and she dodged. They countered each other back and forth, back and forth, until their laughter and breath fell out of sync, and she stumbled to the ground on a mat of forest duff. He fell beside her, and they struggled to breathe through lingering laughter and spinning heads. Slowly the rhythm of their breath neared the rhythm of their hearts. They stared up through sprawling spruce arms at the cloudless sky. Their thoughts danced to a similar tune, separated only by a lack of words and their shared innocence. They let the touch of their sides say it all. Brooke could feel his warmth, and she knew he could feel hers too beneath their shared blanket of sunshine.

When Brooke awoke, she wasn't sure if she'd slept five minutes or an hour. Her heart raced as she felt his leg next to hers. He was stone still and breathing loud. They had fallen asleep.

She lay motionless, hesitant to move. Staring up through the trees, she felt the tingle of passion and smiled at the peace of being young and free.

CHAPTER TWENTY-SEVEN

The Older Brother

▲ ▲ ▲

Mustache Bob was absent for two days before he returned in the night. Tom figured he was prospecting because he had taken his dogs and mules.

After he returned, he came to see Tom, carrying a pot of coffee, which said one thing: he wanted to talk.

When they had visited before, Tom could feel Bob's suspicion about how and why he had wound up in this part of a vast wilderness.

Bob sat down and poured a couple of cups. "So, you worked for Maddison and Howard as an assayer, that right?"

"Yes, worked about two years." Tom answered.

"How'd you get out west?"

"Brooke's mother and I came from Ohio in '64. I was discharged. Union. Teresa, my wife, died not long after we got here. So, Brooke and I moved to Denver, and I took the job with the assay office."

"Where'd you fight?"

"I didn't fight. I was a surgeon's assistant in southern Ohio and Tennessee."

"You a doctor?"

"Not really," Tom said. "I've always just been thrown into doing what needed to be done, and I've learned a lot over the years."

Tom looked at Bob, whose gaze said *go on*. "I got out of West-ern Reserve College in '54," Tom said. "I studied engineering and geology. I guess because I was college-educated, the Army thought I could be a surgeon's helper. I wasn't a helper for long. After a little training, I had to jump in and do what I thought was right. Saved some, lost a few. A lot of them just kids."

Bob wagged his head. "Goddamn the war," he said. "I seen how you sewed up ol' Bow River." Bob downed a sip of coffee then sucked air across his teeth. "So, you come to Colorado for doctoring or for mining?"

"We actually came to farm," Tom said. "North of Denver. We lasted less than two years. We started just before Teresa got sick. She was gone in a couple months." Tom swallowed and glanced over at Brooke, who was cutting hides with Blue Jay. "It was hard on Brooke. Still is. Me too."

"Sorry," Bob said. "Guessing you didn't want to go back to Ohio?"

"No, no. Brooke and I moved into a house with a lady. She was a big help with Brooke, woman things you know." Tom looked at Bob who silently asked the obvious question. "No. We just rented from her. She cooked and cleaned. Other folks lived there too. Brooke was in school, and I got that job in spring of '66."

Tom scrunched his lips and exhaled heavily through his nose. Corky Black came to mind, and he knew that's where the conver-sation needed to go. His brush with Corky nagged at him, and the mystery was as maddening as it was confounding.

The two men fell silent. Tom glanced around the village, and Bob leaned over and stroked the yellow dog's head. Tom took a couple of deep breaths then launched into what he knew he had to say.

"You know, Bob, there are many reasons why I came out here into these mountains, and Corky Black's one of them. That rich sample, him dying — however it happened — I always wanted to explore out here."

Bob shifted his jaw.

"If Corky hadn't brought in that ore and died that night, I

don't know that I'd be here. The maps, the ore, the mystery was just enough to set me out. I never wanted to live in a town, work in an office. Hell, I wanted to be a farmer, a prospector, a builder."

Tom picked up a stick and poked at the coals. "I'm kind of a scientist. I really just want to explore."

Bob matched his grin. "Me too." They shared a short chuckle.

"So, let me get this straight," Bob said. "You came into the mountains following the clues Corky left, and you brought Brooke because she wouldn't let you go without her?"

"That's it."

"And a couple days after you met me, you bumped into Bow River and his son, who bumped into the bear?"

"Kind of. We bumped into the bear that took off and went after them. It took almost a week to get Bow River where he could ride. We were at the upper end of the flats when Loma and half a dozen other men caught us."

"Caught you?"

"Yeah, they snuck up on us at first to figure out what we were up to. Once they knew we were friendly, things were fine."

Tom looked over at the tipis. "Pretty soon, I realized that if we stayed with the band they'd lead us through the mountains, feed us, protect us. I could hunt ore and learn the reservation's boundaries, and the Utes wouldn't be any the wiser."

"How did that work out?" Bob asked.

"It got complicated. I got to know them, and they started to trust me. Even though I didn't deserve it. Now, I want more than anything to earn the trust they gave me. And keep it."

Blue Jay walked past and dipped into her tipi. Brooke's bold laugh rang out from a conversation with Stone Calf.

"I never thought of becoming some sort of a medicine man," Tom said, "Never thought Brooke would read to the kids and that they would tell her stories too. Truth is, I was ignorant — and prejudiced." Tom looked at Bob, who held both bushy eyebrows high.

"They're tough as steel, but that's not the whole story," Bob said. "They love and live and die just like the rest of us. Some people would say they love better and stronger, because their lives depend on taking care of each other — and their whole community. It's a different way of looking at the world."

Bow River stepped out of his lodge and tossed his hand in the air. Bob and Tom returned his gesture.

"They've taught me a lot, and there's nowhere I'd rather be," Tom said.

Bob chuckled and nodded his head slowly as he looked at the painted tipis scattered through the aspen trees. "Looky there," he said as Bow River held up a tipi flap. Out came Stone Calf, who held her daughter's arm as she stepped into the sunlight.

The baby, Silver Star, slept in Star Flower's arms. The new mother squinted against the sun she hadn't seen in nearly a month. When she finally noticed Tom and Bob watching her, she and her parents turned toward the men and beamed big smiles.

"I guess I better go check on my patient." Tom stood, stepped away, then turned back to Bob. "I never really told you I was sorry for you losing your partner, Charles, I mean Corky."

Bob folded his lips together, grabbed the coffee pot and stood up. "He was more than just a partner." He stepped away from the fire pit then turned back to Tom. "He was my brother." Bob walked toward his tent with a dog on each side.

CHAPTER TWENTY-EIGHT

A River of Horses

▲ ▲ ▲

Bob, Tom, Brooke, and Water Bird headed up the Bunkara River, riding four animals and leading two more, packed with enough gear for several days. They were destined for the headwaters of the river, the site of the bear attack.

Bob had reasons to go up-river, but he wouldn't be specific. He and his brother had prospected the headwaters. Tom suspected they'd found a vein to follow.

Tom was eager to return to the Bear Camp too, where he figured he'd picked up the gold he'd found in the surgical pan. Before the night of Silver Star's birth, he'd used the pan when he'd stitched Bow River back together. He'd washed the pan in river gravel, which is where he must have picked up the gold.

The sun was topping the divide when they left Pony Springs. Tom was on Timber, and Bob rode his black mule, affectionately called The Judy Mule.

Water Bird sat up straight in the spearhead position of the group. This was his first time to guide as the only Ute, and the others acknowledged his lead. A single eagle feather hung from his hair and dangled at his chest. He wore a beaded vest with bird designs. Around his neck hung the small pouch on a braided string. He rode Surrocco, the gray stud with apricot spots on his white rump patch. The big horse stepped out with a determined stride.

Behind him rode Brooke, dressed in a calico shirt and a pair of leggings sewn into pants. An owl feather hung from a white headband around the red hair that floated behind her. She rode her favorite filly, Smoke, a medium-sized horse with a quick and playful gate.

The filly was a frosted red roan with a plum-colored mane and maroon-red ears. Her sides were smoky gray with a lavender wash that ran up her neck and across her face. She was a yearling when Strong Horse had brought her into the mountains. Now, she was three and flaunted a coltish nature that reflected the spirit of the woman who rode her.

As Brooke rode up the trail that she'd ridden down a year before, she remembered that uncertain feeling of following those mystical Ute men into a mysterious land. And now a year later, at fourteen, she was fascinated by their world and feeling like she was part of it. Riding behind Water Bird she felt safe and free. Her father rode behind her, adding to her feelings of security. But knowing that Water Bird was looking out for her and would protect her, no matter what happened, gave her a warm feeling she couldn't quite describe.

Surrocco scurried up a rocky spot, and Water Bird twisted around to watch Brooke ascend. The smoke filly studied the steps and climbed with agile grace. Water Bird grinned and nodded. Brooke returned his approval with an unexpected giggle.

About midday Water Bird led them off trail to an area of ice caves and caverns. Tom understood the geology and explained the forces that had created the cave systems to Bob and Brooke.

While they explored the caves Water Bird slipped down to the river, where he sat cross-legged at the base of a waterfall. A mist of rainbow colors floated around him. When the others spotted him, they watched as a small black bird hopped in front of him and then dove into the river. Water Bird sat as still as the stones around him.

Brooke looked to her father, who stared wide eyed. Then she glanced at Bob, who cocked an eyebrow and reached under his hat to scratch his head.

Brooke slid down behind Water Bird and whispered his name. He remained motionless for a moment then turned to her with a soothing smile. When he turned back toward the river, something disappeared below the surface.

Water Bird stood up and returned to the horses where Tom and Bob waited.

They made it up-river to the old camp in early evening. The long days of late June provided them with a couple of hours before dark.

While Brooke and Water Bird looked around the old camp, Bob and Tom climbed a brushy avalanche chute on the south side of the creek. In a side draw, marked by short rocky bluffs, Bob pulled away a brush pile to reveal a trench cut into the hillside. It was fifteen feet long by eight feet deep at the farthest point.

A miner would know it as a "drift," and Tom had no doubt that Bob and his brother had dug it. Bob climbed to the back of the trench and quickly shoveled away the dirt that had sloughed into the cut. When Tom heard the shovel scrape solid rock, Bob snapped, "Come here."

Tom shuffled up the cut and looked over Bob's shoulder as he scraped away the last of the dirt with his fingernail.

"Look, looky here." Bob cranked his head around with a toothy smile. "Ye-he-he-he-ha!"

"Whew! That's it, huh?" It looked just like the ore that Corky had dumped onto the counter in the assay office.

Bob spun around and gave Tom a bear hug, rocking him back and forth. The men's feet were trapped in the narrow trench, and they toppled to the side where they lay, laughing at the sky.

That evening around the fire Bob explained how he and Corky had missed the gold strike the summer of sixty-six because they were working a site around the Pony Springs. That was when they'd met Bow River and the band. If they hadn't been stocked with plenty of coffee and sugar to share, things might have turned out differently.

"It was the fall of sixty-seven," Bob began. "We were headed out of the mountains when Corky panned the first gold down there in the creek. It took us nearly two weeks to find the vein in the avalanche chute, and by then the snow was piling up. We almost didn't make it over the divide with the stock and the dogs before the pass got snowed in. If we hadn't had those fur boots from the Utes, we'd have frozen our feet, and we'd both be bones by now. We killed a bunch of sheep for winter meat and set camp at the Twin Lakes. The plan was for Corky to take the sample on to Denver and, depending on how good it was, he would buy supplies and look for an investor. He thought he'd be back by Christmas. Then, maybe we'd head farther south for the winter. When he wasn't back by March, I knew something had happened. By May I'd given up most of my hope. I didn't come back here into the headwaters of the Bunkara until late summer, and I headed back to Denver in the fall of sixty-eight through the Red Cliff River, where we had a few claims."

They stared into the fire in a long silence.

"Did the Utes have any problem with you prospecting?" Tom asked.

"They never seemed to, just asked us not to build a cabin. So, we didn't."

"Did they have any interest in mining?"

"Not really. It didn't make any sense to them. They weren't going to dig like dogs or wash stream gravel, when what they wanted was horses, guns, food, and water. Maybe a little coffee and sugar and a good woman."

Tom just nodded and stared into the fire then glanced over at Brooke. Her hair stuck out from the top of a blanket that hadn't moved in a while.

Water Bird sat across from the men, leaning against a log. He seemed to be listening, but his eyes were half shut.

Tom pulled a fur blanket up around his neck and kept his feet toward the fire. Bob huffed a ragged snort and repositioned himself to the warmth. The dogs both lifted their heads then laid back down. The camp fell silent except for the rumbling river and a few fire pops.

The next morning, with help from Brooke and Water Bird, the men staked the original claim and laid out five more. Brooke took on the job of naming the claims. She named the original vein Corky's Strike. The others, she christened: The Foundation, The Recovery, Bad Bear, The Independent, and the Two Dogs. These six claims formed the foundation of the new company of Black and Dunagan Mining Interests.

They spent the afternoon on the sandbars and in the rivers panning for placer ore. When the third pan Bob shook produced a beaming thread of gold, he splashed and played in the water like a duck. Tom and Brooke joined him, whooping and slapping the water to celebrate the find.

Water Bird watched their odd behavior from the bank. He'd seen Brooke romp with the little children, but he had never seen this. This was different. He didn't understand how people could get so excited about a pan of rocks and water. A pan of raspberries and honey, maybe, but this made no sense.

When they noticed his confounded look, their wide smiles faded. They stood red-faced in the river, realizing that their rollicking must look bizarre to him.

Brooke locked eyes with Water Bird. He looked utterly bewildered. He was their leader, their guide. He deserved an explanation.

She turned to Bob then to her father. "We need to tell him. He needs to know what these tiny flecks of gold are worth."

Bob pulled at his mustache and stared down the river. Then he turned to Tom, who gave him a look that said he agreed with his daughter. Tom nodded, as Bob reached deep into a pocket and pulled free a leather pouch the size of a fist. He brought everyone around as he opened it.

"Oh. My. Gosh." Brooke's eyes widened.

Bob leaned the pouch toward the small group to reveal gold dust as dense as a stone.

Then he squeezed up close to Water Bird, so he could see into the bag. Water Bird glanced in and shrugged. Bob stepped closer, and Water Bird watched him reach into the bag and press a tiny pinch of gold between his fingers. He held it up and let it fall back into the bag.

"*Soo-ece chah-vah*, one horse," Bob said.

Water Bird's eyebrows ticked up. Bob reached into the bag again, filling the hollow of his palm with gold. After funneling it back into the sack, he held up his clenched fist and let his five fingers spring outward twice. "*Tompsoo-anie chah-vah*, ten horses."

Water Bird's eyes jumped wide, his mouth dropped open, and his head rocked back. Then, Water Bird cocked his head down to get a better look at the size of the pouch. His eyes asked the silent question. Bob understood and held the bag tight as he spread his arms wide indicating that the bag of gold could buy an entire herd of horses.

Water Bird studied the pouch of gold. He scowled then let out a short laugh, thinking they'd been teasing him. But their stone faces didn't smile. Brooke slowly nodded. They watched his eyes look down at the ground, then out to the water, as they all wondered: how much gold was in the river and how many horses could it buy? It was like a river of horses.

Water Bird's eyes came back to the pan that Tom held out to him. Taking the pan, he studied it, as if looking for holes. Then he looked over the rim and smiled. In a single motion, he bounced his eyebrows and tossed his head toward the river. The others were slow to understand his humor, but when he took a step and looked back, they got it and laughed out loud. Again, they were one step behind their leader. The four of them waded back into the river and started panning for gold.

A couple of weeks after the group returned to the Pony Springs, Blue Jay in the company of other women was combing Brooke's hair when she noticed that a sizable cluster had been cut from the back of her head. As a group the women stepped back from her with shocked looks across their faces. A wave of nervous chatter rippled through the group as their eyes darted around the dirt. They dithered to suggest that maybe a ghost had stolen her hair. Blue Jay regained her bearings first and suggested an avenger, probably an Arapahoe had stolen her hair to prove his fearlessness. Whoever or whatever had taken Brooke's hair, the theft was a show of power rather than an attempt on her life.

She begged them not to mention it to her father, who would insist on returning to Denver immediately if he found out.

Honoring her wish, the women hid the stubbly patch beneath a thick braid.

Brooke had felt so safe by the Bunkara, sleeping alongside her watchful father and her dear friend, Water Bird. How had an enemy breached their camp? It must have been someone so stealthy that even the dogs hadn't noticed the intruder.

Not long after they returned to the Pony Springs Camp, Tom surprised Bob with the sight of the nearly pure silver streak on the claim that Brooke had named the Silver Star. Bob had never seen silver that pure, and he was jubilant at the sight of the ore — but nervous too, knowing that a strike like that would create a flood of activity if anyone else should come across it. They named the two adjacent claims the Morning Star and the Silver Queen. Mustache Bob was a prospector. His business was to discover bearing ore, or placer, stake a claim and sell it to the highest bidder. He and his brother had made a living prospecting ever since they'd washed out of the Confederate Army and headed west in '63. Bob was now the sole owner of the claims that he and his brother owned on the eastern slope, and he could sell them as needed.

Tom was an engineer by education and a good one. At Western Reserve University, he had scored top in his class in engineering and geology. Now he owned claims, or at least he would once he returned to Denver and filed on them. He had a knowledgeable partner in Bob, who indicated he would remain a partner and not sell his interests unless he and Tom both agreed to it. Tom intended to take care of the paperwork and seek out capital. The men knew that their claims were only valid if they were outside of the reservation boundaries. Until those lines were designated, they intended to keep their claims a secret from other prospectors. Most Utes remained puzzled by their interest in rocks. The only stones they saw as valuable were the hard ones that could be fashioned into arrowheads and knives.

But Water Bird now knew that the flashy silver and gold-colored minerals in Ute territory could be traded for horse flesh, so he watched Tom and Bob closely — asking questions and passing on everything he learned to his people, who remained skeptical about the practicality of the endeavors of white men.

It was late July when Bob left the camp at Pony Springs. His plans were to go to the head of the Red Cliff River, a tributary that poured into the Bunkara about twenty miles downstream. As winter set in it would be easy for him to cross over and head to Breckenridge, then on to Denver where he would meet Tom.

The morning Bob struck out, everyone in the village was there to see him off. Bow River spoke to him for several minutes before he let the rest of the village say goodbye.

One of the women had his animals packed and ready to go just after daylight. She was the last one Bob spoke to before he rode away. The big yellow dog was reluctant to leave Brooke's side, but when Bob rode out of sight he hurried to catch up.

CHAPTER TWENTY-NINE

Gift of a Star

▲ ▲ ▲

The Trout Moon was waning toward the Hot Moon of late July when Bow River told everyone to go to the Mother's Lake. He, Stone Calf and Star Flower would stay at the Pony Springs, but he wanted Water Bird to go. The Black Eagles would be coming over the divide, and Bow River wanted them to be welcomed by as many people as possible. They would understand why he and his family had stayed at the Pony Springs.

Although Star Flower was stronger, she still had bouts of sickness that were remedied with concoctions and teas. Tom was skeptical of all Ute medicines at first, but the more he watched the results, the more he learned.

It was a clear afternoon when War Raven led the Black Eagles below the Brothers' Peaks and to the shores of the lake. The fanfare was grand with thundering drums and brightly painted people and horses. Good Bear, Loma, and Water Bird greeted the visitors with honor.

Brooke had withdrawn from Water Bird after the day at the waterfall. Her cramps had begun the next morning, so she'd been restricted to the menstrual hut for nearly a week. Although her stay in the hut was uncomfortable, she tried to use the imposed distance to temper her feelings for Water Bird — hoping that the brief separation would put a damper on his feelings too. But her coolness did little to deter him. He hung close and brought her water. He sat outside the hut and talked to her through the poles until Star Flower or Blue Jay shooed him away. Day after day, he persisted. It wasn't that she didn't want to be around him, but rather that she knew she needed to be careful around him. The feelings that had washed over her at the waterfall had been strong and confusing.

Blue Jay and Star Flower didn't make it any easier by repeatedly telling her that she was plenty old enough to get married. Whenever they nudged or teased her about it, Brooke laughed out loud or scurried away. There were simply too many factors working against the pairing of a white woman with a Ute man for her to seriously entertain the notion of a romance with Water Bird.

Brooke still dreamed of going to the same college as her mother, who had graduated with honors and had been active in the women's suffrage and abolitionist movements. Women faced a lopsided situation with men holding most of the power, and the treatment of black people was deplorable. But any rights, let alone equal rights, for Utes or any other tribes, were never discussed. Instead of inviting the native peoples to join other Americans in building a nation together, the government's approach was to corral them on reservations and let them learn how to feed themselves — or die trying.

Most whites in Colorado were in favor of eliminating the Ute and Arapaho people by whatever means necessary. Back in Denver, whenever her father had spoken up about the inalienable rights of those who first inhabited this land, he'd been criticized and threatened or mocked and dismissed.

Even though Brooke was young, she knew she could not allow herself to fall in love with a Ute man. Not because of the difficulties it would cause her, but for the hatred and fury that would be aimed at Water Bird if he "dared" to marry a white woman. Black men had been hanged for far less. Even the slightest misconstrued gesture toward a white woman spelled trouble, and she had no doubt the same fate awaited Water Bird if she allowed a relationship to develop.

Brooke's heart swelled every time she saw or spoke with Water Bird, but she convinced herself that what she was feeling wasn't romantic love. To control her confounded feelings, she needed to keep more distance from him.

The Utes didn't know that her father was making plans to return to Denver in the fall. In about three months they would be on their way back. She knew that she could skirt Water Bird's advances until then. If she kept him at bay but didn't push him away, she could manage her feelings until she escaped back to civilization. Back in Denver, she could finish school and attend college in Ohio. Surely, over time she would forget Water Bird. And he would forget her.

* * *

The Ute summer rendezvous included games and horse racing for the men and trading gossip and goods for the women. In the morning hours the young men, and some girls, hunted. Afterward, they rested until the evening fires were lit. Most girls helped their mothers until chores were done, then they rested or gathered in groups. When the moon was big the young hunters would be out all night, stalking deer, elk, and sheep.

The younger adults and children played and mingled together too. They reenacted the lives of their parents, celebrating hunts, horses, and war games. They built lean-tos and huts and made rafts that they floated in the shallows of the lake. The little children played morning and night until they were too tired to play anymore. At night there were feasts of fresh meat and berries, and afterwards the drums and dancing went on until dawn.

* * *

The little boy, Cricket, had found Brooke soon after they arrived, and he was never shy to seek her out. She was always kind and accepted the gifts he brought her. Each time, she'd offer a snip of her hair to add to his collection.

Brooke saw the girl, Blue Water, approach Water Bird as soon as her family group arrived in the camp. As Blue Water came toward him, Water Bird searched the crowd for Brooke before turning to greet Blue Water.

Brooke thought she looked more beautiful each time she saw her. Her prominent cheekbones and full lips gave her face an angelic appeal, and her rounded figure was distinctive among the Ute people. Someday, she told herself, Blue Water and Water Bird would marry. She knew that plans for a wedding might already be in place if she and her father hadn't been traveling with the Yellow Bears, but she couldn't deny the pang of jealously roused by imagining the life that Blue Water and Water Bird would likely have together.

It was the third afternoon of the summer gathering when Brooke and a group of girls gathered at the edge of the lake. Brooke and Sah-seet were weaving grass mats while other girls were beading clothes and tending babies.

Water Bird and several boys sat nearby working on gear and talking.

Cricket and two other young boys floated in the shallows on three logs tied together. Other younger boys romped in the water, vying for attention from the girls, which clearly annoyed the older boys.

Blue Water was decorating a leather bag with colored Porcupine quills, looking up at Brooke periodically as she talked to her friends. Her glances were pleasant but persistent and made Brooke uneasy.

Suddenly, Blue Water set the bag to one side and came over and sat on the log next to Brooke. Her friends followed close behind her. Blue Water spoke at a nervous pace, but when she realized that Brooke didn't understand, she slowed down and used her hands alongside her words. It took a while for Brooke to realize that Blue Water wanted to see what was around her neck. Brooke caught the word, *Poo-cheeve,* star, and knew that all the girls wanted to see her crystal star necklace. Brooke had forgotten she was still wearing it. Slipping it over her head, she held it out for Blue Water to see. Sunlight caught the glass, and it sparkled with a pinkish hue. A cheerful chatter rippled through the girls. The boys moved closer and marveled too. Water Bird squinted as his eyes shifted between the girls.

It felt good to be with Blue Water and her friends, who were all a similar age and smiling. Star Flower had always provided a level of security, but she wasn't around as much now that she was a mother, and it was difficult for Brooke to communicate without her. Brooke coaxed Blue Water closer and held the necklace across open fingers. She tipped her chin down and her new friend did too, then Brooke lifted Blue Water's long black hair and settled the necklace around her throat. Blue Water looked up with a bedazzled grin, and Brooke nodded.

• • •

Water Bird was the first to look toward the screeching sound that came from the peaks that cradled the lake. The others noticed his look and listened too. In the big village odd noises were common, but this one had the rattle of panic.

Down the shoreline the little girl, Sah-wof, stared across the lake. Suddenly, she jumped and squealed in a voice flooded with panic.

Near the middle of the lake floated logs, the logs that Cricket and his friends had tied together. An arm waved above the water, but no one was on the raft.

Water Bird sprang into action and splashed across the shallows, running for the south shore. As he ran, he stripped down to his loin cloth. He hit the rockslide that bordered the lake and never slowed down. He leapt across the giant rocks like a lion.

He knew the cold water could suck the life out of a man — and little boys had only half a chance of surviving. He launched himself like an arrow and pierced the water. When he came up his arms churned in a race to the raft. Two other boys hit the water behind him and labored toward the logs.

People came running from the village. Men and women

launched rafts that they paddled and pushed through the shallows.

Water Bird's hand slapped the slippery logs where two boys cried and shivered. One tried to speak, but his words were choppy. Water Bird held the raft with one arm and flung the boys, one at a time, onto the logs just as the other rescuers reached the raft. They bobbed along the side to steady the logs.

The older boys snapped at each other like wolves and argued about how many kids had been on the raft. One of the little boys mumbled something, and Water Bird questioned him hard until he finally uttered, "Ah-choo-pits." Cricket.

Water Bird rolled his eyes, emptied his lungs, flipped over, and disappeared downward into the dark water.

Water Bird sank like a stone as the water scratched his eyes and the wetness felt like ice. Powerful strokes drove him down, searching for any hint of a little body. His lungs reared against his ribs for air, the painful cold and the burning eruption inside his chest sent his mind reeling.

He began to lose the strength that drove him on. Everything stalled as the cold wrapped around him. A speck of his mind floated in blackness where everything was missing, his arms, his legs, his breath, his life.

What brushed across his face was coarse as a horse tail and slick as a snake. A brown swirl spun around him then slowly slithered closer. Lilting whiskers floated around the otter's face. Round, black eyes looked back at him with a daring gaze. A flash of color darted between them as Grandfather Trout settled in next to Otter.

Water Bird wasn't cold anymore, nor was his body racked with pain. He floated in the growing warmth of his totems and waited.

From out of the depths, the sacred bird, Wah-we-chitch, shot upward and grazed the tip of his nose. His head flopped back, and he stared upward toward the light. Falling toward him was the bundle of papoose leather he'd been looking for. He had no question about what to do, and he did not hesitate to do it. With a powerful thrust Water Bird shot upward and grabbed the bundle in one arm as he stretched for the surface with the other. The higher he swam the colder it got. The aching in his body spread with every stroke. When he broke the surface, he was next to another raft. The men onboard struggled to stay on top when Water Bird flopped Cricket's body onto the raft and crawled aboard himself.

As the men paddled the cumbersome raft toward the north shore, Water Bird flipped the boy's body face-up.

On the banks of the frozen Bunkara he'd seen Brooke's father, Turtle Wind, push water out and blow air into Strong Horse, and he knew he had to do the same. The little boy's body was tiny compared to Strong Horse's, but he had to try.

With his knees straddling the boy's hips, he placed his hands on his belly and shoved quickly. Water shot from the boy's mouth, and the men on the raft slipped and stumbled around. Again, he shoved the boy's chest and water shot out. Water Bird pinched the boy's little nose and pressed his lips to the boy's cold mouth, blowing in a blast of air. He repeated the belly push again and again, but nothing more came out.

The men on the raft jumped off in the shallow and pulled on the logs. Water Bird scooped up the boy, waded to the shore, and laid him on the sand. With another push more water oozed out. He waited and watched, but the little body didn't move. He could hear voices and screaming coming his way. Within seconds a crowd had gathered. Miketta, the boy's mother, broke through and grabbed at her son. Water Bird screamed for her to get back, and two men pulled her away. She fought like a dog on a rope.

Again, Water Bird blew into the little mouth and pushed at Cricket's stomach, but nothing happened.

"Ah-choo-pits! Cricket!" He blew air into the boy again.

Tom slid in on his knees. Water Bird went back to work. Here they were again with a drowned friend, a loved one, and nothing but hope on their side.

With a mouth full of air, Water Bird moved his mouth back to the boy's lips and saw his eyes roll back. The little body cramped and vomited up water in Water Bird's face. Yelling through a half smile and burning eyes, Water Bird wiped his hand across his face and grabbed Cricket's mouth, forcing in another blast of air. The little boy's arms flailed as Water Bird pumped out another gush of water and vomit. The little boy gagged to breathe, but he was breathing.

The crowd that had stumbled backward snooped closer. Their mouths hung open, and their eyes bulged as if they were seeing a ghost. They covered their mouths and looked at each other, unsure whether to cheer or run.

Miketta stood spellbound for a second then threw herself on the child and bawled.

Good Bear stepped up, bent to his knees, and grabbed Miketta's shoulders as she shook with sobs.

Tom sat on a log then gestured to Water Bird to bring the boy over, laid him across his knees, and push on his back again. Cricket cried out and belched more water. Tom felt hands on his back and turned to see Brooke's red, watery eyes staring down at the boy.

The boy's father, Annico, broke through the circle just as Tom was helping Cricket stand up on wobbly legs. Annico, scooped up his son, and Miketta wrapped her arms around them both. The crowd squeezed in and locked arms while mothers and fathers, children and strangers cried and sighed together.

That evening the drumming continued late into the night. The Brothers' Peaks stood stark against the sky as families made their way to the big fire pit on the bank of the lake.

People visited more than they danced, and everyone young and old was talking about the miraculous return of Ah-choo-pits.

Some thought it was magic. Some knew it was the work of Si-nawav. Others wouldn't say what they believed. They knew only that Tom Gun, Turtle Wind, had the power to blow life into the dead. Now everyone had seen Water Bird do the same.

When Miketta and Annico walked down the path, the entire party cheered, whooping and hollering as the drums rolled heavy. Cricket hooked one arm around his father's neck and held on tight. Children, teenagers, and old folks hurried up to tap Cricket's arms and legs. They all wanted to touch the boy who'd been to the land of the endless spring — and back.

When Cricket saw Brooke coming his way, he leaned into his dad and smiled.

Brooke stepped up, rubbed his leg, and spoke in Ute. "Cricket, it is wonderful to see your big smile. Thank you for coming back."

They all turned and headed down the path toward the fires that glowed golden across the surface of the lake.

Brooke walked to the edge of the water and marveled at the reflection of the Brothers' Peaks across the glass flat surface of the lake. She sucked in a slight gasp when she reached for the glass star string around her neck that wasn't there. Her mind circled back to the moment she had slipped the necklace around Blue Water's neck, just before the panicked alarm that the boys were in trouble on the lake. She realized her kind gesture toward Blue Water was now a gift, a gift of a star.

On a rocky point high above the rumbling drums sat Water Bird. Hidden in darkness he waited for his totems, wondering why they came only when he was at the edge of death. He knew his totems were mind made, they showed up like a dream yet were a guiding force in his life. There was so much he didn't know. But he knew the path that had led to today. If Turtle Wind and Rose Creek had not come to his homeland, his father would most likely be dead. He would never have seen Strong Horse come back, never have heard his words — and he would never have known how to bring Cricket back.

CHAPTER THIRTY

Medicine Circle

▲ ▲ ▲

It was the start of the Fall Moon when the clan gathered the horse herd and loaded the travois for the trip to Yampa Pagosa and then on to Winter Camp.

The first camp downriver from The Pony Springs was the Blue Creek Camp, where the people would find the first of the rich pinon nuts that they so needed.

The second day at Blue Creek a group of hunters returned from the south. Soon after, the village was in an uproar. The hunters were flushed with fright nearing panic. They sputtered as they explained what they'd seen. The more they spoke the more excited they got, and their tension agitated the village.

Tom moved in closer to the ruckus as people went running past him back into their lodges.

Brooke caught up to her father and tugged at his arm. "What is it, Papa?"

"I'm not sure. You understand Ute better than I do."

The commotion was such that Tom began to fear the worst. Enemy tribes, or maybe soldiers were coming.

"Water Bird!" Brooke yelled when she saw him heading toward the horse herd.

"What is it?" She grabbed his arm and changed the question into Ute words.

"*Ah-roo pitch,*" he answered. "

"Ah-roo pitch?" She tried to remember the word. She knew she had heard it before, but when? Then she remembered. At the Yampa Pagosa, Water Bird refused to take her up the river into the canyon. He wouldn't go any farther for fear of ah-roo pitch, ghosts.

Water Bird waved his arms to the south, where the hunters were, spitting out the explanation.

"What did he say?" Tom asked.

"They saw the ghost of Strong Horse on Heart Mountain," Brooke told her father. Bow River was headed their way. Behind him was Star Flower with her baby in her arms. She was breathing hard.

"What's this news?" Star Flower caught her father, and they stopped alongside Tom and Brooke.

"Who said they saw my husband?" Star Flower demanded an answer from her brother. He told her what the men had seen. Star Flower's face wrinkled in bewilderment then crept to rage.

"No. Ah-roo pitch!" she screamed.

Bow River reached for her as she spun and struck his shoulder. Stone Calf threw her arms around Star Flower and kept her from falling to the ground. She bawled and wilted in pain. Her jostled baby cried too. The two women rocked side to side and, when Stone Calf could hold her no longer, they sank to their knees.

When Stone Calf led Star Flower away, Blue Jay carried the baby. The men and women left behind stood frozen.

Brooke could feel her heavy breath across her lips. She looked at her father and the other helpless people. In that moment she saw the Ute people as vulnerable for the first time. They couldn't explain what they'd seen, and they were frightened.

The group broke up and Water Bird walked with Tom and Brooke to the entrance of their lodge then turned and disappeared without speaking.

That evening the village was quiet as everyone stayed inside.

The next morning in bright sunlight a council was called, and the entire village met around a fire pit.

Bow River, Good Bear, and Loma sat together and everyone

else circled around them, waiting for the hunters to explain what they had seen on Heart Mountain. They didn't want to talk but, as they started to, they glanced repeatedly to the south. The men had been riding through the brush up Sow Paw Creek toward the base of Heart Mountain. Just before they reached the aspen trees, they looked on the center peak and could see Strong Horse in the cliffs. Questions bounced through the crowd, and the men explained that it was his face that they could see. Elders in the group mumbled back and forth, and Wolf Song asked more questions.

One of the hunters explained that the rock face of Strong Horse watched them as they turned and rode hard for camp. The ghost watched them until they disappeared into the canyon and even out of sight. They could feel him looking at them.

When Strong Horse died, his body was kept away from the springs at Yampa Pagosa for fear that his spirit would haunt the warm caves. Instead, his stiff corpse had been hauled up the arduous trails to the Hanging Lake to be interred with the other spirits. Now it seemed he was haunting the slopes of Heart Mountain instead of the chasms of Ghost Canyon.

After everyone listened to the stories the three chiefs huddled and discussed while the rest of the village waited. When they came to an agreement, Bow River announced that he and some other men would go see for themselves. Anyone else who wanted to go would not be forbidden.

Curiosity overpowered fear as nearly everyone in the village followed the contingent of men who headed up Sow Paw Creek.

A string of riders wound their way through the colored brush of the lower hills. Behind them many older people followed on foot. Some were towed on travois.

The men who had discovered the sight the day before rode behind the chiefs. Tom and Brooke rode in that group. When they topped a rise and the peaks came into view, the trio from the day before yelled and whooped and galloped their horses back down the trail.

At first Tom didn't see what the others saw, but he could see

Bow River's face drop. The men made the horses so nervous that they pranced underneath their riders.

Tom and Brooke rode up next to Bow River and Water Bird. When Tom made out the strong features of a man on the center peak, he was shocked by the resemblance to Strong Horse.

It was late in the Fruit Moon of early October, and Heart Mountain cut a sharp silhouette against the blue sky. The tops of the gray peaks and the north slopes were dusted white. The face of a man stared down at the valley from the hollow of the center peak on a rocky slope dusted with snow.

An assemblage of rocks, snow and shadows created the image. But why had it appeared now? Tom reasoned it was caused by a combination of snowfall and snowmelt that didn't happen every year, every decade, or maybe every century. Tom knew what it was physically, but he had no explanation for the timing or the resemblance to Strong Horse. All his reasoning would hold little water with the Yellow Bears. Anyway, he couldn't even convince himself that pure logic could explain away the phenomenon.

As the rest of the band came within view of the face, some people hid. Others fell to their knees and chanted in prayer. All the men dismounted and went into council, seated around the chiefs and elders. Tom sat with the other men, elbows on knees, pondering the sight.

When Tom was asked for his understanding, he offered that, in his mind, Strong Horse still lived in the features of this valley.

"Sinawav created all of this," Tom said.

"Sinawav created all of this: the mountains, rocks, forest, ice, and snow. He created us too," Tom waved his hand in a circle to include everyone around. The men tipped their heads and studied him. He reached down and pinched dirt between his fingers then let it drift in the breeze.

"He created us from earth, water, wind, and fire. When we pass on to the land of the endless spring we are still made of earth, water, wind, and fire."

The Sunday lessons of Tom's past were coming forward, and they suddenly seemed to make more sense than they ever had before.

"Sinawav works in strange and mysterious ways within the realm of Mother Earth and Father Sky. Nothing ever really leaves the earth. Instead, it travels in the great circle of life to help bring back new life. Like the grass that rots into dirt to give birth to flowers. And the circle of life continues." Tom looked up at the rock and ice sculpture that showed the wrinkle of a smile, and he remembered the last smile of Strong Horse's life. Tom looked at the faces around him. "Remember, my friends, Strong Horse passed over to the land of the endless spring and returned. And what did he whisper to you?" Tom pointed his finger at Water Bird.

No one knew what Strong Horse had said to Water Bird with his last breath, and Tom and everyone else wanted to know. Water Bird looked side to side at every man and woman. They all hung on his words.

He looked up at the face on the peak and said: "The circle of life is the river that runs through the land of the endless spring. Nothing begins and nothing ends. The river runs on forever."

Everyone sat stone still and stared at the young man. His words curled through Tom's mind, and he marveled that Strong Horse must have known he was about to pass on. In that moment he believed for himself that Strong Horse had crossed over the river — and had come back to impart wisdom and hope to his people, himself included.

Bow River pointed to the face on the mountain. "This is not the ghost of our fallen brother, this is Sinawav, this is big medicine. Let this face remind us of the great power of Sinawav and how his wisdom is for all people."

The next morning Star Flower asked Brooke to go with her and her mother to see the stone face of Strong Horse. Brooke, Stone Calf, and Blue Jay rode up the trail toward the point where the others had been the day before. Star Flower led the way, and most of the women of the village — and many of the men — followed. She wore her white doeskin dress and carried her baby in a cradleboard painted light yellow with beads and ribbons to match.

Bear scat was scattered through the oak brush and a sow bear and cub climbed up on a rocky point to watch the riders before disappearing.

The women sat on the point while the men laid out a large circle of stones around them. The little hill was now a sacred sight protected with a medicine circle.

Star Flower cradled her six-month-old baby while all the women from grandmas to little girls sang songs and shook rattles. Brooke sat in the circle too, with Green Willow and her baby on one side and Sah-seet on the other.

Star Flower stood up and held Silver Star out toward the face of Strong Horse, her father, so that he could see his little girl. As she stood holding the baby, the women snuggled around her and placed their hands on Silver Star. Then, together, they sang.

Tom and the men stood back and watched.

When the women's arms came down, they turned around, and every face was shiny with tears.

As the line of riders rode down the trail, everyone twisted to look back at Strong Horse, who watched them go.

CHAPTER THIRTY-ONE

War Club

▲ ▲ ▲

The cottonwoods were yellow as the clan moved downriver from Blue Creek. Heading west of Heart Mountain, they passed the powerful stone face of Strong Horse. The camp had grown quiet over those days, as the mystery of their short-lived leader had confounded everyone.

The day after they reached the Fat Berry Camp, riders came in from the north and brought news that the White River Agency had been built. The agency's headman sent word that he wanted the Utes to come there for the winter. Those who did would receive rations and presents. The lure of sugar, coffee, and flour was enticing, but the Yellow Bears had heard this before. The riders headed south up the Snow Stone River to carry the message to the Black Eagle and Red Springs bands.

Bow River thought they had enough food for the winter but still planned to hunt the big elk herds that wintered along the Bunkara. He knew that some of the people would want to make the trip to White River for the presents and maybe the rations too. It was a new agency in a new place under a new treaty. Maybe the new policies would be more honest.

After a few days at the Fat Berry Camp, where the women scrounged with the bears for acorns and cherries, Bow River decided it was time to head for Yampa Pagosa.

Tom knew that in due time he'd tell Bow River that he and Brooke would be heading back to Denver after their stay at the hot springs.

From camp Tom could see the eagle's nest that marked the traditional river crossing, farther down the Bunkara. He knew that the clan would find a new crossing to avoid coming close to where Strong Horse had died. A new crossing would be more treacherous but worth the risk to the tribe.

Bow River asked Tom to go to the river and help look for a new crossing. Tom was pleased that Bow River trusted him to help in such matters.

The men gathered at the riverbank and most of them went upstream, but Tom and Water Bird headed down. As they neared the old crossing at the eagle's nest, Water Bird rode on a terrace several hundred yards away from the river.

Tom stayed close to the river and came into a group of trees where there were still large ash piles from the fires a year before, where wet, freezing men had struggled to survive. Without stopping, he rode past the pits where they had burned stacks of wood against the bitter cold. He remembered the chatter as the men talked against the cold, and he could feel the silence as they readied to cross the river with Strong Horse strapped across a mule. He rode out of the trees and through the thick willows then slowed his horse at the old crossing. The slope to the water was scoured down from use. Tom looked across the ripples to the other side and thought of how much deeper the river had been last fall.

He stepped down from his horse and squatted to toss a handful of pebbles into the river, one at a time. His heart hastened as his mind replayed the sights and the sounds of that dismal cold day when Strong Horse had died.

The face on the mountain and all the whispers about Strong Horse made Tom wonder, again and again, how the tragedy had happened. How had the tribe's greatest horseman been thrown from his mount? How had he landed so hard that he'd shattered his skull?

He could still feel Strong Horse in his lap and smell the blood that soaked through his leggings and froze to his skin. He would never forget when the big man's eyes sprang open, as a gentle smile creased his face. Tom felt a pang of guilt for yet another man he hadn't been able to save.

He tossed the last of pebbles into the stream and watched the ripples dissolve. He started to turn away when a sparkle in the river caught his eye. He stepped to the side for a better look at what he thought was a sunken stick, or maybe a bone. Then he noticed a pattern on the lustrous object, and he knew it wasn't natural. Probably a piece of gear that someone had lost. He wrapped his horse's bridle reins around a willow and waded into the river.

He was thigh deep when he reached down for what he thought might be sunken driftwood. When his hand wrapped around the slippery stick, he could feel patterned nubs poke at his palm. The object weighed more than he expected, and he immediately knew that this was more than a stick. When it broke the surface, he saw an ax. The green, stone head was roughly chipped on both sides. The handle was dotted full length with brass studs and had a natural crook at the end. When Tom held it up, the brass studs sparkled like the river behind it. This wasn't like the stone hatchets and hammers of the Utes. This was different. This was a war club. Maybe even an Iroquois club from back east. He'd seen such weapons at the university but never out here. Chances were, it had been traded over hundreds of miles and many years to make it out to the Utes. Someone must have lost it crossing the river. He was sure the Utes would marvel at what he'd found, but he worried that the ax might make them suspicious and wary. He considered dropping it back into the water but reasoned that it might have significance. Maybe it had belonged to someone in the clan.

He looked downriver and wondered how long the club had been there. Not long in his estimation — since the rawhide lacing still held the stone in place. A nervous twist curled in his gut as he looked back up stream. The weapon was probably not as old as he first thought. He waded out of the river and tied the club to his saddle before hurrying downriver to catch Water Bird.

Water Bird was coming back upstream when they met. He was

eager to see what Tom had found, until he saw it. Water Bird's eyes went wide then narrowed. He shouted for Tom to follow. Then he turned and rode his horse in a gallop toward the village.

They were just outside the camp when they met Bow River, Good Bear and two other men. Water Bird handed his father the club.

Bow River ran his fingers up and down the brass studs then slid his thumb across the sharpened edge. He balanced the club in one hand and picked at the rawhide lacing. Then he handed the club to Good Bear.

Good Bear felt the edge of the stone.

Water Bird looked right at Tom. "Arapaho."

"Arapaho? It's Arapaho?" Tom asked.

All the men nodded. When Bow River and Good Bear signed Strong Horse's name, Tom quickly understood. This was an Arapaho war club found at the spot where Strong Horse had fallen into the river.

Tom asked to see the club again, and Good Bear handed it over. Tom balanced the weight of the stone against the length of the handle and knew he could heave it with great power.

As a kid in Ohio, he'd seen men throw axes in competitions with great accuracy. Tom knew that anyone could do the same with practice.

Tom stepped down from his horse and urged the men to watch as he went through the motions and flung the club at a tree, which he hit dead center.

Tom picked up the club and ran his thumb along the edge and remembered the dent in Strong Horse's skull. His fingertips had wedged in the warm gash.

It had never made sense how Strong Horse could have fallen backwards from his horse into the water and split his skull that way on a stone. Tom had never been able to put all the pieces together. Now, his gut curled. Strong Horse had been murdered, and, in his hand, he held the murder weapon.

All the men looked to Bow River, who held up his hands. Tom saw the sign for Henry Eagle, the man murdered in Black Rock

Canyon. Bow River looked at Tom, held up a hand with four fingers, and said: "Four men, Strong Horse, Henry Eagle, Arturo, and Red Elk made the whirling-wind raid. Now, two of the four men are dead. We know Henry Eagle was murdered by the Arapaho with the face of a badger. Maybe this same man killed Strong Horse."

Good Bear told Tom that someone needed to ride to the Black Eagle village and tell them that Strong Horse had been murdered, and that Arturo must be on guard for his life. Two of the four men that had stolen the Arapahoe's horses were now murdered and Red Elk was still missing

Tom nodded his understanding. Three of the six men in the scouting party rode horses from the whirling-wind raid.

Water Bird reached out and ran his hand along Surrocco's mane. Bow River did the same to his spotted sorrel stud then pivoted him toward the village.

The news ran through the village like fire. An Arapaho war club had been found, and it was the weapon that had killed Strong Horse.

With the news came the screech of vengeful women, who lashed out at an unseen enemy. Their wrathful howls rattled the woods and ricocheted off the red-rock hills.

As the yellow ball of the sun lay out across the horizon, the drums rumbled, and the fevered pitch of rage spread across the flanks of Heart Mountain.

Ugly masks and painted faces came out as the clan whipped up a hatred that tingled the spine.

CHAPTER THIRTY-TWO

The Wild Red Mare

▲ ▲ ▲

It was mid-afternoon when the Yellow Bears topped the bluff above Yampa Pagosa. As soon as they arrived, everyone dropped their gear and hurried to get into the water. It was warm and no one worried about standing tipis. They would sleep under the stars in the warm water or on piles of blankets and furs. Fires were lit and food spread out as naked people lounged in the springs like the affluent nobles that they were.

The next morning Tom told Bow River about his plans to return to Denver. The chief scowled then took a seat on a log next to him. The men talked all morning and, before long, everyone noticed the intensity of their discussion.

Tom explained as best he could that he and Brooke had family back east that they needed to see. Tom's parents would want to see their son and granddaughter. Hopefully, his folks were still healthy and alive. Bow River was unhappy, even though he'd anticipated the news. Others, including Water Bird, had not. Bow River was concerned for Tom and Brooke, but he was worried about Water Bird, too. It was obvious how Water Bird felt for Brooke, and her father was sure she was fond of him too. It would be hard for Water Bird to accept their leaving. He had freely fallen for Brooke while she had held back, knowing she would be leaving.

When Bow River told his son, the boy's mouth hung open and his eyes grew wide and round. With words too quick for Tom to catch Water Bird questioned his father, who remained calm and resolute.

Star Flower and Blue Jay were surprised and saddened too. Star Flower was defiant and somewhat perturbed that Tom and Brooke would want to leave the richest of all the Utes. Brooke stood close by and could hear a tinge of fright in Star Flower's voice as she quizzed her father. Brooke had never thought that their leaving could frighten Star Flower —and maybe the others too. Could it be that their presence had created a bridge between cultures that had carried a degree of safety for everyone? The kinship they shared provided a measure of protection that would be lost when Tom and Brooke separated from the tribe.

Brooke was torn about going back to Denver. The thought of civilization with its expectations and biases caused a twist of worry to coil inside her. Life with the Utes was exciting, and she barely remembered life in the city. She wanted to return to school but living with the Utes required constant presence in the moment, which left little time to dwell on the future. Her brief contemplations were restricted to evenings with her pad and pencil. She wondered what people would think of the choice she and her father had made to live with the Utes. She knew that most Americans held opinions that were blurred by misguided notions about unholy savages. Very few whites understood that the Utes were every bit as benevolent as most, and more generous than many. But their environment demanded that they be rugged and protective of their lands and way of life.

The second evening at Yampa Pagosa, fires were lit and the drums pulsed at the heart of the village. People gathered near the fires. First the children and then the grandparents danced to the drumbeat. It was the start of a goodbye celebration for Tom and Brooke that would last for days. When the news spread that Tom and Brooke were leaving, they were crowded with attention and showered with gifts — from horsehair bridles to colorful clothing decorated with beads and quills. A group of young girls gave

Brooke a pair of earrings they'd made by lacing together strands of her blazing red hair with their own silky black locks.

Delicacies like berries and mint mixed with honey were drizzled on everything from smoked trout to biscuits. Elk roasts and turkeys were baked in pits and the meat was paired with choke-cherry juice that bordered on wine.

Everyone expressed gracious appreciation for everything that Tom and Brooke had brought to the band. But Water Bird was conspicuously absent from the celebration. Grandma Chuka curtly explained to Brooke that she would have to stick around if she ever hoped to have a handsome man like her grandson, Water Bird, for a mate. Brooke understood and replied with an understanding look and a nod. Grandma Chuka gave her a strong-armed hug before she stood and walked away with two friends.

As the gathering progressed, Bow River and his family circled Tom and Brooke and, with the help of different translators, they recounted their adventures together.

Brooke watched Blue Jay squeeze in next to her father. The sides of their legs pressed tight together as they adjusted their seating on the log.

As the long-tailed bear in the night sky arched around the North Star, old folks, couples, and droopy-eyed kids made their way toward soft beds. From the biggest men to the sleepy children, everyone came by to say goodnight to Brooke and Tom, who would soon leave them.

Finally, only Bow River, Stone Calf, Blue Jay, Star Flower, and her sleeping baby, remained to watch the fire fade. The log they all shared was less crowded than it had been earlier, but Blue Jay hadn't moved.

When Bow River stood it was time for everyone else to head to their tipis. Together they walked toward their lodges, young boys still darting here and there. As Bow River and Stone Calf turned toward their lodge, Blue Jay turned and continued on with Tom and Brooke. Outside their lodge Tom and Brooke stopped, and it was Blue Jay's turn to say goodnight. She wrapped her arms around Tom and squeezed so hard he had to squeeze her back.

Brooke waited for her hug and wondered if she'd get one. When Blue Jay relaxed, so did Tom, but they both held on. Blue Jay reached up and lay a finger from the base of his nose to the cleft in his chin. Tom breathed in deep as she slid her hand down and rested her fist on his chest. He held her stare, wet his lips, and cleared his throat.

Brooke watched, unsure of what to do. Blue Jay pivoted and wrapped her in her arms. Hugging her off the ground, Blue Jay kissed her cheek, turned, and walked away.

The next morning there was still no sign of Water Bird. When Brooke saw Star Flower step out of her tipi with her baby, she asked where he was. Star Flower shrugged her shoulders, glanced at the hills downstream and nodded.

"Rose Creek," she said, and Brooke looked her way with eager eyes. "You must have known that, when he heard you were leaving, his heart would hurt." Brooke looked to the side and pressed a fist to her lips.

"Water Bird loves you."

Brooke drew in a breath.

"You have been through so much with us." Star Flower glanced down at the baby, as did Brooke, and they smiled. "Brooke, you traveled the great circle with us, something no white girl has ever done. From Pony Springs to Bear Dance and back here to Yampa Pagosa. You are family, the kind of family we could marry."

Brooke looked up the Bunkara at the west side of Heart Mountain, dark with shadow. The word *marry*, which she'd barely said to herself, was now splayed out between them. The glaring statement out in the open felt like an admission, and a weight lifted. Brooke felt a tingle from deep in her nose to the edge of her eyes. She bit her lip to counter her tender feelings for Water Bird. Loving him pushed at the boundaries of polite society. The idea of being with him pierced her heart with little stabs of pain and pleasure.

"I'm sure my brother would ask for your hand if you were to stay much longer."

"But I couldn't," Brooke said. "I'm only fourteen."

"I know, I know." Star Flower took Brooke's arm and stopped her from saying more.

"Rose Creek, I know who you are. I know you must return to the world of your past, a different family, different friends, different boys."

Brooke's chin wiggled as her blue eyes pooled with tears that became tiny streams. Star Flower pulled her close.

"Water Bird's not far away," she said. "He has many horses to watch after, but he won't let you get away without seeing you." Star Flower loosened her hug and wiped her hand across Brooke's cheek. "He may wish to make a promise."

"A promise? What kind of promise?"

"Let's wait and see." Star Flower hugged her again and looked at the river. "Now, let's take this baby and introduce her to the pools of Yampa Pagosa."

It was mid-morning, and the sun was shining bright as they made their way downstream to where the women swam. As little girls grew more modest, they went from swimming naked with all the children to separating into different pools. There were several women and girls in a turquoise pool where Star Flower and Brooke came out of the willows. The women giggled as they welcomed them to the water. On the round rocks they undressed and tiptoed into the pool.

Brooke's skin was swan white next to the other women, who teased her about all her red hair. Her ivory skin turned pink from the warmth and the kidding.

From a rocky point down the river, Water Bird could see the women in the water. They were tiny in the vast scene. He saw Brooke and his sister and knew when they were taking off their clothes. He resisted the urge to get closer. He didn't need to see her to know how she looked. Her eyes were the color of a Pinon Jay, a range of blue from sky to midnight. Silver streaks laced the edges of her irises and dove into the deep pools of her pupils. They were eyes that sparkled in every light, like the shimmer of an alpine lake under summer skies. Across her brow and the bridge of her nose dainty freckles spread out like the Milky Way. His mother called them stardust, a gift from Father Sky. Beneath her narrow nose, rose pink lips turned up at the tips like the ends of an archer's bow. Her gentle smile, like still water, reflected the depth of her soul. Her chiseled chin showed the strength of her father cut to the feminine lines of her mom. But it was Rose Creek's radiant red hair that defined her in the eyes of the Utes. Like the mane of a red sorrel mare, it danced and wove around her neck, spilling over her shoulders like a flash-flood waterfall. The colorful curls of amber and orange changed with the light like a forest of fall oak.

Water Bird reached up to the little pouch that hung around his neck, where he carried a twist of Brooke's hair from that day at the waterfall. How could she just leave? His heart ached with his pride. He'd learned humility from Strong Horse but knew he was wealthy too. Rich with more than just horses and a rifle, he had knowledge and spirit. He had forest helpers. Not everyone did. His totems were mighty, but neither he nor his helpers could hold Rose Creek. For all he had, he didn't have enough. He felt a tortuous twinge at the thought that she would know other men in Denver, and they would probably own horses too, along with other things that he did not.

He remembered the nights in winter camp when they lay on warm furs by the fire, when she'd read her books to the children about faraway lands and strange people. If he'd tried harder to read the words and draw the letters, maybe she wouldn't be leaving.

His throat tightened and he slid his jaw side to side. He couldn't stop the tears that seeped from his eyes and the longing that clawed at his heart. He rubbed his fist across his mouth as he fought the urge to cry. He moaned at the pressure and knew he couldn't win. His face wrinkled at the noose around his heart and tears burst forth. He shuddered and cried out for what he couldn't control. The sorrow he'd corralled for days broke free like a runaway mare.

On a rocky point above the river, he'd surrendered to the wild red mare. Now he must let her go, but he would never let go of the hope that he might catch her eye again. Maybe next time, he'd have the skill to tame her just enough to keep her close.

Through blurry eyes he watched the figures in the pool far away. Straightening his back, he reached for the cedar flute that lay next to him. He touched the stem to his lips and lightly blew a soft tone.

CHAPTER THIRTY-THREE

Pile of Soft Fur

▲ ▲ ▲

Tom planned to leave in two days. He and Brooke would climb north over the big flat-top mountain to avoid Ghost Canyon then head east up the Eagle River. He knew Bow River would send a group of men with them to the Bighorn Fork. They would cross the divide alone headed for Breckenridge. From there Denver was four days away, depending on the snow.

The Dunagans owned a dozen horses and mules, including Timber and the paint mare, Tess. Tom had intended to return to Denver with only five, but when he tried to trade some of them away, he was convinced he should keep them all. Once he assessed the additional gear of gifts, ore samples, and clothes, he knew he would need all the animals.

There was no celebration in the camp that night. The people were busy preparing to move to Winter Camp in a couple days. After dinner, a large group, including Tom and Brooke, headed to the Grandmother's Pool.

At the base of a cliff the long, curved pool was half in the open and half hidden inside a cave. The stone arch at the cave's mouth hovered just inches above the water. A person could swim from the outside to the inside without going under water. A fire was built next to the outside pool and the light lit the cave inside. By the time everyone slipped into the water it was dark but backlit.

Brooke waded through the shallows to a deeper spot before she slid off her buckskin dress. She floated across the pool with only her head above the water and sat next to Star Flower. Tom and the other men sat to one side, and the women lounged nearby. In the dim light Brooke could see the women's breasts but glanced away when they looked toward her. After a while, her breathing slowed, as she settled in, despite the men and boys who soaked only a few feet away.

Brooke's mind wandered to her mother. What would she say about her daughter lounging in a pool with both women and men? Most likely, her mother would have wished to be there too.

As the campfires smoldered the night grew darker, and the conversations faded. Brooke drifted away then jerked awake with a gasp. She glanced at Star Flower, who was half in the water with her baby on her naked chest. Across the pool, her father rested with his head tipped back, someone snored. Brooke folded the skirt she'd left on the bank into a pillow, scooted her butt against the sandy bottom of the pool and drifted back to sleep. The next thing she knew Star Flower was coaxing her to wake and come to bed. She followed Star Flower to her lodge where they slept with the baby between them.

• • •

Tom felt slender fingers wrap around his hand. They closed on his palm with a confident grip. His eyelids lifted to the face he'd expected. Blue Jay's dark eyes shimmered, and moonlight bounced across the high points of her cheeks. Her eyelashes closed and held shut, then opened with fresh sparkle. She was hidden in the water and lightly tugged on his arm.

"Come," she whispered.

Tom looked over her shoulder at where Brooke had been.

"Star Flower," Blue Jay said quietly, tipping her head toward the tipis. Tom looked to his side for Stone Calf and Bow River. They were gone too. He glanced from the moon to the horizon and calculated dawn. Blue Jay nudged his hand. He breathed in and scooted closer to her damp face. Her legs wrapped around his and he felt a tempered pressure building between his thighs. His eyes slid down her neck to the shadow of her nipples. When she arched her back her breasts rose above the water, and she slid her leg up until it firmly rested at his groin. She rocked her hips, and a sensation he hadn't felt in years wove its way through his body. She glided away with his hand in hers, and he didn't resist. The water shimmered silver in the moonlight as they slid under the arch into Grandmother's Cave. She stepped from the pool to a sandy ledge. Steam followed her body to a pile of soft furs. Her shape was smooth and round from her waist to her thighs, as he knew it would be. She laid down and pulled a candle closer.

He watched as his past flashed by. Tamping down the memories, he knew where he wanted to be. He stepped from the pool in a cloud of warm vapor. He knelt beside Blue Jay and laid a finger from the cleft of her chin to the dip in her upper lip. Her chest rose as she anchored her eyes to his. His finger slid down her chin and rested on top of her heart, which thumped against his hand. They shared a smile as his fingers glided over her breasts, circled her navel, and slid lower.

CHAPTER THIRTY-FOUR

The White Pipe

▲ ▲ ▲

Tom was sipping his coffee when Bow River came around the tipi. Tom handed him a cup and reached for the pot. Bow River sat down to drink with his friend.

"Storm's coming," Bow River said as he studied the wispy clouds. They looked back into the fire and their cups.

"Are you still leaving tomorrow?" Bow River asked without looking up. Tom heard a snap in the question. He couldn't force the words out. Truth was, he didn't know his own mind on the matter. Did he really have the desire and the will to leave? The feel of Blue Jay wrapped around him in the early dawn hours still rolled through his mind and body.

Brooke surprised them when she walked up. "Morning Papa," she said.

Tom tipped his head toward Bow River. "He says a storm is coming."

Brooke glanced to the west. "When?"

"A day or so."

"Will it stop us?" Her voice climbed with the question.

"No, no it won't," he said, looking at Bow River. Brooke's eyes bounced between the men.

Bow River sighed as he straightened his back. "Be ready today. I'll send Good Bear and three men with you. You'll need to leave at dawn. Pack your gear today. You'll stay in our lodge tonight."

Tom nodded as Bow River set down his cup, stood up and walked away.

"Okay, let's get packing," Tom said. "He's not happy we're leaving."

"Neither am I, Papa."

It was a drizzly evening when the Dunagans moved into Stone Calf's tipi for the evening meal. Good Bear, Fat Cow, and their kids came too. Brooke scooted over when her father made room for Blue Jay. Everyone watched them readjust before they looked back into their bowls.

The smell of elk stew lilted around the room with streams of wood smoke. Chewing and the clickity-clack of wooden dishes were the only sounds.

Brooke glanced around and caught only a child's eye looking her way.

"What's going on?" All eyes sprang toward her before dodging back down to the food.

"Why is everyone so quiet?" She looked across the fire at the host then turned toward her father. No one spoke. Her face was getting warm. She set her bowl down. "Damn it, what's wrong?" Surprised faces jerked up. "Where's Water Bird?" She pointed the question at Stone Calf, whose face seemed sad as she looked at her husband.

Bow River swallowed and set down his bowl. His shoulders straightened as he folded his hands in his lap and looked at Brooke.

"Brooke, Rose Creek," he started in a calm voice. "Water Bird is away. We know where he is." He paused. "You will see him before —" He stopped himself then started again. "You will see him, Rose Creek."

"We are all sad, Brooke. Including you, I can tell. We are sad because of the great bear."

Brooke scrunched her face slightly and tipped her head.

Bow River continued. "The great bear lives beyond today, beyond tomorrow. We never know where he is until he finds us."

Bow River ran his fingers over the scars on his arm. "The Great Bear hides in the future. Look around. He is not here, but he is always out there. Tomorrow, when you leave us, we may never see you again." Bow River glanced at the fire. "Brooke, the Great Bear is always out there, beyond our ears, beyond our eyes, beyond tomorrow's sunrise. We must live with him. We must live with our fear. If we give the Great Bear room, he gives us room. Rose Creek, we cannot live without the bear, but we can give him room."

Bow River turned and looked at everyone. "If we give him what you call love, we can live together. The Great Bear is fear, but the room we give him is love." Bow River smiled softly, and Brooke nodded. "You know this. Give the Great Bear room." Bow River held his hands out toward Brooke. "We the Yellow Bear people wish you and your father to go in love. We give you room to go. Give the great bear room, and he will help you."

Bow River looked away and nodded to Good Bear, who brought up a leather bag. From inside he drew out the White Pipe. He held it up as anxious faces settled into a new calm. Fat Cow handed him a dish of brown leaves. He ground a pinch between his fingers and let it crumble into the marble bowl. He packed it then handed it to Stone Calf. She touched a stick to the fire, and it quickly ignited. With a long, strong draw she lit the pipe and handed it to her husband. Bow River stood up and drew in, then offered smoke in the four directions. He handed the pipe to his daughter. Star Flower took it with a smile as her baby wiggled in her lap.

Brooke had never seen the women smoke, and she watched with wondering eyes as Star Flower drew in then let the smoke curl out between her lips. She turned toward Brooke and offered her the pipe with two hands. Brooke felt her mouth sag open, and she placed her fingers across her lips. She glanced at her serious faced father who dipped his chin. She looked around at all the faces that coaxed her on. She looked the pipe over. It was heavier than she expected.

The moist cedar stem touched her lips, and she drew a breath inward. The sweet smoke crossed her tongue and fell into her lungs, and in that moment, she transformed from Brooke Rose Dunagan into Rose Creek. She closed her eyes and, lifted by the smoke of a sacred tradition, her mind took flight in a swirl of her past. She saw her mother kneeling before her with a tiny spoon in her hand. She saw baby Silver Star in her own hands, all flush with the blush of birth, then she saw lines of dancers moving to and fro. Then the messenger, Hummingbird, flitted by, and she saw the tiny gold flecks in Water Bird's eyes. Brooke lowered the pipe and felt the smoke flow out. It twirled, as did her world, and she knew that she was part of a ritual that few would ever know. She handed the pipe to her father, and the tradition carried on. From him to Blue Jay then around the room, kinship was tempered by the heat of the White Pipe.

Lightning snapped and thunder shook the tipi poles. The rain fell hard, and Brooke wondered again about Water Bird. She hoped he was warm. She knew he would be happy for her that she had smoked the white pipe. When she crawled between the soft fur of her bedding in the house of her new family, she hoped that he was safe and that he would give the Great Bear room.

CHAPTER THIRTY-FIVE

The Calling Song

▲ ▲ ▲

Brooke woke to the snap of the fire. The little light lit the lodge that brightened as the flames grew. It was dark and dripping outside but smelled of warm people inside. Mothers and fathers set up as little ones still burrowed under their covers. Gradually, everyone worked at the pace needed to prepare for a move. People ate hot stew as bundles were strapped and packs were packed. Only essential words were spoken. When everything was packed, Stone Calf and Blue Jay stepped into the tipi with two large bundles tied tight. They held them out to Tom and Brooke. Bow River stepped up, drew his knife, and cut the twine binding two buffalo-robe coats that now unfolded on their own. The inside of the hooded coats had been tanned white and painted with red designs, and the wooly outsides were thick and warm to the touch. Brooke looked to her father, who released an astonished sigh followed by the words: "*To-we-ock.*"

"*To-we-ock.*" Brooke chimed in to echo his thank-you. They stepped outside in their new coats, and someone placed a round Lynx hat on Brooke's head.

Good Bear and Loma waited with horses and pack mules. Tom's saddle sat atop Timber, and Brooke's waited for her on the roan filly, Smoke.

As darkness turned to dawn the rain lifted, yet heavy clouds hung to the cliffs. Bow River stepped up to Tom. "There will be snow up high. You must ride steady, up and over the divide, big snow is coming."

They stood in front of their mounted escorts, watching the women take turns hugging Rose Creek. Tear tracks creased every cheek. Star Flower took Brooke's face in her hands and kissed her on the cheek. "Rose Creek, we are sisters and will be together again," Star Flower said. Brooke understood every word and nodded back, fighting the urge to bawl.

Blue Jay stood next to Star Flower and took her turn to hold Brooke's face in her hands. "Rose Creek," she said, "Now you are our sister, and where you go, we go with you."

Brooke looked into Blue Jay's eyes, remembering the way she took charge of Silver Star's precarious birth. "I will never forget your strength and courage. I will spend the rest of my life trying to be as brave as you are."

The women then turned to Tom, and Blue Jay stepped up and drove her arms under his. Her face crushed into his beard as his nose laid just above her hair. She looked into his eyes and stood her finger on his lips and chin; he did the same to her. "I'm coming back," he whispered, "I promise."

She smiled, rose on her toes, and pressed her cheek into his.

Tom and Brooke moved to their horses, where Bow River helped Brooke mount up. She sat tall in her saddle, looking over the crowd and then glancing at the hills. Bow River tapped her twice on the leg, and a flurry of women and kids came up to do the same. Brooke giggled at the attention while the Smoke filly fidgeted below her.

Bow River looked up at Tom, "Thank you, Turtle Wind. You saved my life and many more. We will meet again."

Tom placed his hand on Bow River's shoulder, squeezed and nodded.

• • •

Good Bear called out and turned his horse upriver. He signaled Tom and Brooke to fall in line, and the other men followed. The horses struck out at a quick pace. Brooke twisted around and waved at the people between the tipis until they were out of sight.

• • •

Mellow notes from a cedar flute fell from the cliffs. Brooke straightened in her saddle, surprised at what she was hearing. She stared down the neck of her horse and listened. Her breath felt shallow as she tossed back the hood of her coat and tilted her face to the sky.

The pure sound circled the canyon with the grace of an eagle. Brooke followed her ears and searched for the source of the melody. On the point of a cliff high above the river Water Bird stood straight against the gray sky. A pair of feathers dangled from his hair. A bow and a quiver of arrows hung at his back. Surrocco stood still on a cliff above him.

The sight on the cliff and the sound of the music stifled her breathing. She wasn't sure if Water Bird was calling her to stay or saying goodbye. The only thing she knew for sure was that the calling song was for her.

Star Flower had said he would make a promise. Now, in the flute's song, she heard his plea. A promise as she rode away. She felt a pull at her stomach that crawled to her heart, and she longed for that brimful feeling she'd felt that day at the waterfall. Now, part of her own heart stood high on the rocks above her. Water Bird, who had failed to persuade her with words, now made his proposal with wind and cedar.

In the theater of striated stone, she listened to the breeze in the trees like the moan of a cello, the percussion of the river, the tone of the flute, all told her she was in love. In love and riding away.

The smoke filly bowed against the climb and dug her hooves into the gravel. Brooke could hear the polished notes above the clatter of rocks and the rattle of the riggings.

Tom twisted in his saddle. His steady eyes stared into hers. He

283

dropped his chin, turned back around, and pressed his heel into his horse. The stern-faced Ute men around them frowned with bewilderment.

Brooke gazed again at the man on the cliff, who held his posture true. He looked smaller as she rode away. She pulled the hood over her head and folded forward. A tickle on her cheek brought a flushing warmth to her whole face. She fought back the torrent of tears for only a second, then, as if she'd never bawled before, the flood of feelings poured out like water through a broken dam. "Oh! Mama, oh Mama, what is this?" Her months of wonder, want, and denial broke free in the turbulence of lost time. She rocked in the saddle, as if taking fisted blows. Still, the horses climbed the steep trail, as the lonesome lover's song followed behind them, into the mist.

CHAPTER THIRTY-SIX

The Frozen Camp

▲ ▲ ▲

The village split up the next day. Some of the people headed for winter camp and the others went back up the Bunkara to hunt. Bow River had told them to go to the Red Hills Camp where the Bunkara and Snow Stone rivers met.

Tom, Brooke, and their guides crossed over a high flat-topped mountain and made it to the Eagle River in two days. Good Bear led them to the Big Horn Fork where they could see the Continental Divide. The weather had threatened for days, and he urged them to hurry over the pass.

The fifth morning out, they woke to a light snow covering their camp. The Utes saddled their horses and headed back downriver. Tom and Brooke watched them disappear around a bend as their horses pranced and whinnied against their tie ropes. It was the first time in almost two years they'd been without their Ute companions. Tom checked the sky then headed back to camp. Brooke followed behind, watching her steps.

Tom spread out a hide and started stacking supplies. He thought they could be climbing the pass in less than an hour.

A snow squall blew through camp and climbed the ridge to the north. Tom watched the flurry and knew they needed to hurry. He held his gaze on the gray hillside and started to turn away when he noticed a large dark brown patch moving on a ridge. He tightened his gaze at the mysterious sight and realized it was moving, like water.

"Buffalo." Tom squinted tighter before he repeated louder, "Buffalo!"

Brooke walked to his side and looked up hill. "Where?"

He reached for his rifle.

"Up the ridge, just under that stand of spruce." He took a long step. "Let's get closer."

This was the first buffalo herd he'd seen since crossing the plains years before. Almost daily the Utes talked about *tah-ooch,* the buffalo, as a mystic god. They worshipped buffalo for the strength they gave to the people. The Utes were always on the alert for any news about herds entering the northern parks. Tom thought about rushing back to try to catch Good Bear, to let him know about the nearby herd, but he couldn't. They had to keep moving.

They crept quickly along a trail just inside the pines then dropped into a gully and climbed upslope. Their own buffalo coats were heavy, and they quickly got hot as they climbed.

"Brooke, let's leave our coats here."

She paused a moment and stifled a cough. "Papa I'm going to keep mine on. I'll be slower but I'll keep up."

He felt for his knife handle. "I'll keep an eye on you. I think if we get up there." He pointed uphill. "We'll get a good look."

Brooke whispered back, "Will you shoot one?"

"We'll see." Tom turned and stepped uphill.

When Brooke caught up, her father was bent behind a log. He waved a hand to coax her on. She landed next to him, and he pointed to the opposite hillside. "Look!"

Across the canyon, in the sagebrush, over a hundred shaggy creatures grazed. They were golden tan with wooly black mats draping their heads and shoulders. Their front ends looked twice as big as the rest of their bodies. Their eyes were shiny black, like their short crescent horns. They grunted and grumbled as they pushed through the scrub.

Tom looked at Brooke, and they wrinkled their noses at the musky smell that lilted downhill.

"Look," Tom said, pointing at a big bull that surveyed the herd. "They're gigantic."

"Yeah, they are," he whispered back.

"Are you going to shoot?"

Tom watched for a moment and glanced east toward the divide. "I don't think so." He looked at Brooke. "We don't need the meat, and I don't want them to scatter. Our Ute family needs them more." Brooke smiled as she looked back across the canyon.

Ka-bang! A shot rang from down by the river. They spun on their butts.

"What the hell?" Tom rolled back to look at the herd. Every animal stared downhill.

"Maybe Good Bear," he whispered. Another shot rang out.

"Papa, there's someone at our camp."

Tom stretched up and looked downhill. He squatted and gripped Brooke's arm. "Come on." He slid sideways in a crouch. They rushed downhill out of sight then climbed the next small ridge. Tom peeked over the crest and quickly hunkered down.

"What is it, Papa?"

"I don't know Brooke, but it's not good. They're not Ute, and they're in our gear."

Brooke started to stand but he jerked her down.

"Stay down."

Tom looked back up at the buffalo herd that was heading out of sight. He hoped the raiders hadn't seen them. One hand raised his rifle; the other gripped his daughter's shoulder. "Stay with me. We need to hide."

Tom peeked over the ridge and watched the strangers destroying their camp. His heartbeat shook his body. An Indian on a red speckled horse remained mounted and gave orders while the others ransacked the camp. When the breeze shifted, Tom could hear their voices. They were stealing gear and stock.

"Papa, they're taking everything. Who are they?"

"I don't know Brooke. They're not Ute."

Tom glanced up hill where the buffalo had been. "Thank God, I've got my gun." He suddenly tensed at the thought of his coat lying downhill with bullets in the pockets.

"We've got to get closer." He slid left, just inside the trees.

They popped out on a point and squatted behind a log. Tom could see a dozen men, their faces painted black and yellow. He swallowed as a chill crept up his arms, knowing the unexpected visitors were Arapahos. He studied the big man on a speckled horse that watched the others. His face was painted with badger bars. Tom's gut twisted at the thought that this must be Badger Heart. Which meant he knew whose camp he was destroying. When Badger Heart looked up, Tom ducked down, afraid he'd been seen.

"Get down, Brooke," he hissed.

Tom read her face and thought how young she looked.

"We need that coat," he said. "If they find it, they'll have my bullets."

Tiny snowflakes floated in the air.

"Papa, don't leave me."

"We have to get to that gully. Stay right by me."

When they reached the coat, it was dusted with snow. Tom shivered as he pulled it over his back and mashed his hat under the hood. The whinny of horses and loud talk floated up from the group below them. They had to hide, and Tom hoped the falling snow would help.

The draw next to them was chock full of willows and rosebushes. They pushed into the thicket and crawled under the branches of a fallen spruce. They squeezed together and wrapped first one coat and then the other over them. In the darkness of their little shelter, they could hear the snow settling around them. Brooke winced but managed to hold back a cough that strained at her chest.

• • •

The Arapahos had smelled out the empty camp. Badger Heart sat atop a spotted gray horse and barked out orders. He knew whose camp it was. He knew the horses and their owners. The paint mare and the big buckskin declared it the camp of the white doctor and his daughter. He wouldn't search for them now. He'd seek them out on their way back. Without their horses they wouldn't get far. Badger Heart's first aim was to follow the Utes to winter camp and steal back the Arapaho's horses. The Utes wouldn't expect a raid so late in the year.

Badger Heart knew the risk but was undaunted. He'd lost his mother, brother and father and had little left to lose. To win back the stolen horses and take scalps and children would not avenge the loss but would restore some pride to the Spotted Bird Clan.

The marauders took everything they wanted and smashed everything they didn't.

* * *

It had been mid-morning when Tom and Brooke hunkered down in the brushy draw. Once, in the early afternoon, they'd heard heavy steps not far away but hadn't been able to tell if they'd been made by a man or an animal. So, they'd remained motionless, hoping their coat shelter would keep them hidden.

It was late afternoon when Tom looked out on a foot of snow. He waited and listened before he stood and helped Brooke with her coat. Shaking the snow from their coats, they both began to shiver, and their boots slid in the snow that slumped all around them.

As they struggled through the brush, Tom worried about what they'd find back at their camp — if anything. They slipped downhill slowly, studying every step. When they got to where their fire pit had been, they couldn't see any of their belongings, only humps covered in snow. Tom hoped he'd find coals glowing in the fire pit, but it had gone cold. He glanced west to the horizon at a thin pink stripe below steel blue clouds. It would be dark soon, and the only goods they had were in their pockets. Tom hoped to find their mittens first. He pushed at the piles of snow with a stick. With every shove he uncovered something and buried something else. What he really needed was a piece of agate to strike a spark.

He had his knife and, if he could find hard rock, maybe, just maybe, he could get a fire going. He looked at Brooke, who lightly pawed at a pile of rubble buried in two feet of snow.

"Brooke, be careful of your hands." He moved toward her. "Keep them in your coat. Let me do the digging. Keep moving your feet."

Brooke shuffled side to side to clear a spot then stepped from foot to foot.

"Papa, we might be in trouble."

He turned and looked. He couldn't lie. Their situation was obvious, and she was way too smart to miss the truth. She stared back from under the wooly hood, her face cloaked in crooked red curls. He couldn't deny her frank remark, nor did he want to confirm it. He didn't have to. She knew they were up against tough odds. She knew misery was always close in this wild world. Tom swallowed. In the fading light, snow began to fall again.

"Brooke, we'll be alright. We'll get through the night. Things will look better in the morning."

"Papa, what about the horses?" He looked away, unwilling to answer. He cleared the snow at the base of a tree. The light was fading as they crawled under their coats and huddled together. For what seemed like hours they leaned on each other. When Brooke shuddered and went limp and heavy, Tom knew she was asleep. He felt relief that, for the time being, she couldn't feel the cold and hunger. Just get to morning. Then he'd find some dry tinder and build a fire. What if he couldn't find enough agate to make a spark? Could he build a fire with sticks as he'd seen the Utes do? He'd watched Strong Horse build a fire once with a piece of sinew and two sticks. Tom had never done it. He'd never tried. Now he wished he had.

"Papa?"

"I thought you were asleep."

"You know where I wish I were right now?" He took a moment, surprised at her question.

"Where?"

"Yampa Pagosa."

"Yes. I can feel the steam."

"Papa, I fell asleep in that pool the other night. Star Flower had to wake me up. Did you fall asleep?"

Tom waited to see if she had more questions. He had fallen asleep on the ledge in the steamy cave with Blue Jay wrapped around him. He could still smell her wet hair.

"Yeah, Brooke. I fell asleep."

"It was nice there. I even liked the smell, like eggs frying. It was so warm. I wish we could go back."

"Don't you worry, my girl, we'll make it back to Yampa Pagosa. Trust me, we'll get out of here." He pressed his cheek to hers.

She sniffled.

Tom sat still until her breathing slowed. Only then did his chest relax.

CHAPTER THIRTY-SEVEN

The Battle at Red Hill

▲ ▲ ▲

Cimarron coughed a spray of blood, his knees buckled, and he fell. A jagged rock arrowhead had pierced his chest and was now wedged against his spine. Sah-wolf watched a man jerk her brother's head back and slice his scalp to the skull. Unable to scream, she stared until someone grabbed her by the hair and flung her across a saddle.

Shots rang out through the village, echoed by the thuds of clubs and fists.

Wolf Song stood up at the first scream, grabbed his lance and pushed through the tipi flap. He never saw the club that smashed his skull and snapped his lance in half.

Water Bird and Black Fox were crossing the river when they heard shots at the camp. Water Bird kicked his horse onto the bank. Men were raiding the village. Their painted faces told him that the invaders were Arapahos. There were only a few Ute men in camp to protect the women and children. Water Bird heard his mother's screams.

"Go for my father fast," he ordered Black Fox, who jerked his horse around and disappeared into the trees.

Upstream more thieves circled the horse herd. A man on a buckskin horse rode on a ridge above the heist. Water Bird whipped Surrocco into a sprint toward the village. He couldn't stop the thieves, but he could cut off any Arapaho leaving the village. He knew where they'd have to go to escape. He jumped from his horse, hooked the reigns on a stump and ran through the trees with his rifle ready.

At the sound of branches breaking and heavy hooves pounding, he stopped behind a tree and caught his breath. He inched his eyes around the trunk to see four riders racing toward him. The first carried a rifle in one hand and tugged at a leather bundle across his saddle with the other. The next two were loaded with plunder too. On the fourth horse a little child's legs kicked. The kidnapper folded forward, pinching the child to the saddle. Water Bird recognized the little girl, Sa-Wolf. He jerked back behind the tree as the first three riders galloped by. He leaned his shoulder into the tree's bark and readied his rifle for the last robber, who rode a black, bald-faced horse. He timed his breath to the hoof beats that were coming closer. With a big exhale he swung around the trunk and lined his rifle to the top of the horse's head. *Kaboom!* The horse's head exploded mid-stride, catapulting the rider forward. The horse folded, its dead weight landing on the Arapaho. Sa-wolf screamed in pain, as she tumbled and bounced to a stop in a willow patch.

Water Bird ran to the Arapaho, who slashed his knife at the air. He was pinned by dead legs that couldn't move. He snarled at Water Bird, who'd seen only one man die before. Strong Horse. Across the ugly black and yellow face, he recognized the pain of dying, but this time he felt no grief. He stepped on the man's arm and put the rifle barrel at the center of his skull. He resisted pulling the trigger again. The Arapaho must have heard his first shot and might be coming back. His finger felt the trigger just before the man went soft and his eyes glazed gray. Water Bird turned to Sa-Wolf, who bawled her way through the willows.

Ka-bump-a-ta! Ka-bump-a-ta! Ka-bump-a-ta! Hoof beats echoed through the forest. An Arapaho swerved around a tree and his rifle flashed. A blast of air creased Water Bird's head at the crack of the shot. The Arapaho screamed and charged full gallop toward Sa-wolf, who had struggled into his path.

Water Bird's rifle exploded at his hip. He jacked in another shell and was aiming when the assailant flipped backward from his charging horse, knocking little Sa-wolf to the ground.

Water Bird drew his knife and ran to the body of the first man he'd killed. With a sucking pop, he cut the scalp away. He scooped up Sa-wolf and ran for Surrocco.

Bow River and some others heard the shooting from upriver and raced for the village. When they got there, it buzzed like a hornet's nest. Children cried, mothers screamed, and a flock of old women hacked a dead body.

Water Bird was trying to restore order when Bow River arrived. He said Wolf Song and Wood Deer were dead, and the thieves were heading north with the horses they'd stolen.

Bow River barked orders as everyone scrambled for weapons and bullets. Women grabbed their men and hastily painted their faces. Water Bird painted his own, and when he stepped from his lodge, a bloody black scalp dangled from his shield. The men tapped his shoulder and shield, acknowledging his prowess as a warrior.

Within minutes the men gathered, holding back horses that strained for a charge. Stone Calf handed Bow River the last of his gear. Just then, Water Bird rode up.

"Father, it was Badger Heart." Bow River's face snapped toward him, as his eyes grew wide. Water Bird caught his father's arm.

"What?"

Water Bird took a deep breath. "He was riding Timber, Tom Dunagan's buckskin horse."

Bow River said nothing. The two men locked eyes, while their nervous horses shifted below them. Bow River looked over at the men who were ready to ride then twisted his horse to the west and buried his heels in its ribs.

The party left camp at a dead sprint, the opposite direction of the thieves. Bow River knew where the Arapahos were headed, and he knew where they had to go to get back to the Eagle River. He knew that if he and his men headed west then north, they might beat the Arapahos to the pass. They would have to push their horses to near death, but they had to catch the thieves before they crossed into the Eagle Valley. If the Arapahos made it over the pass, they'd split the herd into smaller groups and the Yellow Bears would be forced to lose some horses to save a few.

CHAPTER THIRTY-EIGHT

Shelter Tree

▲ ▲ ▲

Tom awoke before first light, thinking of ways to keep Brooke alive. He'd huddled against her all night under a makeshift tent heavy with snow. Brooke coughed hard, and he worried that her warmth had become a fever.

He had to find a piece of flint. With that and his knife he could spark a fire. Then he'd find water and food. They'd been carrying bags of dried meat with their gear, which had been ransacked. Even if the Arapaho had left something behind, he would have a hard time finding it under three feet of snow.

If he couldn't find the right rock to make a spark, he'd have to try the treadle-and-pan method to build a fire, using three sticks and a string. He'd seen Strong Horse do it, and a few of the women. Getting a fire going was crucial, so he had to try.

When he poked his head out of the tent he'd thrown together, the landscape looked flat. Humps of gear that had been visible the evening before were now hidden under snow.

"Stay here, Brooke, let me see what I can find." He tucked her coat around her. When his hand brushed her neck, he knew she had a fever.

As he struggled to get through a few yards of snow, his pants froze to his legs. After an hour of digging, he hadn't found anything of use. His hopes of finding the little fire bag seemed more unlikely with every passing minute, but he kept digging.

"Father, what have you found?" Tom didn't reply. "Did you find the book bag, Papa?"

The book bag. Of all the things he couldn't find, he hadn't thought of the two years of diaries and drawings that had chronicled their lives. If he could find it, he'd have paper for a fire.

"Did you find the fire bag?" He heard a shiver in her voice that caused him to hesitate again.

"No, Brooke." He turned toward her and fought through the snow.

"You need stand up and move," he said, as he kicked away snow to clear the way for her to stand.

He braced against the tree and, at the snap of a branch overhead, he knew his mistake. Clumps of snow broke free from above.

"Oh, goddamn it!" Tom gasped, and Brooke trembled from the shock of the snow that dropped. Brooke pulled off her round hat and shook her shaggy curls. Tom brushed away the snow that melted at the touch of her skin. She looked up with a half-smile, jumping in place to try to stay warm.

"Good," Tom said. "Keep moving."

"Papa, I'm thirsty." They hadn't had water since the morning before.

"Here, lick a little snow. Not too much." He held his sleeve to her face. She touched her tongue to the snow. Her lively eyes were light blue like her mother's. He pushed the thought away. Thinking about Teresa wasn't going to improve his situation.

"Brooke, you've got to keep moving," he snapped. "I want you to stand right here and move your feet as fast as you can. Just do it," he added in a softer tone.

He looked at the snowfield that hid their gear and knew that buried somewhere lay the key to their survival. If he could find the flint, they'd have a chance. He had his gun. If he could build snowshoes, he could find game. Had the buffalo saved their lives, or had the herd lured them to the edge of disaster? Maybe he could find them again. Tom slowed his anxious thoughts. First things first.

With a broken piece of a saddle, he scraped at the heavy snow. He bowed his back and dug harder.

"Papa," Tom heard the quake in his daughter's voice and looked up. "I'm getting sick," Brooke said, folding forward. Tom pushed through the snow as her big coat slid from her shoulders and she crumpled in a heap.

"Brooke!" He went to his knees and scooped her up in his arms. Her colorless face was dotted with freckles and vomit. "Brooke!" Anger chipped at fear. "Goddamn it!" He cursed his cavalier ego and knew that it was the Utes who had kept them alive. He was hopeless without them. His fortunate upbringing, education and wealth were worthless, and he wished for his Ute friends.

Brooke's eyes fluttered open then quickly grew wide. She coughed hard. "I fainted."

Tom crushed her to his chest, his shoulders shuddered. "Oh God, thank you. Thank you. Oh, thank you, Sinawav." He looked up at the gray sky and rocked her in his lap, knowing he'd lost her for a moment. In those seconds he'd felt a defeat he'd only known once before. There was no pushing Teresa away this time. He let the thought of her warm his heart for a moment.

He hugged Brooke close, staring out across the snow. Feeling her breath on his cheek and smelling her hair, he felt surrender sneaking in. Surrender to their plight, but also forgiveness for the hubris that had brought him here. He carried Brooke to the shelter tree and kicked the snow down to the dirt before he leaned her back against the trunk. He moved her weak limbs like those of a doll. He pulled off her boots to rub her feet. There, strapped to her left calf, was a knife sheath with a bone handle. He had no idea his daughter carried a weapon. A little line of beads told him who the maker was — and probably the giver too. He could imagine Stone Calf giving her instructions.

"Stay with me, Brooke," he said, as he rubbed her toes faster.

CHAPTER THIRTY-NINE

Brooke's Red Shawl

▲ ▲ ▲

Water Bird could see an Arapaho leading a spotted maroon stallion, luring the rest of the horses up a narrow draw. Bow River signaled and his men hunkered down, watching the thieves coming at a steady pace.

Beyond the herd on higher ground, a lone rider slipped through the trees. Water Bird pointed out the rider who rode above the stolen herd. They recognized Tom's buckskin horse and knew the rider must be Badger Heart.

The Utes knew it was Badger Heart who had killed Strong Horse and Henry Eagle. Now the Utes feared for their friends, Turtle Wind and Rose Creek.

Water Bird signaled a warning downline to the other men. Good Bear and Bow River spoke with their hands. Then, Good Bear and three men moved up the ridge and disappeared. When the plan was set, they waited for a signal that would come from Bow River when Water Bird's rifle was aimed at Badger Heart.

The horse herd was directly below in a grassy flat cut by a little stream. *Bam!* Water Bird's rifle went off. Badger Heart slumped and rolled off his horse. The others followed his fire with a rapid blast. Three Arapahos fell dead in an instant. Another dragged himself through the grass. Another volley went off before the thieves knew where to look. Two more Arapahos took slugs as panic set in. The horses milled in confusion, and the Arapahos abandoned the herd and fled for the pass.

"Halt!" Bow River yelled, and the men watched the thieves ride hard to escape. The dead and wounded lay on the flats below. The others whipped their horses hard to escape. A barrage of rifle fire went off and the would-be escapees crumpled under a shower of lead. Cut off by Good Bear and the three men who had moved up the ridge, the last of the thieves lay dead in the grass. The Utes screamed in victory and raced downhill, gathering scalps and horses. Bow River and Water Bird stayed on the hill and watched for any hint of Badger Heart. Searching for the Arapaho leader, they crossed the valley with the other men.

They found the spot where Tom's buckskin had flared away from Water Bird's bullet, but there was no sign of Badger Heart, or the horse. They followed his tracks over the pass and into a thick stand of timber. Badger Heart, not the horse, was bleeding. They didn't want to give up the chase but their enemy, wounded and alone, posed little danger now.

As the shadows grew long in the dark timber, they turned back, needing to return to their camp on the Bunkara to bury their dead.

At the battle site the men stood over a pile of plunder retrieved from the thieves. They paced as Bow River and Water Bird approached.

Water Bird stopped short and stared into the pile. A shawl that his mother had given Brooke lay next to a beaded shirt that had been Tom's.

Water Bird released an exhausted sigh as his shoulders slumped and trembled. He stooped to a knee, and a mournful roar rumbled from his gut.

As the sun crept west, the Yellow Bear warriors headed toward the bereaved people of their village. The clouds that had hovered all day settled across the mountain tops as the west wind stirred leaves across the ground.

Water Bird was the last man on the ground as the others started the horse herd down the canyon. Rose Creek had changed everything in his world. Because of her, he could see a bigger world.

He could see a different world for his people. She had given him hope that his family could live in peace with the whites and free from their enemies. Because of Rose Creek, his sister had all her fingers and a baby too.

Maybe she wasn't dead. She couldn't be. He looked up to the sky through blurry eyes as tiny snowflakes sprinkled his face. He wondered at the wisdom of the wolf and the trickery of the coyote and wasn't sure who held the most power.

The sharp chirp of a water bird caught his ear and he looked to the little stream that cut a course through the flat. A little black bird bobbed on a rock then disappeared into the water.

Water Bird climbed on Surrocco and headed downstream. The next morning, he topped Cow Flats Pass with a few other men as the first streaks of dawn cut the sky. Their horses were wet with sweat from pushing snow that got deeper as they climbed. By evening's gray light they turned around in deep snow with no sign of Badger Heart, Turtle Wind, or Rose Creek.

CHAPTER FORTY

Endless Spring

▲ ▲ ▲

Tom was weak as he struggled to get up from the shallow pit they'd wallowed in at the base of the tree. He hadn't slept for more than an hour, but he knew Brooke had. She was so sick he couldn't leave her for even a short time to try to get to water or kill food. He melted snow in his mouth a teaspoon at a time and spit it into a wrinkled metal cup he'd found. When it was half full, he woke Brooke and got her to drink. They were literally trapped in camp by walls of snow. He couldn't imagine how they might be saved. He wasn't sure the Utes would know they were in trouble, but he knew that the Arapaho would. Their chances weren't good. Brooke had a better chance of survival than he did if the Arapahos came back, but that wasn't a thought he wanted to weigh.

At midday it stopped snowing and patches of blue sky heralded bitter cold coming. He still hadn't found a stone to make a spark, so he resigned to trying the treadle-and-pan method to build a fire. He'd have to create friction with a little bowed stick called a treadle that would spin another small stick, the spindle, atop a flat wood surface called the pan. With the right pressure, speed, and persistence, he hoped to create a hot spot in the wooden pan that could be blown into a flame. He had to make it work, or they'd freeze and starve. He decided he'd prefer to die warm.

His frozen fingers felt like they might explode as he fumbled to make the parts. Every bit of effort drained him more.

The sun was arching west when he got the spindle spinning on the fire pan. The first time he checked the end of the spindle he could feel warmth. He started again with a little more pressure as he moved the treadle back and forth a little faster. After an hour the dent in the pan was warmer but still not hot enough to burn. He pushed on into the second hour and then the third.

Doubt wiggled in and he worried that he needed to go faster, press harder. Maybe he'd used the wrong kind of wood. The Ute women used aspen for the spindle. He'd used pine. But he couldn't stop now.

"Snap!" The spindle splintered into pieces. Tom stared down as he gritted his teeth then slapped the little bow on the ground. He looked up, knew how late it was, held his breath, holding back the tragedy. He shook at the dampness on his back. A fire seemed outlandish.

He'd try again in the morning. He glanced at the shattered spindle, and a dull color against the snow caught his eye. He reached for the reddish-brown sliver of something. As he grabbed it, air climbed into his chest and his mouth sagged open. Meat. He stared at the needle-sized sliver of jerky and felt saliva seeping in his mouth. He brushed away the snow to discover more and bigger pieces.

He brushed away more snow and quickly had a handful of frozen shards of jerky.

"Brooke, Brooke, Brooke." He headed toward her. They had a handful of food that could be the start of saving them both.

She shivered lightly when he uncovered her. She didn't move when he said her name. She was dazed from the cold and what was probably influenza.

"Oh no, come on girl, gotta wake up, Brooke! Wake up."

Tom tipped her up against the tree trunk. She stared back with blank eyes.

He held a piece of meat to her chapped lips. Her mouth opened, and Tom slid it in. He caught it in his hand when it fell out, leaving his daughter chewing at the air.

He winced at her feeble attempt. He'd found some food, but she was too weak to get it down. He slid another piece of meat into her mouth, but she didn't even try to chew it. Her head lolled to the side like a wounded bird. He knew that look; he'd seen it too many times in the war. When the will to live is outweighed by the temptation to surrender.

"Oh no you don't." He put a chunk of meat in his mouth and chomped it to bits. He leaned forward, and pushed the mush into her mouth, massaged her throat. "Come on Brooke, swallow. Swallow. Come on. That's my girl, yes, yes." He sloshed a hand full of snow in his mouth and gave her a drink from his lips. He chewed again and again, giving her a little more to swallow each time. When the last handful of food was gone, darkness set in. He wrapped her coat around them both then draped his over the top. He massaged her limbs until he dozed. When he woke up, he rubbed her hands and feet some more to keep her blood moving.

The fitful night wore on as misery birthed delirium. His hand wrapped around a bullet in his pocket. He wished he had anything to shoot, anything to kill, anything to eat. If he'd had his horse, he would have killed it. Hunger cut at his gut, and he knew it burned Brooke's too. Maybe she was too sick to know the full ache of her hunger. How he wished that could be true.

His mind spiraled deeper into a darkness he'd resisted for years. He knew how to end his own agony. He still had bullets and a knife. Death could come swiftly if he delivered it with his own hand. Faces flashed across his past, the horror then the sudden look of lost and gone. Gone. If he took his life, could Brooke live on his flesh until help arrived? He knew she couldn't. She couldn't even stand up. And no one was coming. Nobody knew they were buried alive in a canyon of snow. Only the Arapahos who had raided their camp. If they knew the pair was there, they'd come back for Brooke's scalp and his rifle. If he killed himself, he'd have to kill his daughter first. After that, it would be easy to put a bullet in his own brain.

"Papa, did you find the journals?"

Her little voice shocked him awake.

"No, Brooke. But we'll find them, don't you worry."

Tom stared into the blackness, realizing that the world was the creation of his thoughts. All the people in his past — the ones he hadn't been able to save would never be saved, and those he had saved would carry on. Only by saving himself could he work to save Brooke.

He remembered Water Bird's words from that day at the Medicine Circle, explaining how the circle of life is the river that runs through the land of the endless spring. *Nothing begins and nothing ends. In the circle of life, the river runs forever.* He surrendered to what he couldn't change and forgave himself for his shortcomings.

"Whoosh-thump, whoosh-thump." The crunch of snow brought Tom's head up from his chest. "Whoosh-thump." Through the walls of their dugout, he could see a half-naked Arapaho standing just feet away. A white stripe split his face and black points marked his cheeks. His burning eyes looked down a rifle pointed their way. A brass studded war club with a green stone head hung at his hip.

Tom felt for the gun in his lap, rolled it over and cocked the hammer. He lifted the muzzle.

"Kaboom!"

Tom's eyes snapped open, and his head popped against the tree. He tightened his mouth to catch his heavy breath and glanced at his rifle, cold in his lap. His senses tingled; his breath cut hard on his throat. He stared into the blackness and sorted out the implausible image he'd just seen in his dream.

Feeling Brooke at his side assured him that she was alive — for the moment. He was alive too. His task still at hand, he fought to rein in his breath.

"Whoosh-thump. Whoosh-thump." Tom could feel the noise as much as hear it. "Whoosh-thump. Whoosh-thump." He shook his head. He wasn't dreaming. Something was outside. He pushed the hide cover open with his rifle barrel, rose to his feet, and stood stark still against the cold, listening.

"Whoosh-thump, whoosh-thump." The sound came from a cluster of pines by the creek. He studied the area until movement narrowed his eyes to a patch of brown hair. Food, he thought, an elk. When the animal moved, he could see black legs below the pine boughs. A half grin crept up his cheeks at his luck. He raised the rifle and aimed at the edge of the trees.

"Whoosh-thump, whoosh-thump." The sounds grew louder, as flashes of hair appeared and disappeared behind the trees. He watched for the first chance to shoot.

His breath caught in his gut. Wait. What was he seeing? An elk? No. A fringed legging, blood-stained leather, an Arapaho boot. Riding a horse. His horse, Timber.

In the next second, his dream was confirmed. An Arapaho man appeared, riding his buckskin gelding.

Timber cut a warm outline against a backdrop of black and white. The gelding halted with his ears pointed at Tom, who held his rifle sites on the Arapaho's chest.

The man stared back, motionless, his rifle leveled across his lap. The white stripe and black lines on his face left no doubt. It was Badger Heart.

Tom's mind rattled. He could feel the trigger but couldn't pull it. If he died, could Brooke survive?

Timber nickered. Neither man moved.

Tom looked through his sites at the most dreaded man in the mountains, but he felt no fear at the thought of a bullet in his own gut. He was the dog in the corner, acting on instinct alone. Here, there was no room for fear.

The painted face staring back looked neither frightened nor bitter but wore a smug smile. A bloody moccasin hung from his wounded leg. Tom saw that a bullet had found its mark. The lone renegade stood testament to many dead Arapahos.

Tom was drawn to look at the contrasting color at the edge of the Arapaho's face. Something seemed out of place, yet familiar. He squinted his focus slightly. A streamer of color dangled in his black hair. Like the mane of a red sorrel mare, points of light lit the colorful twist. Tom's gut tightened. There, at the side of the warrior's cheek hung a long clump of his daughter's hair. How in the hell had Badger Heart gotten it? Somewhere, somehow, he had stolen it from her head, no doubt when she was asleep. His stealth made Tom even more aware of the chilling opponent he faced. Badger Heart had come close enough to cut hair from Brooke's head — and had let them live once before. Maybe he would again. But, for what price?

Tom felt his breathing slow as he lowered his rifle slightly. Badger Heart lifted a finger and wrapped it around the lock of red hair at his cheek. He rose in his saddle and looked behind Tom at the pile of buffalo robes where Brooke was hiding. Tom jabbed his rifle forward, and Badger Heart sat back in the saddle, his rifle still leveled at Tom's gut. Then he turned in his saddle. For a few moments, Badger Heart stared back down the canyon from where he'd come, as if he were searching or listening for someone.

Tom was struck by why Badger Heart would lower his guard and look away so casually. Tom knew this was his chance to kill the killer. He could feel his finger tight on the trigger. If he pulled it, he'd have meat and a horse, but Tom had never killed a man. Throughout the war, despite all the death he'd seen, his job had been to save life not to take it. Bow River's words about fear, the great bear, drifted though his memory. "Give the great bear room, and he will help you."

Badger Heart twisted back to face Tom. The two men locked eyes and Tom recognized the face of surrender. A look he'd seen before on the faces of men in the war. Men that had given up all they had to give. Beaten. Tom saw his own reflection in the face that stared him down. Two men beaten by war and the loss of family just looking for peace from their pasts. Tom felt a tug at the common thread that wove between them, for he knew that Badger Heart too was haunted by the horrors of war. Tom knew he didn't have the will to kill and neither did Badger Heart or one of them would have been dead by now. The two men held their stares until Badger Heart loosened a strap on his saddle. Leaning forward he tossed a weighted bag that disappeared in the snow then he turned Timber and they vanished into the trees.

Tom knew it was the last time he would ever see his trusted buckskin horse again. He stood frozen in the loss of chance. He couldn't pull the trigger, and his only hope of getting Brooke across the divide had ridden away. He felt empty as he trudged through the snow toward the bag that his opponent had left behind. He was confounded yet somewhat hopeful when he looked inside at a pound of dried meat.

CHAPTER FORTY-ONE

The Gift of Life

▲ ▲ ▲

The black dog stuffed his face in the snow and huffed. The yellow dog followed the same tracks and pushed his nose into a hole, snuffling a puff of snow. The dogs struggled up a trench where something had traveled days before. The black dog went to the next dent in the snow, stuffed his face in, and huffed again. Bob watched from atop his mule. The dogs burrowed in the snow, and Bob knew they had found something more interesting than anything they'd crossed in days.

"What is it boys?" The dogs looked up and went back on the hunt. Whatever it was had passed through before the last twenty inches of snow had fallen. The spacing of the nearby tracks suggested a horse and rider.

Bob's mule sidestepped at a rattle and a thud. He looked back in the snow and saw the corner of a rawhide box. He slid off his mount into the waist-deep snow and pulled it up. The blue diamond pattern identified the box as Ute. He folded open a flap and stared inside at several leather-bound books and knew immediately whose they were. He'd seen Tom and Brooke detail their days in those very journals several times.

He opened a book and read: "April 9, 1869, we left the Big Tree Camp yesterday and headed northeast up what I think is the North Fork of the Gunnison (the Muddy Fork to the Utes)."

Bob looked at the string of horses behind him, waiting in the belly deep snow. He'd found them tied up the day before on a ridge above the river. They'd been there a while and were gaunt and weak. They'd been left for dead. He'd seen at least one of those horses in the Yellow Bear herd last summer. What he'd found didn't sit well. The abandoned horses and the box of journals suggested a raid.

• • •

Tom could hear heavy steps in the snow. He reached for his rifle but felt Brooke's arm. He held his breath as the steps came closer. Lost in delirium, he raised his head to face whatever or whoever was approaching.

"Tom!"

At the sound of his name and flash of light, Tom threw off the buffalo robe and tried to stand but couldn't.

"Tom!" His name echoed again through his hollow mind. He gasped and wrenched his face to the light.

"Tom, it's Bob. Bob Black!" The words bounced around in Tom's head as he choked and reached for his rifle. "Tom! Don't shoot. Don't shoot. It's me, Bob!"

Bob leaned in and held him down with two hands. Tom looked up with crazy eyes, head jerking side to side as he grabbed for Brooke, who hadn't moved.

"Bob!" Tom screamed and reached out and jerked him to his face, "Oh my God, oh my God, is it really you?"

"It's me, Tom. It's me."

Tom spun to Brooke and pulled her up. The weight of her body folded limp against his arms.

"Brooke!" He screamed through building panic.

Bob jumped across them, scooted underneath her, and pressed his ear to her chest.

"No, no, no!" Tom raged.

"Shut up," Bob snapped as he pressed his cheek to Brooke's. He shook her then opened an eyelid with finger and thumb. Her eye rolled up, and the lid snapped closed.

"We've got a chance," he said as he hoisted her into his lap and shook her again, coaxing the slightest murmur from her blue lips.

"Get under her. Shake her. Move her. Don't stop moving her."

Bob snapped to his feet and pushed through the snow to one of the stray horses he'd found. Leading her forward, he stuck the rifle muzzle below the mare's ear and pulled the trigger. Kaboom! Dogs cowered and horses jerked as the mare crumpled. Bob grabbed a hind leg and flipped the dead horse over. With a long arching slash of his knife, he laid open her belly. Coils of guts spilled out onto the snow. He ripped off his coat and shirt, grabbed his knife, and reached up into the carcass as deep as he could. Steam rolled from the bloody cavity as Bob raked his knife inside until he tugged out the mare's heart and lungs. He sheathed his knife and marched to where Tom jostled Brooke. Tom looked up in terror. Bob didn't explain. He plucked Brooke up and laid her across the horse's shoulder. The dead horse's body quivered.

Tom scrambled up just as Bob drew his knife. "What the hell are you doing?"

"Tom, this is our only hope. We've only got a little time. I've seen this work before. If we can get her in this hot carcass, she might get warm enough to pull through." Bob jerked off her boots, slid his knife up both of her leggings, then split open her shirt. In just a few tugs, he pulled away her clothes. After staring at the knife tied to her leg for a second, he sliced the strap that held it in place. Then, he hefted her in his arms and slipped her into the open cavity of the horse. Like feeding a big log into a fire, he shoved the girl into the steaming carcass. He pushed her down into the animal's belly, leaving just a slit for her face.

"Get her robe," Bob barked. Together they tucked the wooly hide around her and covered her head. They stepped back and looked at the bloody sight, waiting. The dead horse still quivered.

Brooke was almost gone, weak and frozen. She'd shown no life as Bob pushed her into the carcass. Neither man had checked for a pulse.

"What now?" Tom asked.

Bob looked him over. "Let's see if we can save you," he replied as he reached in a bag for a pair of mittens. "We need wood, lots of wood."

Before long a fire crackled. Tom stood at its edge with his eyes closed. Bob hauled over more wood, coffee simmered, and slivers of horse liver sizzled in a pan. It was early evening before they had enough wood to get through the night. They split the fire into two, building up the flames on each side of the dead horse with Brooke inside. Just before dark they squeezed open her mouth enough to trickle in some broth. She wasn't moving and hadn't spoken. She had to get through the night to have a chance. As night engulfed the camp, sub-zero temperatures followed. Tom and Bob settled in by the fire and waited, desperate for Brooke to stir.

Dawn's silver sliver cracked the horizon by the time Tom awoke to stoke the fires. He piled on wood and stepped toward the horse carcass. As he reached to move the buffalo-hide cover, it moved ever so slightly.

"Brooke?" The carcass wiggled again.

Bob sat up. At Tom's glance, he scrambled to his feet, piling wood on the fire. Standing side by side the men rolled back the buffalo robe. In the firelight a tiny sparkle shone in worried eyes. Neither man spoke. Brooke blinked and a puff of breath slipped from her. "Papa," she said. Tom fell to his knees with his face at hers. "Brooke, it's alright. Don't move."

"Papa, I'm all wet," she whimpered. "It smells. What's happening?" Her voice wobbled, and her chin trembled.

"We'll get you out of there real soon. For now, stay put. Don't move."

Her blue eyes bounced between the men. "Bob?"

"Yeah, Brooke, it's me. Mighty happy to see you. Here drink this." He put a cup of broth to her lips. She choked at first then swallowed.

"Where are your dogs?"

The men looked at each other. "They're right here by the fire. Don't you worry. They're happy to see you too."

Hours later in bright sunshine by blazing fires, they lifted

Brooke from the carcass. They wiped her with soft leather and wrapped her in furs. It would be another two days before she could feed herself and stand. Her moccasin boots had saved her feet and her fingers came around too.

For another two days the trio hung close to the fire feasting on horse meat, biscuits, and coffee. When the men weren't eating or gathering wood, they were stripping cottonwood and willow bark for the horses.

Five days after Bob came to the rescue, they all struck out for the divide. They had no choice. For now, they had plenty of meat and more on the hoof if needed. They had six animals to break trail and enough bark to feed the horses for a few days. They had all the journals except one.

As they started upstream in deep snow, Bob saw the same shallow snow trench that had guided him to Tom and Brooke. He knew that Badger Heart had tossed them a bag of jerky that had kept them alive until he arrived. Now those same tracks, half buried in snow, would guide them across the divide.

By the second day out, they neared the crest.

In the forests the snow was uniformly deep, but in the open stretches above the timberline it collected in drifts. Brown grass and shrubs poked through for the stock to nibble. The wind blew in fits and bursts, ahead of another storm.

When they stopped to switch lead animals, the dogs walked back down the trail, ears perked, noses up. Bob noticed first and nodded so the others would look. The wind had died down, and the gentle notes of a flute flowed up the canyon. Horses turned and pointed their ears to the last stand of timber. As soon as the notes arose, they disappeared. Brooke looked to her dad, who stared downhill with a quizzical expression.

"Papa did you hear that?"

Bob tossed his head toward a rider, bundled in a hooded buffalo coat, who loped up the slope toward them. Two other mounted men waited at the edge of the trees. Tom glanced at Bob, who unsheathed his rifle. Tom did the same. The dogs barked.

The big horse ran strong and steady in a swirling cloud of

snow. His hooves pounded the frozen ground in a resolute rhythm that rocked the air.

"Papa, that's Surrocco."

The rider reached up and tossed back his hood.

"It's Water Bird." Delight spun through Brooke like a warm breeze. She nipped at her lip and instinctively reached for the string around her neck, but it wasn't there.

Water Bird drew the powerful horse toward them, stopping near where Brooke sat. Surprised expressions became subtle smiles.

Bob was the first to say *hello*, then Tom. Brooke drew in a deep breath but couldn't speak.

Water Bird nodded lightly, looked both men in the eyes, then turned to Brooke. He felt inside his coat and brought out a clenched fist. Relaxing his grip, he opened his palm to reveal her glass star necklace, which now dangled from his fingers. He held it out to her.

"Oh my God, oh my God." Brooke pressed both mittens to her chin, shuddering as tears of joy ran down her cheeks.

"Blue Water wants you to have it," Water Bird said. "She's afraid she may never see you again."

Brooke held back as if afraid to accept the gesture. If she never saw Blue Water again, she would never see Water Bird either.

Water Bird bobbed his hand and Brooke pulled off a mitten to let the necklace fall into her hand. She held it to her chest and stared into Water Bird's dark eyes.

The wind picked up and spun the snow into eddies that surrounded them. They all bent into their coats until the squall calmed. When it did, Brooke and Water Bird shared a final glance before he turned and rode away. Brooke shook her shoulders against the cold, pulled her hood over her head, and pressed her heels into her horse's ribs, urging him to cross over the Snowy Mountain divide.

• • •

Tom, Brooke, and Mustache Bob rode into Breckenridge, where a small crowd had gathered to meet them. Travelers along the trail had delivered the news, ahead of their arrival, that the father and red-haired daughter, thought to be dead, were in fact alive and coming to town.

As they turned the corner onto Main Street on Christmas Eve, the town erupted in joy. The snowbound town had little to celebrate at the threshold of winter but knowing that the father and daughter had been found was a Christmas present to everyone. Miners, prospectors, mule skinners, loggers, cooks, bartenders, crooks, and clergy stood on the streets and cheered.

The guests of honor and their dogs were hustled into the warmth of a packed saloon. Tom and Brooke felt awkward and out-of-place as they stood under a wooden roof for the first time in almost two years. Soon, presents came out of the woodwork for them, as if the town had just been waiting for a reason to celebrate. The party, food, and warmth went on until the three new arrivals made their way upstairs to feather beds and blankets.

• • •

The next morning, across the Snowy Mountains, beneath the Roan Cliffs, Blue Jay walked the trail to where the women drew water through the hole in the ice. She filled her water jug and stood up. A butterfly tickle in the center of her belly made her wobble. She took a deep breath, placed her hand against her navel and looked out across the river. She'd only felt that tiny tingle once before, years before, but she knew what it was. A baby. She breathed through tight lips that bent up. Her head swam, and her heart thumped lightly in her chest as she turned to carry water, the gift of life, back to the village.

About the Author

Larry Ray Rather is a fourth generation Coloradan whose grandparents lived among and traded with the Ute Indians of Southwest Colorado. His curiosity in Native American culture and history began early and inspired him to write a tale of romance and tragedy across cultural lines in the wilderness setting of Colorado in the late 1860's. His knowledge of Ute life, paired with his understanding of horses and the mountainous terrain of Colorado, inform his exploration of people from disparate backgrounds forging deep bonds, tempered by the hardships of an unforgiving wilderness.